A BELL RINGING IN THE EMPTY SKY

The Best Of The Sun

VOLUME II

A BELL RINGING
IN THE EMPTY SKY

The Best Of The Sun

A Collection of Writings
From The First Ten Years
Of
The Sun, A Magazine of Ideas,
Published in Chapel Hill, North Carolina

EDITED BY SY SAFRANSKY

THE SUN PUBLISHING COMPANY   1987   CHAPEL HILL, NORTH CAROLINA

Copyright © 1987 The Sun Publishing Company

Manufactured in the United States of America

Published by
The Sun Publishing Company
107 North Roberson Street
Chapel Hill, North Carolina 27516
(919) 942-5282
www.thesunmagazine.org

(Originally copublished with
Mho & Mho Works, San Diego, California)

Library of Congress Cataloging-in-Publication Data
(Revised for vol. 2)

A Bell ringing in the empty sky.

    "A collection of writings from the first ten years
of the Sun, a magazine of ideas, published in Chapel
Hill, North Carolina."
    I. Safransky, Sy. II. Sun (Chapel Hill, N.C.)
AC5.B385   1985   071.56'565   85-10462

ISBN #0-917320-12-3 (Softcover volume 2) ·

ISBN #0-917320-23-9 (Softcover two-volume set)

6 7 8 9 10 J Q K A

Table of Contents

Introduction

A Bell Ringing In The Empty Sky would, we knew, be a big book, in spirit as well as size, a generous collection of the best of the essays, interviews, stories, and poems that appeared in **THE SUN** during its first ten years.

Searching for months through the back issues, choosing and discarding, sifting through a decade of words, then sifting some more, we came up with the best, the very best. It was, indeed, a book big in spirit — but it was, alas, too big: more than 1,000 pages, with as many words as *War and Peace*. Faced with the prospect of yet another round of tough decisions pitting author against author, best against best, we chose instead the time-honored solution favored by parents and politicians: we'd publish *two* big volumes. Volume I came out in the Spring of 1985. Volume II you're now holding in your hands.

Since the publication of Volume I — and, in part, because of it — **THE SUN** has found a widening audience. People are drawn to the magazine because it speaks to the human heart, to our deepest possibilities, to the power of love. It does this not in the language of transcendence — not in new-ageisms and glossy truths — but with down-to-earth writing about people's lives, their sorrows and passions and fears. No less a magazine of feelings than one of ideas, **THE SUN** speaks to who we really are, not who we sometimes think we are. Our lives are a mystery more subtle than words can tell, though words can hint at the mystery.

THE SUN's emphasis has never been solely on polished writing or literary reputation. Some of the people who write for the magazine are well-known; others are unknown. As editor, I'll sometimes pick a story that's a tad amateurish over one that's better crafted. So much "good" writing is soulless, thickening the heart with lies and sharpening the symbols of hate. **THE SUN** favors writing — whether rough-around-the-edges or expertly styled — that embraces human contradictions, honors our inherent innocence, helps us awaken from our clouded dream of fear. It favors questions rather than answers. Not all our questions *can* be answered, and **THE SUN** asks its readers to live with those questions. As Rainer Maria Rilke put it:

"Be patient toward all that is unsolved in your heart and try to love the questions themselves like locked rooms and like books that are written in a foreign tongue. Do not now seek the answers which cannot be given to you because you would not be able to live them. And the point is, to live everything. Live the questions now. Perhaps you will then gradually, without noticing, live along some distant day into the answer."

Weaving together our stories, our visions, our hard-earned truths, **THE SUN** reminds us that no single viewpoint, no one guru, no easy answer can possibly honor us as much as our own searching. We live the questions. We smile ruefully, knowing there's a basic unity to all things, but that we can't name it without distorting and diminishing what *it* is. So we find other ways to express it: words that point the way (since we know we'll be on this path a long, long time); words that hint and puzzle and delight; words that let us glimpse, as if from a distance, who we really are; words in an odd and lovely little magazine.

Here, from the first ten years of **THE SUN**, are some of the best of them.

Sy Safransky
Editor, **THE SUN**

A BELL RINGING
IN THE EMPTY SKY

The Best Of The Sun

A Short History of Part of North Carolina

With Some Names Changed To Protect The Innocent, The Guilty & The Dead

C.B. Clark

US 501

South
in November, stalks of cotton
leaning to the highway.
On the dead grass
white bits drift, unpicked.

And down the road,
near dusk,
a school bus stops
to let the dark, late children
home.

— Jim Wann

Although the distance is only thirty miles, I go home once a year. Once a year, for the last ten years, in August. I always drive at night. I never travel the highway, I take the back roads. I know them best.

The only reason I go at all is Lester. I go to commemorate, in some public way, Lester's death. The others

The back roads are silent, and silence is in our Southern blood, silence and the isolation of the road, silence and running the road alone.

who know why he died understand my obligation. If they themselves observe some private ceremonials, they have not told me, nor would they. I am the outsider now. I chose to leave. Thirty miles is a long way.

Lester is Lester Bone. We were graduated from the county high school in 1955. Lester graduated like everyone else, although he could, by objective standards, hardly read or write. He was graduated in my class, or I in his, along with certain others — friends. Friends and relations. There was Beatty Sims. There was Hasty Nikero. There was John John Johnson (known as JJJ). There was my sister Bambi Clark. And there was T.A.C. Oliver. He was black, the only black male in our class of two dozen. We called him Taco, a name he adopted, and when we went thirty miles to Chapel Hill, the college town, on those clear November nights when football was over for us, Taco tried to pass himself off as Mexican in the restaurants there, boasting his darkness and breed so loudly that he goaded many a college boy to doubt such origin and to pay for such doubt with a bloody face. Taco was a fighter. After graduation he joined the Army. He was a career man. He attained the rank of sergeant before he was shot in pax-marked Korea. "Seoul food," Beatty Sims said. No one laughed or was meant to.

So it's thirty miles from Chapel Hill to Bliven. Bliven has no zip code, no post office, and the gassy tiger has never heard of Exxon, only Esso. The Esso sign rusts above the road. A company truck delivered the Exxon one, but the truck departed in the dead of night and no one hoisted the new sign up or took the old one down. Bliven does have a mill which manufactures thread from which other factories in other towns manufacture stretch socks. The mill uses water from the Haw River. Haw is an Indian word meaning river. So we have the last water-powered mill in North Carolina, using water from the river river. The mill is brick with rows of square windows. Old brick. Brick fired from our Piedmont clay. A blood-hued brick. Beautiful brick, which glows in the late Autumn sunlight before night comes on and the world goes dark.

Bliven has its mill and a few houses. They are not set in any linear perspective along the main street. The houses, mostly three-room, white, tin-roofed examples of Depression architecture, are here and there on the slopes above the roadway. There are no fences. The trees are huge in girth. Old river oaks and hollies. We have no concept of zoning. Mr. Durban sells groceries and hardware. He closes Wednesday afternoons, as well as Saturday and Sunday. Mrs. Croft sells Esso gasoline. When Mr. Nikero, Hasty's father, died, Hasty sold the building which had been an Army/Navy store to Beatty Sims. He sells fishing gear now. On Wednesday night people play cards there. Beyond the last store is the narrow bridge, dedicated in 1928; the road leads across the bridge, up a hill, and out of town.

But I am coming into town, returning on a humid August night down the back roads, past the gaunt pines and the pastures where the scent of blue grass and string grass is sweet. The beams of my truck's lights graze the asphalt, exposing the scars there.

Anyone granted life takes death in the bargain. These back roads are life-giving; deadly too. I guess in Northern cities men drink out their time in barrooms. We don't serve liquor in our bars, and we don't even sell beer in this county. The barrooms in the adjacent county are noisy with country music. The back roads are silent, and silence is in our Southern blood, silence and the isolation of the road, silence and running the road alone. In his manhood, his car is where the Southerner has the world on his own terms. His car, that special one, labored over, cared for better than a child, becomes one with the driver, or the driver one with the machine, and the driver escapes all that is mortal or hateful or irrevocable, escapes for a few moments out onto the night roads; for a few moments the driver controls his destiny, or its illusion. The boy of sixteen who once drove with a girl's thigh hot against his is a man who doesn't ask anyone to go with him. There would be no point in going at all if someone went along.

I can't say I've always liked cars. Beginning at sixteen a Cadillac impressed me, a Chevy didn't. "Damn college smart ass," Lester said, "stick your head in here and look at this work." He was talking about his Model A with the 327-cubic-inch Chevy engine capable of RPMs in the high four figures. "Jesus, Bobby, don't you understand what this is, what you're beholding here?" Although I couldn't name the parts then, I knew I beheld a way of life, one which would haunt me despite my estrangement from Bliven.

If Lester couldn't read or write with any degree of general certification, like the newsboy in Baltimore who had the I.Q. of an idiot yet each day kept, in his head, a correct running addition of the license numbers of passing cars, Lester could read anything to do with motors and act upon his understanding. Lester's game was to bring his Model A to Calvin's BBQ on the highway outside Bliven and wait for a car of college kids to stop and make a bet, their motor against Lester's.

The game had begun as early as 1960, a time when Lester's job as a pickup driver for Sweet Meadow milk had paid him enough to buy the Chevy engine and have the bores done and transform the A into a beautiful, simple, invincible machine. By 1960 I had gone through college at the University at Chapel Hill. Beatty Sims had served a year in prison for running a cop off the road. Bambi had married and divorced and was living alone in a weathered tenant cabin on the field line of JJJ's parents' property, a trace of a hundred acres which they finally sold to the CIA, which built an underground monitoring system there. Bambi told me about the meetings at the BBQ nightlot, and the races out along the narrow two-lane which passed over what we called chicken bridge, another one-lane bridge, this one wooden, ten miles away, so named because whoever refused to keep pace, fender to fender, chickened out.

"What do you get, Lester?" I asked. "Money," he answered. "You ought to know, Bobby. You're there. Those college kids going to school with their year's money on them. I get a bit."

However, in another five years Lester didn't race anymore. He didn't care about the money. I thought he was playing a losing game against diminishing skill. I supposed he took his car out to race by himself to preserve the illusion of a younger man's coordination, the brain-hand-eye precision he had lost to ten years of pills and beer, loneliness and frustration. "You don't know it all, Bobby," my sister said in reference to my speculations.

So in the Summer of 1965, when I was in Bliven for a weekend, I decided to set Lester up. Perhaps I wanted to prove my superiority over him once and for all. I planned to be with Lester at the BBQ when a college friend would drive in and challenge Lester for a bet large enough to entice him. My friend and I had staked a mule around a blind curve in the middle of the road. I was sure Lester, when he saw the animal blocking the road, would quit.

The race was arranged, Lester and my friend starting off and running the first mile even, each doing eighty on the curves. When they came to the blind curve my friend was in the lead by no more than half a car length. The mule heard the motors, and caught in the sudden spray of highlights, the animal moved, unbelievably gracefully sideways so that the animal straddled the center line, allowing just enough room on each flank for the cars to graze past. Lester didn't let up, but my friend quit. He was so shaky he couldn't feel the steering anymore. Lester laughed telling me about it. "But why did you set me up, Bobby? Why, Bobby? My life isn't worth a damn, only my car is. You could have wrecked my car."

A month later Lester killed a man in an argument, cut him up in the C-graded kitchen of a chili parlor near Siler City. Lester never said what the argument was about. "At night out on the road, Bobby, I could get away. Trouble was I always had to come back." He meant Transcendence. For a while Lester transcended his life as he drove the night roads. Maybe he could have maintained the escape. Maybe my cheap trick had soured him, made it go wrong. In any event, Lester gave me the car to own. "There ain't no road to drive in prison." He turned after he had said that and followed the sheriff while a deputy followed him. They had locked chains around Lester's skinny ankles. The faded blue prison shirt and pants fitted poorly on Lester's five-eight body, all of a hundred pounds. "Lester won't come out," Bambi said. She was right. Lester hanged himself in his cell within the year.

So it's my duty. I bring Lester's car back to Bliven once each year. I ease it off the special trailer and park it by the Esso station. News travels fast. The next day everyone knows. Kids who were fathered by my classmates come down to examine the car. They lean over it, they don't touch it; they seem to hold their breath. "Hey, Bobby," one of them asks, "you going to race it?"

"I wish I could give the car away." JJJ and Beatty nod. "You can't, Bobby," Beatty says, "no more than you can ever leave home. You just get to be a stranger in it."

We walk up the hill to Beatty's house. He hands me a flannel rag to clean the grease off my hands. "You've kept the car in fine shape," he said. "I'd even trust you to work on my own."

I answer: "I hate cars." Beatty smiles. He knows that already down the moonless roadway the Southern night-wind is calling my name and though I haven't turned I will. Soon I will power through the darkness, my headlights spreading open the near darkness, holding it away before it closes behind me where I have gone, where Lester has gone, where all of us will go until we vanish forever in the greater darkness beyond.

(May 1976)

Hal J. Daniel III

Seeing It This Way Helps

For every dead armadillo
we see between here and
New Orleans there are two,
maybe three, standing
behind the chain fence.
They stare, claws hooked
in the links, at their
brothers and sisters who
have been crushed by the
radials of the interstate.
Their bicameral brains
understand some armadillos
die so others may live.
The survivors cogitate
their own existence when
they see their kin smashed.
They stare through the
early morning fog with
topaz eyes. The images
they see stay within their
now wise minds. They pass
on the DON'T GET RUN OVER
ON INTERSTATE 59 gene to
their baby armadillos.

The armadillos that get
run over don't pass on
anything but a death smell.
Those that watch the splats
in the pea soup pass on
something worthwhile to
their offspring — the
PEARL RIVER SURVIVAL gene
and that's what it's all
about. The same goes for
cats, dogs, and raccoons.
I'm not sure about possums
and squirrels. Even stupid
fish getting ripped into
the air leave behind some
bright school mates and
memories.

Here's Lake Pontchartrain.

(April 1984)

Hal J. Daniel III

Better Than Being
A Highway Frisbee

The skull is not
crushed. The left
leg is broken. 2
or 3 cervical are
dislocated but the
ears are clear. A
Volvo radial got
him just across the
shoulders. He must
have been about 4
months old, already
a bandit. I saw him
climb down his oak
before he could do
it. Pop. My raccoon
is dead. I'm sad
but smile at its
limp beauty. His
paws and mask match.
I'll dissect the ears
and larynx. George,
in Physical Therapy,
gets the hands (paws).
Larry can look at the

brain. The forelimb
section on the pre-
central gyrus should
be neat. Speech Path
can have the tongue;
Sparky a new pelt.
He cleaned his food
in the dark of last
night's moon. Coon
meat for Plummer.
He'll stew it with
sweet spuds, tell me
it's the best he's
ever eaten. Should
at least be tender,
no dog scare or shot.
Garrett gets the tail
for his 1951 Merc.
Daddy gets a few baby
raccoon oyster pearls
for his tooth col-
lection. It stared
at me on my jog this
morning. The skull
will join a cluster
of road kill bleached
bones, placed in a
Cree Indian style
totem to the carless
Nirvana.

(February 1984)

Black Reaper

Lorenzo W. Milam

Buck didn't know how old he was, that's for sure. We guessed it to be somewhere between seventy and ninety. His head was bald, and shiny. His face was thin, and I was never sure how he could shave it with all the lines and droops and excess skin it contained.

His stance was straight, his figure bony. His skin was chocolate milkshake rendered luminous with the same glow as my dad's fine calfskin boots after my repeated (unwilling) attacks with Booth's Mahogany Creme and chamois.

Buck's eyes were loose-lidded, and the iris of them seemed smudged, as if someone had stepped on a Necco Bittersweet Chocolate Wafer, down on Riverside Avenue, just in front of the Fairfax Theatre where I spent most of my Saturday afternoons in the com-

I know Buck is there at work, his shade hovering over the shiny metal blade, counting in the strokes my years. . . .

pany of Tom Mix, Roy Rogers, and those endless Dick Tracy serials.

Buck would come to garden on Thursdays, arriving sometime between 5:00 and 5:30 a.m. He carried his work clothes neatly rolled in a brown A&P shopping bag which grew shabbier and more wrinkled as the year advanced until sometime around Christmas it was discarded for a new one. I would awaken at 6:30 to the sound of his chopping the grass and the slow, rhythmic "chunk" of his hoe would mix with my waking dreams. "There's a woodchuck in the yard," I would think, sometimes; and at other, darker times, I would think, "I can hear death outside in the bushes, with his . . . . " Being literate, I knew the word was scythe, but being eleven, I didn't know how to pronounce it. I knew the sharp, shiny curve of its blade, and heard it as it cut into my days, there before the sun had but risen, warm and thick and full against the hazy North Florida sky.

I would arise from my child's wrinkled bed, and look down on the faded blue back of Buck's boll weevil shirt, watch his whole body keeping time to a work rhythm from his own youth, never questioning that his was the world fixing other men's lawns, weeding their gardens, trimming their hedges, stooping, as he had done some twenty-five thousand times, in the arc of the sun shining against the sky, blazing down to wrinkle his eyes, thinking unimaginable thoughts of a time when this land was all scrub pine possum country.

Buck got paid five dollars for his 6 a.m. to 3 p.m. stint. He got grits and collard greens from Dilsey the cook about 11:30, along with a twenty-minute respite from his labors. I can hear their slow voices from the kitchen below, mixing with the scent of pot liquor and fatback, o their voices! slow, easy, heavy with the warm juices of the rural South: if they spoke to us now, you most probably wouldn't be able to understand them, but I grew up bilingual, with that child's ability to speak in dialect, and I listen to and comprehend that foreign language.

"Lawd hit's 'bout uh hunnert . . . . "

"Sho nuff. Yew wan mo' greens?"

"How lawn I bin workin? Law, iss newn 'fore newit."

"Disn's nebber bin wurs. Yew wan' greits to?"

"Show. Look how hees grown!"

"Ain't du truuf! Gwine up 'fore yew nossits!"

The alien language of an alien workforce, and every word of it brings back to me those rich Summers in the thick miasmal comfort of sweet-honey youth, before the "ragerie" of knowledge had cut such wisdom and satisfaction from my days. That music out of the Southern black is the music of my innocence, and I ride it still down the halls of my early days, mourning, as we all must mourn, as all mankind must mourn, that we are to grow, and grow in to pain and wisdom.

Just before Buck left for the day, he would get his glass. "I'm goin' naw, Miz Milam," he would say, and my mother would send me to the ornate carved Louis XIV liquor cabinet to get out the Old Mr. Boston. She would take a dime-store tumbler and fill it to the brim with what he called his "medicine."

We would sit at the white porcelain blue-edge kitchen table, Buck with his full-to-the-brimming glass of sunshine, me with a skinny leg swinging back and forth under the table. He would take a sip, just a sip, just to make sure it wasn't tainted, just to make sure it was the real McCoy. And, then, after a smack of the lips, he would move his head back and suck in the whole tumblerful of whiskey. Neat. Ah: if the Old Mr. Boston Whiskey Company wanted a commercial for their product, this is it! Buck becoming measureably more warm, his skin softening with a fine glow, his eyes becoming less dilated, a tad sparkly. Bang, goes the glass on the hard white tabletop, and his mouth moves from a tight pucker, upper and lower lips move a bite over dark, toothless gums; there is a whistled breath, a sigh from the deep ages of dark satisfaction, and my dark friend sits before me, his soul at one with the great comforting forces of the universe that reward seventy years of desperately hard labor with the delight of fire in the pylorus. We couldn't have been more delighted, Buck and I, he in the warm arms of Mr. Boston, me in the warm arms of life in the sunny South, at a time when the shadows were hazy, the sunshine was bright, and the smell of the newly cropped bahama grass touched my nostrils, and the days awaited me breathlessly, endlessly.

My father let Buck stay at the old Timuquana Country Club after it moved to its new headquarters on the edge of the rich, brown, slow-moving St. John's River. I remember the old club grounds as a place of especial peace. The oak trees had become distorted with age, arthritis in the knots, craggy old men with gray-green hair hanging almost to the ground. The one path into the estate was slippery with fallen oak leaves, and pine needles, and the mulch of plants growing and dying at their own pace on their own land. The trees and the bushes owned that land, and Buck and the clap-board shed he lived in were tolerated tenants. The shadowy acres took care of their own — the oustide was hot and thick, but in the grove of the old country club, it was cooler, and all had come to a suspension of time, a cessation of conflict. "There's no life here, " you would have thought, but you would be wrong: the moss was heavy with ants and redbugs and ticks, the trees thick with bluejays, and most afternoons, the bob-whites would shrill their incessant two-fold whistle which, since my own father's name was Bob, seemed related to me: "bob-white, bob-white," and the last word would shoot up, quickly, as if to confirm the fact that my dad was Bob, and indeed, was white, in this land of the Universal Black South.

One time, I was allowed to be dispenser of medicine, my mother gone on some journey, somewhere, and I chose for a medicine jar not the Long's Five-&-Dime tumbler but a more luxurious ice-tea glass from Charles Wells' Jewelers, a glass, indeed, more accustomed to my mother's manicured friends' hands than Buck's gnarled, older, blacker ones. I laid a doozer on Buck, and I recall his eyes, tearful, after he had downed what to others might be a near-fatal dose of medication. He is merry, Buck is, and I become merry too as he tells me about his one short-lived romance.

I can see him now, I can see us, as we gather around the table in that brightly-lit kitchen, the sun's gaze so benign on master and son, as I am initiated into the world of love and marriage for the poor, and the black. I can smell the fresh edge of the whiskey as Buck picks up the glass, licks the rim to be sure that he doesn't miss a bit of the juice of the gods. His pate collects a square of light reflected from the bright outdoors as he tells me about buying sacks of lima beans, flour, hominy, black-eyed peas so she can cook for him.

He brought her, nameless, dark, ethereal her to his once-palatial estate, where the pine had faded, dark, elongated rings turned black amidst the wood gone white and dusty. He bought her clothes with the silver he had saved carefully, so carefully, in the old sock, under the mattress: he had to dip into a thousand yards' worth of work to convince her to stay with him.

Buck is merry, I am merry, he is old and I am young, he is black and I am white, he is the child of the dirt and I am the child of men's tales and we are merry as he tells of his three-day romance. She stayed in the woods for three days, and when she left she took the beans and the hominy and the black-eyed peas. She took her dresses, but left the flour. O yes: she took the silver too, a twenty-year hoard of grass cut in the 100-degree sun: she took however much it was and disappeared north east south or west, spilling out like diaspora from the dandelion turned from sun to moon, spilling out two decades of sweat into the juke-joints and cheap hotels of Brunswick, or Valdosta, or Live Oak.

And so Buck lived on by himself, in the many years (he couldn't remember how many; time is uncounted, unsorted coins saved for the aged) since she had left. He and the bluejays and mockingbirds and bob-whites stayed on in the breathless Summer wait of the old country club, he so pure in his joy at the woman who had pinched his poke there so long ago where the birds whistle my father and the scythe comes down silver and sharp across the land and one doesn't question the strangeness of women, the strangeness of the black man's world, the strangeness of boys who sit cross-and-thin-legged across the table, breathing in the aroma of sharp whiskey and the new-mown grass, watching mouths round in mirth at the fates played by all the gods on the hopes of us, even the poor and the black.

I know what happened to Buck. It has to do with the creatures (winged, four-footed, shadowy) that live in the dark corners of the land, the mind, the universe. Long after I had been shipped off to school in the North, my father sold off the estate to a developer. In a tall building downtown, white hands signed and shuffled sheaves of paper, and the next week, a man (manager, realtor, agent) came to Buck to tell him he would have to move along. There is no protest (only the protest of injustice cries inside), the building is vacated. Within a week a Caterpillar earth-mover arrives and turns the land all askew.

Trees are uprooted, bushes are smashed, vines and flowers are crumpled. The brush country which has been home for rabbit and squirrel and blacksnake for so long is rendered flat and desolate. The old bleach-wood clubhouse, home for Buck, peopled with his memories for so long, is smashed and torn, rendered into crumpled wood and bent nails and torn tarpaper. He has probably moved into town, into a single room in a sagging boardinghouse, and he lives out his time with a single metal frame bed, a washbasin, and the cracked edge of his mirror.

I never saw him again, and those who should have known were not able to tell me where I could find him so that I could bring him one last fifth of medicine. He disappeared into the darkness of the city, disappeared forever. And yet I don't know; I think he may still be in the garden at home. I have to tell you: I was there just a few years ago and I heard him in the garden. I awoke in the room where I shaped my first thoughts and feelings and memories (the memories of the shades are the strongest) and I heard Buck out in the yard. I was in my grandfather's long bed where now my toes peep out of the end, my head banging in dreams against the headboard — and I heard the "chuck chuck" of the scythe outside.

It is that dark-dawn hour before the sky loses its infinity, and I know Buck is there at work, his shade hovering over the shiny metal blade, counting in the strokes my years, calling out to me with its cuttings, Buck calling me out of some imagined place, letting me know that he will be there, always, slow, counting out my days; he, never-ceasing, omnipresent, hacking through the tall growths, gathering in long strands of time, binding together, shaping us as our days run ceaselessly forth. I am scarcely awake in the new day, in my old bed of child-memories, and I hear, for perhaps the last time, the sound of that dark angel, preparing us for the measure of our days, chopping the hours and days and weeks and months, parsing out our moments as easily as the sky comes to be broken now with the last remnants of our days.

(May 1982)

David C. Childers

The Elements

I've quit waiting
on the great siren
to blow us an end.
I look back on wasted time.
Humanity stands up
like the guy out back
who looks toward the sky
and lets a song escape him,
doves
out of the restaurant window.

2 minutes later, he's back
on knees, hands, face,
back on the old black Earth.

Ah, the stars,
the red necklace on the street of the bars.
Bringing magic,
a woman comes up from the bridge.

Death be fucked!
Let the end go quick where it goes.
When I see you there,
2 more of us will know.

(April 1976)

Us/Readers Write About . . .

Parents

In each month's US section, readers are asked to write about a different topic. It's a modest effort to provoke conversation about questions on which we're the only authorities.

Writing style is less important than thoughtfulness and sincerity.

— Ed.

My parents' friend, Joe Gottchauk, took a picture of them soon after they were married. (My father was just a little older than I am now, my mother younger than my sister.) They're sitting on a couch in a room with just one light, looking together at a book. Their heads are turned down, but you can see my father's sensitive sailor's face and my mother's shy farm girl face. My mother's hair is long and loose, as I've never seen it in life, and there is about the photograph a strong feeling of romantic love.

The picture is different from the other pictures in my parents' photograph album — it's much larger and more at ease. (My father likes to line people up in front of monuments.) It's also different from what I've seen of my parents' life — my father serious and indrawn, almost bitter, my mother strident and cheery, avoiding the world by attacking it. I never saw my father kiss my mother with pleasure. Were they really in love in that photograph, I used to wonder, or was it just a trick of lighting?

Since my sister and I left, things have changed a bit with them — they've noticed each other again. My father admits to himself (if to no one else) that he needs her. My mother has experienced him not just as Her Man, but as a kind man. I think they even talk to each other, when no one's looking.

After thirty-four years, love doesn't mean anything, my mother says.

They may not like each other, or even love each other, but they've survived each other. In one sense, this has made them free.

Sparrow
New York, New York

(June 1983)

Three Photographs

Priscilla Rich

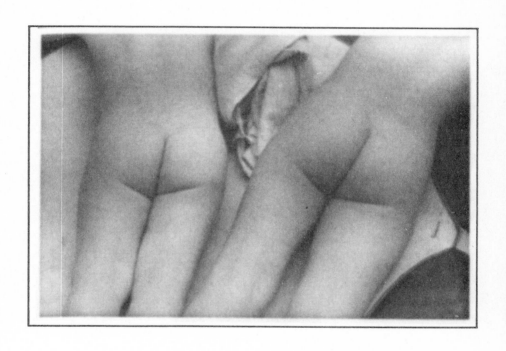

J.W. Rivers

Carl

When you're an only child
but still not Number One Son
you've got to wonder
if you shouldn't have been
Adonis or Hercules
Robin the Boy Wonder
or a dashing sultan
from the Barbary Coast.

You can't run away from home
the J.C. Higgins has two flats
no foxtail and somebody
stole the rear view mirror,
you could hide out
among the Japanese

but you don't like rice
and fishheads or hara-kiri,
if you had relatives in Cheyenne
you could go there
if you had bus fare but
you don't even have a pot
to pee in.

But if you had
a smaller slower stepbrother
or live-in cousin from Canada
you'd be King of the Hill
Prince Charming on an Arab stallion
Head Man among half pints
and shrimps.

(March 1978)

J.W. Rivers

Death Bed

Ma's quit moaning,
she's quiet for now.

The minister's
at the kitchen table
having homemade wine with Pa.

He came in his sport coat
and Lincoln,
said the Lord's prayer
and a few good things
about Ma's life
in five minutes flat,
has been in the kitchen
for twenty
drinking homemade wine with Pa,
tells about last Sunday's birdie,
new construction at the church
and radial tires
that go forever.

(March 1978)

J.W. Rivers

From Burnside to Goldblatt By Streetcar

You're only really safe in Burnside,
Right here in Hungarian Village, Uncle Oscar
Lets you know before your first streetcar solo
From 94th and Cottage Grove to 63rd and Halstead
To see Ma during break at Goldblatt Department Store:

keep an eye out for Jews
who'll snatch your underwear;
Poles who'll take
your Tom Mix whistling ring,
finger and all, and your
Captain Midnight secret decoder;
the Italian neighborhood
is so hot it can blow any second
like a Chicago pineapple;
those Germans brained two nurses
and a nun just last Sunday;
the Japanese carve kids
with swords all the way
from head to toe,
toss pieces on front doorsteps
with the milk and morning paper;
the chocolate drops from Africa
blow poison darts with rusty barbs,

steal your change,
streetcar transfers
and baseball cards, dance around
as you lay dying forever;
when — and if —
you get to Halstead Street
watch for Mongolian perverts
under manhole covers,
Armenians in the awning
with deadly piano wire,
avoid basements and Ukrainians
with beards and damp knives

And you wonder just how much you want a chocolate soda
At the soda fountain with Ma
During break at Goldblatt.

(March 1978)

New York Diary: Amazing Flesh

Sy Safransky

I read, in the newspaper, about a man who is dragged from his car, knifed repeatedly for the few dollars in his wallet, and left bleeding in the gutter. My mother says her friends don't go out at night. It's an old story, old as the city's tired and dour expression, old as the dry and wrinkled hands of a man trying to remember better days and remembering nothing but bone.

□ □ □

I am staring, through an opening in the curtain drawn around his hospital bed, at my father's swollen belly. The nurse is changing the bandage. I force myself to look: at her black hands on his white flesh, moving gently, expertly, uselessly; at his face, yellowed with jaundice and etched

And soon I will be the elder, still struggling with these bad habits, dragged across the years of my life like a rusty plow. . . .

with new lines and suffering this new insult as he has suffered so much before: with a look compounded of dumb amazement and mild amusement, as if there were a joke appropriate to this, too, if only he could remember it.

□ □ □

Back at the house, in the room which my mother has turned into a clothing store, I spy a customer undressing. She is wonderful to look at, like those statues and tapestries I saw at the museum yesterday. Such economy and such extravagance of gesture. Common; classic; divine. The shape of woman. Flesh, amazed and amused at itself.

I marry his body to hers. My father and this stranger. Swift corruption and sweet allure.

□ □ □

At the neighborhood movie theatre where, as a child, I was nourished on the romantic and the improbable, nothing but X-rated films are now shown: explicit and crude and flavored with their own improbable romanticism — of sex as its own definition, its own expression, its own end, somehow apart from the rest of human experience. Like dying, which becomes, in this culture, the ultimate obscenity, at least to the living.

□ □ □

On the street, I'm invited to a feast at the Hare Krishna temple. "I'll be there in spirit if not in flesh," I assure her. She eyes me reprovingly. "Be there in the flesh," she says. "You never know what your flesh will be the next time around. It could be the bark of a tree." I tell her I like trees. She's not amused.

□ □ □

A girl I dated in high school is on my mind. I call her mother, who tells me she's married, with three children, and would love to hear from me; it would remind her of when she was a pretty young girl. Yes, so pretty I could look at her for hours; and what now? Fat and sunken like the rest of those suburban housewives? Her flesh a burden, rather than a pleasure and an endless entertainment? But how can I ask these questions, or call without knowing the answers? Without knowing if there is an amazement, or a tiredness, in her eye? Without knowing if she is married to life, or to death? Of course, I am being foolish. She is probably quite happy, quite in love, quite diligently counting her calories.

☐ ☐ ☐

Jogging around the block in the morning, once again caught up in an enthusiasm for self-renewal. Next year I'll be as old as my father was when I was born: a reminder of my own mortality. We are wondrously more than flesh and bone, but flesh and bone still. And soon I will be the elder, still struggling with these bad habits, dragged across the years of my life like a rusty plow; still yearning for clearer sight and so a fuller heart; still, in other words, being me. My father's son, some might say.

☐ ☐ ☐

Remembered at the museum: a bronze Buddha in a glass case, small and perfect, the ultimate celebration of contemplative wisdom. The eyes impenetrable, the smile compassionate and ever-so-mocking. I stood and looked at it for a long time. But for the glass, I would have touched it.

(November 1974)

Michael Shorb

My Father's Garage
On Christmas Night

Back after all these years and older,
The silence better, more like
Friendship, two neighbors
Rooting for the same team.
Rafters are filled with the detritus
Of mutual lives: a tent we used
For camping at the lake, a punching bag
No one hits now, my sister's furniture.
And your workbench is piled higher
Than ever with a hundred
Accomplished or forgotten
Repairs and adjustments,
Power sander and soldering iron askew,
A wood box filled with broken things
Waiting to be renewed.

This is what you ended up with.
A garage domain, a world of certain things,
Perfect fits. I don't question it anymore.
Perhaps, half lost in worlds of ideas
And perplexions of beauty, I even envy
This yoga of wood and metal tightly joined,
Of things held down by nuts and bolts.

Admiring this platter you once fashioned,
Quail in flight on smoky plastic, I praise
It perhaps too much, or awkwardly, meaning
A hundred other appreciations left unspoken,
Meaning to say you weren't what I thought,
That you never understood the anger
Of your sons, the drugs, the grasping
For roads. America has nothing
    to do with this.

There's just the two of us, looking
More alike than we realize, feeling
What we don't know how to say.

(March 1983)

Waiting

Elizabeth Rose Campbell

". . . the Hebrew word timshel — 'Thou mayest' — that gives a choice. It might be the most important word in the world. That says the way is open . . . 'Thou mayest'! Why, that makes a man great, that gives him stature with the gods, for in his weakness and his filth and his murder of his brother he has still the great choice."
— John Steinbeck, East of Eden

1960

I am in cut-offs and tee-shirt reading comic books. She is in her underpants and bra with an unbuttoned shift draped loosely around her, reading *The Ladies' Home Journal.*

We are sitting beside her fishpool where clusters of waterlilies hide oversized goldfish and tiny ones flash like gold omens when our shadows dance across the water. The locusts whine, the magnolia rustles in the breeze, and the swish-swish of my grandfather's plane on mahogany soothes us from his shop nearby.

We share this spot for hours,

I began to feel increasingly like her shadow, a time bomb that would go off in her lifetime, blowing to bits her world of blueblood and breeding and small-minded Southern snobbery. . . .

satisfied with the scent of roses, gardenias, camellias, and fragrances for which I have searched for years and can only find in this memory. She turns to me suddenly and says, "You can do anything in this world you want to. You know that?"

I put down my Archie comic book to look at her and she holds me there; I nod tentatively at her puckered brow, demanding eyes, lips taut with tension. I am an eight-year-old imposter, small and ridiculous before such total affirmation.

She is emphatic: "You'll write a book some day. And illustrate it too. You've got too much of your mother and Katy in you not to."

My mother has written no book. And her sister Katy has not illustrated one. My grandmother is being outlandish again, fantastical, presumptuous, as she often is when it comes to her family, their abilities, their success, their influence. But I am moved, feel tender towards her, get up and hug her from behind, offer to answer the phone which is clamoring in the back hall of her house.

"For you!" I cry. She grunts, hoists herself out of the folding chair, curses, "Who *is* it?"

She is a chameleon, crossing the lawn in her enormous underwear and sagging bra, glancing furtively at the lane nearby as she clasps her shift to her front, plods into the house to become the gracious Lady, feigning delight when she picks up the phone ("Oh, *Yah*-uh, Hal-loo Flawwrence"), speaking loudly into the receiver to convey sincerity, talking in a rush of volume and warmth and hanging up with a bang, never giving Florence a chance to respond, oblivious to the transparency of her mask.

She routinely does this, refuses conversation unless it is on her own terms, at her own convenience, and most preferably with herself or her family center stage.

"Whew!" she cries when she returns to her chair, as if she's been clever, kept the wolf away from the door, defied the same social obligations she revels in when *she* directs, plays hostess, is the star.

She is the classic Leo, a preoccupied extrovert in defiant colors, her cup running over with uncontainable pride and goodwill. She is the irreverent fairy godmother come to disrupt my grade school class, knocking on the door as she opens it, wearing a once stylish, now tattered hat, wordlessly scrutinizing the class for her suspect, jabbing her finger at me when she finds me, and accusingly, triumphantly announcing, "There she is!" Her glee is contagious, the other children giggling and hypnotized by her presumptuousness, my face red with embarrassment and pride in her dramatic presence. She is the hearty lioness in need of an audience to receive her grandiose generosity, to share in her hilarity, to laugh with her, not at her. And that is who I am for her, receptive to her foolish glamour because I see a child in her eyes, looking mostly for love.

When did her charm become a burden? When I began to talk back, ask pointed questions about what she felt, what she thought. Her answers were too quick, too proud, too thoughtless, and my reaction was to recede into myself and mock, pity, or ignore her.

But she could not tell me what she did not know, what she'd never asked herself. Her depths were uncharted; she had never learned to listen, to sit faceless and still, to love the spirit satiated in silence.

I began to feel increasingly like her shadow, a time bomb that would go off in her lifetime, blowing to bits her world of blueblood and breeding and small-minded Southern snobbery that thrived on fear. I was becoming foreign, even to myself, as I let go of sleep and the status quo. I was repelled by the short-sighted visions, the calcified values, stiff and ingrown, and was attracted by all that I'd been taught to ignore: the inner worlds, the metaphorical meanings, the "coincidences," dreams that came true.

I hid this from her, and was shocked when I realized I was imitating her when I hid. Had I inherited only the worst, not the best in her?

To accept the best and the worst, the full inheritance, I would have to forgive her again and again for the closed doors, superficialities, the absent humility. And if I did not, I would never know the best in her, her grace, her struggle, her emancipation. Or my own.

I wanted to speak of it, make her know I was there, but she had no ear for the telepathic night where neither of us needed words, glory or opinions. So I cultivated unorthodox styles of waiting for her, for her revelation, her truth, everything unseen that might come up unchecked, unveiled from behind her masks. I waited almost twenty-five years before I understood it is a mistake to wait. This patience is of no service to her or me. And when I give it up, I may know who she is.

August 1980

So profoundly does the ocean affect those that live by it that it follows them, forever, and so it was that my first memory of the ocean's influence was given to me in the inland Piedmont of North Carolina where my grandparents had settled, three hundred miles north of the South Carolina coast they grew up on. They talked around the ocean, never describing it directly, but instead handed me a conch shell to put to my ear, which whispered why: the ocean is space, no walls, the singing source, the Great Mother. You cannot describe what comes out of the sea, a womb so sensitive, so graced with possibilities that it could engender millions of life forms. But you can hear it in two persuasive syllables: ooooosssshhhhnnnn.

It ran in my grandparents' veins, that ocean presence, life that must withstand hurricanes, the flooding, high winds.

It is a near-tropical Eden, this section of the South Carolina coast, with singing insects and alligators and ancient oaks covered in Spanish moss, myrtle bushes, marsh, and the Waccamaw River winding its way to the sea, which splashes and foams against what the commercialists call "the grand strand," from Charleston to Myrtle Beach, purportedly the widest beach on the east coast.

I have many dead here: great-grandparents, great-great-grandparents. People I never knew, who lived here for a reason, shaped their children by this ocean, died here.

One of them was a reverend called Isaiah, who according to his obituary, "with little advantage in the way of education yet became a plain, instructive, and somewhat interesting preacher; and occasionally his efforts were attended with considerable manifestation of divine power." He died in 1878, leaving behind eighteen children (he had two wives), three hives of bees, one loom, two nut trays, a grape grinder, cider press frame, six quilts, seventy-eight sheep, six dry cows, two cows, two calves, two family Bibles, two dictionaries, and an assortment of tools.

My grandmother is one of his many granddaughters, and it is her first cousin Lenora, another granddaughter, who has been the center of the wheel of extended family. It is she who has stayed closest to the ocean, converses with small children, puts no stock in social sophistications, but in her sciences: plant life, animal life, sea life, the rhythms of the earth.

Lenora is my mother Skate's bosom buddy, confidante. They

are the same age, but Lenora most closely resembles my grandmother — Punkin, as Lenora calls her — in exuberance, acting
ability, humor and sheer life force.

Lenora is Punkin's potential filled out, the generosity put to use,
the large gestures followed through with purpose and sunny
courage. Lenora knows who she is and what she wants, is seasoned
at sixty, ageless, with an instinct for strong character in others, a
keen compassion for those less alive.

I am about to see them, Lenora, Punkin, Skate and other kin,
making the five-hour drive across the flat and sandy land between
Chapel Hill and South Carolina, pine forests monotonously flaking
the highway. I strain for a glimpse of the ocean when I am still a half
mile away from it, before I've hit the beach road. Even from a
distance, I can see the water's movements, the indisputable logic of
emotion, with no up or down or east or west, churning waters of insatiable creative impulses, foaming, dissolving, regenerating. I think
about Punkin — will I be shocked at her deterioration, will she cry
when she tells me about the nursing home she lives in now except
for family vacations? Will I?

It takes a day for me to settle down, accept the sand in my bed,
the hum of family conversations, the zigzagging of lives. I watch
Punkin carefully, touch her every chance I get, hold her restless
hands, try to get her to talk about herself. She is overweight, seems
bloated, her hip bothers her and she can't take long walks on the
beach anymore.

She sits in a folding chair under an umbrella in sunglasses and
sunhat, rubbing sunscreen on her large nose. Skate insists Punkin is
"better, herself again," with the family around her, not "confused,"
as she becomes when she is alone or ignored.

I work on my tan on a towel beside her and we watch Skate and
Lenora swimming beyond the breakers. I leave Punkin to join them;
the three of us hang onto a raft together in the warm ocean. Lenora
declares she doesn't feel a day over sixteen. Skate says she doesn't
either. Lenora teases me, "What do you think maturity is?" I hem
and haw and tell them I think it's knowing you don't know
everything. They both whoop and declare they are mature.

I get off the raft and swim nearby, watch Skate, feel my respect for
her, resurrect an eight-year-old memory of a skirmish between Skate
and her sister, of the moment when Skate suddenly blurted out,

"Well, there are a lot of things I used to know and I don't know anymore, about what's right and wrong, what's proper, and what's not."

She was fifty-two then. She was barely fifty when my father died three years after my grandfather's death. She was forced then to decide, "Do I grow old with memories and Mother or do I start over?"

She started over, left a hometown that wanted to keep her, moved to Chapel Hill where she knew no one, and never regretted it. She does not understand Punkin, who cannot bear to be alone, wants to escape from herself, is always in search of some diamond, something to warm the body and the soul, imagines her children possess it, imagines that without them she has no validity, no meaning.

Skate feels guilty: "I am her oldest daughter, I *want* her to be happy, but even when she's with me she can't find what she wants; she looks for it everywhere — when I put down a book I'm reading, she picks it up. When I get a phone call she wants to know who it is. When I go into another room, she follows me. She looks for it in food, everywhere, but I don't have it, I can't give her what she wants!" Skate has bitter tears in her eyes and I know her sisters feel the same way.

I go sit on the beach with Punkin, beg her to come to the water's edge with me. She won't. I pick up a *National Enquirer* at her feet and read aloud to her.

The *National Enquirer* reports: eight years of aptitude tests show no difference between men and women on most tests, and women are better than men in fourteen areas. In only two areas did men excel over women: in structural visualization and grip! (Punkin: "I don't believe that, do you?")

The *National Enquirer* reports: the amazing ostrich boy! A fifteen-year-old Brazilian boy who swallows live pigeons, razor blades, ping-pong balls and brings them back up! "I've never seen anything like this!" Dr. Neto tells the *Enquirer*.

The *National Enquirer* reports: a baby in Austria was born prematurely on March 10, 1980, assumed to be a stillborn. It was carried to the morgue, and almost a day later was heard crying, was rescued, and reunited with the happy parents. Punkin sighs, says, "I like that one."

The sun is setting but still warms us. We doze together, she in her chair, I on my towel with Steinbeck's *East of Eden* for a pillow.

Punkin and I share a bedroom that night. I roll over and look at her facing me in her bed, smile, smack my lips in a kiss. The porch lights illuminate her face through the window. She smacks back at me. "Love you the mostest my darling," she says, and closes her eyes tight.

The next evening, Skate, Punkin and I attend a family wedding at All Saints, a small church near Pawley's Island. A grandniece of Punkin's is getting married. Many of the people attending are locals who recognize her, step up to speak. She becomes flushed, pumping hands and introducing herself to strangers as if she were a visiting dignitary. We are seated on the front row; Punkin talks in a stage whisper to everyone that joins us there.

I am ready to go back to the cottage after the wedding but to miss the reception in Georgetown would be to deprive Punkin of too much. When we get there, Skate and I exchange smiles as Punkin coasts through the crowd, in her own territory now, a Southern belle who can charm, entertain, dazzle like a seasoned gambler cutting cards.

It is said that she was very beautiful as a young girl, and I see her tonight talking with this man and that, not as an eighty-two-year-old woman but as a girl of eighteen, deeply happy among attractive and well-bred young men.

November 1980

Liza and I borrow a truck, hit the road to Wellman in response to Skate's call: "Mother's house has been sold. We have to get everything out of there this weekend."

Liza drives — sunlight in her hair, fiery blue eyes, features that haunt. Our mothers are sisters; we share the same name — Elizabeth — and she wryly accuses me of having been angry with her for it when we were children.

The ride passes quickly; we drink wine, talk of men, sex, marriage, matriarchs — Punkin in particular. We talk about family festivals, the food, how the children ate in the kitchen, the thrill of graduating to the dining room, the grownups' talk, our grandfather's abbreviated prayers. "Thank you Lord. Amen," he'd say, from the head of the table, his daughters and their children on each side, Punkin facing him in red wool, earrings and elegance.

It's been years since either of us has been back to this rambling old house that stabled so many — my great-grandmother, my grandmother and grandfather, all of their children, and at times their children's children. The yard has grown up, but the magic is still there — the white-railed front porch dappled with sunlight, back porch covered in ivy, the high ceilings, wide windows, attic mysteries, basement subterranean terrors: a furnace, a fire. The hall stairs groan with my weight as I head for the bedroom that was mine the year I was eight. I am not looking for things but for views; I want to memorize what I can see from every upstairs window: the church steeple through treetops, the magnolia, the crepe myrtles, the house on the hill my parents built after their first was destroyed by fire.

We spend the afternoon emptying the house — find antique toys, peacock feathers, World War I cavalry leggings, my grand-father's stiff-necked shirts. Memories beg to be cried over, but no one cries. We hide in the work to be done.

I dig blindly in the flower beds overgrown with weeds for everything I remember being there: spider lilies, tulips, and jonquils. I take cuttings from the fig bush, pomegranate tree, Sweet Betsy bush, the forsythia, wild cherry, the pecan, the camellias, gardenias.

There is a cry from the back porch: "My glasses, oh Lord, I've put them down and I don't know where!" It is Punkin in a familiar crisis, putting down her eyes, sending us all off to scurry until they are found. We find them and get back to salvaging, sorting, loading, worrying about flat tires on the trip back.

I have a camera, call Punkin out to the front porch, squat on the sidewalk to focus, my back to the street. I snap the shutter and a gentle familiar voice calls to me from behind, sending chills up my spine. "Is that my Betsy Rose?" It is my second grade teacher who lives across the street, who does not believe in teaching without hugging. My eyes are damp when I kiss her because I remember how happy Betsy Rose felt when Mrs. Johnston called her that in 1959.

Punkin calls me back to her. "Look at the light coming through those dogwoods. Isn't that gorgeous? Look at that red!"

It is getting late. We need to finish loading, carry Punkin back to the nursing home, drive back to Chapel Hill with Skate following us, unload at her house. I check the truck where Liza, Uncle Wilson and Aunt Katy are haggling over a problem — the rolled-up porch screen is hanging off the back, unanchored; we must take everything out and repack, says Uncle Wilson. We all have different solutions, all talk at once, and Uncle Wilson erupts into a fit of temper, politician's dignity set aside. He shakes his head like a badgered bulldog and curses, "Gawwdamnsonofabitchtoomanycooksinthekitchen!" and scrambles out of the back of the truck in his three-piece suit. It is perfect. I am happy to be home, and heave with hysterical humor, hanging on to the side of the truck.

We finish, the truck is loaded, Skate and her sisters check windows and doors, lock it all up. I feel drained, weak-kneed, stand beside the back porch door and swing it back and forth and listen to the music it makes. It squeaks: home, home, home. I look for Punkin. She has already found me; she is standing alone by her empty fishpool; her face is caved in with grief, cheeks wet; she is shaking her head at the house and me. When I reach her I am crying too, take her in my arms. She whispers in my ear, "It is the end of the world."

I hold her with my voice, the way she once held me, tell her that her life is worth living, that she can't escape it, not even through death. It is the end of *a* world, not *the* world, and it's only unbearable if we can't find within ourselves what doesn't die. Find that, I say, and you'll know that everything that has ever been in this house is alive, in you, in us. We're going to spread that kindness — the Winter fires, the rain splashing in on your bedroom curtains in July, the kitchen's warmth, the light of the chandelier in your eyes, your moonflowers, your roses, the red in the dogwoods. I'll give it away again and again and you do the same, you hear?

We are laughing and crying at the same time, stroking each other. She takes my face in her hands. Her heart is full, untouched by the ship breaking up under her, the dark waters swallowing her past.

She whispers, "I leave everything to you. My estate. To you."

The waiting is over. I let her go. I am not waiting for her awakening, will not again. She has her freedom, and I have mine, and that is enough.

(December 1980)

David Citino

The Funeral

When you need them most, to ask
where to go from here, your hair
growing brittle as February grass,
they're gone, singly or united,
under stone in a safe place where
the stranger who cares for them,
pulling a mower behind his
International Harvester
to trim the grass they lie beneath,
setting poison out
for the mice and squirrels and weeds
that mate nearby, knows them
better than you, seasons laboring by
like old city buses against the wind,
but too far away to disturb
a parent's rest, their reward
for teaching you that being their child's
the same as being no one else,
that mourning them's the final thing
you have to learn.

(May 1981)

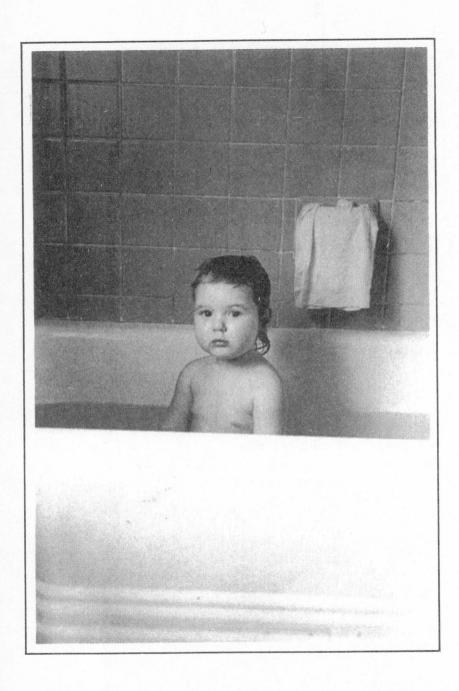

US/Readers Write About . . .

Childhood Fears

I am eleven years old. It is late for me to be out; but here I am, just leaving the local movie after three hours of horror films. Dr. Cyclops, The Werewolf? I can't remember the exact films because the experience isn't isolated; yet the feeling, the events are as regular as the passing of the weeks into Summer.

Ahead of me is the long walk home. Behind me are the grotesque, gray creatures of a nighttime movie world. Between the two I move on legs that seem to be controlled by something outside of me — a spirit in the old, abandoned house that I must pass beneath before I reach the streetlight by the railroad track, and the last, dark stretch of tree-shaded street that I must go down to make it home.

The horrors multiply as I go. All the stores I pass are haunted, of course. People have passed their lives within them, discontented and disappointed by life. They linger on in the places they still hate in death as they did in life because now as then they do not know what else to do. The laundry, the clothing store, the sudden alley to the shoe-shine shop, the dentist's office — I pass each as quickly as I can without running. To run would be to admit I am afraid. That has caused me trouble in the past. Being afraid has kept me home when my brother went to see Frankenstein or the Creature from the Black Lagoon. It has cost me my masks which my mother has either hidden or destroyed because I sleep some nights with the lights on, or don't sleep at all. It has brought forth derisive laughter from friends when I hesitate before certain places in the night.

The night! How could a God of love and mercy create such a place? I leave the stores and the invisible widow's house behind. Ahead, though I cannot see it, I know there is the old abandoned house, once the fine home of a mill owner whom people in the town won't talk about now. Used for a while as a semi-hotel for transients, it has quickly gone gray and rotten in the last year. The early Spring wind rustles through the huge trees around the place. *That's all the noise is*, that steady thud from a form light won't acknowledge.

I know there is discontent brooding within those walls. I have been inside the place in the daylight. With two older girls I explored its dilapidated elegance, laughing and mocking the fear I knew then it could generate. Then my mind had not been on fear, but on the nicely developed hips and breasts of the two girls. "They heard my thoughts, I know. The ghosts heard me thinking as I watched the girls move through the tiny rooms and narrow halls. Now they have their chance, now they are rushing down those same halls, down the collapsing stairs." I pass into the twisting, huge shadow of the house. My mouth is cold, my hands are cold, my stomach is an abyss full of devils and man-faced reptiles with dog feet. My heart! Is it there?

Before I can scream or run, I am suddenly out of the shadow and gradually entering the glow of the streetlight. Fear flows out of me like stagnant water from an overturned bucket. I am proud of the unfearing me as I cross the railroad track and the highway. Down the tunnel of trees above the street, I see the light of my house. My parents are there, and food, and warmth, and the TV light. But then I remember there's also the house where the man came home one snowy afternoon and dropped dead with a bag of groceries in his arms. Poor man, laid out dead among eggs and cereal boxes, bills unpaid, son growing up wrong, wife gone Catholic.

Now I am running. If only I can make it to our door, at least they'll know I'm there and they can help me live to do it all again next Friday.

David C. Childers
Lillington, North Carolina

When I have fears that I may cease to be.
— Keats

Death often colors our childhood far too subtly to understand at the time. When I was seven, my grandfather died in our house. I can still recall my father's slow, heavy tread on the stairs, and the growing fascination with which I watched him carefully count out a handful of coins, medals, and rosary beads — the contents of my grandfather's pockets. Even as a child I was shocked to think that this was all my grandfather had to show for his seventy years — that the dead had only this parting gift to bestow on the living. I clutched those few coins and cried fiercely before venturing downstairs. I can remember brushing against the soft folds of a black cassock and smelling the wax and incense I even then associated with death, standing and staring at my grandfather, his face already strangely unfamiliar and growing more distant.

My Catholic upbringing made death my constant, unwelcome companion. In school it was driven into us that we might die at any moment and be called to account for our life. Every day we listened to gruesome stories of unsuspecting, proud sinners cut down by a speeding car or crushed under a pile of storm-loosened slates. Where life to some children is an unbroken expanse dotted with minor setbacks, mine, because of these insistent stories, was pockmarked by gaping holes in its very fabric. I don't exaggerate when I say that my life seemed a moment-by-moment affair. The ground might open at any time and swallow us whole; the play might suddenly halt and the backdrop fall away to reveal a crowd of grinning faces of our own death masks. Our greatest fear was that, just before this happened, we might be tricked into some sin that would make us forfeit eternal life for the pains of everlasting damnation. Yet even at that time, we had figured out that there was such a thing as being too good. It seemed obvious that the devil would find such goodness irritating and irresistible and that God would probably let him torment us with terrible diseases, family deaths, and bitter disappointments — confident that the results would only redound to his greater glory. Knowing this, we felt like marked men tempting the fates by our excesses. Sinning a little seemed the best way to assure our anonymity.

This emphasis on last things took its toll. I can remember spending nights huddled in bed, afraid that the last judgment might catch me unaware. I would pull my sheets as tightly to my chin as I could and lie there shivering in those early Summer evenings, afraid that the faint glow at twilight might really be the false dawn supposed to herald the second coming. It seemed unfair that the world should come to an end before I had had a chance to test my dreams. Nonetheless, such thoughts made me extremely sensitive to how fragile and tenuous life seemed to be. One example stands out in my memory. I had heard on the news of a mid-air collision in which all had died. That night I replayed the tragedy in my mind dozens of times. Each time I could see the planes on their collision course. Each time I would brace myself for the sickening shudder as they touched and I would imagine that I could feel the intense heat from the mounting fireball. But worst of all, I would thrill to the horror of that final second when, suspended thousands of feet above the earth, each person might have realized how utterly helpless he was to avert his sudden and horrible end. I listened to my heart racing after that, morbidly fascinated by the thought that God might choose this moment to end my existence and so make me a spectator at my own death. Only my mother's arms could shut out the cold and darkness which seemed to be lying in wait for me.

From that time on I used to have a recurring dream. I would be lying in a field looking up through the waving grass. Next to me would be a small ditch. The ditch would quickly swell, becoming darker and deeper, until suddenly I would find the ground slipping from under me and myself falling, falling — while all the time I could see in the distance my house, which I feared I would never again enter.

Paul Linzotte
University Park, Pennsylvania

(June 1980)

Stealing Souls:
Thoughts on Photography

John Rosenthal

A few years ago, on a cool Fall afternoon in Central Park, I sat down at a bench and watched an odd man playing the drums. He was playing on the lip of a tall wastebasket, drumsticks in his hand.

"Baba-la-bop," he kept saying over and over again, synchronous with his play. "Baba-la-bop."

Somewhere down the line he had become a weird person. Who knows how long ago? Not him. In a gray trench coat he looked like a large man who had, inexplicably, become smaller; his head was oversized and dense. Then I realized something else that was different about him: he was wearing makeup, layers of it, and he had blacked in his hair and sideburns with paint or shoe polish. He was Mr. Show Business gone loco.

As photographers, we find those persons most alien to our bourgeois training . . . and we "document" them, as if the sole intention of their suffering and aimlessness was to earn them the right to become an "interesting" subject.

"Buddy Rich!" he shouted out, and in the clicking of his sticks he made a fine adjustment.

There was something shocking about him, a zone of outrage and defect which distilled all the air between you and him. His face had a depthless quality, cartoonish; he was a Central Park doll who made certain noises when you poked him in the right places. And he was good at his drumming, for lunacy has its perfections, too.

I was only beginning to take photographs then, so I started to wonder how I would photograph him. Should I even photograph him? Did the world need another such photograph? At the time I couldn't believe that it didn't, so I set about preparing myself for the adventure — a certain push to the nervous system which would allow me to step out of my anonymity into the public world; a few adjustments of shutter and aperture.

Would Cartier-Bresson take this picture? I wondered.

Then I noticed that standing behind the drummer was a woman in a full-length fur coat talking to someone seated on a bench. Beside her a small poodle on a red leash stood prancing on little clicking feet. All of a sudden the poodle started jumping in the air, straight up, brief little nervous jumps, making no noise going up or down.

It was too irresistible. I slid off my bench, approached the drummer — who once again modified his drumming technique with the declaration, "Gene Krupa!" — crouched low, framed both the leaping poodle and the mad musician, and fired off a number of frames, maybe twenty.

What was I after? I had yanked two odd realities together, the way photographers do, and thought that was enough. Was there going to be a secret heart to my image?

Years later I realized that a poodle's nerves and a crazy park minstrel have nothing in common except to the witless. Of course I could always claim the imperatives of absurdism . . . but hasn't that been claimed enough? And is it even true? This absurdism which the lens loves to capture — isn't it ultimately sterile and flat, the imposing of an aesthetic usually in the place of tears? For the most part, these dark demi-statements of the camera insinuate a potpourri of beauty at the heart of our tense world, a beauty which is there only because the camera found it. They make us seem profound at the exact moment we are being trite. Trite? Yes, of course, for what did I offer this man but a context in which all his sadness and loneliness were neutralized by my delight in the capricious. Much better by far to photograph him simply and let his own face tell a story.

A few years later I stopped again to rest on a bench in Central Park a few yards away from the zoo. By then a photographer, I had been walking around the city for a few hours in search of certain images which had so far eluded me. My assumption was that the photographs I was looking for were just around the corner, and all I had to do was find the corner. It was not a bad notion really, for it built up the legs and taught me the joys of strolling, something I had never learned in thirty years of travelling by car. And I was learning to see too — not as of yet with any real clarity, but at least with the gradual sense that there was something to see, something, at any rate, beyond what I had already seen, something just around the corner. It was where this corner might be that was to occupy my thoughts as I sat down on the park bench.

I also sat down to look at a woman who was sitting on a bench directly across from me. She was an old woman, at the most seventy, in a black cloth coat, and she was covered from head to toe with birds, mostly pigeons, though there were a few sparrows hopping about her knees. Her coat and her red cheeks told me she was a foreigner, but I would have guessed it also from her open way with the birds, her conversation with them. She was chatting with them and cajoling them in an endless stream of bird-chucks and half-mutterings. There were criticisms, terms of endearment, feathered confidences, jibes about what they were doing today and what they did yesterday. She had names for many of them and would personally consult with a few special ones about their comings and goings. Out of a small white bag she fed them seeds while constantly reminding them of their manners, which were none too fine.

She was obviously of that breed of people, not so rare, who prefer the company of birds to that of people. In New York City where there are too many people and not enough birds, her like can often be found sitting in Central Park on warm afternoons. And on this day lots of people were in the park taking advantage of the lovely weather: elderly overweight ladies with little dogs, ears twitching with the news, lying at their feet, and old men with parchment skin dressed in neat threadbare suits, eyes closed to the sun, their starched white shirts bright like snow in the noon sunlight. Couples and families wandered by — the American families in unwrinkled clothing, cramming in as good a time as they could in as short a time as possible, the children whining and bored, and the European families, mostly couples, alert as birds and handsome in leather and lace, talking melodiously to each other. Down the way a drunk who looked like Rasputin slept fearfully on a bench. His green linen suit was stained and he was shirtless beneath his jacket. On each side of him a couple of feet of free space had been granted; an unwholesome presence.

I was not prepared for what happened next. A plump man wearing a shiny green short-sleeved shirt and madras pants, carrying a camera case under his arm, passed the woman feeding the birds, fiddled with his camera for a moment, and then, whirling around, took her picture. There was suddenly an upheaval of birds, an explosion of clucks; it was astonishing how quickly the bird-woman had detached herself from her charges.

"What are you doing? What are you doing?" she cried, advancing toward the photographer, one accusatory finger pointing directly at his face. "What do you think you are, taking pictures like this?" she shrilled in a loud querulous voice, her accent Germanic. "You think I don't see you taking my picture? You think I don't know you going to take my picture? I know before you know!" she yelled, still moving toward the poor fellow who was in a state of real confusion.

One knows that New Yorkers are famous for confrontations, but no out-of-towner can ever be ready for one. They are always thirty seconds behind the retort they would like to make, the one they would like to recall when they get home. And our photographer, probably a Midwesterner, was no exception. Exposed as he was to this unexpected assault, he blushed deep scarlet, stammered, stepped backward, his camera clutched at his side as if it were something unclean. What is more embarrassing than when we have been caught peeking? In his confusion one could see a blow to his virility — which was wilting in front of the eyes of thirty people. And let it be said that this was no ordinary assault or anything resembling a dispute — it was an obsession provoked and let loose. And she wasn't even finished.

"You give me that film!" she demanded. "You give me that film, or you pay me money! You want the picture so bad you help pay for food! I know what you do when you go home to Ohio! You put my picture in the magazine or newspaper! You help me pay for food and then you put me in a magazine!"

But by this time the photographer had realized that the punishment did not fit the crime, and mumbling something about a crazy old woman, he walked away. She, mumbling something about stupid tourists, went back to her bench where the birds, soon reassembling, joined her as if nothing had happened.

This scene was to repeat itself a couple of more times in the next thirty minutes. After a while I could anticipate her dashing up from the birds as some innocent tourist began to point a camera in her direction. And her complaint was always the same: her photograph was going to be put somewhere, and for it she would receive no compensation, not even enough to pay for air, for bird seed.

At that moment I recalled a scene from a movie I had seen at least fifteen years before. It was not the first time I had recalled it — in fact, I have thought of it so many times that I now wondered if I hadn't dreamt it. (Which of us, after all, hasn't remembered an experience in detail which never occurred — an experience we needed perhaps, but never had? Did we end up having the experience? I wonder.) The movie was *Lawrence of Arabia*, and in the scene a native, perhaps on top of a train, gestures furiously to someone below not to take his picture. Someone explains, "The natives believe that if you take a person's picture, you steal his soul."

I don't know why I've thought of that scene, real or imagined, a hundred times since I saw that movie. I suppose that I thought at the time it was somehow true, that an act of appropriation could take place when a photograph is taken — but surely in my life as an American young man no point of view I ever encountered would countenance such a notion. Yet why did that scene keep coming back to me over the years — why, more particularly, as I was sitting across from the woman with the birds?

A process of revelation began for me at that moment which it would take me years to conclude. I haven't gotten to the end of it yet. It came from looking closely at the woman and her birds, looking without a camera, without the hope of anything other than the look. It was partially epiphanic, one of those bright, seemingly-divine moments when a crowd of isolated thoughts and notions fuse into a single perception which changes everything. It was also a moment earned — after all, back in North Carolina a marriage was clamoring for attention I was putting elsewhere. And wasn't I, sitting here languidly on a park bench in Central Park, the only one in the world who wanted me to be here? There was a hint suddenly that nothing of importance would ever come to me if I weren't sitting on a park bench somewhere by myself, and that I was absolutely right to be here today — far away, all at once, from everything, all the good things and all the bad things, all the responsibilities and the distractions, all the choices which had ended up so unclearly, and all the urgency which would soon force me to make new choices. I was, simply, available; and my dukes weren't up.

Yes, it was true — something was being appropriated, but I didn't know what. I would find out what it was. A woman sitting on a bench was having her picture taken by men and women she didn't know. Inside a camera an emulsified surface had received a scattering of light — and somewhere down the line this emulsified surface would be bathed in chemicals. An event which occurred in time would be converted into an object which occurs only in space. This is pretty close to magic, even if it can be explained — and if not magic, then at least something strange, very strange. What could be stranger than an odd old New York lady's image appearing suddenly in the troubled waters of an Ohio darkroom? *Particularly if she wishes it not to be so.* To me, sitting in the bright New York sunlight, such an image seemed very strange indeed. What is she doing, after all, in that water? What is her image doing there? Outside the darkroom an angry woman may be cooking dinner, a rerun may be playing on a television a few rooms away. Shouldn't we ask what is going on here? Why has she been thus converted? And for whose benefit? All we know with absolute certainty is that it is not for her benefit — since she has established it most ferociously in our minds that she has never received a penny for her birds, and that's what matters to her. I mean, if she is to undergo conversion, if a woman sitting on a park bench is going to be converted into a two-dimensional image, we might ask why.

The question was particularly close to me in those days. Why take photographs? Or to put it another way, is the impulse to take photographs an artistic impulse, that is, one which tries to enlighten, to disclose, to make meaning, or does it come from a semi-voyeuristic inclination to make thrills by stopping time, by perpetuating an event beyond its natural closure? And if photography is an art, how do you make it one? Running up and down the city as I had for the past few years, I had come up with a number of interesting images, but I wasn't sure that according to my own inner measurements they were worth very much. I wasn't sure they said anything real, and, never being a cynic, I was afraid they contained very little of that feeling for life which I consider basic to the truest instincts of art. As of yet I hadn't been able to take out of me *feelings* and get them into a photograph. Even the best of my images partook of that impersonality which is the curse of the medium. All this machinery in front of us — it's so unlike a brush and paint, paper and pencil, which conveys, without our choosing, who we are and what is the disposition of our heart. Where, I wondered, was my theme, my true subject? Robert Frank had found his America — where was mine? Cartier-Bresson's photographs were saturated and explosive with his curiosity for place and his passion for the historical event. Steiglitz took photographs of New York City and made them look like photographs of a mind. Even Diane Arbus, claustrophobic, addicted to Halloween and nightmare, had nevertheless made the world her own. Hell, I wasn't even able to get in my photographs the specific kind of joy and energy which one constantly comes across in the photographs which friends take of friends. Why we take photographs was no small question for me, playing, as I was, in the suburbs of art.

It is true of course that one of the oldest traditions in photography is the taking of photographs which portray the odd and exotic. This is the information-gathering aspect of photography. In the nineteenth century the search for the exotic had led brave men like Frances Frith up the farthest reaches of the Nile and Samuel Bourne 18,000 feet up the Himalayas. The initial impulse for these projects sprang from a legitimate curiosity about the things of this world, a world, which due to the limits of transportation, was still largely unknown. We forget in the modern world, where everything is accessible to everything else, where helicopters routinely land on the top of mountains, where "information" can be instantly retrieved, where already millions of images have accumulated in both our archives and our memories, that in the nineteenth century, a person, providing he had a curiosity, would have very few restraints placed upon him. Knowing as much as we do, we lose joy of getting to know. A hundred years ago the shape of the modern world was taking place in our minds, and this had greatly to do with a photographic quest for the exotic, the unknown.

But the modern manner of taking photographs — not of the exotic, but of the merely odd — is a different matter altogether. It is similar to the difference which exists between the nineteenth-century notion of "taking the tour" and the modern notion of tourism. The issue is one of seeing slowly, or rather, of not seeing too quickly. As moderns, we simply see too quickly, which is a way of saying we don't see at all. Our camera sees for us: it frames up a scene (a family, a historic building, a landscape), converts it into a two-dimensional image by the push of a button, and allows us to live under the illusion that in "having" something (a photograph) we have "done" something (an experience). And we learn too quickly too — for no matter how hard the apologists for the high-tech industries try to convince us that "knowing" is the same thing as having information at our instant disposal, nothing of value has ever been learned except by enduring the tests of time, its cruelty and its surprises. No painting can be seen and comprehended quickly, and no woman can be loved too rapidly. This is as true as anything I know. That which is rapid and accelerated may be necessary to people who have to speed things up for the purpose of making money or scoring some kind of goal, but it has nothing to do with the act of "knowing."

The modern tourist, having become saturated with images of the "unknown" world, is really without a curiosity, that is, without a passion for the unknown world. An earlier curiosity for the exotic, hungry and innocent, has given way to the legitimate feeling that the world is too much known, the world has become boring. And this is especially true in America where a large and depressing conventionality, amounting almost to the blunting of curiosity itself, dominates the national psyche. But who can blame us? Since our birth we have been overwhelmingly subjected to the insistence and presence of images, an insistence which has ended up destroying our interest in photographs themselves, or anyway, in the content of photographs — which happens to be the world itself. Buy our camera and tickets, charge through the landscapes of Europe in an air-conditioned tour bus, wrap it all up in a week, file our slides and snaps in boxes labeled "Europe." Done. We've done France. We might as well eat a meal in one bite in order to compliment the chef on his subtlety.

What is tragic in all this is that the truly exotic, the unusual, and the unknown still exist in our world, but we have lost our capacity for them. Our assumption is that we know our world, that because *communication* has improved, so, too, has our knowledge of things. Instead we have become like those friends of mine who took speed-reading courses because they wanted to hurry the process of understanding. The result was that even though they could read *Moby Dick* in a day and retain for a few weeks a breezy recollection of the whole book, their involvement in the tale came to nothing — whereas other friends of mine slowly endured the book, crawled through it, sometimes taking weeks, savoring the odd Elizabethan language and allowing the mythic elements of Ahab's search for the white whale to illuminate their own quests. Eventually, the speed-readers, in order to explain their own lack of interest in Ahab's obsession, decided the book was an exotic antique and went into various high-speed occupations like advertising or "communications." I can't say that my other friends became poets, but it is remarkable how few of them became frauds.

(What a journey I was on, sitting on the bench in Central Park. Yet all around me were the signs that I was on to something. Just over the wall I could hear nothing but the steady honking of cars stuck at red lights, not even stuck, just stopped for a few seconds — the sound of acceleration, of anxiety, of tedium, of purposeless agitation, like cows on drugs. And who was I, resting now on a park bench, having run up and down the city in search of some fugitive image?)

It seemed to me (as the bird-woman fed her birds once again, no tourist with a camera in sight) that the speeding up of things had cost us nothing less than our real curiosity for real things as well as our respect for the differences among those things. Photographs, those bright rectangles, had somehow managed to replace experience, unshapeable except by the best part of ourselves; images of mystery had replaced the long, arduous course of mystery itself.

What American child wouldn't rather go to Disneyland than to France? We see things so quickly that we begin to prefer only those things which are quick to experience — romance novels, simple and cynical art, fast sports, video games, cocaine, and my own private lament, bad photographs; namely those meaningless large-format "nature" photographs which are nothing more than a sentimentalizing of the disappearing American landscape — or even worse, that species of "documentary" photograph, taken by white, middle-class photographers, of the sad and the derelict, usually black, men and women too ill to smash the lens or too ignorant to question the motives of a person with six hundred dollars worth of equipment around his neck.

Sitting in the park, myself a tourist watching other tourists go by, I realized that a hunger for images of an unknown world had given way to a delight in the picturesque, a much milder form of curiosity. The distinction seems minute, but underneath it I caught a glimpse of an immense loss. One of the richest traditions in photography, the venture into the unknown, had been converted into ogling. The tourist with a camera, almost anybody with a camera, was not taking photographs out of a wonder for what he didn't know; that was long gone. This photographer believed he knew all he needed to know — from there on out it was easy wonder and easy laughter. What our tourist was trying to take home with him was a real old lady in a park who had been converted into a two-dimensional joke. The hidden statement beneath the photograph he would take was really a remark, and it went something like this: "New York is filled with oddballs. This is one of them." Uncurious about the real woman, he snaps her picture to validate the normality of his own life. She has become exotic to him because nothing else is. It is from the deadest places inside ourselves that we take most of our photographs. Going neither to the bottom of the Grand Canyon, nor to the bottom of ourselves, we settle for the *exoticism of class*, the hills and valleys which exist between us and our fellow citizens, the poor, the drunk, the confused. Make no mistake about it (I told myself), these photographs are not meant to illuminate whoever will look at them someday. This is not Walker Evans looking as closely as anyone ever looked at something he had never seen before. This is the high-speed American with high-speed film taking a quick snap of an actual woman as if she was a weird-looking building or a pretty sunset.

Was a soul being stolen? I didn't know.

As I watched the old lady in black continue to fuss with her birds, I saw — this day was a day for seeing! — that even though she might seem exotic to the tourist with the camera, she obviously didn't seem exotic to herself. Exoticism is not of those terms we apply to ourselves. It is always to some other person they apply, some person who is exotic when compared to us. At home with ourselves to some extent, we judge our acts to be commensurate with our needs. I don't feed birds because I am strange, but because I am lonely or because I love birds or because my father raised them when I was a child or because I read Robinson Jeffers at the right time and remember his saying, "I'd rather kill a man than a hawk." We always have our reasons which are concealed only from someone who is not ourself. To ourselves we are perfectly clear; only others, with their concealed intentions, their unexplained behavior, seem opaque.

Unless she was chasing off a tourist with a camera, the bird-woman seemed quite sane, sitting on her bench and chatting with the birds.

In fact, from her own point of view, she was doing exactly what she wanted to do. It was the tourists who were crazy. And in what way? Well, in my real willingness to be sitting there in Central Park, sensing the early tidings of a world about to unflower, free of concerns which could never include this woman, I found myself in sympathy with her, not in the intellectual sense of being on her side, but rather as if I could see through her eyes, as if her difficulties were my difficulties. That's not an easy thing to do; it requires something akin to sleep, a drifting kind of wakefulness, and it's especially hard for someone like myself who lives too often in the abstract world where thinking about someone means not thinking *like* them. But here in my leisure, floating among my thoughts, willing to be slow and then slower, proceeding snail-like beside what seemed like a large glimpse of how things are, I wrote a monologue in my head which came from this woman's need but used my words. It went something like this:

How can you maintain a friendship with birds, how can you maintain anything with birds, if someone is taking your picture? It is this constant interference at my peripheral line of vision, my concentration! To photograph me, someone "stops" me, not only literally on film by a shutter speed over which I have no control, but also by "stopping" the atmosphere around me. If, as I feed my birds, life is flowing around me, an afternoon or morning tidal flow, then a photographer breaks all that up, he interrupts the casualness of things. You see, it makes me self-conscious, which, when I am feeding birds, is nothing less than a crime. Do I need it? Content and cajoling, easy among my birds, doing nothing but what I want to do, I don't need a photographer taking my picture. Should I be chronicled? What for? Before the photographers came, my friendship with the birds was without self-consciousness. This man, this person with a camera, has invaded my right to exist on my own peaceful terms. Friendship, remember, is never easy, not with your next-door neighbor, not with your brother, and certainly not with a park full of birds.

Was a soul being stolen? Suddenly I thought so. On every level possible this woman was going to lose. And she was going to lose big. She had already lost much. What she had worked out for herself in the middle of this difficult city, what friendship she had managed with a number of birds, what primitive means of assuagement was hers, was being ransacked by a legion of wide-eyed tourists with cameras. To them she could have been a creature in a zoo. Making her self-conscious, they destroyed her peace of mind, which is, after all, what we have to work with. Lacking all imagination (having no time for it, really) they pretended she was there for them and their hungry cameras, and they stole her image. For what use, we may ask? Only the worst. These tourists, like most Americans, assumed they knew what was what, what was proper behavior for a human being, what was not, what was beautiful, what was ugly. And they were out to build a monument to their assumptions. Each slide they took of the bird-woman, hell, each slide they took of the Grand Canyon, was another brick in place. This is crazy. This is pretty. This is poverty. This is an Indian.

It takes years to create any kind of real clarity. All that brave woman did for me was to end my search for a particular kind of photograph. Her refusal to accept gracefully the right of anybody to discredit her own eccentric world by the puny (yet momentous) act of taking her picture made me realize how unprotesting are the objects of our dangerous gaze. And also how truly unexamined is that gaze. As photographers, we find those persons most alien to our bourgeois training — the hapless, the homeless, the tacky, the truly marginal; that is, people most unlike ourselves — and we "document" them, as if the sole intention of their suffering and aimlessness was to earn them the right of becoming an "interesting" subject. In my own case, I knew that, if it was true that I no longer felt obliged to take photographs of "happy" children *because such photographs told me little about the lives of children*, I also had no reservations about taking "serious" photographs of strangers, men and women who would not protest against the categories in which I would (for the purposes of getting a grant or having an exhibition with a good title) place them — Ukranians of the East Village, transvestites, suburbanites, the Hopi Indians, the Irish. And yet when compared to the size of lives, to the actual differences which exist between people who might be "gay" or "Irish," these images ended up telling me just as little about the lives of the people being photographed as did those photographs of children licking ice cream cones. These categories (nets) were purely academic puffs which disappeared two seconds after they were examined. and so too did general agreeability, the false family-of-man atmosphere, which these categories almost automatically produce.

Learning what you don't want to photograph is only half the battle, though a large half. It's also the half which can be put into words. The other half — which consists of one's photographs — can only be depleted by any attempt to set up a verbal equivalent of whatever power they may have, what intentions. However, I don't mind saying that after I left the park that day — having observed for half an hour or so the old woman and her refusal to be photographed, and being chastened by my own realizations — I never took quite the same kind of photograph again. From that moment on I regarded the taking of a photograph as a personal act, as personal as the writing of a poem — deep and perilous, intellectual and beautiful. A photograph, or a grouping of them, would be as mysterious as this woman and as complicated as my own mind. I would never document anything. I would hope for luck, but I wouldn't rely on it. I would hope not to diminish things.

I got up to leave. The old woman was still with her birds. She looked up at me quickly (having seen my camera bag), so I held my empty hands against my face, palms out. I couldn't help but break into a laugh. And she laughed too, nodding her head vigorously, though not enough to disturb the birds.

(March 1983)

Sy Safransky

Recognition

The world becomes another
story. I see nothing so clearly
as myself, and that
smudged. The mirror I took
for a wife has run off
with my eyes. I stuffed
the sockets with newspapers.
I ate the radio. I became
a headline, inappropriately
handsome, for the facts of my
life. Read between the lines:
I am the obituary for the sports
page, I am the coffee break
and the broken bones of time —
once free, now tamed to meaning,
pacing the human cage, wall
to infinite wall; a prisoner
of space, no less; no more.

(February 1976)

On Women

Cindy Crossen

Many times in my life I have felt like a new person. My cells are subtly dying, rebirthing, regrouping all the time, so that I can never pinpoint one moment of metamorphosis. I am everchanging yet constant, like a river. I now live with a little girl with a big belly who laughs and cries often and with abandon; and I know I was once a little girl nearly the same. I watch wrinkles grow around my eyes and I know that I am getting younger, circling around my center to my beginning. As I think of womanness, I meditate on my own changes.

My sister and I played in many fantasies. There were fairies, and kingdoms in the clouds that warred with each other during violent thunderstorms. The sky would rain huge drops; the streets would flood;

As the hair on my legs grew longer, I would idly play with it for hours, knowing that to the world's eyes, and still even to my own, it was "disgusting."

then we would wade in the water, forgetting kingdoms and fairies, finding washtubs and inner tubes for floating down our newly-created river.

There were infinite adventures to be imagined, and we enacted them as we played, making all we did exciting and romantic. We formed secret clubs and became blood sisters, pricking our fingers with a needle, squeezing out a drop of blood, and then touching fingertips to become bonded forever. We created our rituals and religions, and felt no compunction about abandoning them for others as we flowed along.

I committed myself to Christianity when I was about ten. It was a time of exultation and confusion for me. I made glorious resolutions in my diary, such as not lying anymore, followed by an entry praying for another chance, making another promise when I slipped. That was the year I first learned what the word "fuck" meant, and this secret knowledge troubled me very much. I felt, since my parents hadn't told me about it, I shouldn't know. I was filled with God often, and just as often with guilt. That year began the questions which I would ask myself, in varying degrees of intensity, for a long time. Why are we so concerned with clothes when it so clearly tells us in the Bible not to be? Why do we wear lipstick? Should I date boys? How should I live? The way I saw it, if I were to follow Christ truly, I would wear robes and bare feet and give up money and be humble and help people. And be a social outcast. My world pulled me in another direction — toward a concern for my looks (I was very vain), a desire to have boyfriends, competitiveness in all I did, achievement. It's only now that I'm beginning to feel answers to some of those dilemmas.

As I live with teenage girls now and look back to my own experiences, I realize that a girl's inner confidence that she is really a woman is tenuous, so she bolsters it with externals. The inner pressure for me to fill the feminine mold was strong. All the firsts were important — first bra, first bra with cups, shaving of underarms and legs, stockings and high heels, menstruating, wearing lipstick, being kissed. I was so conscious of these things. I would round my back and lean over my desk so that the boy behind me would be sure to notice I was wearing a bra. On a Girl Scout camping trip a friend told me, "You aren't a real woman until you have your period." Upset, I denied her words; I had not yet "started," but

I asserted that even so, I was still a woman. Secretly I had my doubts. On the day I first menstruated I was proud, and happy. Surprised, too. I felt I was very lucky; I was initiated. The secrets of a woman were mine now.

Shaving was never as much of a joy for me — I just had too much hair, and it kept spreading. I didn't like wearing bathing suits, but what could I do? I shaved it all off. Sometimes my hair follicles would get red and infected, which was a disastrous effect in a bikini. We had so many tribulations about our flaws. My first act of liberation (an internal movement) was cutting my long, all-boys-prefer-it-that-way hair. I was free! The next act, some years later, was letting all the rest of my hair grow. I felt even freer. As the hair on my legs grew longer, I would idly play with it for hours, knowing that to the world's eyes, and still even to my own, it was "disgusting." I loved it like an ugly child. Thick and abundant, it rippled in the wind and felt nice and soft after years of unmanageable stubble. People on the streets stared. I was in the thick of adventure again after the repressing years of trying to be beautiful. The trappings of femininity were dropping away and what was left was pure woman, and also some little girl.

Growing older means growing older and growing younger. If I live, I will be an old lady. My cheeks will be soft as silk. My breasts will wrinkle; my voice will tremble. I hope there'll be a light in my eye. I used to believe I'd have perspective at the age of eighty, but as I get nearer, I think I'll just have a different perspective and more experiences. I begin to let go of past identities, and take on new adventures, with the creativity and sense of play of my young girlhood. Having passed the serious business of proving I'm a woman, I'm free again to be anything I choose.

(November 1975)

Barbara Street

Living At The Edge

Living at the edge
isn't easy. Still,
I prefer it. My dragons
they're friendly beasts
some days. They wear
tennis shoes, smoke Gauloises,
they watch the evening news.
They speak to me in even
tones: Girl, we're taking over.
Fine, I say. I'll go. I'll bake
a cake. I'll write postcards
to my friends today.

Thanks a lot. It won't last
long, I know. See, they're
dragging out the broken glass
now. Kisses for your fingers,
they purr. Ice cubes for
your red hot veins.
They rub it in. Those dragons,
they know how to win.

The edge is here. I search
for paper clues in the *Herald*,

anything, anywhere. Smoke
dope. Read my horoscope.
I'm earth. I'm dirt. I must avoid
travelling in planes. Lemon bleach,
I read, takes out stubborn
stains. Why not mine? Express
yourself in spices, lady. I will.
I am chives. I am the marjoram.
The women's news — that's me.
I'm stained. I'm ink.
At odds with death, a dwelling
place, if you will, for these dragons,
their fierce hot breath, their stink.

(November 1975)

US/Readers Write About . . .

Good Marriages

As an outsider, it is probably presumptuous of me to comment on a "good marriage." On the other hand, outsiders have different eyes.

My experience of good, long-term relationships is that somewhere along the line there comes a tip-over point, a magical abyss into which criticism, praise, analysis and description fall and become . . . helpful, perhaps, but not entirely relevant. Too much time has passed; too many difficult and wonderful events have come and gone; the fabric is made and comment is not quite adequate. There is a connection. It has rough and smooth edges, its needs are met and unmet, and its corners can be dark or lit. Whatever the case, there is a kind of factualness that confounds the perfect commentary.

Two things seem to me indispensable in a good and lasting relationship. One is laughter and the other is a deep sense of wishing a partner well on his or her own terms.

By laughter I mean perspective. The perfect (fantasy) mate does not exist, so it becomes necessary to forgive what is "missing" and then, if what is "missing" is badly needed, fill in the blank with situations or people outside the relationship.

A woman artist I know has had a series of unsuccessful liaisons with other artists because she thinks a sympathetic hearing on the subject of work is necessary. I said I thought she was missing the point. "Why don't you try to find someone who is moderately interested in art but who really likes you? You can get your art support outside the house and the security at home." She laughed and agreed in principle and promptly went out and got herself another artist lover.

The second aspect, wishing a partner well on his or her own terms, may not be so easy. So many relationships in our society are based on *quid pro quo* that it may be difficult to break the habit in important personal dealings. Of course, you-do-this-for-me-and-I'll-do-that-for-you or you-don't-do-this-for-me-so-I-won't-do-that-for-you may work for a while — perhaps a lifetime — but it strikes me as narrow and unpleasant in the long run. The mercantile approach, sometimes described with the oozingly inaccurate term, "sharing," is so ingrained at gross and subtle levels that the best a person can manage in some instances is to admit it and laugh a little. With luck, a partner will laugh too, recognizing in himself or herself a similar capacity in other circumstances.

To wish someone well on his or her own terms requires respect, trust, and clarity.

The respect may come in the form of a strange distance — distance in proximity, a willingness to know that another human being is and always will be a secret. Why it is that human beings who are wise enough to know they cannot know themselves persist in thinking that they can adequately or accurately analyze others is one of the nonsensical wonders of the human race.

Trust is too often touted as something to be placed in others. It is better to begin, with care, closer to home.

Clarity seems to me to be the willingness to say "yes" and to say "no" — with affection. I do not mean the socially acceptable "yes" or the much-praised "no." "They," even the ones closest, may have very strong and persuasive opinions. Good for them. But, as one fellow put it, "Better your own truth, however weak, than the truth of another, however noble."

So much for words. So much for formulas. The blessing for the day is that if people had anything to do with formulas we'd all be in the soup and bored silly.

Adam Fisher
New York, New York

(April 1983)

I visited my Uncle Jimmy and my aunt Joan in the Summer of 1978, in Concord, California — the last stop on the BART line from San Francisco. I was on my way to the Rainbow Gathering.

Jimmy and Joan were both in their forties and both had bright blond hair. My uncle had a big smiling beard and an almost sur-realistically large mustache. Joan had the slightly lean, slightly plump female body that one describes as "attractive." She looked like a secretary, which she was.

As I recall, my uncle picked up a side of beef on his way back from the railroad station. He apologized, knowing I was a vegetarian, but later said something like, "Man does not live by sunflower seeds alone." He treated me with a mixture of wariness and warmth appropriate to a nephew he hadn't seen for ten years.

Part of his ambivalence was due, I think, to his own bohemian years. When he and Joan met, twenty years before, they were both living in tenements, listening to jazz music — their friends were drug dealers and prostitutes. Uncle Jimmy wrote poetry — strange poetry.

Now they lived in an apartment complex on the last stop of the BART line, and Jimmy was preparing to go into business teaching people how to write resumes. (He said the secret was to "sell yourself.") Resumes are a type of poetry, but a rigid form, more strict even than haiku. Also, Truth doesn't have the same importance it has in other poetry.

I remember them pouring some wine, putting on the *Saturday Night Fever* album and dancing sexily around the apartment. (In my memory, I was eating sunflower seeds at the time.) They were in love.

I found all this a little disturbing. I hitched off a few days later, thinking that California really is like everyone says.

Four years later, Jimmy got a brain tumor and started to die. Joan became his nurse. She was close to my parents, and wrote them let-ters. In them, she talked about watching the man she loved turn into a child, a happy and very sick child. She really respected him — I think she said that he was the person she admired most in the world. His medical expenses were enormous, the insurance ran out, and she couldn't both work and take care of him. Most of their friends fell away; they couldn't handle the situation. Jimmy lost his memory and lived in the eternal Present. In a few lucid moments he would realize what was happening to him. One by one, his organs began to fail. All this took most of the year. His wife was by his side continually.

Joan survived through a combination of **rage** and devotion. As for me, I was no longer separated from them by my fear of middle-class stability — theirs had vanished. In its absence, I could see their love for what it was.

Sparrow
New York, New York

(April 1983)

Sita and I have been married twelve years. We met on one day and moved in on the next; sort of, "Ah, so here we are again; let's get on with it." No big romance or trips. I was nineteen and she was twenty-two.

To us, marriage is only a vehicle for going to God. Monks go solo, and married couples go as a tag-team; one can't get even a step ahead at the other's expense. If the couple truly become "Dharma-mates" then there is never the question of separation or divorce. This Dharma marriage is quite different from a marriage based on social/psychological principles such as peace, happiness, liberated woman, liberated man in the popular sense. The Dharma marriage is a raw, no-holds-barred journey in which neither partner has any "rights" at all or spaces to uphold and protect. Ram Dass used to query us, "Do you want to be right, or do you want to be free?"

Rather than developing a context which maximizes the daily peace and harmony, the Dharma marriage shows both partners all their uptightnesses, weaknesses and insecurities so that they can become free rather than just comfortable. Many marriages in our culture dissolve because the discomfort becomes too great for our model of what marriage should be like. Ironically, there's a tremendous joy in giving up even the slightest model or anxiety about having a happy marriage. There's an old Buddhist saying, "Ah, the joy, to discover that there's no happiness to be found in this world."

If I want to be free, then anything that Sita does that gets me uptight is simply one more opportunity for me; it has nothing at all to do with her. If our life together is pleasant, that's fine; if it's not, then that's fine, too. Our union is a precious opportunity to come to God; who else other than your wife or husband can pick apart all those deepest, subtlest ego spaces? Why give that up so that we can hide better? In a sense this is the difference between *bond* and *relationship*. Sita and I have a stronger *bond* every day, *because* our relationship dissolves more each day. Relationship implies specified ways or guidelines within which two people deal with each other; agreements, more or less, about what goes and what doesn't. The more defined a relationship, the less the union can evolve and change; the two people only have a certain context with each other;

there's a built-in stress in the system right from day one. The less defined the relationship, the scarier it is, but the stronger is the bond which develops. One year may be filled with romance, the next year may be totally platonic, in a third they may seemingly be going in different directions, in a fourth they may be driving each other crazy. The Dharma-mates don't freak as their space changes, because they're not clinging to a model of how it should be. It all becomes fascinating to experience — quite humbling as well. The Love deepens and grows too much to remain personal, and becomes Love for God instead. There's no husband or wife, just two intimately connected beings becoming free together, for thousands and thousands of years, crossing gender and cultures and times. . . . Change comes only with time, and Love defeats time. A relationship which depends on certain things changing or not changing is not one in Love.

Children become part of the marriage. The husband-wife-children thing is just the brief passing support system this time around. We honor that level, but also live more as two brothers and a sister on the spiritual journey. Laxmana, Sita and I are a marriage which we enjoy and appreciate more than words can describe. One of the definitions of "marriage" is "an intimate union." The literal definition of "Yoga" is "union." In answer to your question, "What is marriage?" it certainly is an intimate Yoga — one intricate, exquisite vehicle for going to God.

Ah, the grand humor of it all. . . . Here comes the wind, the warm, dry night wind, and who are we?

Bo, Sita and Laxmana Lozoff
Durham, N,C.
(August 1978)

Steven Ford Brown

Pockets

Pockets have travelled all over the world carrying nothing but grains of dust & darkness. Pockets have also carried gold, opium, watches, knives, string, money. Rain in the pocket of a farmer in Kansas as he steels himself & his land against the worst drought in memory. The gigantic dustbowl of the Midwest becomes a pocket of sorrow & hard times as the crops are blown across the desert like Conestoga wagons sailing for the West Coast. Astronomers carry maps that chart the darkness pinpointing small glowing worlds of light that hang out there in the distance of space. The President carries speeches in his pocket. The words of these speeches forget the meaning of the alphabet & gather together in a clump on the pages like small dark animals. When he pulls his speeches out to liberate a country in Southeast Asia or to levy a new tax, the words run away. A small child picks up a white stone, stuffs it into the black country of his pocket. The stone thinks it has died or been transported to a cave, to a black country where nothing breathes. The stone dies a little bit thinking of the breathing clock of the earth. The stone rides around in the pocket dreaming of home. Even the open mouth of the child when he sleeps tonight will become a pocket overflowing with darkness.

(December 1978)

Steven Ford Brown

A Few Sky Things Explained

1. Thunder is an old man with a club foot who drinks a lot, stares at the rain, limps around & rumbles mournfully at his absent wife.

2. Lightning is a woman born ugly who ran away from home to the sky where she covered herself with mirrors & now spends her time flashing light out to the edges of the universe, while back on earth astronomers fall in love with this strange new star.

3. The sky is the dark side of whalebone, at night it grows a thin stubble of beard, comes clean with the sun. Sometimes this whalebone opens & everything falls out.

4. Wind was driven from the sky by thunder. Wind dreams of returning but at present works a very dull job & leads a boring life. Sometimes the wind can be seen leaping among the trees, blowing up off the water of lakes.

5. The sun is a crabby old cab driver with a long ragged mustache of solar coronas. He always has a stubble of fire on his chin & when he gets angry his muscles bulge & his hairs flare. He carries a pocket watch of gold but if trapped in the desert or out of gas in Milledgeville, if need be, he can tell time by the stars.

6. The moon is a thin slip of a girl who once fell in love with a sailor. The sailor had come across seven oceans in his twelve-league boots, his cape of invisibility. He gave her exotic presents from the Far East but one day left her. Her light dulled & she hacked off her long hair. As she lay sobbing on the edge of night she faded down to a thin rim of light.

(December 1978)

Hard Learning: A Diary

Stephanie Mills

September 11. Male and female created he them. What is the truth, the mystery of that difference?

September 17. He held me and called me his buddy. Funny. I hadn't thought of him as a friend so much as a lover.

September 23. Sometimes I wonder if I am trying to manipulate even God with my good girl strategems.

October 6. I say I want a lover. I suppose to have one I must be one first.

November 1. Is it him I'm interested in or am I interested in being interested? The man himself or the fact of his manhood? Why must I relate to men so differently than I do to women? (Maybe because they *are* different.)

November 6. I besieged him with honesty and self-revelation, attempted

I gave him criticism on the overweening masculinity of his style. He responded with detailed instructions on how to fuck in the sun.

to fascinate him with a glimpse of the molten gold at my core.

November 16. The illusion was that he's impulsive like me. The reality is that he's scared like me.

November 22. What do I want from a lover that I can't give myself? Understanding. Correction. Intimacy. Touch, sound, holding. Contact with the sacred heart of another.

December 4. The more deeply I penetrate my motivations, the more ego dynamics I find, the more tricks and traps for the soul.

January 1. He was talking about his ego problem. His ego problem held the floor three times as long as mine.

January 2. I gave him criticism on the overweening masculinity of his style. He responded with detailed instructions on how to fuck in the sun.

January 3. I feel remorse for hurting his feelings, if I have, and regret that I probably haven't hurt them much at all.

February 12. My simple failing is to wish that this peak could last a lifetime, and that my lifetime may be long.

February 14. Feelings pass in an instant and their memory becomes awkward, an embarrassment.

February 27. I hate to think that our joy in bed was a triumph of technique over skepticism.

February 28. We were disconnected from the start, a reality that remained unaltered by our competent, loveless sex. Highly instructive disillusionment, but not worth what it cost in sleep.

March 6. I didn't believe that in his self-confession he spoke the truth, had no idea how that truth would feel in practice.

March 13. Today I pondered the difference between delusion and deception.

March 14. Which of us was the wiser? And what's wrong with a surrender to passion? It's as good a thing to do as fulfill an obligation, but there was no way for us to do both.

March 19. Did he feel like someone had grabbed his image like a doll and run off to play with it? Did he stand there horrified, watching the doll thrashed against the wall for not responding?

April 27. How could I have been so blind to the man's essence? It was the vaporous opium of sex. I always confuse it with love. That's a lot to ask of either.

May 1. My vanity was injured because my self-revelation, my skilled dissection of my outsize half of the relationship, didn't beguile him.

May 2. There are bunches of us, so infected with our individuality that we just won't commit to another, no matter how hard we think we're trying to do just that.

May 13. I think what he was saying last night is that he likes me too much to love me.

May 21. My hopes metastasize into expectations too often. Hence I quaff this bitter brew at the no-holds bar, nursing a grudge with a self-righteousness chaser.

June 11. I have let myself be entered by them, and changed. Their withdrawal is painful. I don't want to be left, but I'd rather be alive than insensate, so I'll take it all as part of life's sweetness.

June 12. It takes bad pain to drive me beyond my fear of that unknown on the other side of change.

June 17. Slowly I'm coming to understand pain, not as a mark of failure, but as the emblem of risk-taking humanity.

July 4. Why not sympathize? Why not comfort? Is anyone's suffering deserved? Does withholding kindness or judging another's mistakes benefit anyone? No. Our job is to love and empathize and then do that some more.

August 6. Far less touching in my life. Sleeping alone all of a sudden. I wonder what that's doing to me at the levels where my mind won't go?

August 7. The relationship worked until it didn't, after all. I guess I should remember that.

August 23. Too much turmoil in my life. The death rattle of old habits of thought, the clinging to expectations. There's no way to detour around the shit pile, no way out but through.

October 29. It's panic that kills swimmers on the night-sea journey.

November 4. Slowly I began to love the storm, seeing it as a manifestation of the goddess's transcendent power, infinitely wise and no doubt right, but wholly unreasonable, unseasonable, and inconvenient to mere mortals.

November 5. I will definitely keep trying, keep on turning over those rocks, giving myself over to the big chance, never mind the fears and betrayals and departures and absences.

December 25. Now I'm accommodating reality, making the pearl, laying down nacre on the provoking grain, making it beautiful, mine, and whole within me.

January 1. God. Please let me learn how to pay attention, just pay attention to the other person, and to become transparent myself.

(February 1984)

Leslea Newman

In Defense of Van Gogh

for Rachel

Even if it was only the tip of his ear
and she was just a gin-soaked whore with old thighs,
the point is at that moment
to him she was more beautiful and more rare
than a thousand perfectly cut diamonds
or a field of royal blue irises
or you in your red parrot dress.
And if I ever love anybody even half that much
I'll gladly cut off my whole head for them
if they ask, and even if they don't.

(March 1981)

The Lucy Syndrome

David Koteen

Time, a pallid fiction; a courteous sycophant come to prate of future reward. And yet, the only vibrant thread visible throughout the entire tapestry. Lucy. A cousin of one of my college professors; he drove her over to the house we (four others and I) rented. Everyone else left for the dance and I was waiting on the third floor in our common room. Jerry, our pet squirrel monkey, sat on the window ledge eating peanuts, throwing the shells at whoever walked by, or nobody. The kindly prof brought her up the wobbly fire escape, our habitual ingress. Lucy Olinsen: rosy-haired, blue of eye, straight nose, round cheeks, beautiful smile. Honestly feminine. The apparition of my choice. She walked like a duck. Whatever my shortcomings were, she forgave them. We drank something for a while, the

What we take with us when we traverse the veil is awareness — a slight shift in consciousness. The whole story may be for a single hard lesson.

three of us. Jerry got drunk, tried to jump to the lampshade, and fell to the floor. Lucy laughed and the monkey bit her thumb, which caused a few drops to come down her cheeks. I was immediately in love. The way her hair curled around her Scandinavian neck, the fullness of her nineteen-odd years in hips and breasts, the way her cotton skirt clung to her thighs. Young and hot and exceedingly loose to begin with, how was I to know this was the beginning of an inconspicuous sequence which was to follow me like a tail of lead. A little alcohol and a lot of youth; all I could feel was this intense vortex, effluxing from Lucy's woman center, sucking me to where I wanted to go. And, she was there the whole time. We were dancing and I fell back on the couch. Happenstance. Abruptly, her goodness came tumbling after, duck legs and all. With her rump in the air our friendly monkey seized his chance, and leaped on it, chattering all the while, sniffing and scratching at her undergarments. Then in counterpoint to the previous movements came a taut whisper: "When I was seventeen I got raped, and pregnant; and I wanted to have the baby. I was rejected by my parents who made me give it up for adoption. (Jerry ejaculated.) My friends condemned me. (Now a rain of tears were falling on my face.) So, please understand this; you're wonderful, but I can't let you come inside of me. I'm too afraid!"

Later, after graduation, I moved to New York, Lower East Side of Manhattan; very cheap apartment — sixty dollars a month. I lived with Robert, one of my college roommates, whose sister resided in Brooklyn. He was very Jewish, and not surprisingly, so was the sister: Lucy Hemmen. Also very uptight. Slender, angular with high cheekbones, light brown eyes, cropped red hair. The two of them had a long-standing flirtation going — touching, innuendos, lots of tongue-on-the-lips action. He told me that all her experiences with men were cut short and unfulfilling. With a Ph.D. in English literature, she was a recluse, eking out dollars proofreading for *Reader's Digest*. She was contracted and in permanent hibernation. Immaculate two rooms, blue and gray. Of course, my heart went out to her. When you're the way I was — three months of rent in the bank, no responsibilities except to give the day everything you've got, floating and flowing, back to the wind, sails billowed with tasting and touching and seeing, alive with give-and-take, skimming the cream and licking my fingers, always higher and higher — no thought entered of why I was interested in this cold woman. Robert was very jealous of his relationship with Lucy, but one weekend while he was gone, around eleven at night, I wandered over to Brooklyn, saw the light on, rang the buzzer, and got a reticent invitation up. She knew why I was there, and greeted me as warmly as she could (like the string beans do when you open the freezer). Same tight and trim outfit; not that I expected a negligee or something. Coffee, she offered, at 11:30. Somewhere down in my subconscious cellar, behind the aging red wines, there was knowledge that before me stood a debt to be paid. Preferable would be passionate frolicking on the kitchen floor. Uh-uh. Strictly business. So when she went to the toilet, I raced quietly around her cupboard like a mongoose, finally uncovering some scotch and brandy. Took a long draught from each bottle, returned the scotch and asked her through the door if I could have a drop of brandy. She would sip a little too. At last she led me at 2 a.m. to her bed where "I made love to her." Only due to the double Taurus in my astrological chart was I able to arouse enough emotion for both of us. About an hour trudged by, guilty and sober. I asked her did she feel all right? Could I get anything for her? She invited me to sleep on the couch.

So, Hell has many vestibules. Teacups of flaming brimstone can be a relatively potable beverage. The couch was comfortable; but listening to Lucy's wide-eyed pathetic thoughts, cacophonically ticking with the kitchen clock, left me empty as an abandoned tortoise shell. And not hungry. "Would you like to go out for breakfast?" I asked, several hours later. Nothing like a hot pastrami sandwich when your intestines are knotted up, and nausea has backed up your esophagus to the base of your throat. Maybe there'll be some flaming brimstone tea?

When I bumped into Lucy Olinsen in the Glass Department of Macy's, it was north and south poles of two magnets approaching each other. It was as if we had gone to sleep that night and were just awaking, still in embrace. My hands were on her buttocks and her legs were spreading, only restrained by the tightness of her skirt and social propriety. Waiting for 5 o'clock, I walked through the muddy Winter city in shirtsleeves. Snow-mush around my sneakers. We drank Spanish wine on the subway downtown. Then slaloming through the overflowing cans of trash in front of the Ninth Street apartment building, rose up the stairs on passionate vapors. Avoided the many who frequented our small flat, gathered cozily around the electric stove oven. Did the landlord ever turn on the heat? It didn't matter. I led her into the back storage room, six-and-a-half by eight feet, curtained, frost on the soot-fouled window, facing the next blackened brick building. Still a virgin. Except once. (She had snuck up to Massachusetts and climbed an old wisteria vine to peep at her sleeping child without adopted parents knowing.) More than I, Lucy O. understood why we had re-met. I never quite saw the ramifications of my actions, splashing out along the curved side to return one day; one day not too far off. Heating the room as we went, until from a hollow distance came that little voice: "Don't let it go inside of me! I'm still scared!" Iron echo. So with a mixture of conflicting feelings, she lifted my twisting auger onto her belly as it was at the end of its course. When the liquid heat hit the soft flesh she screamed like a panther breaking loose from its manacles. In the background the soothing laughter of my friend Robert, saying, "Don't worry. We keep it chained up to frighten burglars." I took her home uptown, where she had a room with her better-to-do relatives. I never saw her again. Lucy called me the next day to say she had been severely reprimanded, as her carnal sin radiated boldly from her face. A good lesson: don't show happiness. Her aunt and uncle asked her to be gone by the end of the month. What did that have to do with me?

When Spring emerged in NYC, it was time to go; thumb in hand I landed in Berkeley, California, which offered plenty of stimuli, and 3,000 miles from the Atlantic Coast. One adventure faded into the next; the less you remembered, the better off you were. I was writing a little but mostly chasing the sun. Whatever was of import, day or night, this year or the next, was not it. Lucy Whitman was five or six years my senior, a dance teacher who bounded about the streets of Berkeley, leaping and lunging where she would. She was some kind of queen, who exuded regality with every step. She asked me to her modern dance class which was an hour and a half of incessant transformation from rigorous exercise into improvisational, whatever works movement. Married, but living alone. The morning after the second class, she stopped by where I was staying, invited me to the beach — a picnic. I was surprised and elated; we went off in her Rambler station wagon. She was very West Coast; I held her in awe. Below my curly black hair there was a great deal of fear, which I kept at bay with the whip and prod of faith. California beaches around Point Reyes are magnificent. I was honored by the invitation and delighted with the sunny sands of the Pacific. Lucy and I ran and played along the shoreline. We climbed a steep cliff to eat; I sensed a change in the weather: with malevolent fingers the sea spray reached toward us; sharp rocks scraped my skin as I climbed; as we went higher up the sheer ocean side of the cliff, Lucy's features hardened. I shivered slightly. The ocean was leering and a voice came out of it, and said, "Why don't you dive on to these rocks? I will protect you from being injured, you know. Try it." Such a clear and seductive Voice. Squatting, I gazed into the crashing waves below, wondering whether I should jump or not. Lucy asked me if I wanted some yogurt; I looked up at her; she was huge. Her face was very far away; blouse wet; her nipples were little tongue tips beckoning me. Waist-length hair, blowing and winding about her sensual body; I thought it was seaweed and she, some kind of evil mermaid — part of the plan to get me to jump into the sea. She wore loose-fitting sailor pants with a large hole right above the left knee. She was the Temptress all right, and I knew it! At the end of her extremely long arm was this small purplish container. My jaw was set as I took it from her (now she was the witch from Hansel and Gretel, fattening me up for the oven — or in this case, to hurl me on the sharp rocks below). I lifted up the lid and spun it into the sea, and stuck my middle three fingers into the fruit at the bottom of the yogurt — boysenberry. And very slowly, gazing continuously into her green eyes, I slipped my hand full of yogurt through the slit in her bell bottoms, slid it up the inside of the thigh and began working it into her woman's opening. Back and forth like a house painter; and then I came back for more, up through the slit again, working it much more vigorously, always with eye contact, until finally, the spell was broken; the ocean let go of its menacing ways and Lucy returned to being a woman. On the thirty-inch ledge we made love so deep, so intense, that the sound of the sea was silenced.

Lucille, Louise, Louis, Lulu, Lucifer, Lucy. Because we come from such a stiff-necked race (as Moses puts it), the cycles of our self-debilitating behavior — the ones that keep us firmly rooted to anxiety and frustration, year in, year out — to us are always subtly obscured. All the passing show, the glittering patina, possessions and wealth, and what-have-you remain on the earth when we drop off. What we take with us when we traverse the veil is awareness — a slight shift in consciousness. The whole story may be for a single hard lesson. The petite orgasms along the path act to keep us on task. Everyone has his own signs, sarcastic quips which demarcate the turns at the crossroads, reminders of our shortcomings. For me the trail has been blazed with Lucys. This excruciatingly lucid bit of information has barely penetrated my mind after fifteen years. It has nothing to do with the individual females who don the name; it has only to do with my genetic, personal, and historical derivation. Well, perhaps a little more. There are two aspects of the Lucy Syndrome. The classic double-edged scimitar. In the Judeo-Christian tradition they are personified by Lucifer — the bearer of light; i.e., Venus before the sunrise. Lucifer, also, is the fallen angel, he who rebelled against God. He is of colossal pride. Lucifer — the cross of *light* and *pride*.

Another shape to this dualism comes out of a pair of Lucys who haunted the Sixties. B.B. King, the monarch of hard blues, has a guitar named Lucille, which he makes love to; rather she is the female sexual persona — the body of woman. When I first heard him sing, "I got a sweet little angel/I love to see her spread her wings," I knew he was singing to me. I gotta get me some Lucy! For those leaning on the intellectual came the Beatles with their portrayal of the same angel, only more abstracted — Lucy in the Sky with Diamonds. Unlike B.B. King's Lucy, this one is not a sex-object, but the ideal partner or helpmate that is promised to every son by his parents.

My father hated my grandmother, his mother-in-law. "A selfish bitch!" was his favorite epithet. The major manifestation of the schism in my parents' marriage was this loathsome creature: Louise or Lulu. Not only was the active detestation of Lulu present in my upbringing, but both my sisters were named after her (how far we bend to break our back): the elder was Louise; the second, Lucy. Thus, it is readily comprehensible to see why the Lucy Syndrome pervaded my being; I am its natural heir.

Not long after I finished my first book, I went to France. Too cold. To Spain, and eventually, the romantic and traumatic island of Ibiza. From there a motorboat would take you to the serene isle of Formentera. I was on it. As was a red-haired Irish Lass, freckled and pug-nosed: Lucy Reirdon. When we docked, she took me home. Formentera is flat and rocky. Rocks piled in rectangular fashion for fences and to form small agricultural plots and pastures. A few roads and mossy labyrinths of rock walls. Lucy was strong of arm and will.

After we wound through the maze and arrived, she insisted that she wash my hair, which desperately needed it. (I hadn't realized that this lady was the fourth non-familial Lucy in my life; nor that all of them had red hair. When you're me, you're pretty dense!) "Strip!" she commanded. From the cistern she pulled up a bucket of icy water and methodically poured it over my head. As the water reached my loins, whatever flickering was occurring there was immediately squelched. Lucy Reirdon was her own woman; talked very little; knew what she wanted. She had some type of intense Irish shampoo and sharp fingernails. I asked her if she had considered torture as a profession. Then came the icing on my scalp — about two gallons of cold water. I was in shock; one large mass of goose bumps. She took pity and wrapped a towel around me. And then some strong tea with milk and honey; and goat cheese and bread. Then a little onyx pipe with smokeable matter within. I hardly knew where I was in the first place, and what she offered in this burning vessel took care of the remaining fragments of my memory. She led me inside the white-washed house, which was really an altar — pictures of Christ, Krishna, Buddha, and many-armed goddesses with lotus flowers. Pillows and fragrance everywhere. A fever of fear shot up my spine: I was to be sacrificed! Quickly, I turned, expecting to see her with an ornate, sacrificial knife . . . but no. She had disappeared for a moment, dropped her army pants, and returned in an emerald green satin robe. As we sat quietly together on an assortment of sheepskin and Moroccan rugs, I perceived very clearly that Lucy Reirdon was a goddess. At the base of my skull a surging of energy gathered and was steadily rising like a thermometer over an open flame. Lucy un-moved, eyes closed, lips barely parted. Throughout the room a vague, undulating orange glow. Then that old distant Voice: "Welcome home, lost one. You were right the first time; you are the sacrifice. Sacrifice yourself. It takes a long time; begin now. Now!"

Five years squeeze through the hour glass. Lucy went her own way. For me marriage and children and a farm in Oregon. What is begun is always completed. Sooner or later. As my marriage deteriorated, sexual frustration mounted. It became a malignant tumor in my head which grew and grew. It was cut out. You always get what you deserve. In this case I certainly did. Lucifer wields a decisive scalpel. But still my consciousness lay unaltered. One night around three a.m. — the hour of Lucy — I found myself in a deep cavern. There were three cots; on the left was an old emaciated friend of mine, named Louis, rapidly demising. On the right, a bull-necked, bulging-muscled man. In the middle was the succulent-bodied Ms. Lucy, her backside raised up like a cat in heat. And I — the ego of this vision — was floating above her in conspicuous coition. The heavy duty male leans over and in a gruff, throaty voice says, "Lucy. Louis is dead. Nothin' can stop me now. I'm coming to get ya!" Lucy weeps out, "You fucking coward! You're too chicken to do anything!" "Don't say that about me! I'm coming to get ya, right now! Look out honey! I'm comin'!" He leaps from the cot toward Lucy, who turns in fright. And what of our hero? I see the dead Louis and the raspy-throated bull, snorting fire. So still deep inside of Lucy, just as he lunges, I shove my foot in between his neck and shoulder. With the thud of foot against neck, I sit up in bed and look over at my wife, curled up asleep. My eyes close and that familiar Voice starts up: "You proud and lustful fool! Lucy. Lust. Lulu. Lucifer. You know how language works! I've warned you many times before! A word to the wise! You fool! This is the last time! We'll take this body from you, if you can't use it properly! Remember! Remember well!" And with that I was awake, staring into the chilly, dark room, sweating profusely. With the speed of a computer all the fragments of this story raced through my mind. Slivers from my childhood and my parents' relationship — thousands of translucent slivers. The letters *L* and *U*. Grandma Lulu, the wedge. The quartet of redheaded Lucys. Why are we cast in this incessant drama? We stare at it and don't see it.

And so, like Adam of the earth, I cry out, "Lord. Here am I, eater of apple." And in the palm of my hand a single seed of understanding. Not much, after all these years, since I first met Lucy. The inexorable pride that haunts me, the fever of gluttony, and lust that would forego God for an ecstatic moment are the gas, grease, and oil that lubricate this hell-bent vehicle. They are tears, the sperm that race up the tube; they excite and terrify but they will never, never save me. This jot of being who I am is a poor student. On the great scale the drop of awareness truly balances the vast weights of pain and frustration. Hours on the operating table pass; decades of unconscious days, they too pass. The moist dark gem awaits its proper season. And finally like a thin shaft of light I am ready to nurture it. Finally. Ah! Lucy. You beautiful creature! Beautiful, beautiful creature! Good-bye.

(August 1983)

US/Readers Write About . . .
My Body

My body will turn thirty-five this Summer. I think of thirty-five as the age at which you discover that all the while you've been thinking that you were breaking your body in, you find that all you were doing was breaking it down.

Look at this. The dimples in my cheeks that all my aunts used to find so cute have turned into creases. My scalp reflects light. Every morning when I harvest stubble from my face, I have to stretch sections of skin to expose deeper furrows to the razor. And lately I have found stiff, gray hairs growing out of my ears and nose. It's a little hard to believe that this is the same body that was nearly thirty when its owner was asked to prove its age at a bar. Now it looks as if it *owns* the bar.

I'm not a kid anymore, that's for sure.

Then why do I still feel like one?

I think it may be because I was never an athlete. I never crossed a physical peak, so I never had to face a decline. At my age, most sports stars have long since passed into the front office or the restaurant business. Meanwhile, my outside shot (the only weapon I ever had in my basketball arsenal) is about as good as it ever was, which is to say more or less okay as long as nobody defends against it.

I remember the shock a few years ago of learning that Bob Kaufman, a 6'8", 250-pound bruiser who used to set the best picks in the NBA and a college classmate of mine, had retired to the front office at the age of twenty-seven because of arthritis. *Arthritis.* I also remember the shock of learning, in my twenties, that other high school and college classmates had died of causes other than war or accidents. Cancer. Leukemia. Tumors. Heart failure.

I was sure, back in those days, that IT was going to get me. If other clearly superior samples of my species were made victims by age and disease, what were my chances — me, with my colossal appetite for leisure and garbage food? I figured I was good for thirty-one or thirty-two, tops.

Then one day, half a year past my thirty-second birthday, I was seized at work by chest pains. Couldn't breathe. Felt a weak and rapid pulse. Dizziness. Fear of death. They took me to the doctor's office where my friend in the white coat wore that look of reassuring concern they give you when they're about to tell you that they'll have to amputate only one of your legs. "You have a suspicious electrocardiogram," he said, before sending me to the intensive care unit in an ambulance.

Three days and $1,600 later I was free again, the recovered victim of some spontaneous disorder that did a good job of faking myocardial infarction. Turns out I'm just one of those people with a funny EKG. Next time I'll know not to panic.

In the course of this adventure, I discovered that my main cardiac risk is "family history." This is reassuring. True, my father died of a heart attack, but he was seventy and started killing himself with cigarettes in his teens. His mother is still fine, and she'll be one hundred this year.

I also discovered that my thumper isn't too bad after all. It pumps along at a leisurely fifty-six beats a minute, and I have the blood pressure of a teenager. I have kept my system safe from abuses by cigarettes and alcohol.

So while my neck may crunch when I turn my head, and one day I may find more hair in the sink than on my scalp, I think I've got something to feel good about. As bodies go, the one with my name isn't a bad place to live.

David Searls
Durham, North Carolina

□ □ □

I nursed my second daughter for fourteen months, long past the time usually expected of any mother — working or not. It was a most natural and comfortable duration, and until she was ready, I saw no need to end what had become an unencumbered exchange of human warmth. The Summer suctioned us together in sticky sweat and hunger, the milky-sweet smells rising to interplay with the season's humidity. Winter I recall as best, we two wrapping ourselves around each other like fleece blankets to keep away wolves and cold nights.

During those milk-and-honey days I felt in perfect step, in such tune with grander cyclic certainties that once I had merely viewed from outside their framework. Those days are now gone, and my three-year-old dreams of ways to aggravate and enchant me. The feelings, however, still surface when I seem to need their comfort most. After all is quiet some nights and I drink hot chocolate or Sanka before bed, the steaming liquid soothes my throat, but often detours in its path to the stomach. The old needle-like sting, the tingle, the heaviness returns as the heat trickles down into the fibrous system of unused milk ducts. It's as though my body speaks kind reassurance to me, saying, "You're no less of the moon, tides, heavens than you once were. Your milk lies not barren or dry, but deeper within, underground and waiting."

Linda Burggraf
Knoxville, Tennessee

□ □ □

I get up in the morning because I have to. It's a hard struggle to pull up from the sticky fingers of sleep things enough to reground me. I feel old and empty; it is only the morning. There were dreams of a deep blueness with the feeling that my body was there somewhere. The guts, the bones.

At midday I drive past the body of a young black girl asleep face down on the side of the road. What's her story? The hot sun softens her asphalt bed, yet she has bruises and the little pebbles stick to the palms of her hands. In this highest and hottest sun I feel my stomach and wonder how my body will betray me.

In the evening I piss and shit behind closed doors. Who and what is it that makes this substance? It feels good to piss and shit although I'm usually far away in a book of history or poems of the nineteenth century.

Dreams of the body with nightfall. Small motions of sex that sometime complete, sometime don't, remind my heart to beat faster. But my dreams are of my grandfather's body. As he lay dying in the hospital, he looked at my mother with tears in his eyes and said, "I want to go, mama." Through the cigarette smoke she says she knew he was dead when his lips started turning blue. My body, my body, when will you forsake me?

Brian Adler
Athens, Georgia

□ □ □

My body is the house in which another little body dwells, swelling my tummy while the ligaments supporting the uterus pop and spring like rubber bands. I am not burdened by this physical responsibility yet, although I know that I shall be, having been this way before. Nothing grounds you into the physical like being pregnant. Soon my brain will begin to live in my uterus until I can no longer think with my head, only my womb.

There is something we humans deem sacred about a pregnant woman. However, I do not feel sacred. At first I felt invaded. It is always so with me even though this child was conceived by choice and not an accident. Now I feel vital and alive. This little one flutters and jumps, swims freely in her warm sea. Soon she will curl up tighter and tighter until each movement seems like a violence and I will think of nothing but the time when she will be out of me. I will relish the idea of the wrenching and opening that is necessary to make way for her to pass through — until it actually happens. Then I will undoubtedly wish to be burdened with her weight again just to escape the incredible pain.

So, my body is a house for now but it is more. I am not my body but I experience my reality through this amazing creature. I think my body has a consciousness all its own. How else could it function when I am away from it? How else could it behave with such seeming independence, thumping and pumping and twitching without my conscious awareness? It has an awareness of its own, almost but not entirely separate from me. My body and I work together in such perfect harmony that I become it and it becomes me. Together we are me — for now — but I know this is a temporary state of affairs. I perceive with my intellect that I will one day take leave of this body and live a life without it. Although I know this, I can't say that I understand it. I am so accustomed to seeing the world with the abetment of my body that I don't really consider what it is like to exist without having to think and act in physical terms.

What does one think about if not food, clothing, shelter? What can it be like to live without eating, evacuating, washing, dressing, and (heaven forbid!) sex? I know that I spend time away from my body nearly every night and yet when I am awake and aware as a physical being I don't think that much about it. I intuitively know that I live somewhere in a realm where my body has no bonds on me but I choose not to remember it most of the time — undoubtedly because the joys of being physical would seem puny if one were to recall fully the joys of being non-physical. Also, it would be pretty distracting. Our awareness is better concentrated on the job at hand, that of being physical beings in a physical environment.

Ami Bourne
Isle au Haute, Maine

(August 1982)

You Eat It

Sy Safransky

Is there a right way to eat?
Is there a wrong way to write about it?

I'll take the second question first. I've got an apple in one hand, a pen in the other, and my mouth is moving as fast as my mind. Is this as bad as talking with your mouth full, or is it the boldest kind of personal journalism? It's not academic; consciousness swings on a chemical hinge — another way of saying we are what we eat — so a description of my eating habits is no less revealing than a catalogue of my sexual preferences, and the analogy is hardly haphazard. Michio Kushi, the leading proponent of macrobiotics, goes so far as to assess the Presidential candidates on the basis of their physiognomy, and helpfully suggests that George Wallace would do well to cut down on meat and eat more grains and vegetables. If

I'm as uncomfortable with the vegetarians as I am at Hardee's.

there's a wrong way to write about politics, this may be it. But since Mr. Kushi admittedly had no previous knowledge about the candidates or their policies — a blessed but odd turn in an election year — his conclusion that none of them has the stature of a world leader is all the more remarkable. Now, you don't have my picture before you, but if I told you I drink coffee and sometimes smoke, you'd get some ideas. Unfortunately, so does Mr. Kushi. If you've ever gotten sick eating nothing but brown rice, you'll want to chew that over. (In macrobiotics, they tell you to chew everything at least fifty times. I tried this once, but before I was half done I was chewing my gums.) But this is the wrong way to write about macrobiotics. If you believe in it, and it works for you, these thoughts are as nourishing as a maraschino cherry. If you're prejudiced from the start, I'm only reinforcing your conceit. Don't think you understand macrobiotics, because most of those who follow it don't. George Oshawa, who popularized it, is to the written word what Kushi is to political science, and a philosophy of eating which begins with the principle that "everything is the differentiated manifestation of one infinity" is about as helpful to spiritually gullible Westerners as Sophie Portnoy's dictum to eat, because it's good.

Eating pure, whole foods that grow naturally in your area, chewing well, and avoiding bad combinations is the basic macrobiotic idea; like many other worthwhile notions it has been turned into something forbiddingly esoteric. My friend Bruce, who's seven feet tall with a kind face, understands it better than anyone I know. He was quietly amused, I'm sure, when I barrelled into a ten-day brown rice fast without proper knowledge or preparation; I went down for the count on the seventh with the worst headache I've ever had. Discharging poisons, he later explained. About to die, I insisted.

But when it comes to food I've always been an extremist. For four years, I was a strict vegetarian. Humans are not biologically carnivorous, I explained to whoever would listen. Meat, I went on, is the dead flesh of an animal in a state of decomposition. Besides, it's riddled with harmful chemicals. Finally, what right do we have to kill other creatures?

Persuasive arguments, especially when everyone is concerned and confused about his health, and, more generally, about how to live; not a few of my friends were convinced, changed their ways, applauded my example.

No one's applauding anymore. I'm as uncomfortable with the vegetarians as I am at Hardee's. When they asked a Buddhist monk why he didn't eat meat, he allowed that the vegetables are no less alive than the animals, but the animals make more noise when they're killed. Nearly as much noise as the vegetarians. If this offends you, because your pantry has no meat, only honey, robbed from the bees; and natural yogurt, made from milk the cow would naturally have stopped producing when she naturally stopped nursing; and sprouts, which are eaten alive; if this makes you so hopping mad you want to take off your brushed suede jacket and teach me a lesson about right and wrong, I'll ask you to calm down, because the plants in the room are shrinking from your violence, and the Gates of Hell, hinged with a high-protein meat substitute, are yawning wide. From where I'm standing, I can see Arnold Ehret, father of the no-dairy mucusless diet, being licked head to toe by a transvestite cannibal in peacock feathers, and Robert Rodale, father of the organic gardening movement — who laid the blame for John Kennedy's assassination squarely on sugar, in a tract that pictured Oswald holding a bottle of Coca-Cola — neck-deep in a vat of hot fudge, being stirred by a benign-looking CIA operative with a double chin.

We outgrew economic determinism and, with barely a pause for air (fouled by a proletariat that had settled for Ramblers rather than Revolution), moved on to nutritional determinism. We search for the right food with the same zest as scientists looking for the cure to cancer, and what we forget — but I can't say it, can I? This is already too offensive by half, and God's a mouthful.

(June 1976)

Death and Other Cures

Sy Safransky

Editor's Note: Dr. Lobsang Dolma, forty, is chief physician of the Tibetan Medical Center of the Dalai Lama in Dharmsala, India. She was born in Keron, Tibet and was a physician for eleven years in Keron, Katmandu, and Dalhousie. She visited Durham, North Carolina to exchange ideas with doctors here and tour several hospitals.

Her hands are graceful, forceful, certain. They move through the air like swift, impassioned birds, emphasizing her words, as she explains about medicines of flowers and fruits for craziness, diagnosing pregnancy by feeling the pulse in the ring finger, the difficulty of curing heart disease when there are evil spirits, the importance of the doctor's own dreams before the patient arrives, and, with the same matter-of-factness, about cancer. She is sitting cross-legged on the pillow, her eyes dark and active, her voice calm: why tumors grow; karma; the presence of evil spirits.

Sympathy is written all over his face like a bad check, but I suspect there is a more profound forgery somewhere, back in the schools of medicine, back in the long, sterile hallways of Western thought. . . .

I can't remember the exact words. Probably something trite, and over-ly dramatic. Doctors watch too many movies, too, wear the same mock-heroic masks as the rest of us, masks of compassion and wisdom and bravery. Upon them rests the awful obligation of making dignified sense of what they can't understand. They are the high priests of the culture, and perhaps it is the awful pomp of their office that makes them look so unhealthy. Overworked and overfed. Not to mention overpaid. Of course, I am being unfair, but as the doctor himself suggests, life is unfair — other-wise, how explain my father's suffering. Sympathy is written all over his face like a bad check, but I suspect there is a more profound forgery somewhere, back in the schools of medicine, back in the long, sterile hallways of Western thought — proud, antiseptically rational, and immunized against whatever virulent germs of intuition, faith and plain common sense linger in the blood.

All pleasure and pain has mental origins, she explains, and so no disease is unrelated to mind. Specifically, the balance of winds, phlegm and bile within the body determine how healthy a person is. Imbalance leads to disease. This is similar to the idea of bodily humors prevalent in the Middle Ages. In Tibetan medicine, which is faithful to Buddhist philosophy, any imbalance is a result of desire, hatred, and confusion — the basic ignorance arising from false perception.

"Illness," she says, "is caused by your own actions in this or a former lifetime. Killing, stealing, and lying can draw illness to yourself." In one out of ten illnesses, she continues, an evil spirit is present. "We don't attack spirits. We handle them with compassion. We give the spirit something else to feed on. When a spirit is taken out of someone's body, it dissolves like a cloud. It no longer has a reason for being."

A physician may recite a mantra, or magical chant, 100,000 times to effect an exorcism. Other rituals that are attached to the giving of medicine act as what Western science might call psychotherapy.

He thought the pain was from intestinal gas. "Why can't they do something for the gas?" he asked, over and over. It wasn't gas: it was the tumor growing, fouling his intestines, advancing on his liver, and cruelly upsetting the delicate chemistry that we, who enjoy it, take for granted. The doctors assured him they were doing all they could — except, of course, telling him the truth, which he eventually figured out for himself.

In Tibet, she explains, there are 1,500 medicines, made of minerals, leaves, bark, earth, roots and fruits. Medicine is used before other treatments. Surgery is rare. The instruments are burning cones and needles, similar to those used in acupuncture. When a tumor is found, a needle is inserted, and a cone with burning incense placed on top. The tumor dies, and is expelled.

"Are you afraid?" I ask.

"Of what?"

"Of dying." The word, once said, doesn't seem so evil. Why won't anyone else talk about it?

He shrugs, as if the answer is obvious — or perhaps simply impossible, as if the kind of introspection I'm demanding is worse than the pain already lacing his insides. "I'm just sorry," he says, "we didn't get to be together more."

An imbalance in the body, usually because of non-digestion of food, leads to disease, she explains. "If you avoid eating bad foods and bad combinations of foods, diseases can be avoided." Some foods that are healthy become injurious when mixed with others. Some bad combinations, she says, are radishes and mushrooms; fish or meat and butter; red or black pepper and orange juice; ice cream taken after meat. Meat and fish are not innately harmful, although mixing them is. Also "there is great fault in eating until your stomach is full. Think of your stomach as having four sections. Fill two with food, one with drink, and leave one for the winds to circulate."

Thinner than I'd ever imagined I'd see him, the intravenous feeding keeping him alive now. His lips are dry. My mother sends me to the grocery to buy him a soda. Years earlier, I had pleaded with him to change his diet, to stop eating foods with preservatives, to cut down on meat. He sat there, sipping a Pink Grapefruit No-Cal, challenging every statement, as I grew more shrill. Once again, we were arguing less from conviction than from that fierce, dimly understood need to change one another, to shape each other's lives to designs more of our own choosing. Downstairs, I buy him two bottles of No-Cal, flavors I hope he'll like.

"Sleep on your right side," she says, "with your head to the North and your feet to the South. Your head should not face the South. The Lord of Death is in the South."

He is lying on his right side, uncomfortable, yet too weak to move. He asks me to help him turn over. I want to help, of course, but I hesitate. His flesh is sagging and yellow, tattooed like hospital meat with needle marks and small bruises. It is a body mortgaged to death and, like any animal, I would rather give it wide circle. But we have surrendered so many of our animal privileges — living naturally, dying naturally — in order to go poking among the crumbs of what we call our common humanity for other nourishment. The animal within notwithstanding, I am as hungry to help as he is for it. I lift him, the gift of whatever strength he has nurtured in me finally returned. It is, save mourning, the last thing I do for him.

After studying medicine for nine years, a Tibetan doctor spends three years studying the pulse. A diagnosis is made by placing the three middle fingers of each hand on the patient's pulse and also by sight from a urine specimen. Someone in the audience, whom the doctor had diagnosed earlier, is said to have winds in his stomach, making it hard for him to digest milk and sweets. A friend who knows him whispers that this is true.

He doesn't look any different. His eyes are half-open, his mouth small and tired, the early morning sunlight bathing him. He seems almost relaxed. It takes me a few moments to realize what has happened. "Mom," I say, stepping away from the bed, "I don't think he's breathing." I reach for her, as much to steady myself. I am frightened, I think, by the sheer mystery of it. It's as if his lifeless body is a kind of vacuum sucking all meaning from the air around it, all the explanations, all the medical terms and medical excuses and medical prayers — everything, perhaps, save the medical bills. My mother calls for a doctor, who takes one look and tells us to wait outside. As we stand there, another doctor goes in. And another. It's ten minutes before one of them emerges to tell us what we already know. I can't remember the exact words. Something about how they tried their best. I believe him. Not believing sours the insides, makes you old before your time.

(June 1975)

My Father's Dying

Virginia L. Rudder

I thought you could not die until the sun stopped
and Summer's shifting air parted into light's opening doors.
I never believed you would die until I stood clutching
the steel bed railings. Fragile flesh cracked
like a dropped egg. Your straining lungs heaved,
wheezing like a lumbering combine lurching through ripened wheat.
Your sunken chest, my first safe pillow,
fluttered up and down like a frightened partridge.
Your hazel eyes clouded; speech trembled upon your lips.
Eternity slipped between us. You stared up at me
like a puzzled child and then turned back.
Your eyelids quivered shut. The hiss and spit
of oxygen stung my ears. It was the hardest work
I ever have known, covering your thin shoulders
with the sheet, squeezing your fingers, fumbling,
letting your hand drop and walking away.
It is harder now, letting go.
I greet callers at the front door in your place,
accept bags of ripe tomatoes and platters of grapes.
I pick out the softest bones from table scraps
for your bewildered dog. I nail the smiles on my face,
go hide, huddle on the running board of your pick-up in the dark.
I walk down to the pond, stand chainsmoking on the dam,
looking out over the water. Tomorrow at the family graveyard
we will plant your true seed, charred chips and broken shards

of shining bones, deep in Earth's womb, with carnations and spider mums.
Daddy, you are the first man I learned to love,
the one man closest to a god I have ever known.
Foxes bark from the silent trees.
I flip my cigarette into the reeds, giggle, marveling again
how your Scots blood, your huge highlands heart,
cheats the undertakers. Somehow I knew it,
all the time; how you have finished living,
how you will never die.

(March 1981)

Gently Changing

An Interview with O. Carl Simonton, M.D.

Lightning Brown

D r. O. Carl Simonton doesn't look like much of a revolutionary, but his work with cancer patients — focusing on their ability to help themselves get well — has sent widening ripples through the medical community.

Trained as a radiation cancer specialist, Dr. Simonton is so relaxed and warm in person that I was surprised — at a conference in Tampa, Florida on the healing potential of the human brain — at his obvious authority on the podium.

The increasing professional attention and respect for his work — in identifying and modifying lifestyles that are associated with cancer and other major diseases, and using meditation and imagery exercises to combat illness — is obvious, too. During the next year, he will be involved in two major research studies — with the Kaiser Research Foundation and the National Cancer

If we change too quickly, it creates anxiety. . . . You can take people who are functioning pretty well, and with a little well-intentioned help leave them where they are not functioning worth a damn.

Institute — to document his approach.

Dr. Simonton is the medical director of the Cancer Counseling and Research Center in Fort Worth, Texas. With his wife and co-worker, Stephanie Matthews-Simonton, he has co-authored Stress, Psychological Factors and Cancer *and* Getting Well Again. *A third book,* Gently Changing, *is in progress. Cassette tapes outlining the Simonton method are also available.*

A profound change in his work came about through his treatment of his father, who died of cancer. Two and a half weeks later, Dr. Simonton addressed the Tampa conference, describing the application of his techniques to ease his father's death. The personal immediacy of Dr. Simonton's presentation shows the courage and truthfulness basic to his work.

The Cancer Counseling and Research Center is located at 1300 Summit St., Suite 710, Fort Worth, Texas 76102.

— Lightning Brown

SUN: Your method of cancer therapy puts patients to some extent in charge of their own healing. How do you do this?

SIMONTON: I think your point is that I have a very deep regard for the person's ability to influence his own health, much more so than I was trained, or than is now being taught. I believe very strongly that what an individual does and how an individual thinks has a significant influence on his health.

SUN: People create their own illnesses?

SIMONTON: We develop our illnesses for reasons. The words that we use to communicate these concepts make it seem as if this happens consciously, when quite the opposite is true. We don't know how this very complicated process happens. We aren't aware of the stresses, of the things that don't fit, which play a role in our bodies breaking down. And then we are not aware of the secondary gains, the good things that happen to us as a result of getting sick.

The more we look at this, the more it appears that illness is a coping strategy, a way of dealing with difficult issues in life. Illness winds up being one of the acceptable ways of dealing with incongruities, with things that don't fit.

SUN: How do you help patients to identify the causes of an illness?
SIMONTON: What we have our patients do is to take the symptoms of cancer as the illness, and to look for the five biggest changes that they can identify in their lives in the eighteen months prior to the diagnosis being made. If they have had subsequent flareups, they look at the six months prior to each flareup. Then, they look at their emotional reactions to those changes. Finally, with each episode, they look at five good things that happened to them as a result of the diagnosis or of each flareup — what they get out of being sick.

SUN: Cancer brings fringe benefits?
SIMONTON: We tend not to be aware of what our needs are. We block out our needs because we learn early that we have to go to school in order to achieve, so that we will eventually one day be successful, and then automatically happiness will follow. This is a common thing, though we may not all buy into it equally. In order to become successful, we have to numb ourselves to what we want.

It is important for us to appreciate that secondary gains are very good for us. What we get through illness is very important to us, and the statement that illness makes is that the illness is the best way that we can see to meet those needs right now. The objective is to see what we are getting, and to continue to get it through the illness until we can find more effective ways of getting needs met.

Information about stresses and secondary gains is for lifelong use. If indeed I believe that my health is related to my reaction to the events of my life, and that a lot of why I get ill is to get things which I don't have internal or external permission to give myself, then, for the rest of my life, I will look at my health differently. My health is now a feedback device for helping me take a temperature of what is going on in my life, how I am reacting to it, and how well I am getting the important things I need. So it changes the whole dynamic of my life.

SUN: How does this lead to cures?
SIMONTON: In general, I believe that our health is a reflection of the way we live our lives. As we begin to look at improving our health, we take stock of the healthy practices that we have used up to this point, to try to strengthen those, and gradually to incor-

porate possibilities that we have not been using. If we have been very conscious about food, then diet is the central focus; if we are creative thinkers, then we will emphasize meditation. Meditation tends to be a strange word for some people, but a lot of people like to sit around and think, and for me, that's meditation, too. If we like to talk things over with someone else, then we are using counseling.

SUN: Is there a scheme of healthy behaviors which you encourage in your patients?
SIMONTON: I divide relevant practices into six areas: exercise, diet, meditation, play, counseling, and purpose in life. I find it important to acknowledge that none of these are inherently healthy. Any of these practices can be used in healthy ways or unhealthy ways.

SUN: Two years ago, when we spoke with your co-worker, Stephanie Matthews-Simonton, your emphasis seemed to be on relaxation and visualization, on the practice of meditation. Have you now expanded from this?
SIMONTON: In the beginning, meditation was the only tool that we were using, at least the only tool I was labeling. I believe it is a very important tool. With time, I have appreciated other aspects of health. But, as with so many things, what we do first tends to catch the eye, and it's kind of flashy — whereas diet is relatively new for me. I have really only involved myself in the nutritional aspects of cancer treatment within the last three years. I consider all of the practices to be very important.

SUN: What does meditation do to promote healthy living?
SIMONTON: The way that I view imagery and meditation is that meditation is a central way, and a relatively direct way, of changing our beliefs. As such, we can use meditation to change the way we live our lives, because if we change our beliefs, we automatically change our lives. If I think I am a certain sort of person, then I will live my life accordingly. If I want to change the way I live my life, one way of doing that is to change my beliefs about myself and my universe.

If we look at the specifics of what we are trying to do with cancer patients' beliefs, then we should look first at basic societal beliefs — that cancer is a very powerful and devastating disease that eats me up from the inside out, that comes upon me for no good reason, the treatment of which is very hazardous and against which my body has very little potency.

I ask my patients to focus on the aspects of cancer that we understand to be true, and which counter those strong societal beliefs. We focus on the cancer being weak and confused, composed of weak, confused, deformed cells, focus on the treatment as being helpful to my body in regaining health, and on my body's strength and ability to destroy the cancer cells. What I am attempting to do is to help the person dramatically change his beliefs about the situation by focusing on the aspects that we want to change.

SUN: Can this sort of meditation be dangerous?

SIMONTON: All of this is a lot to ask a person to do. It can be devastating to the individual to do this, because we are doing a lot more than talking about just the nature of cancer. We are talking about the nature of the individual, about the nature of health and illness, about life and death.

If we change too quickly, it creates anxiety. This is something I did not appreciate until just a few years ago. It may be very unhealthy for a person to meditate on cancer in the way I just described, because the change may be too much, too fast, and result in much anxiety. And as a result, when the person sits down to meditate, what they come away with is a sense of fear and depression. If a person comes to meditate and leaves feeling this way, the conclusion is not good for their health. We must honor the way we feel.

SUN: Does the same apply to diet or counseling?

SIMONTON: You can't talk about good diet in the abstract any more than you can talk about any of the other aspects of health in the abstract. If we take, for instance, the Texas pig farmer, who is eating chicken-fried steak, meat and potatoes, and pork chops — a salty, high-fat diet — and you take that person and put him on a "healthy" diet, low-fat, high-vegetable and fruit, low-salt, that person is going to die much faster because he will not be getting the nourishment from his food. It's too big a change. I didn't appreciate that before. You cannot divorce the program from the lifetime habits of the individual.

As a society we are taught to put ourselves into someone else's hands when we are sick, to become infantile and to turn over our own potency. In my counseling, I ask patients to own their own potency and to ask for help at the same time. This goes against a large societal form, and that creates lots of difficulties. We are not necessarily doing anybody a favor when we approach this, and that is why our work must be couched in terms which do not create more problems than they solve for the individual. That is a real possible hazard in doing counseling, that you can take a person who is functioning pretty well, and with a little well-intentioned help leave them where they are not functioning worth a damn. It's important to realize that this is a hazard.

SUN: You summarize these awarenesses and developments in your method as "gently changing."
SIMONTON: I think that we make consistent changes if they are gentle. If we don't, if we make changes that are not compatible with the long-term living of life, the changes stop.

SUN: Is that a definition of wholistic?
SIMONTON: Definitions of wholistic are hard to come by, but that is not one. Many times, the wholistic movement tends to be militant in its dicta, and some of the processes which have been developed out of the wholistic movement have been detrimental along exactly those lines, in trying to get people to make radical changes. That has been a problem.

SUN: Yet, in common with the wholistic movement, you reject therapies which are invasive or foreign to the individual's life. Do you place yourself somewhere between wholistic medicine and traditional practice?
SIMONTON: Certainly, I place myself between those two camps. In certain instances, the wholistic movement has been in reaction against traditional medicine. I don't like that. I like to try to use what comes out of traditional medicine, and to realize that, for certain types of people, traditional approaches are best. If that's what they expect, if that's what their whole lives have been oriented

around, then for those individuals that's the best approach.

SUN: How many patients have you treated through your program?
SIMONTON: I began treating patients in 1971. You are talking about several thousand, about three thousand.

SUN: You are now in the midst of major transition, personally and professionally.
SIMONTON: A little over two months ago, my father was diagnosed with advanced malignancy. He died two weeks and two days ago. The family called me in to take charge of the situation. I know that, in all likelihood, he died much more quickly as a result of the counseling than he would have without it. He commented to the family that the experience would test my beliefs and abilities.

I feel solid with who I am and what my work is about, but I am in a state of transition with regard to how I am going to move about in the world. There are certain transformative changes in my method that were precipitated by my father's death. But at the same time, my experience underscored the validity of what I had been doing and of the direction in which I am going.

SUN: Your father was your first patient to ask you to help him die. How has your experience in working with him created new directions for your work?
SIMONTON: The new direction I would like to see things go would be to help people clarify whether they wanted to live or die. If people wanted to die, we would help them die more quickly, comfortably, and under the circumstances they prefer to die. If they want to die in the hospital, then in the hospital; if they want to die at home, then at home.

I didn't know whether Dad would want to die in the hospital or at home. My guess was that he would want to die in the hospital, but the opposite was true. I was very glad for that, but I didn't expect it. So many things happened that were unexpected for me. Not the least of these was how fast he clarified that he wanted to die, and die in a hurry. That was unexpected. I expected him to die fighting, to die a fairly miserable death. I didn't know about the length of it — it had the potential for that — but certainly I imagined it would be one of poor quality where he would be struggling and putting up the superficial appearance of fighting as he was dying.

It wasn't my job to change the way he died. That was clear to me. My job was to try to help him and to help the family, and to take care of myself.

SUN: But you did succeed in changing that for him.
SIMONTON: No. I think that's the way he wanted to die. I think I helped him to clarify a lot more than he might have if I hadn't been helping. I think I helped him to clarify the issues. He could have avoided it; he faced them. I helped. I think I made it easier for him and for the family.

SUN: What reasons are given in medical schools against doctors treating their own families?
SIMONTON: The rationale is that you lose objectivity. I said this to the family. I wanted to maintain objectivity, and for that reason I would not anticipate staying there more than two or three days at a time. I said that if I stayed there longer I would get caught up in the prevailing emotions of the situation, and I would lose my effectiveness. I needed to leave and do other things so that when I came in I would have some perspective.

These are difficult issues. I can't say that this is the way to do it with any other person, but I knew I had twelve years of experience to bring to bear on the situation I was coming into. What I attempted to do was my best, and to know that I could only do so much and then I had to expect help. I did a lot of praying, and I got a lot of help.

SUN: Carl, you are extremely brave. As a physician, you are brave to face death on such personal terms, and not to objectify or deny it.
SIMONTON: Someone pointed out to me the other day that fifty percent of medical bills are spent in the last thirty days of life. I had no idea it was this much. But it is obvious that we are doing more and more to try to keep people alive. We as a society are doing this; medicine is a product of the society. And this fear of death, and this tendency to do anything that we can to keep someone alive, is an incredible economic burden, saying nothing of the emotional burden of our inability to look at death as part of life.

We in medicine and the other helping professions have put

ourselves into the position of having to stop a very natural flow of events. And from that standpoint, we are always going to have difficulty, by looking at stressful events as things we can't integrate, seeing every death as a failure.

SUN: Are there medical models for these new directions in your work?

SIMONTON: There are very few therapists involved in the treatment of cancer patients who openly talk about death as an option. That's appropriate, since, in our society, there are very few places where death is talked about. So it is not good all of a sudden to be taking people who have been diagnosed with malignancy and telling them that they have the choice to die. How often do we as individuals hear that we have the option of dying? It's just as true for us as it is for the patient with malignancy — it's just that they are faced with a situation that makes it a lot more pertinent.

It is important to appreciate that making a lot of drastic changes which might theoretically sound good can be terrible if we don't sensitize ourselves to the ramifications of such changes and the devastation that they can bring upon patients.

I think that it is important that doctors function where they are comfortable functioning, and not to ask doctors to do a lot of changing. What I'm looking at is to find my best way of functioning as an individual, and for us to look as a society at how we want to function.

It is not necessary to have doctors administering what we are talking about. These are things that families can involve themselves in. I wouldn't want a large percentage of other physicians to try to start practicing medicine the way I practice medicine. I don't think that it would be good for them, or for society. What I would like to do is to give voice and acceptance to the large numbers of people who have similar beliefs to mine, and a method for operating so that they can be more involved with their own processes.

SUN: Last words?

SIMONTON: I would hope that as we are trying to move away from a mechanistic and depersonalized mode in medicine, we would also be moving away from a depersonalized way of living life. I hope that we will move toward a more harmonious blending with nature, medically and societally.

I would like for us to beware against believing that we are in control. I think that this is a dangerous and inaccurate leap. We are not in control. We did not create ourselves. But being open and trusting to the forces that did create us and our universe, and attempting to operate in harmony with them — this is the struggle for me. We must move toward love and harmony with Earth. More and more, this is becoming meaningful for me.

The final thing is that, when we talk about these things, about change and directions for change, and ways in which we want to change ourselves, it is very easy to put things into words. It sounds so nice and simple. We begin to assume that what sounds simple will be easy. It is important for us to appreciate that many of these changes tend to be difficult. When the changes don't come easily, we must avoid becoming overcritical and self-deprecating. We must be gentle with ourselves.

(November 1982)

A Father's Death

O. Carl Simonton

These are excerpts from Dr. Simonton's talk in Tampa, Florida.

My father did not become ill by accident. I had watched his health deteriorate over the last several years. Three years ago, in the Summer of 1979, after having multiple illnesses, heart attacks, end-stage liver disease and encephalitis, and after not being expected to live, he was one of the most exciting medical case histories I had ever known.

I had always referred to him as my favorite patient. This became particularly true after he began using results of my work to improve his own health. At age sixty-seven, in 1979, he qualified in the senior men's timed events in the national finals of the National Rodeo Association. For almost anyone, he was at that point in excellent

My oldest niece said, "Obviously, you're sick because you don't want to be here." "Right," I said.

health, particularly for a sixty-seven-year-old man who had been near death.

After that Summer, he stopped riding. There were several big events which precipitated this. The largest was the suicide of a grandson in February of 1981, almost to the day eighteen months before he died. We always look for special events six to eighteen months before a diagnosis of cancer. He held himself responsible for his grandson's suicide, who was only fourteen years old.

When we were together that Fourth of July, it was clear to me Pop was dying. I had not seen him between February and July, and it was very clear to me that he was moving toward death. I started including him in my schedule, one weekend a month. He lived 220 miles from me, and I wanted to spend time with him. There was a lot I wanted to get to know prior to his death, and I knew that might not be far off.

Then, in November of 1981, just before Thanksgiving, a great-granddaughter died of crib death. That was very hard on him. She was about a month old.

I hated to go home that Christmas. There were three major crises going on in the family, and I didn't want to be spending my Christmas in that turmoil. But I went, and I was ill. I had awakened ill at four in the morning, and by six I was throwing up. I knew that it wasn't going to keep me from going, that I was just going to be sick, and that I was going to show them how to use illness. The family asked me why I was sick; I knew they would ask me because they are all familiar with my work. My oldest niece said, "Obviously, you're sick because you don't want to be here." "Right," I said.

It was a very difficult and a very rich Christmas. We held the first of a series of family meetings to discuss Pop's dying. My older sister said that Pop was having a rough time, but that after all these many illnesses, he would come out the other side of it. She was the oldest, and she knew best. I liked hearing that. Mom and Pop's fiftieth wedding anniversary was coming up the following November, and none of us thought he would have the guts to die before then. We were wrong.

His seventieth birthday in February was a very big event. He talked about being seventy as being as long as a person ought to live. He continued to go downhill, mostly stayed in the house and continued his retreat from life. He didn't want any serious discussions — after one major attempt to bring up a serious topic, a terrible experience for me, I decided that I would spend time with him on his terms.

He was worse in June. In July, he was hospitalized with fever of unknown origin. On the twenty-fourth, the four of us kids and some of the in-laws met again. No diagnosis had been made. We said that the problem was not *what* he was dying of, because he had been dying for a long time. The problem was *that* he was dying. Only a week after that, he was diagnosed with advanced malignancy. We knew that was a distinct possibility.

I didn't know if Dad would want me to be involved with his care. I was prepared for him not to want me around as he died. But his reaction to the diagnosis was that he wanted to fight to get well, and that he wanted me to help him. Over and over he commented to the family that this would really test me, and my beliefs, and my abilities.

I proceeded to think through all I had learned over the past twelve years, and how it might apply to his treatment. I was pleased with what my work had developed, and excited about going ahead. And I was scared. I knew that it would be a sonofabitch of a job.

He was diagnosed on a Saturday with advanced widespread cancer extensively involving his liver. No treatment was appropriate. On Tuesday we had another family meeting. I saw that it was going to be a difficult time whether he got well or died. He hadn't gotten sick by accident. I had dealt with many people who had regained health from such a situation, and I knew that it was hell, that it involved real transformations of life stances, that it involved the whole family. I outlined what I wanted the family stance to be. I wanted us to believe that he could get well, though I knew we all had our own beliefs. Having dealt with the recoveries of a lot of people a lot sicker than Dad, it was easy enough for me to believe that he could get well. That was not central, though. What was central was that it was okay with us that he might die, even though we wanted him to get well.

Because I knew him so well, I took the liberty of setting the goals and plans for his program. Meditation was the first thing, because he had used it over and over, and had confidence in his ability to use it. He had incorporated meditation as a health practice and had taught it to patients in hospitals and nursing homes where he was a Baptist chaplain. His physical activities were simple: he was just to get dressed three times every week. We set some goals for his diet, and discussed the important element of purpose in life. Dad was to record in a journal what he was doing.

Six days later he had only gotten dressed once. He had gotten cranky and cantankerous, and hated to have anyone remind him of what he was supposed to be doing. We got together again and had a family meeting. We all agreed that he was making only a token effort at regaining his health. We agreed to confront him with it, and to see whether he wanted to continue. So we did. We presented it to him straight: he wasn't doing nearly enough to get well. He agreed that he wanted to give it another shot, that he wanted to try to get well. And so he did for another four days.

He had been a boxer in his youth. He began to use a phrase I never heard him use. He said he was going to throw in the towel. And from that time on, he didn't show the ambivalence I have seen in so many patients. Dad became peaceful, no pain. He was really loving and expressed a lot of love. When I got home the next time, he asked me if it was okay with me for him to die. I said that wasn't what I wanted for him, and reassured him that I was willing to work with him to die, just as I was willing to work to help him to try to live. He said that he wanted to get it over in a hurry.

It made sense to me that, if he were going to die, he should die quickly, painlessly, and comfortably. He said he didn't know how to do that. I told him that I thought that one can use the same tools in dying as in living.

Most persons I have dealt with don't want to ask the questions, don't want to actively involve themselves in dying. He kept asking me how. I told him that one can meditate on dying just as one can meditate on living. I was amazed that he was asking such important and clear questions. No patient had asked me this; families had, but I had never been forced to formulate a response to a patient. Dad was a preacher. I told him to relax himself, to think about turning loose of life and going to be with God. It seemed to make sense to him.

He proceeded to die comfortably and quietly. He was dead five days later.

(November 1982)

Irving Weiss

Man Is

the only animal   who

> Files things away for reference
> Has lost his external soul
> Thinks TV is real
> Dassnt flip his mother
> Can botch his own suicide

> "Only man,
> supererogatory beast,
> Dame Kind's thoroughbred lunatic, can
> do the honors of a feast." (Auden)

                         who

"is given the necessity of having always to do something
upon pain of succumbing." (Ortega)

       who

"labors." (Marx)

                         who

"does not without effort know what he is." (Mumford)

"But though nothing is more distinctively
'human' than a scientific laboratory in one
sense (for no other species but man is known
ever to have made and used one), it is the

kind of 'humanity' we get in mechanization
(a 'part of' man that became so poignantly
in industrial routines, 'apart from' man)."
(Kenneth Burke)

        who

   Lives as if

      "The desire to take medicine
      is perhaps the greatest fea
      ture which distinguishes man
      from animals." (Osler)

       the only animal whose

"condition is that of 'individuality
within finitude.'" (Ernest Becker)

   "Of all the distinctions between
   man and animal, the characteristic
   gift which makes us human is the
   power to work with symbolic images:
   the gift of imagination." (Bronowski)

"Alone
of all
the animals
man knows
he
will die."
(J.M. Cameron)

"Man is the only"

      who

"Man is the only"

               who

"animal who blushes or needs to." (Twain)

   ("According to an extensive study
   carried out in California in 1966,
   pigs are the only other mammals,
   aside from man, that are capable
   of getting sunburned.") (Paul Sterling Hagerman)

"Carlyle, however, celebrated the virtues of silence through
thirty volumes. Why is this a joke? The language of
paradox is as old as human consciousness, an integral
part of its most complex functions. No animals can think
or utter: 'I do not exist.'" (Ihab Habib Hassan)

"The difference between men and animals is,
we are told, that men can count, and Ida
can count beautifully up to ten again and
again and everybody listens." (Donald Sutherland)

who

Is beastly

but

"Human beings owe their biological supremacy
to the possession of a form of inheritance quite
unlike that of other animals: exogenetic or
exosomatic heredity." (P.B. Medawar)

"What distinguishes man from
the other animals is that in
one form or another he guards
his dead." (Unamuno)

"Biologically, man is still the great amateur of the animal
kingdom: he is unique in his lack of anatomical and physio-
logical specialization." (René Dubois)

who

Is not chronically afraid
"the only" who "amateur" who "animal"
"all the others are professionals." (C.S. Lewis)

"Action alone is the exclusive prerogative of man; neither a beast nor
a god is capable of it." (Hannah Arendt)

Marx: "who labors"
Adam Smith: "Propensity to truck, barter and exchange
one thing for another" distinguishes man
from animal.

animal whose

"behavior causes activation of the limbic
pleasure regions of the brain, *not* as a
result, primarily of the sense organs,
but primarily, as activity of the brain's
thinking region." (H.J. Campbell)

"On all the other planets I have known,
animals were never afraid of machines.
They are not afraid of things they have
never seen before." (Stanislaw Lem)

who

Says man is the only animal

who

(January 1979)

The Silent Mind

An Interview With Jehangir Chubb

Sy Safransky

When I noticed courses on Eastern religion being offered around town by Jehangir Chubb, a retired professor of philosophy from the University of Bombay in India, I was intrigued. Was he another dry intellectual or a genuine teacher, with something to say to us all?

We met and talked, and I was even more intrigued. He is an intellectual — he earned his doctorate at Oxford in 1937, headed the department of philosophy at Elpehinstone College at the University of Bombay from 1948 to 1965, wrote Assertion and Fact — The Categories of Self-Conscious Thinking and many papers on philosophical subjects. But in addition to being a philosopher's philosopher, he is steeped in the spiritual wisdom of ancient and modern India. His manner is formal, his words precise, his presence calm and

> You don't set up an ideal of what you want and try to become it. You become aware of what you are, and in that very process you become or realize the ideal.

spacious. Even when turning away a question ("What is the mantra?" "One doesn't tell the mantra.") he is gentle, respectful.

The collected works of Sri Aurobindo, one of India's great mystics and philosophers ("the greatest," Dr. Chubb says), line one wall of his modest apartment in Chapel Hill. He has been here since 1975, teaching courses through the extension division of the University of North Carolina at Chapel Hill and more recently through the Community Wholistic Health Center. He has also been a visiting professor at Temple University in Philadelphia and Case Western Reserve in Cleveland, Ohio. He left India in 1969 to "continue my research work in a more vigorous intellectual climate." He is seventy-one years old.

—Ed.

SUN: There are many people who are not ostensibly interested in philosophy, but who are interested in whatever philosophy has to say about how to live a happy, full life. What has your study of philosophy taught you about that?

CHUBB: The role of philosophy has been understood differently in India and the West. It basically stands for a theoretical understanding of, among other things, the nature of reality. That is how it has been understood in the Western tradition. But in India metaphysical philosophy has always been regarded as a transitional stage leading to spiritual realization. In that respect philosophy in India is practical. But the term practical again is a little ambiguous because one can be practical in two dimensions. One is the horizontal dimension, where you use philosophy to organize social institutions. Now there, the West hasn't much, if anything, to learn from the East. The West is much more practical in that respect. But practical could also mean a movement in a vertical direction where philosophical theories are regarded merely as maps or guides, provisional formulations of the truth to be realized. So I distinguish two senses of the word practical: one in which the movement is horizontal — philosophy flowing out into the world and organizing human life — and the other in which it is vertical — philosophy transcending the intellect and its concepts and culminating in a direct realization of the truth.

SUN: Is fulfillment possible on the horizontal level?

CHUBB: This is usually denied in the religious outlook, though, following Sri Aurobindo, I would say that there has to be an integral fulfillment, first in the vertical dimension and then spreading out into the world of space and time. In traditional spirituality what I have called the horizontal dimension has been overlooked. The gaze is fixed on Heaven, Eternity or Nirvana and the world is regarded at best as a training ground or an antechamber to our eternal home. The idea that this collective, embodied existence may have its own mode of self-fulfillment is rarely given serious consideration. There are two major figures in the contemporary world who have had this wider vision and have spoken of and sought to bring about this collective realization. One is Teilhard de Chardin, a Jesuit priest, who spoke of the Christification of the universe, and the other is Sri Aurobindo, who believed that the goal of evolution is the establishment of a divine life in a divine body here on Earth.

SUN: For someone who looks to spiritual teachings for clues as to how to live a more satisfying life, are there truths that can be shared in so many words?

CHUBB: I think the emphasis should not be on truths which are there to be accepted as creeds or dogmas but mainly on the change in one's personal life and existence. If one is disturbed about the world in which one lives, one is not going to change it by preaching another philosophy but by changing oneself. It is, undoubtedly, a very long process, but it's the only way. To change the world one has to begin with oneself. And then from that center influences emanate and radiate outward.

In the Buddhistic approach — I mean in accordance with the teachings of the Buddha — creeds are not important. What you believe is unimportant, because our beliefs are conditioned by past experiences, our environment, heredity, upbringing. So they have only a very limited value. What is important is a process of knowledge of oneself, without reliance on any beliefs or theories. And this process is described by the Buddha in his teachings concerning mindfulness, where one is mindful of the entire process of the psycho-physical personality without any theorizing about it. And through this mindfulness there comes into being a radical change in consciousness, self-knowledge and the transformation of human personality. And this is not in accordance with a preconceived theory.

SUN: What is the relevance of the teachings of the Buddha in the world today?

CHUBB: In the world today there is a strong tendency toward agnosticism. Belief in God doesn't have a very strong hold, except among the orthodox followers of a religion. But generally speaking, belief in God, theism and the religious way of life have lost their appeal. In such a world the Buddhist teachings would sound refreshing because the Buddha doesn't ask you to believe in anything. For him there are no belief systems at all. He says: look at yourself, be mindful, be aware of everything that you do and say and think, and through this awareness there comes about knowledge of the self, and also, ultimately, the realization of Nirvana. Mindfulness is the only way, he said, for the purification of being, for the overcoming of torment and sorrow and for the attainment of Nirvana.

SUN: What does the concept that we create our reality with our beliefs mean to you?

CHUBB: I would say that we organize our belief systems, and therefore take things as real, in accordance with our past conditioning, so in that sense beliefs create "realities." But when there is direct self-knowledge, once again quoting the Buddha, we see things as they are, and we see ourselves as we are.

SUN: That suggests that there is an absolute reality behind the phenomenal world.

CHUBB: The process of mindfulness does not start with that or any other assumption. That would be just another metaphysical theory. One may discover such an absolute reality through the process of mindfulness, but it will not be set up as an ideal which one has to realize. Buddhism bypasses all theories.

SUN: The notion that we create our reality or realities — that we choose, because of past conditioning, those phenomena we are going to call more real than others — seems to be a potent tool for change.

CHUBB: One does not choose. To understand what the Buddha said and to practice mindfulness does not imply that we must make a list of things that we have to hold onto or discard in order that we may begin the process of understanding. One doesn't start by discriminating between things which one regards as good and those which one regards as evil, and eliminating the latter. One starts with what one is. And if we find that there is any relationship which is helpful, which brings about peace and harmony and satisfaction, that's all to the good. Through the process of mindfulness, one discovers that one's life and thought processes and actions are frequently caught up in obscurity, confusion and internal contradiction. And then one can, if one becomes aware of that clearly and directly, straighten that out. It's not a question of giving up anything, but straightening oneself out. And if, in that process there are certain goods which are permissable, we hold onto them, but after a while we may realize that these goods are not really worthwhile and we outgrow them.

For example, a person may find some satisfaction in going to the club every day to gossip or play cards. But after a time he may come to realize it's not really worth it, that he can find a better use for his time. But it should come spontaneously; he doesn't set out to eliminate something by using the surgeon's knife. There is a constant self-fulfillment, where you become more and more integrated, and there is an inner guidance which you follow, in accordance with which you reorganize your life.

SUN: Within yourself how does that inner guidance manifest?
CHUBB: Inner guidance is really inner; you cannot ask for any external signs of it. If it manifests, one knows that there is inner guidance. But if you look for an external sign then it's no longer inner guidance.

SUN: Are you saying that it ceases to be inner guidance if it's described?
CHUBB: It can be described in the most general way, but not in a way which would be helpful to anybody, which would make it possible for him to acquire this inner guidance. We can say that discrimination, the discriminative faculty, has developed. And so one discriminates between things without having recourse to rules and regulations. And without having the need to go to somebody else for guidance. That is the most general way in which one can describe this inner guidance.

SUN: Without having someone else to go to: does that suggest that those who go to gurus for guidance are not hearing their own inner messages?

CHUBB: I would use the word perceptions rather than "messages." But to answer your question, there are two reasons for going to a guru. One may be to get guidance. But that is not the deeper guru-disciple relationship. The importance of the guru is that from his personality there radiates an influence which enters into the disciple and helps him to grow and develop by himself. So I don't think that these two — going to a guru and being guided from within — are inconsistent. More and more one relies on the inner guide, the Antaryamin or the dweller within the self; he takes over and guides from within. One goes to the guru not so much to ask him what to do or not to do, but to live in his presence and open oneself to his influence. The change in personality doesn't come about by the application of rules. It is a process of being born, as it were, and there are many incalculable factors that enter into it.

SUN: Do you consider Sri Aurobindo to be your guru?
CHUBB: Yes, Sri Aurobindo and the Mother.

SUN: Who is the Mother?
CHUBB: Sri Aurobindo's co-worker. Her father was a Turk, but she was brought up in Paris, so she was practically French. Independently she had the same realization as Sri Aurobindo and had the idea of "making heaven and Earth equal and one," to quote Sri Aurobindo. And when she met Sri Aurobindo, in the early part of this century, she realized that her place and life's work were with him. After the First World War was over she came and settled in Pondicherry where Sri Aurobindo was, and they were working together to bring about this new stage in human evolution.

SUN: She is still alive?
CHUBB: No, she passed away in 1973.

SUN: And he died when?
CHUBB: 1950.

SUN: So she continued the work after he died. And did you ever meet them?

CHUBB: Yes, but Sri Aurobindo had withdrawn in a sense. He did not want to get involved in meeting people and talking to them because that would have distracted him from his inner work, which was not really for himself but for bringing about this new order of existence. So one could only have his *darshan* [spiritual meeting] four times a year. And I became acquainted with Sri Aurobindo's teachings in 1946, just four years before his passing away.

SUN: How did you become familiar with his teachings?
CHUBB: I was in the army during the war, until 1946 when I got demobilized and I had three months' leave before joining my old post. I wanted to go and spend some time in an ashram. A friend of mine who was familiar with the Sri Aurobindo ashram made arrangements for me to go and stay there. That was my first *darshan* of Sri Aurobindo. I then read his magnum opus, *The Life Divine*, and then I kept on going regularly. During those four years I had about six *darshans* of Sri Aurobindo. The Mother I met frequently and also privately. She used to give interviews and I met her several times. She helped me a great deal.

SUN: How did she help you?
CHUBB: I put some personal problems before her and she talked to me about them and she talked to Sri Aurobindo also about them. And both of them gave me their force, as it were, to deal with the problems. I wouldn't be very different from the influence any teacher, who is really a teacher, exerts on his disciples. Something passes from the teacher to the disciple, a kind of force which helps the disciple to reorganize his life. These things I think are quite common; they're not peculiar to Sri Aurobindo and the Mother, this kind of silent force that emanates from an individual.

SUN: Did you ever meet with them on levels other than ordinary waking reality?
CHUBB: Not the Mother, but once I had a very vivid dream. It seemed to be more than a dream. During that period I was worried about death. There was also fear attached to these thoughts. In this dream I saw myself lying on the bed and Sri Aurobindo walked up to me. I didn't get up from the bed, I didn't think it was disrespect-

ful, it all seemed quite natural. He came and sat beside me. And I asked him a number of questions about death which he answered. Later on I realized that these answers were the same as those given by him several times over in his letters and other writings. Then he suddenly put his hand on my lap and said, "But why are you afraid of death? You are living eternally in the heart of Sri Aurobindo." That was the end of the fear of death.

SUN: When was that dream, how long ago?
CHUBB: Many years ago.

SUN: So you have no fear of death now. [He nods.] How about dreams? What do you make of dreams?
CHUBB: There are many theories about dreams and I'm not an expert in this subject. Some are merely reproductions of waking experiences. Some may be wish-fulfillment, as the Freudians say. Others may be prophetic or occult. There are different kinds of dreams. There's not one single explanation which will account for all dreams.

SUN: If we experience being somewhere in a dream, do you accept the explanation that our consciousness has in fact left our body and is in a . . . .
CHUBB: It's possible.

SUN: A dream world that is as vivid and compelling on that plane as what we call reality on this plane?
CHUBB: Yes, it's possible. I know people who have had that experience vividly and continuously. But I'm not interested in this phenomenon; whether it is true or not true is not of much importance.

SUN: Do you feel that way generally about what are called occult or psychic phenomena? Do you feel that they're detours or distractions?
CHUBB: Here one has to be a little careful. They can become distractions if one gets attached to them. And then the energy is diverted from the main purpose. Then the ego begins to function and you get a sense of power and importance. And in the Yoga system of India it is explicitly stated that these occult powers will

arise but they should be ignored completely, otherwise you get side-tracked. On the other hand I'm not one of those who dismiss the whole occult field as having no significance. I would say, following Sri Aurobindo, that for the perfect and complete life, all the powers of human nature and the universe have to be mastered and fulfilled. Occult powers are part of the total energy of nature and they too have to be fulfilled. But it has to be on the basis of a spiritual equanimity. Otherwise, going into the occult would be an ego trip sometimes and it could be dangerous.

SUN: Do you do any formal meditation?
CHUBB: Largely the Buddhist, but it is not formal, because formal meditation would be in accordance with rules; you concentrate on an image, you do certain breathing exercises, or you try to control this or that thought or impulse of the mind. But in the teachings of the Buddha, meditation consists in becoming aware of the total process of the mind. It's not exclusive concentration on any one part of the mind. And I think I should have said earlier that this type of meditation is to be found also in Hinduism in the *Samkhya* system. The *Samkhya* recommends adopting the witness attitude. One steps back from the processes of the mind and witnesses them. And so there comes about an inner detachment. But there's nothing formal about it. You are either able to occupy that poise of witness consciousness where you become aware of the total process of the mind, without identifying with any particular movement, or you're not. It's not by following any rules of discipline that you can do it. It's a process of waking up. And there are no formal rules for waking up.

SUN: What does love mean to you, and how does and doesn't it relate to romantic love?
CHUBB: I think that spiritual love, which is a total self-giving without any thought of return, is the true nature of love. Then it may take a different form when, as it were, it enters into a restricted field of consciousness. There it may become romantic love. And it still retains its value in that particular expression. It is only when romantic love becomes possessive and thoughtless that there is degradation and distortion. So romantic love can be a very helpful thing, even in one's spiritual life, if the two people help each other to grow. But that should not degenerate into possessive love, where you become all-

important. Then love turns into a form of exploitation.

SUN: From your observations, how many people in romantic relationships are able to manifest that more spiritual love?
CHUBB: Well, it happens in India, we have that tradition there; if the two partners are both spiritually inclined, they help each other. Many of our sages have said the same thing, that such a relation can be very helpful indeed. But love in itself is its own eternity. It doesn't require any response from anybody else to sustain itself.

SUN: So the beloved is all existence; one doesn't need a single object. In fact, in having a single object, love can turn into something other than love.
CHUBB: Not other than love. I think that the qualities which we regard as values — love is one of them — exist in their absolute form in themselves or in the Divine and they can manifest under conditions of relative existence, where love, to take one quality, doesn't cease to be love but becomes a lower and diminished form of the absolute quality. This is because there is an analogical resemblance between human qualities and their divine equivalents and this justifies us in using the same word: love, wisdom, knowledge, power. But the divine quality is qualitatively different from the human quality. It is not merely a higher degree of the corresponding human quality. When we pass from the human to the divine quality something new comes into being, something incomparable and ineffable. So romantic love is still love. We don't need to use another word.

SUN: If the romantic love we're absorbed in is not the same as the deeper spiritual love we would like to feel, what do we do about that predicament?
CHUBB: Why should it be a predicament? These things are permissible in the sense that they are helpful, in their own way. So why should it create a problem? The predicament would be artificial: I want to love in a spiritual way, but I don't. Now that is an artificial demand.

SUN: How is it artificial?
CHUBB: Because you are setting up this ideal of spiritual love and saying this is what I must achieve. But according to the Buddha all

growth should be spontaneous and natural. You don't set up an ideal of what you want to be and try to become it. You become aware of what you are, and in that very process you become or realize the ideal.

SUN: Doesn't mindfulness itself become a goal?
CHUBB: It is not a goal but a process, a purposive movement or mode of awareness that does not rest on a theory of the self — the ideal self, or any other theory. So it is free of all conditioning. It is not the Cartesian process of doubt but rather of detachment, which carries one beyond both belief and doubt. Further, it doesn't posit any goal which one is trying to reach.

SUN: Such as divine love?
CHUBB: Yes, it is merely a process of being aware of oneself, being alert and watchful of all that goes on in the mind, not leading an existence which is half or three-quarters unconscious.

SUN: Are you fully conscious?
CHUBB: Not fully, no.

SUN: How do you perceive the gap between where you are and what you imagine it is to be fully conscious?
CHUBB: You are asking for a kind of spiritual confession?

SUN: I am interested in anything that would illuminate that. Whether the details are personal or not doesn't matter. They might be interesting.
CHUBB: I would then answer by approaching the question from a different point of view. Indian sages talk about realization and they also talk about a settled realization. And realization is something that comes; you perceive — to talk again in Buddhistic terms — the total process of the mind and you're detached and there's integration or wholeness. But it may not be a settled experience. One would have to keep on practicing the process of mindfulness. In those terms I would describe my own condition. It is not a settled thing, but it is more or less constantly there.

SUN: Was there a particular experience somewhere along the line, a singular dramatic experience for you?

CHUBB: Did you say dramatic or traumatic?
SUN: Either or both. An awakening that you can identify with a particular time and place?
CHUBB: The first experience was after I had a talk with J. Krishnamurti. That was in the early Thirties when I was working for my master of arts degree.

SUN: And where was this, in India?
CHUBB: Bombay, yes. I had some problems. I won't go into that. And after talking to him, one day I went out for a walk and one sentence from Krishnamurti came back to my mind. "Don't indulge in this desire, don't control it either, but understand it." Then suddenly all the mental processes stopped and I found myself in a state which is described as the silent mind. All mental conflicts and, indeed, the mind itself, came to a stop. I had achieved what the *Samkhya* calls the witness consciousness and I was abiding in that. That was my first experience of the silent mind.

SUN: Was that an awareness which faded or has it remained?
CHUBB: It went and came, went and came; it is now more in than out. That has been my story and I repeat what I said earlier that it is not yet a settled experience.

SUN: So you regularly remind youself?
CHUBB: You mean practice mindfulness? Mindfulness is not a process of reminding oneself of anything. Yes, I meditate every day, but it is not formal meditation. Besides, meditation need not be restricted to a particular time. Recently I discovered that the silent and continuous repetition of a mantra is also very helpful. The Mother had given me a mantra way back in the Fifties but only now, in the last few months, it occurred to me to use it.

SUN: What is the mantra?
CHUBB: One doesn't tell the mantra.

SUN: What were your impressions of Krishnamurti?
CHUBB: I came to understand Krishnamurti much better after I

read Zen Buddhism. I find that he is in the Buddhist, particularly the Zen Buddhist, tradition, though he doesn't follow that or any other tradition; he is an original. My only reservation about Krishnamurti is that his teachings are not sufficiently comprehensive or compassionate. Having discovered a path, which may be called the pathless path — if one can use that paradox — every other approach is for him a waste of time. That negative aspect of his teaching I do not accept. But otherwise his teachings are very original and profound.

SUN: Why are you in America these days?

CHUBB: In pursuit of another strong interest, and that is intellectual philosophy. I always wanted to return to the West because the intellectual climate here is more vigorous in the field of theoretical philosophy than in India. I have a great respect for the intellect and do not play it down because I see the truth in spiritual philosophy. According to me, these two, intellectual and spiritual philosophy, can and should be integrated for a fuller development of human personality.

SUN: Is there much suffering in your life?

CHUBB: No.

SUN: Difficulty?

CHUBB: Yes, I think I have had my normal share, to put it mildly.

SUN: But would you describe yourself as a happy man?

CHUBB: There is no real happiness that is dependent on external circumstances, but there can be a discovery of a center within whose very nature is peace, self-existent peace, independent of all changing circumstances. I have touched that center.

(July 1981)

Birdseye

Pat Ellis Taylor

Winter in Dallas, Chuck and Morgan and me all tucked into an efficiency apartment with a murphy bed, smoking marijuana in a large walk-in closet that also doubles as my writing space because Shorty the landlord says if he catches you smoking pot he'll throw you out. Shorty is king of this straight baptist red-brick apartment and square lawn in the middle of a block of black chicano-low-riders and jesusfreak vans with holy fire painted in orange running off the front fenders, gunshots at night and sirens in the alley behind the supermarket, taxi driver asking on the corner have you seen that blonde hooker that's always here, flat brown bottles on the sidewalk when I walk to work past the park in the morning, everybody asking me are you sure you should be walking to work?

Hal says that something flies out of his right eye, Jewel Babb tells him that something left, and he says does it really happen that way, does it really fly out?

And we're all working. In the morning everyone up at six-thirty, Morgan into the bathtub, blowdrying purple punked-out hair, red suspenders, gray corduroys for the carwash, catching the Abrams-Mockingbird bus but still having to walk three miles at the end of the line. Chuck and me working kelly girl, Chuck bumming out fast from so much joking around — Chuck the kelly girl, Chuck the poet, Chuck the man who comes home and watches tv with a quart of beer at night, completely wiped out.

And me, walking along the downtown sidewalks, underneath the North-Central Expressway, past the liquor store black men waving brown package out, say don't you talk to black men *huh?* thinking about when I used to live in the desert, when I'm going to be rich, when I won't have to be a kelly girl anymore, when I'm going to tell just the right story. It's going to come to me, and it's going to be the right story for everyone. Walking back past the park where Chuck says the winos come at night and pool their money and buy the bottles I'm always seeing on the sidewalk.

But in the late afternoon the birds come before the winos, hundreds of blackbirds, grackles, swirling over the park, resting in the tops of the trees like large black leaves come to cover the bare branches, the sidewalks white with grackle guano, and here and there in the grass the dead stiff body of a grackle, died in his sleep waiting for the Spring to come a little more before following the wind on to Kansas and Illinois and wheat fields coming ripe all the grackles dream about. After dark the winos will come, grackles and winos occupying the branches and roots each to his own, watching the moon in its phases barely clearing the Dallas skyline.

And before grackle park, I walk along the sidewalk, thinking about everything. But when I get there it is half past five and the sky is turning red and gray and the grackles are flying down into the branches, finding each other, making the hiss-whizz-crack-and-cackle thousands of times. I stop thinking about everything except grackles and grackles, my head filled with them like the trees. One day I stop in the middle of the sidewalk. I think that I will try and call to one of the grackles with my mind. I will call out come to me, come to me, come to me, and I will try to think of the motion of a grackle flying through the air and landing on my shoulder. So I pick out a bird by himself at the top of a very tall tree. I look at him squarely and think as loudly as I can, come to me, come to me, concentrating on the motion. But he continues to sit, looking in the sky, in the branches, at the other birds, never at me, until the energy is gone and I stop thinking at him and continue walking along the whitened sidewalk, the litter of dead birds and leaves in the gutter and the swirl of birds high in the sky. Blocks away from grackle park I forget the birds completely, wondering if Morgan scored roaches from the ashtrays at the carwash, wondering what to make for supper.

There is a woman named Jewel Babb who lives in the desert. When I talk about her I call her wise, I tell people she is eighty years old, that she lives with goats, that rumor has it she can heal people with her hands. And suddenly it is February, I am saying this about publishers and that about contracts, and maybe I will write this up I am saying and I will even print this *my*-self, swaggering around in the apartment talking to anyone who will listen, fast and loud — oh there will be a meeting with this woman in the desert, I will bring champagne, I will make arrangements, get money, so many telephone calls to make and to receive. At the same time Chuck is becoming confused and disheartened. He says there are not enough windows in the apartment, there are not enough rooms or beds, and he wants to leave me. He has told all our friends, I can hear it in their voices solicitous and curious on the telephone. So when he leaves me alone one evening at the apartment, closing the door without saying if he will be back, I sit down in a chair in front of the television feeling too large and heavy and awkward for anyone to want to keep around. Besides,

there is no money, no check in the mail that was supposed to come,

and there is no grass, not even seeds or roaches,

and there is no Morgan, he is at a movie or a punk rock club, gone somewhere leaving me alone alone alone.

Sitting in the chair in the apartment in Dallas, watching the little brown cockroaches roam around the cheerios box above the television picture which is fast becoming a black and white blur, the sadder I become, the more loaded and heavy with responsibility I feel. I think that I have taken on too many people to care for and that I won't be able to go to the desert after all, and that the photographer (who is Anne) will be so disappointed because this is her first free-lance job and it is falling through, and that the artist (who is Hal) will be so disgusted because I have told him I am going to make a book with his paintings of the woman and the goats in the desert. And I am thinking I am crazy, I am crazy, I have lost my train of thought, I have made myself believe that there is some good to writing stories which are only dirt in my mouth, too much marijuana has filled my brain with strange ambitions, and on and on until I am gone completely, the apartment is gone, the floor melts the walls melt, I see the delicate ice crystal structure that everything depends upon, that the universe rides on, and then the ice melts and I melt and everything is terrible. All sense has completely gone.

But the next morning the sun is out and I get up and have a grapefruit and a cup of coffeee. I'm feeling better even though my stomach is messed up and won't digest anything before eleven o'clock in the morning, serious symptoms. I will die of nervous ulcers before I am forty-five. Then Chuck comes in the door wanting to go the desert with me after all, tossing around money, even willing to pay for the airplane tickets until my own check should happen to come. That is the way it is, living with Chuck: one day he is a regular-sized man, then the next he becomes big and lion-hearted, a man of large proportions, elastic seams.

So that night I am settling into a Southwest Airlines economy seat, a cardboard box of files on my lap, Chuck tucked in on the wingside with a yellow plastic bag of grapefruit and peanut butter, provisions for the trip, and the plane takes off above all the lights that are Dallas, lurching a little in the air currents, making me think of my own death as airplanes always do, of what everyone will say, that I died before my prime, that I still had quite a bit to say, and I wonder if people who die in airplane accidents always have a head full of plans right up to the time of fiery consummation. I decide that they do, just like me. Then we are very high and the night is black and somewhere above the desert we start slowing, coming down.

Hal's new red car is going to carry us all. He is packing his watercolors, a large pad, sleeping bags for everyone, gloves and a knife so that he can look for peyote. He isn't sure there will be anything else — are you sure she'll be out there? he asks me, are there going to be goats? And I answer always yes, I'm sure. I am getting good at pretending. Hal is having some problems at the house with his wife, she says well ex-cuse me! and he says I've had it! He walks out, but Chuck and I don't look up from the packing. Then we pick up Anne, who just came back from Guatemala. She has her cameras and bags, doesn't have a job at the photo lab anymore and is shy and doesn't know me very well, and I am amazed again that these people are going with me to a place I have named in the desert to see a woman who I have assured them is supposed to heal people with her hands. But then it is the twentieth century, we're not going for the laying of hands, we're going to lay hands on. If Jesus Christ were living I would write a story about him and get some people out for photographs and sketches, some close-ups of the miracle of laying on of hands, and sell it to a magazine. Chuck has divorced himself from the pilgrimage. He is going along for the ride, he has forgotten his camera, his writing tablet and his pen. He will look out of the car windows and count the yuccas while I try to remember what road to take when.

And where are we going? We are tracing out a vague pattern of dirt roads south of Sierra Blanca winding through the Quitman Mountains toward the Rio Grande. I know that one dirt road goes to the woman's cabin, which is alone on a ridge looking out over Mayfield Canyon, and another dirt road goes to Indian Hot Springs which is down by the river. It is special country, all red rock and huge tumbled stone and mountain cliffs studded with caves first used by river- and-rock loving Indians, now by coyotes and wet-backs. I can remember one area, the river plain spreading out a white crust on the ground instead of sand, marking out an area of hot springs bubbling out of the ground into twenty-two pools, which the Indians declared forever neutral ground. There is a rope bridge across the Rio Grande there, that Mexican villagers cross to get to the springs to bathe, although the border patrolmen shoot men in the legs for doing it. Even if they are only villagers coming across for the baths, they are nevertheless wetbacks when they cross the river. A border patrolman is a visionary, taught in geography classes to hold the map of the United States firmly in mind, so that even when he works for a living in a desert which stretches to infinity and upholds a river from both sides, he can still see the clear black line that cuts it cleanly in half.

I don't want to go all the way to the river and the hot springs, I want to remember when to make the turn away to the woman's cabin. I tell Hal to take a turn and then another one and then we get lost in a maze of little arroyos criss-crossing roads which have become paths. In the low parts we all get out, Chuck and Anne and I put rocks underneath the wheels of Hal's red car so that it will drive over the washed-out places without getting stuck, and we push and Hal revs the engine and gravel comes out, the smell of burning rubber comes up, there is dust, it isn't very funny that we're stuck and lost in the desert. Finally at one arroyo the three of us push very hard so that the car becomes unstuck again and Hal drives away in a big cloud of dust, Anne and Chuck and me standing there. The engine fades over the hill and the desert is quiet, big yuccas bending over us, little scrubby greasewood here and there, lots of sky. We walk until we get to the top of the hill and he can't be seen. We walk some more and we walk about a mile, then there he is, the red car stopped in the road, Hal sitting down on a rock beside it. He isn't smiling when we walk up. It was sure good to get away from you for a little bit he says. We drive on.

The sun is almost down when we finally round a turn, the tumble of pens and sheds appear on a ridge above us and we make the last climb up the road into a cleared area, a quiet dark cabin in the middle. It looks like nothing is going on. No cars. There are some chickens picking apart a mattress close to the porch door. There are half a dozen horses standing bunched together in the mesquite which grows along the edges of the yard who are giving us the look-over, and in the back of the cabin somewhere, although I can't see them, I know there are a great number of goats. Chuck and Hal and Anne start wandering around the yard, sniffing around tentatively like humans do trying to get their bearings, trying to locate this and that, peering into the distance at the hills, shuffling through the dirt of the clearing discovering rocks and rusted nails, making mental notes of the road where we were before, the large yuccas, the dog with a blue eye and a yellow one who flaps his tail around in a circle when I come up to the door and knock. Someone is stirring in the darkness of the porch, but when the door opens it isn't Jewel Babb, it is an old man thin and brown, white grizzle for a beard, old blue stocking cap, two black teeth set between two brown ones in the gums. Jewel Babb, he tells me, no esta en la casa, she was earlier, he says, but she isn't anymore. Well, she would be back sometime, I know that, or maybe she won't be back, but what can we do? We can stay, we can wait, we can look at the goats.

The old man says his name is Evaristo, he herds the goats which, he waves toward the back, are all in the pens. So I wander outside and there they are, hundreds of goats, all different colors and sizes, but more babies than large ones, standing, sitting, bumping each other, watching Anne and Hal and Chuck who are leaning at individual places around the pen. I find my own place and stand and watch them for a long time. They are such beautiful animals, the shades of their coats strange colors, their eyes with the pupils slanted sideways some blue and some gold, and their mouths smiling goat-buddha smiles. Watching them I see that I have come to a place where the four-footed far outnumber the two-footed and where in the large space of sky and canyon even that little differentiation breaks down. So I stand and watch the goats just like they stand and watch me, no more, though, than they are standing and watching each other, and then I watch Anne and Chuck and Hal, all of us watching not saying anything, part of the general herd.

At night the four of us walk into the desert in a loop of goat paths, the moon bright enough so that we can see exactly where we are in relation to the path, the rocks, the hills and the greasewood. The stars swim straightforwardly in a band which sweeps across the night as we walk the eye of the kaleidoscope, enjoying our own black silhouettes jutting out from our feet in the sand. Hal says that he has been rolfed and Chuck asks what that means. Hal says it's like zone therapy a little bit, the rolfer finds these places in the body that are sore, then you yell and cry and talk about what you are thinking. Hal says that rolfing is a wonderful thing, that everyone should do rolfing, and Chuck believes that Hal has fallen in love with his rolfer, and right after telling about rolfing, Hal mentions love, that we're taught not to do it. Anne agrees, but she doesn't say too much because she doesn't talk as much as everyone else, although she says yes yes intently at times and nods her head. Chuck is agreeing too, that's true, we haven't been taught to love, and I say yes, that's true, because everyone's afraid that if it's okay to love everybody then we'll all wind up going to bed with our fathers and mothers as well as our neighbor's wife. Everyone agrees with that, so we are quiet and think about it for a while, walking along the path of illuminated rocks, crunching along, someone picking up something, rubbing it in the palm. Look, Hal says, let's sit down together and make a cir-cle, so we sit down together and make a circle in the path but it is silly, we hold hands but Chuck yawns, I hunker down, feel like the stars are breathing down my neck, crunch rocks, cough a little. Finally Hal says maybe we should get up, Chuck says it's just that I've got a little stiffness in my back. Walking is better Hal says, Anne agrees.

Then the clearing edge again, the four of us stepping into its circle, three of the horses stepping into it from the other side, look-ing at us, us looking at them. Two gangs. They are spread out in a semi-circle, the middle one white — white in the moonlight like an apparition, like the horse of a thousand stories, charmed, made from wind or the foam of an ocean that the desert used to sit at the bot-tom of. It seems to me that they are saying something to us, or maybe they are waiting for us to say something, and I am looking at the white one, in the middle of its head, but there is no more than a general concentration between his head and mine, lowered at each other. Then he bows and turns into the desert. The other two brown ones leave, too, and we go into the cabin where Evaristo is already preparing for bed. He shows Anne that she can have the couch where he himself sleeps. It is up against the wall of the kit-chen, piled with a brown scrap of blanket in the darkest corner, lit only by the kerosene flame in the lamp that Evaristo holds while he shows her where it is. Anne declines, it is too dark, the folds of the rags too mysterious. She shares the mattress on the porch with Chuck and me, Hal sleeping at the side of the bed in a sleeping bag, sounds of shifting animals outside the screen, Evaristo's horse taking a long piss right by the door, finally Anne snoring, Hal breathing loudly, Chuck's breath on my neck.

The morning comes before the sun. It is gray and rose, the black and white rooster is crowing, he is sitting on a yucca near the porch, he has a bright brown neck and red wattles. When I walk out in the yard, there are little chickens, a solitary duck, an eccentric of his own kind taken to the desert, and two guinea hens. Also cows, silly and brown, wandering across the lot. There is the smell of coffee which Evaristo makes in a charred pot, there are the goats in the pen, butting and baaing, rustling, kneeling and gazing, the babies by their mothers, the young males leaping and kicking, everyone waiting for Evaristo to come and open up the gate so they can go. Then the sun is up, Evaristo saddles his horse, his stocking cap slung to the back of his head like a blue flag, and he lets out the goats, they tumble through the clearing, beating up the dust. Chuck is suddenly running down into the desert with them, zig-zagging through the mesquite and over the rocks, he is a goat himself with his own long legs leaping and flapping. And the cows can't go, Evaristo is beating them away from the path the goats took down the arroyo with a stick, the rest of the day they peer out over the mesa, not knowing quite what to do with themselves because they aren't goats and aren't allowed to go with the herd. Then the clearing is quiet again and Evaristo is gone on his horse. Chuck comes walking back up the path, the rest of us looking out over the hills to the last of the goats disappearing around a bend, and the sun is all the way up. There is no Jewel Babb but there is the desert, there is sun, there were goats until just a few minutes ago, their dust and smell and images still in the air.

And in the afternoon Jewel Babb comes. Before she came, I was worrying, I was thinking Jewel Babb is not a wise old woman, Jewel Babb is a silly woman, sometimes she repeats herself and sometimes she makes wrong decisions, and really I have never seen her heal anybody, I have seen her touch them, but I haven't seen anything. But on the other hand, does that matter anyway? Anne asks me if Jewel Babb really heals people and I tell her that I don't know. For photographs it doesn't matter anyway. But then Jewel Babb comes.

Her body is still solid and good, she has a heavy scarf on her head, I remember now that she always wears it over her hair like that, although I had forgotten it, her eyes are blue and she is smiling and happy to see me although we are suddenly shy when we hug each other. I tell her this is Hal and this is Anne, she hugs Chuck because she knows him. So that afternoon Anne tells her to stand there and stand there, and she stands, and then Anne tells her to be by the goats which have come back, and she is by them. She picks the little ones up, and Anne takes photographs of that, and she puts them down, and Anne gets that, too. Then Anne tells her to heal a person, and Hal sits on the chair. Jewel Babb puts her hands on his head and on his back, she sits and looks at him a little, then she moves her hand on his shoulders. Hal says that something flies out of his right eye, Jewel Babb tells him that something left, and he says does it really happen that way, does it really fly out? Jewel Babb says sometimes it does, flying out of an eye or the mouth. Then Chuck says Pat, you should tell her about your stomach, and I say yes, well, I've been having a nervous stomach, I can't eat in the morning. So Jewel Babb tells me to sit in a chair. She sits near the screen, the rooster looking over her shoulder, Anne snapping photographs, Chuck getting some coffee, and suddenly I am farting, I am belching, the juices in my stomach are rolling and roaring, I am getting louder by the second, belching and farting and growling, I put my head down in my hands because it is very embarrassing. Anne is laughing, Chuck comes out of the kitchen to see what is going on, Jewel Babb is looking at me smiling, she says do you want me to take that away now? I say of course. She tells me to lie down on the mattress on my back, she passes her hands over me from my head to my toes, then shakes her fingers at the foot of the bed, shaking all the noise away, everything finally quieting down, my stomach stopped.

Finally there is no more film and Jewel Babb is sitting in her chair on the porch eighty years old telling about the goats, what they've been doing, rolling her eyes, her friend Agustín drove her out to the camp she says (he's out in the yard talking to Evaristo — a little brown man who cuts hair and plays the fiddle for a living in Sierra Blanca) he tells me he's going to leave and go be with his children in Del Rio, she says, but maybe he won't go. I get out the bottle of champagne and everyone drinks some, Evaristo comes in, a little for Agustín, Hal, Chuck, Anne and me, the first champagne Jewel Babb has ever had, the first alcoholic beverage in eighty years of life, my responsibility, I'm tampering here with history, major anglo heroine legendary Jewel Babb, anglo curandera and desert wise woman, turns to booze at the age of eighty years, toxifies her system irreparably, her delicately balanced system of healing turned to a jumble of pickled nerves. But Jewel Babb takes some sips, gets happy, we're going to make some money on this book, Jewel Babb says. Maybe you'll stay here, I tell Agustín, maybe you won't want to be taken care of by your family after all. May-be, he says, always may-be.

Sometimes I think about Dallas while I'm sitting in the back seat of Hal's red car with Anne, looking out the window at the Rio Grande, driving along. I wonder if Shorty will have stopped outside the apartment door, sniffed the marijuana and busted Morgan, thrown him out, barred the door. Probably not. Maybe so. The road is gravel, the adobes of Mexican villages and single desert farmers along the other side, rocky cliffs on our side, red canyons, dry creek beds running to the river in a tumble of rocks, the air blue, the salt cedar feathering green for spring along the river, the desert red and brown. Then I am thinking about the Rio Grande itself, how it is just a trickle of water, barely visible through the screen of salt cedar that stretches out between the riverbed and the road. I have read that when the Spanish missionaries first came to this valley, the river was so wide, they could barely see the other side and the grass was tall as a man's head. I am thinking that some day someone should dynamite all the dams on the upper Rio Grande and let the water come down as it should, flooding half of Las Cruces, all of El Paso downtown, a terrible large roll of water which would eventually settle itself into a wide-running band, to make all of this desert green again. And I am looking out over the river when a bird comes down. I see him suspended in the air, his wings spread out, only moving them every few seconds once or twice to maintain his spot above the riverbed.

Well we all see it, Hal sees it, he slows down, I grab his shoulder, Anne says wow and look at that and Chuck cranes his head around, we're all looking at that bird, the sun on such a beam above us that it illuminates his wings to translucent red and brown, his head completely white, it has to be an eagle. It's an eagle, I say, it's really an eagle, I can't believe it is an eagle, maybe it's a hawk of some kind, Chuck says, no it's not, it's an eagle, I tell him. I'm looking at it, everyone's looking at it, and the eagle is looking at us, he is suspended in the air and he has a direct eye on what must appear to him as a wonderful shiny red object full of chattering animals which has stopped in the middle of the road. Hal comes in a little closer, and the bird moves in a little closer. Then when he stops, we do, too. High above him there is another one just like him that appears, circling at the same distance but on a higher plane.

We know something at the same time — we need to get out quick, Hal is already out, and Chuck is out on the other side, Anne and I are scrambling out, then we're in the middle of the road in a little group, all looking at the illuminated bird. As the bird stands still in the air, I get an old ecstatic feeling of being overcome, like when holy fire comes down in a church service and the people cry out, tears in their eyes, falling down on the ground, until I can hardly see the bird anymore. But I realize what is happening and I think no, no tears, damn it, I want to see him as clearly as I possibly can. Then, just in that instant we are face to face, on the same plane somewhere very high, and I am eyeing the eagle the aztec bird coasting over the two-headed stream of red and blue which is the stream of the desert and the stream of the river, one embracing the other and the sky embracing everything. Then the bird swoops down almost into the water he had been hanging over, then angles in front of us, crosses the road, swoops behind a hill, back up, above us, around us, and away. Then he is gone. We are standing, looking up at the sky, in the middle of the road.

(August 1981)

O Marie, Çoncue Sans Pêché

Kathleen Snipes

On my calendar there aren't any more social engagements or shrink appointments or movies to catch up on. It says here: "Monday. Get up. Eat. Floss teeth. Go to bed by 10:00." The little sparrow who's sharing my breakfast says, "Phew-twee. Pep. Pep. Pep. Pep," and stuffs his beak full of bread, so that it's hanging out both sides. "Don't get choked," I yell after him, but he's long gone, chased by a friend.

Old friends, old friends. My dad starts to cry as he hands me a radio. "I just picked this up," he says, "at the PX. They were on sale. Do you have a radio?" "No," I say truthfully. "No, I was just thinking how much I wanted a radio. You need a radio these days. There might be an emergency. Or . . . weather. You need a radio." I nod, smiling. Thanks, Dad. Old lovers, old

Who's fooled by the changing face of time? Grandma knows. The old prayers are the best. And the old gods are the wisest.

lovers. They grow up and have babies without you. With someone else, with someone else's body. Suddenly you see it all in the supermarket on Saturday morning, the whole family together, her kids (by two former marriages) and his own son riding on his shoulders. Run away and cry your eyes out in an aisle they'll never come down. (Try dog food, but watch out, they may have a dog waiting in the car.)

Live and learn. Under next year's budget write: "October. Buy wood. $45.00." No, cross it out and write: "Buy wood. $50.00." No try again. "$55.00 . . . November." The price has changed, but old stories are still the best. R. loans me a book called *Love's Pagan Heart* about love and sex and war in the Islands. See the beautiful girl on the cover with a blossom through her hair and a colored cloth tied around her hips? She's the girl you always wanted either to be or to have. I read the whole story. The Pope would never approve. Thanks, R., I enjoyed it.

Were you the progeny of Catholic matrimony and did you ever carry Holy Cards around in your wallet (backside to Babe Ruth)? This one I have says on it: "Oh Mary, conceived without sin, pray for us who reach out to you." Who's fooled by the changing face of time? Grandma knows. The old prayers are the best. And the old gods are the wisest.

After Dick and Jane and Joan of Arc, the first book I remember is Plato's *Republic*, standing like a temple of truth in the middle of Dad's bookshelf. Dad told me the plot. Now that I know more plots, it's interesting to see how Milton and Dante and, yes, even the Vedas are like Plato's *Republic*. A certain awesome conception of the universe. Cephalus speaks concerning old age:

> . . . when a man thinks himself to be near death, fears and cares enter into his mind which he never had before; the tales of a world below and the punishment which is exacted there of deeds done here . . . .

These old stories are powerfully astounding in all their similarities. In an auto wreck, while unconscious, I see a huge spindle stretched upon a brilliantly lit thread which crosses the vast expanse of the deep, dark void. Afterwards, I can't stop talking about it. I'm still half-zonked in the operating room, or talking through a fog on the telephone, or about to be offered a bedpan — but that doesn't matter, I just keep telling everyone exactly what it was like, the awesome panorama of the skies. Finally someone says: "It was just your concussion. Your psyche did all that to make you feel safe." Yeah.

In the *Republic* Plato writes of a journey, a pilgrimage of a thousand years:

. . . another day's journey brought them to the place, and there, in the midst of the light, they saw the ends of the chain of heaven let down from above; for this light is the belt of heaven, and holds together the circle of the universe, like the undergirders of a trireme. From these ends is extended the spindle of Necessity, on which all the revolutions turn . . . .

"Spindle?" When I get to that word my eyes jump out of my head. And then I read, following, an exact description of what I saw. And I see it all again. "This is it," I yell, leaping up and jumping around on the bed. "This is it! I saw this. I *saw* this. *This* is what I saw." I throw the book up in the air. Who can I tell? My mother? Mothers know everything already, anyway. "Eureka," I yell, listening attentively, and then pounding on the wall. "Eureka, Rat, I saw the universe. Hooray for Plato and ancient history and boo for anything less than the whole truth. Did you hear that, Rat?" The Rat who lives inside the wall climbs over the bathroom sink and drops down to the floor. "Going airborne?" I shout, throwing a pillow at the wall as he, somewhere concealed, climbs upward again. "I saw the universe, Rat. Drop on that one," I whistle as he, still concealed, flings himself to earth with a small thud.

Jumping off the bed, I light a candle and pick up my card that says: "O Marie, conçue sans péché. . . ." Old prayers are the best prayers: "Turn most gracious advocate, thine eyes of mercy towards us and after this our exile . . . pray for us who turn to you."

Later on, in a dream, she kisses my forehead. "There's more," she says, lightly, "more to come," and smiles like a snowflake melting into the sun. When I wake, the room is filled with light and the Rat is curled up asleep in my Nike shoe. "You must be pooped," I say, bending over the edge of the bed, nearsightedly, but he doesn't move a whisker. "There's more to come, Rat," I whisper into his dream. "More to living than walls and holes and getting snacks for Winter. You do a good job, but don't think this is all there is." He raises his nose slightly and then burrows it back under his paws.

"You have a long nose," I say, lying back and staring at the ceiling. I can still see the Universe, as clearly as ever. "We'll take it all in, together. It must be a big place, the universe. We'll need a map, and friends. Lots more of them." I can still see the Holy Mother, too, and she's still smiling, as if to say: "Don't worry, we're all in it together." I think: "There's only one boat, Rat. We're all in it together." His tiny heart is pounding away like an engine. My eyes close again. "Don't take anything but the *whole* truth too seriously, Rat. That's the secret. One day you'll look back over all the holes that you've gnawed and see what it all meant. Everything . . . nothing. What's the difference, really, whether you go right through the wall or around the corner?" For a few moments his heart stops beating. "You can really drop though, Rat," I go on, curling up and rolling into a ball around my pillow. "I'll say that's pure art, dropping. But don't get too fascinated there, either. That's the key. The middle road is the safest path. I'll never forget you, Rat." And I fall asleep, too, forgetting once again everything . . . or *almost* everything.

(*October 1981*)

Memoirs of a Professional Killer

Some Sea Stories from The Big Deuce

Art Hill

Once they gave a war, and everybody came. They called it World War II, and the entire basis of this essay is that one man's recollections of it — necessarily different from every other man's — are worth preserving.

I am not a professional veteran (although rather a gifted amateur). Until recently, I had not spent a lot of my time thinking about the war. I occasionally told stories about those years, as soldiers do. But I displayed no souvenirs, I never joined any veterans' organization, I do not correspond with any old comrades in arms. Still, the war is always there, cutting my life in half as sharply as the three-quarter pole divides the Belmont Stakes. Like a good sprinter sent beyond his distance, however, I am taking a lot longer to finish the second half than the first, and laboring slightly in the

We start out with every expectation of becoming heroes, but we finally settle for a career in the Third Laundry Platoon. And . . . we don't mind so much provided they don't call it the Third Laundry Platoon.

This essay is included in Art Hill's Booze, Books And The Big Deuce (South Shore).

stretch.

It is sometimes a bit unsettling to me when I mention the war and someone asks, "Which war?" In England, when you refer to the war, they know the one you mean. In America, we have many to choose from.

I call my war The Big Deuce. I didn't make up that name (I wish I had) but I like it. I feel it has just the blend of utility and frolic appropriate to characterize a war which has receded far enough in time to be warmly regarded. Because what I remember about The Big Deuce is that it was very fine indeed. Now, that is a monstrous statement, the only defense for which is that it is true. I don't think it's true of more recent wars. The pleasure factor seems to have been missing from Vietnam, even in retrospect.

A very old friend of mine always used to refer to *his* war as "the Great War, not the late war." He couldn't bring himself to call it the First World War. That sounded like a mere preliminary, whereas for so many years it had been the undisputed heavyweight champion of wars. By the time the Deuce came along to challenge it, he had grown fond of it, so he devised a light-hearted designation to identify it as his. In contrast, what do the Vietnam veterans call their war? Nam. Short, sharp, bitter — and it may be that this will never change. It wasn't a nice war, and it seems unlikely that it ever will be.

Not, God forbid, that we thought our war was any fun while we were doing it. War is hell. Everybody knows that. Like all wars, ours was full of dirt and boredom and incredible exhaustion and death. And the fear of death, which may be worse, although there is no way to check on it. We were scared, and we prayed (assuming the Deity to be on our side) for it to end. We thought it never would, and in endless wars the law of averages is inexorable. In short, we hated it.

When I look back on it now, though, it is usually with affection. The incessant bitching we did seems to have acquired an almost lyric quality. The insensitivity and obtuseness of the professional, thirty-year soldier comes back to me as slapstick comedy. The bitterness is gone, replaced by something very like longing. I don't want those years back. (I am an intelligent, educated man, so it follows that I am against war.) But I don't want them to be lost either.

I grieve for the veterans of Vietnam, who did what they understood to be their duty, and then returned to find their presence embarrassing to their fellow citizens. When we came home, we were regarded as heroes, although few of us were. That was nice while it lasted, which wasn't long. From what I've heard and read, most of those who fought in Vietnam think of it as one long uninterrupted horror. I don't believe I have ever thought of the Deuce as one long anything. The war has no unity for me. It survives only as a collection of almost unrelated memories, with nothing in common except that they are, to me, The War — events, places, perceptions, even isolated words and phrases. These are the fabric of which my sea stories are woven.

"Sea stories," incidentally, is the naval name — in the Army, they're called "war stories" — for the lurid tales men tell each other during the long nights aboard ship or in barracks. Anyone can tell them, whether or not he has been to sea or to war. The terms carry a strong implications of exaggeration, but sometimes the stories are almost true. Naturally, all mine are gospel, and they are "sea stories" because I was in the Marine Corps, which borrows its occupational jargon from the Navy, often with ridiculous results. We called the floor and even the bare ground "the deck," for example. That at least has the virtue of brevity, as does "head" for what the Army calls a latrine. But "bulkhead" for wall — any wall, including that of a quonset hut — is sheer nonsense. The vocabulary is firmly ingrained in all regular Marines, however, so we non-regulars used to delight in using the civilian terms in their presence. Nothing so infuriates a stiff-necked regular Marine colonel as to tell him that you "have to go to the bathroom."

The Marine Corps is a branch of the Navy, and the insistence on the Navy idiom probably dates from the days when many of the Corps' grandest officers came from Annapolis. The Naval Academy graduates had "command presence," which is supposed to mean that their manner automatically inspired respect. Sometimes though, it simply denoted a slavish adherence to formalized trivia. A military education, although it trains you to *act* like a leader of men, is not always the best preparation for being one. The career officers who were not from the academy knew the difference. They called the Annapolis men "trade school boys" and it could be either a term of approval or a sneer. You had to listen carefully for the inflection.

I did not have command presence. I tended to giggle at obvious absurdities, for one thing, and since absurdities are an integral feature of military life I failed to impress my superiors (who never, never giggled) as being ready for serious responsibilities.

I seem to be implying that I was a cynical, sophisticated civilian, compelled by an innate sense of decency to serve my country, but contemptuous of military chicken (the generic term for the petty nit-picking which every soldier learns to endure; short for "chickenshit"). Totally false. I desperately wanted to look and act like the tight-lipped, clean-shaven men in the movies I had grown up with, who obeyed without blinking and never slouched. But it just wasn't in me. In the Marine Corps, neatness counts, and I simply did not look like an officer. I took orders well enough, thanks to my training at the Bijou, but the movies had not prepared me to *give* them. The trouble was that I couldn't shake the impression that this *was* a movie. I kept expecting Rita Hayworth to dash in weeping and tell me that John Wayne had flunked out of flight school. We were taking part in the greatest war in history, and I felt like an atmosphere extra in a B picture.

When I went into the Marine Corps, I wanted to command troops in battle. But the Marine Corps knew better, and I became a supply officer in charge of a small group of highly competent NCOs (non-commisioned officer: sergeants and corporals). I wouldn't say they looked up to me, especially since several of them were older than I was, but they liked me alright, and that seemed to work just as well. We won the war. (I just gave away the big finish.)

The Marine Corps was right about me, you see. (In such matters, it usually is.) Friendship, mutual esteem and dedication are fine when all that's required is hard work — and it was often shockingly hard. But it takes something quite different to order men to die, and I didn't have it. I'm grateful for that now. In fact, though I would have been embarrassed to admit it then, I began to be grateful long before the war was over, but for a more selfish reason. In our kind of war, in which we walked ashore and faced the enemy head to head, the best combat officers had the shortest life expectancy. It wasn't fair, but in war, despite the adage, very little is.

Although I wasn't made of heroic stuff, I became a captain at the age of twenty-three, before I had even been overseas. This illustrates the wisdom of getting into the war on the ground floor. In the Marines, every officer has a number, and when his number comes up promotion is automatic unless he has some black mark on his record. Any little *faux pas* which might impede promotion is called "taking your finger off your number." Getting a wee bit too drunk at the general's dinner party would be an instance. Making an obvious pass (especially a successful one) at your CO's wife would be a more serious one. Among reserve officers, failure to be promoted on schedule was merely embarrassing. For the career officer, it was a disaster, and he lived in constant fear of taking his finger off his number. If he offended a senior officer (and there were *so* many ways), the curse would hang over him forever. It might not interfere with his promotion next year, but he would spend the rest of his career wondering if it was going to prevent his becoming a general. And it might.

(Although I may use the present tense, because I am confident that some things never change, it should be understood that my sworn testimony is valid only for a period which ended more than thirty years ago. All I know about the Marine Corps today is what I read in the papers.)

One morning, during the battle for Iwo Jima, a major whom I will call John Smith refused to move his battalion. Major Smith had become battalion commander through the violent death of the original incumbent, and he turned out to be too human for the job. Half his battalion had been killed or wounded, and the troops he had left were devastated by fatigue and shock. He pleaded with the general to give them a few more hours of rest. (The rest you get while under sporadic fire and lying in a shallow hole in the sand is fitful, but it's better than nothing. Far better.) The general said no. The Marine Corps credo is "keep moving." The theory is that you will take fewer casualties in the long run if you maintain constant pressure on the enemy. The theory may well be correct, but it does not take into account the appalling mental and physical agony of men who have been in close combat for several days without a break.

After a number of exchanges by radio, Major Smith told the general flatly that he could not obey the order to attack. Now the general was in shock. Smith was a career officer with a spotless record, but he obviously had the soul of a goddam civilian. He was promptly replaced, and put under arrest. The men moved. Some of them died and some of them didn't.

A few years later in New York, I was having a drink and exchanging sea stories with Barney Rafferty, an old friend from the Fourth Marine Division. "Did you hear what happened to Johnny Smith?" he asked me.

I said I hadn't, but I assumed that he had quietly retired from the Marines, his service record in shreds but his conscience intact.

"He's doing eight to ten in Portsmouth," Barney said.

I gasped. "My God!" I said. I hadn't known Major Smith except by sight (he looked like a Marine officer), but I admired what he had done, not least because it was such a futile gesture, and I knew there were others who shared my feeling. Stunned, I made a bad joke. "That's really going to hurt his career," I said.

"Yes," Barney said softly, "he took his finger off his number."

I remember something else Barney Rafferty said, under different conditions.

The day before we landed on Iwo Jima, our commanding general issued the usual pre-battle call to arms, mimeographed and handed to every member of the invasion force. The gist of it was that invading this ugly little heap of sand (it had been so heavily bombed and shelled that only a few scrubby bushes were left standing) was a privilege for which we should all be grateful. "It is," the statement ended, "your birthright!"

On about the sixth day of Iwo Jima, I found Barney Rafferty sitting in a hole in the middle of a bleak, shell-blasted field. He had been through the worst of it from the beginning, and he looked it. Filthy, unshaven, bleary-eyed, his face reflected the sort of weariness that makes simply not moving a sort of ecstasy. I thought to cheer him up with a bit of mordant wit. "Didn't you know this was your birthright?" I asked him.

"If I had," he said, "I would have sold it for a mess of pottage."

Now, I like a literary allusion at any time, but to produce one under those circumstances, I have always thought, showed real class.

The battle for Iwo Jima, as vicious and deadly as any ever fought, might serve as a paradigm for war. Four thousand Americans, and several times that many Japanese, died on an island five miles long. In 1968, the United States gave Iwo back to Japan. When I read that in the paper, I realized for the first time that The Big Deuce was officially ancient history. Not because of the act itself, but because the reporter felt obliged to explain that "Iwo Jima was the site of a major battle of World War II." To me that was like explaining that Lincoln was once President of the United States. I remember the faces of the dead, their valor now celebrated in a parenthetical remark.

A soldier's view of combat depends upon his temporal relationship to it. Beforehand, there are cold sweats, nervous jokes and, rarely, heroic bluster. Afterwards, there are horror stories, anger and the inevitable laughter. (Funny things do happen in battle, but one laughs primarily because one is alive.) As to how a soldier feels about war while the shooting is on, I'll settle for Barney's apt and graceful comment under pressure.

Between operations (for some reason we never called them battles), our division was stationed on the Hawaiian island of Maui in a camp on the slopes of Haleakala, the world's largest extinct volcano. It was the only spot on the island where it rained constantly. (Real estate agents with useless land to peddle always seem to see the government coming.) Maui is now a lavishly advertised tourist paradise, replete with Hiltons, Holiday Inns and championship golf courses. I'm sure I would be lost there. But we knew it when it was a tropical backwoods, its population almost doubled by the arrival of fifteen thousand Marines. It is, I believe, a commendable trait, lauded in the better faiths, to be content with what you are given, rather than lamenting what you have missed. So I suppress my regret that I never got to Tasmania, and rejoice in the memory of Maui when it was still one of Earth's narrow corners, known but to a few. I have seen the hula dances by sloe-eyed girls wearing skirts made of real grass (ti leaves, actually) instead of shredded cellophane. True, it was at the USO in Haiku, but who's quibbling?

Where else but on Maui could you sit in a mess hall and look out over vast fields of ripe pineapple while eating pineapple, possibly grown in those very fields, shipped to the mainland, canned, and shipped back to your table?

Wailuku was Maui's metropolis, with a population of about five thousand. Everything else was small. Lahaina, the old whaling capital of Hawaii, was a sleepy little village known mainly for "the world's largest banyan tree" and an ice cream parlor where you could get marvelous chocolate sodas. Regrettably, this place was closed in the evening, virtually forcing us to drink other stuff, which resulted in many court-martials — none of them, by the grace of God and my firm friendship with the entire MP company, my own.

From the beach at Lahaina, you could look south and west to the wide channel called Kealaikahiki. It passes between the islands of Lanai and Kahoolawe, and it is one of my favorite American place names. *Ke ala i kahiki.*

When the first Hawaiians made their miraculous canoe trip from the South Pacific, they brought with them a language spoken, in countless variations, over millions of square miles of ocean. By a common but mysterious process known in linguistics as the consonant shift, all the Ts in the old language became Ks in Hawaiian. Thus, "man" is *tane* in Tahitian, *kane* in Hawaiian; "forbidden" is *tabu* in Tongan, *kapu* in Hawaiian. Tahiti, the ancient homeland, is *kahiki* in Hawaiian, so the channel through which you go south from Lahaina is *ke ala i kahiki*, the road to Tahiti.

As a lover of words, both foreign and domestic, I find this information so delightful that World War II seems a small price to pay for it.

What passed for high society on Maui consisted of a coterie of white Americans, all claiming blood relationship, however remote, with one of the five families which ran Hawaii. (The so-called Big Five companies, which still dominate Hawaiian commerce, were all built by descendants of the old New England missionaries who brought God and sin and disease to the islands, and of whom it was said, "They came to do good, and they did well.") High-ranking officers mixed happily with this sort, but my own civilian associations were largely with the multi-racial proletariat, who gave livelier parties, although they seldom made the papers — which was, in some cases, just as well.

I managed to crash this set through my friends in the MP company. Enlisted MPs in a war zone, like policemen everywhere, always know where the most interesting action is.

It was at one of these parties that I met a man whom I still think of as a character from a Damon Runyon story, because we were introduced during a crap game and his name was Walter Waikiki. Even Benny South Street and Nathan Detroit, the Runyon reader assumed, were aliases, but Walter assured me (and his friends confirmed) that his name was legit. I treasure it.

It was on Maui, too, that I received the letter from New Zealand — several times. Written by a young woman, it came in a tattered envelope addressed to Major Arthur Hill, Fleet Marine Force (a vague designation which included most of the Marine Corps). It began:

Dear Major Hill. I am writing to tell you that your daughter is almost a year old now and she is a beautiful baby. You would be proud of her. Diane refuses to write to you but I know she still loves you and would marry you if you came back. I know you can't come now, but when the war is over. . . .

And so on. The old sad story. The writer was apparently Diane's sister.

I was never a major, nor have I ever been in New Zealand. I returned the letter to the division post office, but two weeks later I got it again, and a month later a third time. Since there was no return address, nor even a last name, it could not be answered or returned to the sender, so I finally kept it.

From time to time throughout my life, I have suffered mild distress at the behavior of people with the same name as mine. (In college, there was an Arthur Hill who persisted in writing his name in public toilets.) But I doubt that this was quite the same thing. Surely, if "Major Arthur Hill" ever existed, the Marine Corps post office would have found him. After all, it kept finding *me*.

I sometimes wonder about that beautiful baby, now in her thirties. Did her mother ever tell her that her father was a major (questionable in itself) named Arthur Hill (most unlikely)? And what about the gallant "Major Hill?" Is he still alive, and if so does he ever repent of his duplicity? It is quite possible that he was dead even before his daughter was born. The First Marine Division, which spent some time in New Zealand, went from there to Guadalcanal, where it did a lot of dying.

There is, I realize, nothing unique about this story. It is all too common. But it touched me in a strange oblique way, because some Marine, in a moment of lust tempered by an unseemly prudence, made up a phony name. And it was mine.

One should not write about the Marine Corps without mentioning the language. The official written language was the eerie English favored by all military organizations, in which a spade is not a spade but a "tool, entrenching." Even in death, you could not escape it. When a man was killed in battle, the cause of death was recorded as WGS or WSF, for "wound, gunshot" or "wound, shell fragment." I don't know how they handled "terror, sheer" or "attack, heart." There must have been a few of those.

But I am more concerned with the spoken language, which was vulgar in both the ancient and modern sense. It was the common, everyday medium of communication, and it was obscene. (Someone once defined "fucking" as the Marine Corps adjective.) It was also loaded with color and metaphor, much of which I have never seen recorded anywhere. The classic wake-up call of "Drop your cocks and grab your socks!" is now in universal military service, but it deserves inclusion here because it was my welcome to the Marine Corps. When bellowed by an eight-foot-tall sergeant at 5:30 a.m. while you lie cowering in bed on your first day in a strange and frightening place, it is anything but funny.

Whenever a Marine, usually in response to the news that he was wanted for some distasteful duty, left the scene hurriedly, someone was sure to say, "He took off like a striped-assed ape." Or, in more genteel company, "He took off like a great bird," which has a certain haunting beauty. And when the sky suddenly turned from light blue to ominous black, the obligatory comment was, "It's gonna rain like a double-cunted cow pissin' on a flat rock," an observation which, I think it is fair to say, makes up in imagery what it lacks in elegance.

The standard Marine Corps insult, routinely hurled at anyone deemed to have voiced a stupid opinion, was: "You talk like a man with a paper asshole!" This is my favorite because of its surrealistic quality. I know what it means. It means, "Don't be a jerk!" But why? What is the mysterious origin of this expression? Any reference to that part of the body (note my delicacy when I am not being documentary) suggests sodomy, I suppose, but why paper? Iron would be more to the point. (Which brings us to "pogey-bait," the common term for candy. It dates back to the days of the wooden-ship navy when, presumably, fuzzy-faced recruits could be induced with visions of sugarplums to submit to an unnatural act, the verb for which was "to pogue." Hence the popular epithet "candy-ass" for a weak-willed or indecisive soldier.)

I think of these phrases as peculiar to the Marine Corps, but the truth may be that their derivation, in most instances, is what the better dictionaries style *Southern U.S.* Dirt-poor Southern families contributed more than their share of sons to the enlisted ranks of the Corps. They made the best fighters, according to popular belief, because they had so little to lose. (There were plenty of Southern officers, too, but they usually came from a different social stratum. All of them, it seemed, had attended the University of Virginia, and they vied with each other in claiming the greater number of ancestors on General Lee's staff, which must have been enormous. Many of them, honesty compels me to add, were superb officers.) In the case of the word "hockey" as a term for solid human waste, there is no doubt about its Southern origin. Most of the Southerners I knew during the war affected to think Canadians slightly eccentric because of their skill playing a game whose very name was unacceptable in mixed company back home. A staple of Southern repartee, the word was in continuous use in the barracks, generally in admonitions like "Don't give me none of your hockey," or "Snap out of your hockey," a common variant of which was "Snap out of your shit." The latter was my key to the meaning of "hockey." I had at first thought it simply meant fooling around, the official Marine Corps term for which is "playing grab-ass."

Foul language did not distress the Corps' image-makers but dirty clothes did, so in 1944 they invented the Third Laundry Platoon and sent it to Maui to clean us up. Since we were the Fourth Marine Division, and since there was presumably one laundry platoon per division, it might have seemed more logical to call it the Fourth Laundry Platoon. But the military has always played tricks with unit numbers to confuse the enemy, and that may have been the strategy here. Conceivably, the Joint Chiefs of Staff hoped to lull the Japanese into reckless overconfidence by intimating that we didn't have enough laundry platoons to go around.

The CO of the Fighting Third was Second Lieutenant William Jones, Jr. He had a cushy job, but for one hideous drawback. His mailing address was: Third Laundry Platoon, FPO, San Francisco. This sort of tipped off the folks back in Roaring Rapids that Bill, though a certified professional killer just like the rest of us, was not in fact storming the shores of Tripoli. It was certainly no help in getting girls, which was one of the main reasons one joined the Marines. They practically guaranteed it at the recruiting office. They never mentioned the Third Laundry Platoon.

Since he controlled the only reliable source of hot water in the division area, Jones was immensely popular with bathing addicts, who plied him with gifts of food and booze in exchange for the use of his shower. People back home were impressed that servicemen had all the cigarettes they wanted, but they couldn't identify with an abundance of warm suds. Even a mother who might brag about the money her boy was making on the black market in Paris would be embarrassed by a son who was the hot water king of Maui.

There were thousands of Marines whose jobs were even less dangerous than Jones's, since no scalding water was involved. But none of them was so obtrusively labeled. If only they had called the laundry outfit, say, the Third Special Action Platoon, Jones and all his sweaty troops would have preserved their honor, and the shirts would have come out just as clean. Probably cleaner.

There is no punch line to this story, but I have deduced a moral. When the war ended, and the world had been made safe for men of good will everywhere, I came home determined to write a novel. My subject, it hardly seems necessary to say, would be Life. I never wrote the book, but I thought about it a lot between drinks, and I did come up with a title. I was going to call it *The Third Laundry Platoon*, which had struck me as a poignant metaphor for Life as most of us live it. We start out with every expectation of becoming heroes, but we finally settle for a career in the Third Laundry Platoon. And, once we've resigned ourselves to it, we don't mind so much provided they don't *call* it the Third Laundry Platoon.

All is illusion and revelation. My comrades may not have shared my cinematic fantasy but neither could most of them quite believe in the reality of what we were doing. I remember the diffident wonder with which we read about ourselves in *Time*, a week or so after our first operation, the invasion of Kwajalein atoll. The story referred to our commanding general as "jut-jawed Harry Schmidt." When we saw our leader, whom some of us had actually spoken to, described in *Time*'s imitable style, it finally hit us that we were the stuff of history. We called him Jut-Jawed Harry for the rest of the war. Not to his face, of course, but maybe he wouldn't have minded. He probably had that *Time* clipping in his dispatch case through it all.

There were some among us, though, who had discarded their illusions about the reality of war long since — the survivors of Guadalcanal. As vividly as anything in the war, I recall a conversation with a legend. There were too many legendary figures in those days for all of them to receive the carefully programmed adulation they deserved. But Bert Rogers was an authentic Marine Corps *intra-mural* legend. In the finest tradition of the low-budget movie, he had volunteered for a perilous mission behind enemy lines, and had brought it off brilliantly. In the process, he had killed four Japanese soldiers, one of them with his bare hands. The courage which this sort of thing calls for is beyond the comprehension of the average person, and those of us who were average were somewhat in awe of him.

We stood on the deck of a Navy transport lying in the great Lahaina Roads anchorage off Maui. A warm moonlit night. The division had sailed from San Diego just a week earlier, bound for Kwajalein. The ship was full of nervous people, secretly in fear of disgracing themselves in their first encounter with the enemy. We sought reassurance, hoping Captain Rogers would tell us we'd be all right when the time came.

But he wouldn't talk about it. Quietly and politely, he brushed the subject aside. Someone suggested that modesty was unnecessary in that company.

"Modesty?" With a small gesture of the hand, he neutralized the word. "I killed four men." Pause. "I will not kill any more."

"But they were Japs!" someone said. I cannot place the voice for sure, but I fear it may have been mine.

"They were human beings," Rogers said.

This was news to us. It would be fatuous to say that we thought of the enemy as animals or devils, but neither did we think of them as human beings *like us*. They were mad, irrational killers (as opposed to us rational killers). It is fair to say that this assessment of the Japanese drew as much upon their own propaganda as upon ours, and it was in large measure shared even by other Orientals. As a boy in the Philippines, I had listened to endless fearful talk about what would happen "when the Japanese attack."

"I will never kill anyone again," Rogers said. He spoke quietly, expressionlessly, used few superlatives and no profanity (a Marine Corps first). To the unspoken question, he responded. "I will try to avoid killing situations, but if necessary I will refuse a direct order."

In war, most people kill from a distance, impersonally. (Sorry, pal, nothing personal.) Rogers was the only Marine I met who "knew" the people he killed, the only one close enough to see the look in their eyes. And the only one who took an oath never to do it again.

I thought of him a few years ago when I read a statement by a young, articulate spokesman of the Vietnam protest movement that anyone who served in the Marines would probably be "insane" for the rest of his life. Conceding the demands of polemic, I read this to mean that the man who spent time in the Marine Corps would carry the effects of it for the rest of his life. This is patently true, as it is true that a man who hears distant thunder at twilight or takes a walk in the woods will never be quite the same again.

While we are at war, we believe that the moral sanctions against killing are repealed, because it's them or us. If we are suddenly made aware that they *are* us, as I was by Bert Rogers's passionate vow, we don't like it because it imposes a disturbing moral dilemma just when we need it least.

I never killed anyone. I never fired a shot (although I had enough of them fired at me to feel that I had paid a part of my dues) but I don't doubt that I would have if the need had arisen. And, as the young man so strongly implied, I came out of the Marines a different person. But I'm not sure it was a worse one.

Dulce et decorum est pro patria mori? A dubious premise. Death is seldom sweet, and no sane man ever willingly dies for his country. But there is a hint of nobility in the willingness to *risk* death in a far place for the right reasons. The irony is that when the soldier does risk it, and perhaps loses, he never thinks of himself as doing it for his country, but for the friends on either side of him. Think about that. He joined up to fight for his country, and found that a bunch of people he didn't even know when he enlisted had become the only thing worth fighting for. What is almost impossible for him to understand is that the soldier across the way is doing his best for exactly the same reason. When we have absorbed that simple verity — and not before — we will have taken the first real step toward abolishing war.

It is correct to call Marines "professional killers," but foolish to say it with disdain. Every soldier is, by definition, a professional killer — even if he only runs a dryer. If we resent having so many professional killers on the public payroll, the solution is simple — make peace.

For rhetorical purposes, I have pretended that there is some mystery about why I recall the war years so fondly. But, of course, I know the reason. I know why men gather in disorderly groups and wear funny hats and tell stories about those days. I do not join them, but I understand them. Old soldiers have selective memories.

The fear and anguish have been worn away by newer, more pressing anxieties. What we remember is the freedom from normal responsibilities, the sense of being united in a worthy purpose, the exhilaration of just being alive, the certain knowledge that the nation thought well of us (so essential to a soldier, so lacking in Vietnam).

But, you wonder, are those reasons enough? Men died. Yes, we remember the dead, but we no longer mourn them because we no longer know them. They are just kids.

So were we, then. And that's the real reason.

NOTE: Most of the names I have used are, for one reason or another, fictitious. The exceptions are: Barney Rafferty, Walter Waikiki and Jut-Jawed Harry Schmidt.

No doubt, you will have noticed that I spelled Marines with a capital M throughout. They told us to.

(October 1978)

Man of Silver, Man of Gold

Leslie Woolf Hedley

The library was five long blocks away. In that east coast city, hated with multiplying resolve over years of my life, street blocks were tons of poured flat concrete, expressionless gray and black tar from lamppost to lamppost. Some blocks were more dangerous for people to walk than others, but no street was free of ethnic dangers. It was a city without human or natural landscape, other than locked apartment hells surrounded by larger hells.

Every object appeared foggy gray or dark brown with blood of cockroaches. Having discarded the ability to behave or respond reasonably about anything, people usually spoke in loud gunlike voices without punctuation as if to overcome their own grossness. In that terrible city people always shivered. They shivered in

History, generations of history, pushed down on us. Life had suddenly become a collection of tragedies.

Summer and Winter. They shivered because life had become nauseating. Fear was glued to daily climate.

Except at the library. That library was my sane house, safe-house, a cool tomb of potential freedom and soaring reaches for my twelve-year-old imagination. Getting to that marvelous place, however, meant that I had to survive one innocent-seeming street near a worn-out park where the grass choked, lifelessly anemic, under trampled newspaper, candy wrappers, empty cans and bottles, all such American rubbish. Anything could happen during that excursion, so I always raced the last avenue where the library waited.

Books tied with a leather belt, swinging like a Viking's weapon, I would run past that decaying park and past an already decayed Victorian house of rotting wood. Monstrous dry strings bunched together in its front yard reminded me they once had been living bushes. The house was decrepit, time-ravaged, stercoraceous, hump-backed. It stood next to the library, waiting to be torn down for expansion. Waiting, meanwhile, like a symbol of disease.

That small house assaulted my nerves. But I wasn't afraid of the house. Humans, my peers, those I watched out for with a specially developed psi factor. They might attack, several at a time, strip some boy of books, pen, pennies, sweater, those quick robbing locusts, and vanish either into the park or up buildings, over rooftops and away. These young guerrillas attended a small parochial school near-by. To them we were outsiders, alien, perhaps religious heretics. These Catholic boys were positive their intolerance was superior to everyone else's intolerance.

One day when leaving the library a jagged explosion of white paint caught my eyes. There, crudely drawn on that festering sore of a house, were two swastikas. Three boys from the school, laughing nervously after their act of political-racial Halloween, were appraising their art. My European parents had already branded me with the meaning of swastikas and those lessons leaped into the muscles of my arms and legs. Swinging my weapon of books, I lashed out at the trio. The impact of surprise and my fury became an advantage. Having been taught to box — "In America," my father warned repeatedly, "every day is violent" — my left jab bloodied the nose of one boy, his bleeding adding weight to my attack, and I punched another in his mouth, hearing the chilling click of a tooth snap. They retreated, pail of wash spilling like dirty milk over the broken sidewalk. My lungs ached and my right fist was bruised. Adrenaline gushed inside me. I grabbed for breath, dropping my heavy books on the ground of a thousand grassless Winters.

A hissing sound entered my ears. A human hissing. Weak air from weaker lungs. I hadn't known anyone still lived in that rotten house. Now the front door opened and a slice of waxen face was visible. "Hey, little boy! Little boy!" A cracked voice coaxed me.

I shivered.

"Come here a minute. Don't be afraid. A brave little boy like you." His voice waved like a flapping old flag.

Picking up my books I stepped gingerly over spilled paint, uncertain, observing the old man's rasorial fingers. I entered the house, barely sliding through a narrowly open door.

The room was dark except for a leakage of misty light through chinks in walls and muddy windows. Secret miseries clogged the air and its fetid pungency overcame me. I exhaled, "Whew — "

"Don't worry, *boychik*," the scraggy man said. "It stinks in here and it stinks out there." His voice was a roller coaster of inflection. "So what did you expect? Maybe an ice cream parlor?"

I stared, enthralled, partly exhilarated from my fight and rapid victory. His mouth was a bloodless old wound on a face past defining. Dressed in shiny black, except for a collarless yellowed shirt, deep lines trenched his cheeks and his wet eyes were decorated with red dots. Uncombed hair was mostly gray. While speaking, his ragged calyx beard vibrated pale streaks of lightning. I thought of Socrates, Moses, John Brown.

"So what are you gaping at me like that?" the man asked. "You think I'm *meshuggeh*? Do I look *meshuggeh*? God forbid, maybe I am. But you, little *boychik*, you're also mad. You're mad because you attacked all alone those three *goyim* Nazis! I spit on them!" And he spat on the floor.

Then I sensed that inside his parched head something blazed, a furnace of tension and perhaps — I hoped — vision. His protuberant eyes, like spiral nebula, grew and shrank as he spoke, and quickly he would appear drained of words. His sentences came in quavering leaps and bursts. Any minute now, my nerves told me, something, anything at all, might happen.

"No," I began to apologize for staring, "but you — "

"Listen," he hissed, while his hand patted my head, "I see you from the window upstairs, with your bunch of books, two maybe three times a week, running to the library. Such a reader! Maybe you're a *Yeshiva bocher*?"

"What? Oh me!" I fidgeted. "I'm just — "

"So don't be so nervous," he coughed and sat down on a creaky chair. "You weren't so nervous when you charged like a lion out there." He gargled a lugubrious chuckle. "But you still think I'm *meshuggeh*. So let it be." He waved his hands. "All right. So for what you did, I thank you." He started to rock slowly back and forth. "Anyway madness is in the air, the stinking air. Europe — you know where Europe is? So good. Europe has gone mad already. Germans were always mad. So help me, the American Jews are also mad because they don't believe what's happening!" His body was a pendulum, a black ax swinging in darkness.

I wondered. "What?"

"*What?* What?" he said sarcastically. "Listen, brave *boychik*," and he took a deep breath of fusty air. "*They're going to kill all the Jews!*" The sound escaping was a long scratch on a blackboard.

Killing meant something out of Hollywood or my history books. I knew, however, that Nazis were being discussed in current events. The word had captured headlines. I tried to formulate something intelligent. "Historically — "

"*Historically!* What a word he uses!" He threw the word against the dirty wall. "*Boychik*," his face, a damp sail of flesh, closed nearer to mine, "when anyone tells you that you're living in historic times — *watch out!* That means murder." He stopped. "History is an excuse to commit every crime."

I had nothing to say.

"Everywhere on Earth," he proceeded to rock dithyrambically, "they're going to kill Jews. Not just in Germany. Not just in Poland. Not just in Austria. Not just in Hungary. Not just in Russia." He swayed, a gloomy prophet. "But everywhere there's a Jew, there's going to be a grave."

I shook my head.

"Go on! Go on! What do *you* know? A *boychik*, and he thinks he knows!" His hand on my head was gentler than his biting voice. "So what do you think I'm doing here? Hah? You think maybe I'm playing? I'm hiding, little *boychik*. I'm hiding from them, the Nazis. You see how they begin? You see the dirty swastikas? Hah? Believe me this is only the beginning. Only you should wait and it'll get worse."

"But this," I managed to concoct something, "is America."

Truncated laughter bubbled inside his frame. "You're too young. You don't understand." He tried to gather his breath and febrile thoughts, then wobbled his head. "America? America is a baby, like you. What does America know? To accept madness is even worse than madness. America accepts madness as long as it's good for business. If killing Jews is *good* for business, so then America doesn't care. If killing Jews is *bad* for business, so then America cares."

My brain ached.

"Never mind. So take this." He pushed against my chest an object shaped like a cup, silvery in that dingy atmosphere.

I hesitated.

"Take it! So take it! This isn't a gift," he explained. "This is a thank you present from me to you, because of what you did . . . out there . . . to those young Nazis. Take. Take. *Zei n't kain goylem!*"

I held the reward in my hands, rather pleased, as though I had won a game. Wasn't the world a game?

He expelled staleness from his lungs. "Sooo, now go home. Take care of yourself. Be careful."

Naturally my father questioned my story about the silver cup and my mother told me not to fight. The knowledge that certain boys my age were painting swastikas disturbed them. Both parents sensed an electric political charge and almost everyone we knew felt a threat of some unnameable kind, Jews or not. I was allowed to keep my prize, as though in possessing it I had somehow staved off the threat for a while.

Now this new element of danger captivated me. I read every thing I could about Nazis, Fascists, Hitler, Goering, Mussolini. I was intrigued knowing that walking up a certain street had become doubly dangerous because political daggers were now drawn. History was becoming more real each day. We all knew life was no longer a Vienna waltz or a day in the British Museum. I dreamed of rescuing that frightened old man, of saving whole populations of driven refugees. That deteriorated house, that gray-blackened structure of wooden bones, skeletal, tired and sick, became something needing protection. That crumbling house with its rusty iron fence, like a disillusioned spider's web, became important. Even its blotch of drained soil, discolored and long sterile, was a symbol of warfare. This spelled out a larger drama of the world I was just beginning to realize I was living in.

From then on houses on that particular block, that no-boy's-land leading to the library, my library, weren't ordinary ugly brownstone buildings any longer, but brownshirt barricades, fortifications behind which assembled the worst enemies of civilization. To me civilization meant free books, sports and composers whose music I heard over the radio. Now I was waiting for zero hour.

Emerging from the library several days later, my skin tingling alert, I saw the new plan of attack. This time four boys, two carrying a pail of whitewash and two armed with baseball bats, were getting ready. Their reedy adolescent voices cried: "Hey, you old sheenie!" "Come out, come out, you lousy kike!" The house remained mute. No adults were around, or more likely no one wanted to notice. I had to act fast. First of all my aim had to be that offensive white paint.

My burst of speed kicked the pail upward, a wide arc of white vomit over the four boys. But one bat managed to nick a corner of my ducking head just before I vaulted to the porch and through the quickly opened door. Once inside a garbage darkness surrounded me.

"Ow, my head!" I gasped.

The old man's voice rustled like paper. "See, didn't I tell you? It's madness! Madness!" He pressed a cool metallic object against my forehead. "Here. It's only a little bump. Don't worry."

"Why? Why?" I mumbled.

"The biggest question in the world, he asks: Why?"

"I didn't know there were so many bad people around."

He nodded. "Yes. Yes. But good or bad, they're people."

I didn't understand, but noticed through partially blocked windows that a series of ghost white footprints dwindled down the empty street.

He was quietly pressing my swollen forehead, as though ordinary communication wasn't required or perhaps no longer possible, maybe no longer desirable. We were two phantoms in a dark room. His hands were trembling slightly.

"I'm no longer a human being," he tried to explain in an exhausted voice, "because I'm persecuted and live in fear. No Jew is a human being any longer. But those boys outside, because they don't live in fear of persecution, they're still human beings." Emptied, he stopped. "You want to learn something?"

Shadows that had never known sunlight stretched over us. Sticky darkness clung to the walls, floor and ceiling. A cloying odor almost numbed me so I tried to breathe with small intakes. Something rancid had glued itself to that house. I shivered.

"So listen. Maybe this way you'll learn and remember."

"Yes."

"The American Jews don't want to believe what I'm telling them. They don't want to believe that all the Jews in Europe and maybe the whole world are going to be killed. If not today, then next month, or next year, or in five years." Silence. "Which madness is worse?" Silence. "When nobody listens, when nobody cares, when nobody believes. That's worse madness." Silence.

I imagined prehistoric shadows were strangling the remains of whatever threads of light dribbled over our bodies. Darkness was butchering even the smallest fleece of light. Only half-understanding, I nodded.

He sat, moaned and rocked, damp pallid skin in dim clothes, a violent chiaroscuro of flickering intensity before my awed eyes. "I was there. Over there. I saw the beginnings. But who believes me? Maybe a little boy? Maybe." Silence. "Everywhere Jews are dying. Everywhere." He rocked. "In almost every city and town and village in Europe, another Jew is being murdered." Silence. "Do you know what death is?"

"My grandmother died."

Silently he swayed, a black locomotive straining on tracks of chilling reality. "Let this burn into your mind forever, *boychik. Every Jew is born already waiting to be murdered.* For sooner or later Christian politicians turn against the Jew." Silence and my desperate hunger to comprehend this mystery. A blade of terror ran through me and I was sweating.

"Why," I whispered, "don't you run away?"

His head shook back and forth, eyes like pyropes. "*Boychik,* maybe you can run like a fox. But I can't run. I can't even crawl. I'm cornered. Millions of Jews are cornered." Rock. "There is no place to run." Rock. "And no one wants to know." Rock. "This is my last refuge." Rock. "From here I can't go." Rock. "This is my next-to-last territory and it's shrinking." Rock. "I'm retreating each day into a smaller and smaller space." Rock. "Every day I take up less space." Rock. "I feel myself shrivel." Rock. "Soon I'll vanish entirely. Then I'll be safe." Rock. "You're born and you die." Rock. "And nobody knows you're alive and nobody cares when you die." Rock. He motioned with both hands. "Jews have no friends on the Left or on the Right." His voice was almost inaudible. "May God forgive me. Life is a big lie from beginning to end."

Smallish tigers ran up my spine. Silence now blanketed us with oppressive weight. History, generations of history, pushed down on us. Life had suddenly become a collection of tragedies. A feather of thought tickled alive in my childish mind, telling that all persecuted are related by the blood of their wounds.

"Here," the old man said in a low voice. "I want you should have this."

Whatever it was appeared luminous and cool to my touch. It was the metal he had held to my sore forehead. Embarrassed, I pushed it away.

"Take it in good health," he instructed. "I don't need it. Someday you may need it. Who knows? So take it and goodbye. You don't want your mama to worry."

With a small gold serving dish glistening in my hands I ran home to radio news and neighbors talking about military invasions in Europe, street battles everywhere, a release of political epiphenomena, barbaric and strong, which exuded cinders over that space of my boyhood. None of us is prepared for growing up.

Days later when I again ran heroic streets to the library, the old house was already demolished, that area a large square of gloomy earth, like a mass grave. Of course I never found that old man again and life was no longer the same for anyone.

(March 1982)

Christopher Bursk

Lies

My son and I kiss the same woman goodbye.
We are meeting thousands in the dark Capitol.
This is the first lie:
that I wish to bring peace to anyone
beside those with me now in the lamp's small territory.

Soon we'll be marching down a wide street
    ending in flags
and marble — and dawn, huge and official,
turning the white stone glistening.
We shade our eyes, march into the dazzle
as if light were another kind of government.

This is the second lie:
that the men inside the building hate the light,
have been hurt so deeply they'd have the world hurt.
With them are my father, my brother,
gentle, considerate men,

and though I love them, I rise with others
    against them.
This is the third lie:
that we have weapons they don't — a love for children,
a concern for the planet.
My boy and I welcome the sun
    on the backs of our necks,

we need it there
as we walk into the darkness between buildings.
The police wait for us.
Soon they'll raise their arms and bring down
the shadows we expect.

This is the fourth lie:
that these men like to wield the darkness.
The fifth lie: that they have chosen to.
Mother and wife, the person we love
        most in the world,
has sent instructions:

keep away from the violence.
This is the sixth lie: that we can.
The seventh: that we wish to.
We move closer to the damage, lurk in its shade
as if hearing the screams

seeing the blood, we might understand.
The eighth lie is that we do.
We'd thought by walking in great sunlit masses
before those who began this war
we might end it. We lift the sun in our hands

as if to show the men in small groups
        gathering at the windows
there is another government.
The ninth lie is that they do not know this,
are not grateful like us for free passage on the earth,
the sun's generosity.

The tenth lie is the hardest.
That we are in no danger from these men,
that you are in no danger, my son,
from the faithful, the earnest, from friend, brother,
or father.

(September 1983)

Three Photographs

John Rosenthal

We're All Doing Time

An Interview with Bo and Sita Lozoff

Howard Jay Rubin

From the outside, Bo and Sita Lozoff's Durham home looks like any other: cars and bicycles in the driveway, Bo returning late from coaching his son Laxmana's soccer team. But inside the similarities end.

On the living room wall hangs a picture of Hanuman, the monkey servant of God in The Ramayana, and a photograph of Neem Karoli Baba (Maharaji), known in this country as the guru of the American spiritual teacher Ram Dass. In the center of the bedroom, which doubles as an office, is a devotional area, what Hindus call a puja table, laden with incense, pictures and beads.

Their business? For almost a decade, Bo and Sita have run a nationwide service called the Prison-Ashram Project, though it has little to do with traditional concepts of prisons or ashrams.

The project, part of Ram Dass's Hanuman Foundation, helps prisoners

I don't see the streets as being so much better; I don't know anyone who's not suffering. . . . We're all doing time. The highest compliment in prison is, "He knows how to do his own time." How few of us do.

take advantage of the opportunities for spiritual growth inside prison. Bo is the director and runs the prison classes and workshops, while Sita handles the office work and answers most of the fifty to 100 inquiries that arrive each week from prisoners.

Along with a personal note, prisoners are sent, free of charge, copies of Inside Out — *the project's guidebook for inner growth — and pamphlets on karma, meditation, and spiritual groups in the prison.*

The project also helps prisoners form yoga and meditation groups by connecting them with teachers from various traditions and by sending on request a set of nine ninety-minute cassettes on "Prison Yoga."

My interview with Bo and Sita felt like an intimate, friendly conversation. Bo's answers were relaxed, candid and often funny. Sita spoke little — "Bo's the mouth of the project," she says, "I just hang out in a space of love during the sessions." Although she may appear to take a back seat to her articulate husband, she is fully a partner in the project.

In the most recent project newsletter Bo writes:

"The philosophy behind the Prison-Ashram Project is simple: we don't pretend to know what prisoners need. We offer and share a lot of teachings, methods, viewpoints and ideas so that you can taste many things and decide for yourself what feels right. . . . You have all the answers you need somewhere within the quietness of your mind and heart."

The address of the Prison-Ashram Project is: Route 1 Box 201, Durham, N.C. 27705.

— Howard Rubin

SUN: How did the Prison-Ashram Project get started?

BO: In 1969 Sita and I spent almost a whole year working on a sailboat cruising the Bahamas. The captain was trying to get up enough money to sail around the world and concocted an idea with my brother-in-law to smuggle in 1,400 pounds of pot from Jamaica. That didn't feel like a good way to earn the money to us because the reason we were on the boat was to get out of the paranoia we had developed over the years in the Sixties with civil rights and labor organizing. So we sailed down to Jamaica with him and then we flew back before the pot got on board. Everybody in that whole thing was busted and got probation, but then they did it again right away and got busted again. My brother-in-law got twelve to forty in a federal prison.

Within the next couple of years we went further into meditation, and when we went up to visit my brother-in-law we got really keyed into doing some sort of service in the prison world. We had been in touch with Ram Dass for a while and were bringing him here to speak at Duke; that was in 1973. I had already started talking with the Federal Bureau of Prisons about doing meditation and yoga in the new prison at Butner. Ram Dass told me that he had been corresponding with some prisoners and a month or so after he left he wrote me a letter asking if I would take over his prison correspondence and send out copies of *Be Here Now*, and maybe some project might develop out of all this. He started sending me about a hundred dollars a month out of his pocket to pay for postage, printing and sending books out. It was a project before we knew it.

We didn't have a very succinct idea of what we were doing. We thought at the time that the people we were going to be dealing with would be mostly white, fairly well-educated, middle-class drug abusers or psychedelics manufacturers. At that time Tim Leary and other people that Ram Dass knew were in prison. They knew what ashrams were and what meditation was all about and they wanted a support line outside the prison. Within the first six months to a year it was amazing how different it was from what we had expected.

Prison's an extremely difficult environment to turn into an ashram if you've only got a year or two to serve there. It's much easier just to stay stoned and play basketball and shoot pool and stay out of trouble. We learned that of the thousands of prisoners who wrote to us, most were thirty-five to forty-five years old and had been in prison up to twenty-five years already. They were people who had less than an eighth-grade education. Many of these people didn't have the slightest interest in hatha yoga. They were desperately looking for something to hold on to, something that could help them remain sane and reopen their hearts.

At first we had a very generalized idea that prisons were like ashrams. But as I began going to more prisons, I found that this notion was at best slightly naive. Prisons, more often than not, are very harsh and brutal. Many prisoners, as they began meditating and trying to back off from the con games and jive of the institutional personality, started getting a lot of heat and pressure. Prisons are unlike monasteries in more ways than they are like them. In prison there's an atmosphere of hostility, hatred and suspicion. So you have specific things to work on. We became specialists. We tried to say, "Have a sense of humor, have a calm and clear perspective. . . . All you're trying to do is open your heart and quiet your mind."

We had to begin thinking, well, what do you do, how do you handle somebody with a sixth-grade education who's asking you to explain what karma means? In fact, I wrote a booklet on karma because we got a letter from a guy doing nine death penalties, he'd killed nine people, and he said he really didn't have an understanding of karma.

SUN: How does the project function now? What roles does it play in the prison?

BO: Well, right from the beginning Sita, Ram Dass, and I have thought of the project as an available resource, not any sort of mission or campaign. None of us have within our nature an evangelical feeling of wishing more prisoners would meditate so that they could see the light or so that they could be happier. We just want to be a bulletin board for prisons. Early on the prison authorities wouldn't allow it. You'd say yoga or meditation to the warden and he'd just laugh you out of the prison. All we wanted to do was get credible so that if an inmate wanted to find out something about Zen he had the opportunity. Now we answer about fifty inquiries a week and send them all of our material free.

If they're in a group, we send them a set of nine tapes that include me and Ram Dass, Krishna Dass, Soma Krishna and other teachers. We explain that there is nothing to join, no movement, no sect. If anybody wants to find out more about a specific tradition that they hear about through Inside Out, we try to connect them with people from that tradition. If people want to find a commune or an ashram to live in when they get out of prison, we can usually find one for them. I don't know of a prison in the country where an inmate might become interested in this kind of stuff and not know about us.

SUN: How did you get that credibility?

BO: There's a lot of rascally con in our spiritual lineage. Right from the beginning there was a touch of Maharaji's con and madness. When I applied for a job as a guard at Butner, the warden said that he wouldn't hire me because I wasn't the type. I finally laid it on the line and told him, "Well, I'm a karma yogi and that means that my vehicle for getting closer to God is service and I thought that being a prison guard would be a pretty good vehicle." Within ten minutes he was asking me to write a proposal to become one of the sub-wardens at Butner and run a fifty-man ashram community in the prison. Then he got me up to Washington to talk with the director of the Bureau of Prisons. There I was, an old SDS radical, drop-out, hippie, and suddenly there was an official memorandum in the prison grapevine saying if anyone is interested in meditation or yoga contact Bo Lozoff.

We began to build on that credibility. Later, a woman called me from the New York Department of Corrections and we built on that one, too. Soon we had worked with many state bureaus and had growing credentials. The credibility is sort of a good-natured spiritual con; it strikes us as exactly Maharaji's humor. The doors to all the prisons in the country flew open. All we had really wanted to do in the first place was to be available, and now we are. We get letters from all over the world with never any idea about how they found out about us. People write saying things like, "We found a copy of *Inside Out* in a bush."

SUN: What do you do in your workshops with prisoners?
BO: On one level, the workshops give us an opportunity to meet "backstage" in the play of our lives. Backstage there is no difference between me and the other people in the room; I'm no freer, no more fortunate; all those roles are parts of the stage characters. Backstage there's just nothing to do except to be. It's a vehicle for being in love together with the prisoners who want to be with us in that consciousness. When I walk into a prison room and see ten or thirty or 100 prisoners expressing their desire for this love just by coming to the workshop, the purity in the room starts blowing me away before the thing even begins. It's an amazing feeling to be in that group, coming together for no other purpose than to play in the spirit; there's no college credits, no brownie points toward parole, no naked women or movies or music; just to sit in the spirit, just to play with words about truth, to examine our own souls and maybe to touch hearts. By the time I've sat down and cleared my mind and opened my eyes, it's like looking at so many angels in front of me, beyond space and time. When we sit in this love together, there's no prison and no inmates and no me and no . . . nothing other than love.

So the talk goes on, and the questions go back and forth and I do teach a few meditation techniques and breathing practices in case someone ever wants to use them, but it's all just going on as the play, as the excuse, really, for being together. When we look at each other at the end of the night, when those rough, tough, scarred "criminals" look at each other affectionately or come up to hug me or grasp hands for a moment, the look in our eyes is not, "Wow, were those great techniques!" or "Wow, can you teach yoga!" The look is simply, "Wow, does it feel good to be in love!"

SUN: As an outsider, are you viewed with a certain amount of distrust at first?
BO: It depends. I've never run into any serious hostility. I try to remember as I walk into a prison that I really don't want anything from them such as wanting them to like me or to cop to meditation.
SITA: I think that a lot of guys come out of curiosity. They've heard a little about it and are just kind of squinting and waiting to hear what he has to say. It could take five or ten or fifteen minutes and there's a breakthrough. You can feel it, a change in the room. It usually happens through humor. The whole room starts to relax, the hearts begin to open and open and open. By the end of the workshop I'm usually crying. It's so beautiful.

SUN: Have you ever felt threatened emotionally or physically?
SITA: Never.
BO: That's because feeling threatened is not the way we respond. Every time I go into a prison I remind myself that if what I say about my prison work is true, one of these times Maharaji may test me by having me fall flat on my face. That's got to be all right also. If I think that my going in open and not wanting anything means everything is going to always work out well, that's just a subtle form of wanting something.

SUN: What is your most heartening memory of the prison work?
BO: I went to do a workshop a year and a half ago at Bridgewater. As the fates would have it, they'd circulated the poster for a talk I gave a day earlier on "Toward a consciousness of crime and punishment," a talk I gave at Harvard about how bad prisons really are. I never talk about that in prison; there's nothing that the inmates there can do

about it. I talk about how they can work on themselves.

So, the thirty-five people who attended the workshop weren't the people interested in meditation and yoga. They represented all the prison ethnic groups and they were all angry. Also, this was a unit for the criminally insane. I didn't know any of this when I sat down. This was also the only time I had ever brought a Buddhist monk with me. He was sitting there next to me with his long robe and shaved head.

I began by saying, "We can talk about many things. We can talk about yoga, we can talk about meditation." One man stands up and says, "I came to talk about this fucking goddamn prison system" and he holds up the wrong poster. I said, "Gee, that's from my talk at Harvard, not today's," and another guy stands up and says, "It's the fucking fascists at Harvard you should be talking to about yoga. Then they wouldn't keep places like this going." They started really letting it all out. They were so angry. We went back and forth for an hour and a half screaming. I went right in it. I was having as good a time as ever. We were really doing battle together. I was saying, "Hey, don't treat me like some white middle-class asshole who doesn't know what's going on. That's your problem, because I'm not."

At the end of the hour and a half I said, "Listen. The same guy just stood up and talked about the fucking fascists at Harvard. That's how we started, so let's take a five-minute break, and if any-one wants to learn how to meditate, come back. I'm sorry that there was this mix-up. But no harm done. I love you all."

Twenty-four out of the thirty-five guys came back. Within minutes these angry, crazy, political convicts were being led by the Buddhist monk in meditation, sitting perfectly straight looking like angels, with all their scars and their ugliness and their anger. It got so stoned in there, I almost left my body. It ended just the way they all do, with people coming up and hugging us saying, "Right on, let's keep in touch on this. Put me on the mailing list."

SUN: What effect has the prison work had on your own lives?
SITA: Everything. It's taught me to love and be open. I see people that I would never meet under any circumstances. It helps me to get through the barriers and see that they're just people who want the same things out of life that we do — to love and be loved.

BO: I can line up two double-murderers face-to-face, one with his eyes closed and the other looking at him, and then switching the roles, and say, "Just look at this being and see if you don't see another person who just wants to feel good, just wants to feel safe." Really, we're all exactly alike on that common denominator. Everybody who draws breath wants to feel good. People have a crazy way of going about it. Some people kill nine people thinking that's going to make them feel better, but there's no other reason that they did it except that they want to feel good and they want to feel loved.

We've met some of the most unusual people we could ever want to meet. It has opened us to what Kahlil Gibran said in *The Prophet*: "The lowest that is in the lowest murderer is also in the highest saint and the highest that's in the highest saint is also in the lowest murderer." There are a lot of people who think they might not be able to commit murder, and I know that's garbage; many of my dearest brothers have committed murder, and they're no different from you and me. Somebody that I just hugged the night before last raped a seventy-year-old woman and killed two people, and he's just one of the most beautiful people you've ever known.

When we started doing work in prisons we wore white clothes and our prayer beads and were very strict vegetarians. We had a lot of very firm ideas of what living spiritually was like. Walking into Attica, Joliet or Leavenworth, you see how many things can be taken away from you. You still have the exact same spiritual opportunity when you're not able to be a vegetarian, when you're not able to be gentle, when you're not able to just hang out with nice people. It started maturing us very quickly in terms of spiritual materialism. All we have to do is ask ourselves, "How would so-and-so in Joliet feel about this?" and suddenly it up-levels the whole thing and we realize just how caught we are in this tiny little middle-class sliver of existence, thinking that something is a big issue, like whether your granola has sugar in it.

SUN: What would you say is the main difference between doing your *sadhana*, or spiritual practice, in prison or on the outside?
BO: Everybody turns out to have exactly the same chance. The things that make it easier also make it harder. Prison is an absurdly difficult place to live. It's like walking into a time warp and being back where there are dinosaurs, and no rules and no ethics. It's just

incredibly harsh and brutal. I've walked out of places and cried. As much as I know about non-attachment and "it's all perfect" and "it's all maya," within the relative reality of it, it's as hard as sitting and watching somebody die a very painful death. It's an absurdly harsh environment. Picture being locked up in a space smaller than this living room with eighteen adult males, all from really hostile, angry, brutal backgrounds, all of them with radios, and you're talking about doing *sadhana.*

It's harder in all those ways, but somebody who begins to work on himself in prison can experience in six months the sort of maturity and benefits that it would take you and me twenty-five on the streets to experience. Because in prison, every day he's faced with things that you and I maybe face once in a lifetime, like somebody wanting to kill you, somebody wanting to rip you off, somebody wanting to rape you. What you can get out of it by trying to do it all spiritually is incredible. We'll get one letter from a guy who sounds like a completely illiterate, spiritually immature child. Six weeks later he'll write us back sounding like Norman Vincent Peale or something. It's amazing.

SUN: Is there any advice you give to prisoners about working with the violence and ridicule that they experience?
BO: All that I really feel I can advise anyone about are states of mind. I tell somebody right up front that I don't live there and I know it's really rough. I don't know whether he should defend himself physically or try to be non-violent. I don't know whether he should pursue somebody who ripped off his radio or his cigarettes or whether he should just let it go. I don't know any of the daily, practical ethics of living in that particular prison. What I do know about is the common denominator that he and I have, the opportunity to live in an attached way or the opportunity to up-level it all and live in a non-attached way. I speak about this and then he applies it to his own situation.

People ask me about getting gang-raped and whether they should defend themselves or submit. I can't say to somebody, "Submit and don't worry about it," and I also can't say, "Defend yourself and die." That's his choice to make. Mahatma Gandhi could and would have submitted because he was so non-attached to his body there was no degradation there, there was no indignity. And yet on the other hand, Chief Joseph of the Nez Perce wouldn't have submitted. He would have said, "Ah, this is a wonderful day to die."

I'm very critical of yoga teachers who do classes in prisons and don't take the time to realize the rules are very different for people in prison than they are on the streets. I've known prisoners who've been given advice and tried to follow it and have almost starved themselves trying to be vegetarians, which is idiotic to do in prison — a vegetarian on what, five-year-old canned beans and rotten potatoes?

There's a whole different country here, even though it's not outside our borders. All the rules are different. It's much more different walking into Leavenworth than if you had to go live with pygmies in Africa.

SUN: Some psychologists speak of a prison mentality. Is there any type of consciousness you find more of in a prison, any difference between people who get in and people who stay out?

BO: It's not our business. That's not what we're looking at. Ram Dass is a bisexual, drop-out Harvard professor, LSD experimenter, wandering vagabond, fifty-year-old. Maharaji sat around on a table for the last 300 years of his life. How healthy is that? Most of the people we know are out of the norm and maybe that's why prisoners love us so much.

SUN: Are you saying that there's no difference?

BO: On the highest level there isn't. They're all us. But you can generalize. People in prison tend to have a lot of things in common; not from before they went to prison but from the shared experience after they got there.

I think the book *The Criminal Personality* is dead wrong in that it stereotypes prisoners as having a certain personality. I don't want to even imply that prisoners are more alike than people on the street. Because of the experience that the prisoners share, they seem to have more insight into some very fundamental parts of human nature. A prisoner can meet someone and feel a certain trust or distrust of them that usually turns out to be right. The old saying is true; you can't con a con.

One of the main failings of the concept of rehabilitation is that it tries to turn prisoners into conformists. If there's one trait that people in prison tend to have in common, it's that they are by nature non-conformists, usually somewhere between outlaws and hippies. That kind of rehabilitation is less than useless.

SUN: How would you react to prison life?
BO: We'd be able to do time. Anyone can. That's what we're trying to tell people. Someone will write us saying, "I'm serving the first month of a forty-five-year sentence, and I don't think I can do it." We say, "You can do it, it's up to you."
SITA: You just have to take it a moment at a time.
BO: Imagine finding yourself in a six-by-eight space and knowing you're probably going to be there until you die, there's never going to be the street again. And it's really ugly and horrible and everyone around you hates you and goes out of their way to make you feel bad. It's about as bad as you can imagine, but the choice is really still yours, whether you're going to be a survivor or not.

The people we see are mostly the survivors. I know a lot of people who aren't. When I say they aren't survivors, I mean that they go crazy. They tune out of their rational minds and end up doing their time that way.
SITA: A lot of them would be a little crazy on the outside also.
BO: I don't see the streets as being so much better; I don't know anyone who's not suffering. In prison people spend part of their day feeling pretty good, part feeling bad. It's the same thing that you see in the "free" world. I can say that there's more illusion on the streets in many ways. There's more illusion of going somewhere. In prison it's more honest. Life is basic, just here. We're all doing time. The highest compliment in prison is, "He knows how to do his own time." How few of us do.

SUN: Some say that all prisoners are political prisoners and should awaken to that. Have you ever been accused of pacifying people?
BO: Sometimes outside political people say things like, "You are an agent of the state. You're pacifying prisoners. The healthiest emotion that a prisoner can feel is anger." To that I say bullshit. I used to be a radical also. I was sitting around in a basement in Atlanta in 1968 planning how to blow up draft boards. I carried a gun for more than a year in the movement. I used it too. I shot across Peachtree Street in Atlanta, on a Sunday evening, without the slightest

thought that somebody might walk between me and the car that I was firing at. I could easily be doing the rest of my life in prison on a manslaughter charge. I know personally that anger doesn't help anything. It is not a healthy response to anything. I don't think that it reflects the humor of the spiritual level. What Sita and I both lacked in the political movement in the Sixties was any sense of humor. We thought we had one. What we do with people in prison is help them to regain their humor. What political people are angry about is that they don't want people to regain their humor. I know many people in prison who are doing much more effective political organizing than ever before, because they're operating from a clear, loving space. Love and clarity don't tend to create passive robots who enjoy prison; they create spiritual warriors.

SUN: Does the Prison-Ashram Project support you financially?
BO: Yes. We're supported by the Hanuman Foundation, which has three projects: us, the dying project and the tape library. At first Ram Dass supported the project out of pocket. Now we work on $50,000 a year and that all comes from unsolicited donations. One lady in Canada sends us $2,000 every few months in an envelope. I've never gotten her to write a word of explanation.

SUN: How did you get involved with Maharaji?
BO: Sita picked up *Be Here Now* around the turn of the decade, handed it to me, and I was moved to write Ram Dass a letter. The first time that Ram Dass came to visit, he was such a familiar presence; it was like meeting a lost brother. When he was leaving he said, "We've got so much to do together." It was that automatic. At that time Maharaji was his guru.

There's a certain presence inside that is telepathic. It's exactly the same for me, for Sita, for Ram Dass. That love that I bring into prisons I call Maharaji, because I don't think it is coincidence that this is the identical love that Sita puts into her letters. It's convenient to call this love Maharaji.

SUN: Was he still alive when you got involved with him?
BO: Yes, but just barely. He died in September 1973, which was the year that we started corresponding with Ram Dass, long before we thought of going to India. His presence is a living presence. Guru is a

method. For us, that method is using the being of Maharaji for seeing everything as God.

Being a businessman is part of God also but not my path. That's the difference between dharma and adharma. When you do something dharmic it is something that is in tune with your nature. As you soon as you start doing something adharmic you know it. You can resist the knowledge because it's something that you want, but when it all tumbles down around you and there's suffering, you say, "I really knew it from the start." Maharaji is an *it* more than a *him*. Maharaji is that vehicle for us toward a dharmic quality of experience. If it's there then we do it. We can have a relationship with someone that turns out calamitous, but we'll know that it was a necessary calamity. Others will turn out apparently smoother, but we'll know that they weren't right or necessary.

SUN: Do you communicate with Maharaji in verbal form or is it something that you just end up knowing?

BO: It's a whole body feeling. You ask a question, then realize your body already knows. Ultimately Maharaji is just a part of ourselves that we're still playing a game with by calling it Maharaji because we're not ready to say, "I'm going to go to the God in myself." That game is a vehicle. It's all part of the process, and it will end. The Buddha's first noble truth is still true: there will be inherent dissatisfaction in everything. But I think part of waking up and becoming a conscious being is consciously enjoying the process. I'm in spiritual junior high and it's a nice place to be. There's nothing better about being in spiritual graduate school. I think the first stage of enlightenment comes in accepting yourself exactly as you are.

It takes a long time to rid ourselves of these ideas of spiritual ambition. There has to be an underlying ambition. Ramakrishna says the attachment to liberation should be the last to go. You don't want to throw aside that attachment while you've still got a whole lot of others.

I still have that underlying drive toward liberation, but within that context, I don't have that urgency. I used to feel like I had to be liberated next year. That kind of childish urgency isn't the same as a spiritual drive. I know that I still want to be free, but I'm enjoying the earth plane and being in a body more than I ever have because I'm relaxing.

SUN: You've been together for fifteen years, longer than most couples can imagine. Why do you think so many couples don't last?

BO: People break up because that's really what they have to do.

SITA: I don't think it's better to stay together than to break up. It really doesn't matter because it just gets down to whatever your dharma is. It could be somebody's dharma to have several mates in a lifetime and do work with each of them.

BO: Sita and I met in one day, moved in the next, and got married several months after. There was no big deal about it. We've been through many incarnations together in our marriage, and each one we identified with totally and thought that was all we we going to do for the rest of our lives. For us being together has been a wild rip-roaring adventure for fifteen years, but I think it can be dharmic to be in a relationship that doesn't last more than a year. Most of the struggle and suffering comes from the unwillingness to see clearly that it's over, and that the connection isn't really there.

I think that one of the reasons the divorce rate is so high is that, in the west anyway, it's much easier to find a new mate than to work through the pain with your present one. People say they're looking for a relationship, but their hearts are looking for a bond. I think that it's very hard for a relationship to work over many years if there's not that bond. You don't form a bond by coming to it with a concern that your partner help you protect and nurture the ego-image of yourself that you've created. That concern is one of fear, not of love. What most of us have on that level is not worth nurturing.

When we got together it was with the realization that we really didn't know shit but could look for answers through our being together. We joined together for a no-holds-barred adventure. The bond is formed by all of the radical and unpredictable changes that happen along the way, which involve a constant shifting of both our senses of self. It isn't formed when you come to it with a humorless set of unspoken rules about relating or respecting the other's space. There's no humor if there are ways that you can't step out of, or roles that you have to play.

We're not concerned with "relationship," or fairness, or keeping our own space. It's beyond that; that still implies a conscious pulling back. In a no-holds-barred bond there can be no rules. For us it's involved going through the worst pain and the greatest love. It's certainly not easy. It can get pretty scary when you make someone more a part of yourself than any other. If I can suggest anything it's that people reflect on whether they really want a relationship that protects their image of themselves, or a bond. If they want a relationship, that's fine, but if they're disappointed that they can't break through with the other person, it might be because of the boundaries they're putting around the relationship with their clinging to a limited self-image.

(December 1981)

Jimmy Santiago Baca

What's Happening?

At this moment, fires of a riot are everywhere.
The men call into the smoke, We Want Justice!
Eyes blear from smoke.
In a cellblock the size of a moderate community church,
fifty, sixty fires are spewing everywhere.
My eyes are crying . . . .
The water is turned off, the air-conditioner off,
a sandwich for lunch, no breakfast, no supper.
The men scream, We Want Justice!
And this morning a Mexican is shot to death,
two weeks ago another Mexican was critically shot,
and the Black gangs are locked down,
the Chicanos and Whites are locked down,
and fires burn and burn before each cell,
voices scream and scream, We Want Justice!

The entire prison population quits working
in fields for three cents an hour,
in the factories for a dime an hour,
and fires engulf the tiers,
illuminate cell after cell
long deep eyes stare from.
Behind the flames and arms cloaked in smoke
is the cry, We Want Justice!

My cell fills with smoke, I can't see anyone or breathe,
and six hundred men cry, We Want Justice!
The fire! The fire! And men cry out, Strike!
Viva La Huelga! La Huelga!

Music is playing above the flames, above the smoke,
and I am weeping with my hands over my face.
My cell fills with more smoke. I can't see the bars.
The whole cellblock is a huge billow of smoke.
Over the floor sewage reeks ankle high. Urine and feces.
Everywhere, flooding, and the water is turned off,
garbage piled up for weeks catches flames high. High!
Smoke and more smoke and more smoke!

No one can see anymore, but hear the raging cries,
Viva La Huelga! We Want Justice!
Men are screaming in their cells, behind the bars,
behind the smoke, flames and weeping, men . . .
we live like this . . . this is rehabilitation!
Grotesque murderers! Ignorance! Waste and blood!
Beatings! Robbery of dignity! Sickness of soul!
And through the smoke men's voices call,
How you doing over there? You ok?
And some yell, Play the song I like, I love!
Play the one about the man that lost his woman!
About the one that fights for his freedom!
Through the smoke! The fire! The murderers! Play! Play!
Let my soul feel once more the shudder of those days
when I was free and human! Let me hear it and weep.
And the songs play, and the men sing along,
old sad faces and voices alive in the fire,
in the smoke and bars in their cells, they sing.

From far away in the night, you can see the big cellblock,
a sparking mountain of rock, jutting up, higher
than the mainyard walls, up, with six hundred men in it,
you can see the square windows filled red with fire,
from the flues on top of the roof shoot sparkles,
sprouts gray smoke,

at the windows red against the night flames jump,
pouring flames through broken windows,
expelling black gray smoke,
in the night surrounded with blackness,
and inside in the fire and smoke,
in foot deep sewage, are the cries, We Want Justice!
Viva La Huelga!
And the weeping, and the hate, and the blood!
And the despair, and rehabilitation!

Inside this furnace are the men, human beings, voices crying,
screaming and eyes weeping.
Poor Whites, poor Blacks, poor Chicanos, poor Indians,
who yell, turn the water on!
Let us flush our toilets! Let us drink some water!
They bang against the bars, shuddering rows of steel cages.

They bang against steel bars with broomsticks.
In the midst of flames and music and blood,
in shit and grime and smoke and scars and new wounds,
they scream, turn the water on!
And I am weeping. I am sick.
I have had enough, and yet every day I go on,
while this poem is read aloud by someone,
I am going on, and the sky is filling with black smoke,
the windows are filled with flames,
and I weep! My eyes burn! My lungs are black with smoke!

(February 1983)

Jimmy Santiago Baca

Who Understands Me But Me?

They turn the water off, so I live without water,
they build walls higher, so I live without treetops,
they paint the windows black, so I live without sunshine,
they lock my cage, so I live without going anywhere,
they take each last tear I have, I live without tears,
they take my heart and rip it open, I live without heart,
they take my life and crush it, so I live without a future,
they say I am beastly and fiendish, so I have no friends,
they stop up each hope, so I have no passage out of hell,
they give me pain, so I live with pain,
they give me hate, so I live with my hate,
they have changed me, and I am not the same man,
they give me no shower, so I live with my smell,
they separate me from my brothers, so I live without brothers,
who understands me when I say this is beautiful?
who understands me when I say I have found other freedoms?

I cannot fly or make something appear in my hand,
I cannot make the heavens open or the earth tremble,
I can live with myself, and I am amazed at myself, my love,
my beauty,
I am taken by my failures, astounded by my fears,
I am stubborn and childish,
in the midst of this wreckage of life they incurred,

I practice being myself,
and I have found parts of myself never dreamed of by me,
they were goaded out from under rocks in my heart
when the walls were built higher,
when the water was turned off and the windows painted black.
I followed these signs
like an old tracker and followed the tracks deep into myself,
who taught me water is not everything,
and gave me new eyes to see through walls,
and when they spoke, sunlight came out of their mouths,
and I was laughing at me with them,
we laughed like children and made pacts to always be loyal,
who understands me when I say this is beautiful?

(February 1983)

The Rev. Ben Chavis, a civil rights worker in Wilmington, North Carolina, was arrested with nine others in 1971 for the firebombing of a store during a period of racial unrest.

The controversial conviction of the Wilmington 10 — which many insisted was racially and politically motivated — was widely protested. Evidence surfaced after the trial that cast doubt on prosecution testimony, but motions for a new trial were repeatedly denied.

Finally, North Carolina Governor James Hunt reduced their sentences, while denying them a retrial. Rev. Chavis was granted study release in 1978 to enroll in Duke University Divinity School, and paroled in December, 1979, the last of the Wilmington 10 to be released.

This interview is excerpted from a book called We Are People *put together by three foreign social workers who spent several months talking with inmates of the Orange County Prison in Hillsborough, North Carolina.*

Mariam Nassadien and Vernon Rose, South African social workers, and Wolfgang Bischoff, a West Berlin psychologist, led wide-ranging discussion groups at the prison.

We Are People

Ben Chavis

I have been arrested some thirty times, but I have only been convicted once. We (the Wilmington 10) were put in prison even before we were tried and convicted.

Being involved in the civil rights movement for a long time, one of the things that your are aware that could possibly happen is imprisonment. You certainly don't want that to happen, it's something you don't look forward to, but when it does happen, you sort of fall back on the realization that it was inevitable. If you are trying to seek social changes, real dents to the structure's system, the history of this country has been that the system resists change and will, in fact, eliminate anyone who is trying to promote change. One of the means of elimination is to put you in a prison so, you know, that's why I say I did not know the time, day or hour it

The public is not in the cell with you. The public does not make up your mind whether you are going to hit the guard back when he cusses or spits on you and tells you to take your clothes off and bend over.

would happen, but I understood fully why it did happen.

When I first went to prison, I didn't go in with an attitude that I belonged there. That's very important! When the judge stood me up and sentenced me to thirty-four years, I rejected it the moment he sentenced me. I have never accepted it and I will never accept my conviction!

I decided that I was not going to escape. We were sent to prison from the county jail and while I was riding on the prison bus to Central Prison, from Wilmington to Raleigh, that's when I made up my mind not to escape. When they first put me on the van, I was looking for some way to get out right then. It's a natural human instinct to reject captivity. It took about one hour and a half, maybe two hours, to drive from Wilmington to Raleigh and on the way I thought about it, about what I was going to do. I decided escaping would be wrong. Not necessarily for me, but it would be wrong for the movement. I decided to concretely struggle against that existence, from the inside. That's what I've been doing ever since. I'm not the only prisoner that has been doing this; there have been a lot of others.

I went to Caledonia Prison in 1972 and I only stayed there a month and a half. They put me in a hold down there because I was organizing the prisoners. Caledonia is a large prison farm in the South. It's one of the largest farms in the South. The farm is almost the whole county. They have a fence around the prison. When you work out on the farm, there are guards riding horses with shotguns. They could have a tractor to mow the grass; instead, they have prisoners out there with swing blades. That's not me, useless. See, I am trying to explain to you the process. First, they put you in isolation and observe you, then they send you someplace like Caledonia, give you orders to see if you will obey their orders. Then, if they think you have been conditioned and molded, they would send you to minimum custody and get you ready to go back out in society. That's what Hillsborough is supposed to be. Start off at maximum and go to minimum. I refused to work in Caledonia, I told them that I read that the Supreme Court had decided that mandatory prison labor is not constitutional. A prisoner is supposed to work if he wants to work, and so I selected not to work. Of course, they threatened me at first. They said, "No, if you are given a direct order, you are supposed to work." I said, "I am not going to work." I was in grad school at Howard University at the time. I wrote Howard, and had them send me my books. I studied while everyone else worked. Now, I could have gone on out there and worked, but I was not going to do that. I was not going to work for the State. They make a lot of money. Caledonia is a multi-million-dollar profit complex. Caledonia provides a critical service to the State of North Carolina and the critical service is not just keeping these dangerous prisoners locked up, the critical service is making that money.

When I first came to Caledonia the prisoners were glad to see me. Most prisoners had heard about me before I went to prison. They wanted me to come to their prison because they knew we could make some changes. I helped them to get in touch with a lawyer, helped them to write writs to get back into court. I had books on prisoner rights. I shared the books with them. I held religious meetings. My religious meetings were always geared to struggle. The prison guards never liked what I said because I talked about brotherhood; black and white prisoners struggling together. They didn't want to hear that because there was a lot of division at Caledonia. They wanted the blacks and whites to be at each other, prisoner against prisoner. If you have that, then the prison system benefits from that, divide and conquer. When all the inmates stand together, there's power.

I have found more humanity in prison than I have in the streets. That may be hard to understand. The first day I went to Central Prison, these elderly inmates pulled me off to the side, and for an hour told me certain things that I needed to know, the dos and don'ts of prison. They didn't have to do that. The reason why they did it was because they were concerned, they wanted to share the benefit of their experience. That was very important, and that has helped me survive. Some people say, "Well, Ben, you survived because you have had so much publicity on the outside," but it has been more than that. The public is not in the cell with you. The public does not make up your mind whether you are going to hit the guard back when he cusses or spits on you, and tells you to take all your clothes off and bend over. You have to make some decisions, and you have to decide whether or not you are going to let the prison system break you.

I think we need to get to people who are headed to prison, before they get into prison, before their first arrest or trial. It's obvious they need to be talked to, to explain a certain kind of counter-orientation. Now when you go to prison you are oriented, but I'm talking about a counter-orientation. That would get them ready for this experience because a lot of young boys, teenagers, and young men go into prison unaware. They fantasize, are very naive, and gradually they become molded into a person without any control over it. That's why I encourage study.

Caledonia is hell on Earth if you let it be. Caledonia is a little hell on Earth because the prison guards made it that way and so did some inmates. Most of the cutting and stabbing and killing each other was instigated by the prison system, snitchers. They would have one inmate that would tell something on another inmate. The prison guard would go back and tell the inmate population that the guy is a snitcher, so when he goes to sleep, they kill him. You can't make it at Caledonia alone. I got along with everybody. I refused to join one clique. The prison guards and the administrators provoked us. I've been in prison four years. I've never had an argument with a prisoner. No one has ever pulled a knife on me, no one has ever threatened me, no one has ever hit me with a chair. I have taken some knives away from prisoners. One inmate was getting ready to cut an inmate and I stopped him.

I have seen inmates torn apart because their families won't write them, or their loved ones won't write them. By the same token, I've seen them, just talking with them, identifying with their problems, being really interested on a deeper level than the false level out here in the community. People say, "Well, I really care a lot." I've seen inmates really care about one another, in a way that most people who are caught up in the intricacies and complexities of life aren't able to care. You have to suffer in order to really care. I'm not saying that I'm glad that people suffer, but I'm saying suffering enables you to have the quality of caring on a deeper level because you have been through that experience. Amidst all these negative things, there is some human goodness that comes out. There's something different. There is a communication that is not put into words. There is some feeling there, there is an exchange, there is a give and take.

One incident which led me to leave Caledonia was at the recreation field they had at that time. Usually everybody was wrapped up in playing basketball. On this particular day no one played basketball. The guards panicked! Everybody sat in the bleachers and the guys were reading the poetry they had written, whites and blacks, everybody was clapping at the poetry. We were having an inmate meeting, that's what we were having, but the guards panicked. No one was trying to escape. No one was trying to turn over anything. Everybody was very orderly. That orderliness, that togetherness among inmates, scared the guards. They went to grabbing billy clubs; over the microphone they ordered everybody off the yard, to their cells. They ordered me to come to the front office over the microphone, you, know, called my name out. I refused to go!

There are two things they'll call your name for to get you to the front office: either to get on your case about something, or to call you to snitch. I was not going to allow the prison department to put me in that position, to make it look like I was going to tell what we were talking about. So I didn't go. I went back into my cell. They came to my cell, got me, and took me. They forced me to go to the front office. At least everybody knew then that they were going to take me to punish me for something, not to get information out of me. They will try to use you that way. Anyway, they carry me to the front and the superintendent cussed me out. Nigger this. Nigger that, stirring up these prisoners, not going to tolerate it, going to kick my ass, so on and so on, you're not in Raleigh, you're in Caledonia, they bury prisoners here and they never will be heard from, no one has ever done this and never going to allow anyone to do it and just wanted to get you straight right now! They wanted me to sign a statement saying that I'd maintain a low profile at Caledonia Prison. "I'm not signing nothing!" They didn't put me in the hole, they just sent me back to my cell. I think they were just trying to scare me.

They sent me to this prison hospital, prison sanitarium, where prisoners have tuberculosis. That's where they sent me, where I stayed for three years. Six months of the time I went on a hunger strike and they brought me back to Central Prison because I protested conditions. I didn't think it was right for healthy prisoners to be in the same place as people with tuberculosis. Also, there were a lot of mentally disturbed persons, prisoners that were given these behavior drugs, prolixin, thorazine (which make them act like zombies all the time). That's the kind of environment they put me in, in rodent-infested living conditions, and in a room with six men. One time they tried to give me drugs. I refused. The nurse made a mistake, see, they go by your bed number, they don't even know your name. If you're sleeping in a certain bed, they give you these drugs. I told the lady, "I just came in. I'm not supposed to get these drugs." She called the officer and he recognized that I was a new inmate.

When I got to McCain, I was unaware that it was a prison hospital. The prison superintendent said, "You are in medium custody, you have to go up on the medium custody ward." So they took me up on the ward. When they opened the door, I saw guys with masks on. I didn't know what was going on. No one told me, until after several hours, I finally asked one guy, "Why are you wearing that mask?" He said, "I've got tuberculosis." That was very upsetting to me. At Caledonia Prison, I could sit down at a table with my family and visit with them. At McCain Prison, because it was a sanitarium, because it was unhealthy, because of the contagious diseases, they wouldn't let me touch my family. I had to talk to them through plate glass.

I had to protest the conditions of McCain. First, though, I wrote up this grievance form, because I always found you had to exhaust the existing channels to prove they didn't work. So, I wrote the little grievance form and, ironically, they held a public hearing on the grievance I wrote about. They concluded that the prison was right for sending me there. However, they did, after that, agree to allow contact visits for prisoners who were not sick. But still, that was only a partial victory.

I decided that the only privilege I had was to eat, so I decided to give that up. I didn't have the privilege to drink because at that time they didn't have a water fountain at McCain Prison. So I decided to stop eating as a political protest. It was really my first hunger strike, I hadn't studied up on what I was doing, but after a few days I really got concerned about health, because I wasn't eating or drinking. After seven days, my body became dehydrated from lack of water, so I started drinking water (by that time, they put a water fountain upstairs in McCain Prison for the first time, so I had access to water). I was lucky, because there was a doctor at McCain from India. He had just been hired. He didn't have any allegiance to the State. I didn't want to get him in any trouble because he was scared he'd be deported, but privately, he would almost encourage me. He had experienced the philosophy of Mahatma Gandhi and how Indians look at spirituality, and the struggle with the inner self. Also, Dick Gregory, who had a lot of experiences in fasting as a political protest, called me. At that point, after around the fourteenth day, I consciously changed my hunger strike, which was in the form of a protest, to a fast, to a spiritually strengthening fast, which is a big difference. All the while I was on this hunger strike, I was angry. I wanted to get back at the system and that was just my way of getting back at the system, but actually I was winding up doing negative things to myself by having this anger inside me and not eating at the same time. Once I decided to change it in my own mind, even how I conceptualized what I was doing, I wrote up a statement about why I was going to continue on this fast. I began to get people to send me books on fasting, strengthening. I began to let the doctor take my blood pressure, so I would know what it was every day and my temperature too. I began to write down the number of ounces of water I was drinking and the number of ounces of water I was excreting. I kept up with everything because I knew it was going to be a long struggle and I was prepared for a long, extended thing. I decided I would go as long as I could. Over the three or four months that I stayed on this fast, I didn't become an expert, but I read about 100 books on fasting. I became very strengthened spiritually. I began to put my mind on positive things and not the negative. I began to pray a lot. I was really strengthening myself. At one point, my blood pressure got down to maybe fifty over thirty, which is dangerously low. Then, even though I wasn't eating, it began to increase. My metabolism rate slowed down. I was at peace with myself and had the understanding that what I was doing would be positive. By that time it had been blown up, a lot of people had gotten involved, besides myself, and I was winning. What I mean by winning is the doctor at Central Prison said, "Chavis, you are not going to live past sixty days." On the seventy-fifth day, he came in and shook his head. When he came in, I was doing exercises. I was doing yoga positions. He thought I was unconscious. They locked the door and put a guard in front of the door because they felt somebody was sneaking food in to me. They didn't believe I could do this. So, they locked the door to make sure I wasn't getting any food, and I guess they thought by locking the door and putting guards there that I would give in. That only made me stronger because I was winning. When I started the fast, I was weighing 165; when I stopped the fast on September 21, 1976, I weighed about 100 pounds, but I was strong.

They sent me to Central Prison and I continued to fast. They thought when they moved me from McCain to Central Prison that I was going to stop fasting. The fast had become more than just my little personal gripe with the prison system. It had become symbolic of a lot of concerns. I knew that the National Alliance was going to have a march on Labor Day. (I am one of the co-chairmen of the Alliance.) I decided, in my own way, I was going to go as long as I could, but I hoped I would last until after that march. People used my fast to organize the march. People from around the country came to Raleigh on Labor Day to march.

It was while I was on this hunger strike, in August of 1976, when I got a letter from Allen Hall, saying he didn't want me to die. He was the State's witness who testified against me. His conscience was bothering him. I wrote him back to say I didn't want to die either, certainly not before the truth comes out and I said, "I am praying for you." A week later, he announced he had lied. That's when the case broke open. He hadn't admitted he had lied until he heard about my hunger strike. It bothered his mind. The press was saying that Chavis is dying. They didn't know I was getting stronger. I lost weight, but spiritually, my heartbeat was strong. I only drank water. (I drank a gallon of water a day. I worked my way up to a gallon of water and day and two ten-ounce cups of pure orange juice). I got all the minerals and everything I needed from the orange juice. It was a victory, I succeeded. I beat them at their own game; not only beat them, but allowed folks to organize a movement which was the most important thing. There were thousands of people who came to that march, one of the largest marches in North Carolina's history.

By that time, Allen Hall had recanted; the other two witnesses then admitted they had lied. So the whole situation changed. When I got back to McCain, I began to do more to build up the movement around the Wilmington 10. It's easy for me to say, "I'm not guilty, I didn't do it," but it's a different thing when the people who said you did it admitted they had lied. It gave me a whole new platform to stand on.

I try to encourage the inmates not to lock themselves in another prison, a psychological prison. They have to break out of that. Physically, the prison has me nightly, but that's the only way they have me. Spiritually, I'm not in prison; psychologically, I'm not in prison. I never will be. I will die first; and then when I die, I will still be free.

(September 1980)

Release

Jimmy Santiago Baca

After five years in Arizona State Prison, Jimmy Santiago Baca has been released, and is now living in Hurdle Mills, N.C.

We've corresponded regularly during the two years his poetry has appeared in THE SUN. *It was a joy to meet him when he came here. And a challenge. A touching of hands through different bars, the intimacies of written words contrasting with the newness of a "stranger."*

Being published in THE SUN *was an inspiration for Jimmy, and he was an inspiration for me. I asked him to write about being free.* — Ed.

I cannot write how it was. The world shifted me too fast, with each event passing before me, inflicting my nerves with flash-bulb rapidity. I was quietly startled at the fresh novelty. Numb still to the fact I was leaving, disbelieving, an embryo in limbo, sins forgiven, the time-lessness suddenly and violently mean-ing something concrete. A thickness at

It was a fine thing to have one's own house, to up and go when one desired, to eat selected foods, to dress up, to mingle with friends. Still, what I felt in the world about me was that people lacked a certain reverence for themselves.

the gates, divided by the gates, a heavy pushing through the thickness as though it were fate, staring at me with its warrior's eyes, a victorious man it had to release. And once through the thickness of its invisible armor, leaving my print on its shield like a savage blow of an ax, I came upon a new beginning, a reliving of an old dead thing, with my name, me.

Dressing out in the visiting room, it was the first time in five years I had worn anything else but prison-issue blues. In my new shoes, my tan corduroy pants and a cheap flashy shirt, the guard took me out and ordered me to wait in the bull-pen. Overhead were ancient medieval spikes. The sky was blue.

Yes, Time had been crimped for my passage. Looking with an air of a puzzled child, both my hands gripped round black bars, I stared back through the gates, into the prison compound. I was looking at a friend. . . . I recalled the first day they brought me to this prison, late September, a wind spewing up dust across the starfish network of sidewalks, surface dust blown up and below it hard ground, swept hard with the crisscrossing of so many years of marching convicts. Dust was my destiny, from dust to dust. And from the sight of this dust, on a very gray afternoon, with an edge of chill in the wind, I saw myself for the first time, alone.

And now I looked at prison as a friend I was leaving, that knew all my weaknesses, one I swore oaths by, one that saw me getting older, one that knew me stripped clean, shivering, to the bone, and it was there where we parleyed and gambled life away, in the bone. Flesh was an unfeeling thing, agreed upon by all, a garment to be used to one's best ability in the contest. The bones took register of life's coldness, aloneness. And in the very air hung the omen you would fare against: the omen, the time, the place, and you.

The guard called me and I was boarding a prison van. I was leaving a friend who quartered my life off, fenced it in, for five long years. He now released me, a homing pigeon, expecting me back. On the way out I met the new warden, who had been a captain for twenty years and knew me for five. He said, "Will we see you back for Christmas?" Lifting my box of books off the table with both arms, and heading for the open gate, I turned and said, "Yes, I'll be back for Christmas."

On the way down to the bus station, bright and early, I passed the prison fields. Chicanos in brown groups, bandanas about their necks and foreheads, sweating, working with hoe and shovel, stopped and looked at us passing by. I felt nothing for them, only the truth, that each one would fight and the weak would lose, the strong would destroy themselves. What life was forced upon us must be lived. Very few would lie down and die; rather we became cruel, purposeless and mean, constructed a little personal world, with different rules and punishments, where pride was both the sanctuary and hell for all.

Whatever was done, had to be done. So, with my head filled with a million incidents, dreams, deaths, violence, hardships, unity, savage pride, struggle, friendships, unbearable mental torture, with this in mind, we were leaving now and turning down a blacktop road toward town, the first blacktop road I had seen in five years, the first time I believed, now, I am free.

A world now burst upon my sight. No image I had conjured up in years past could compare with the real. Trees and gardens took on a festive importance. The world was innocence, a peak of clean snow seen at dawn after a deep sleep-filled night. No single item or structure could be singled out for thought; everything flooded by as we sank deeper and deeper into the city. I saw a boy riding his bicycle. I saw a young girl in tight pants walking; then fast successions of business shop doors, and signs, and people in cars. All the while I was thinking how little we knew what went on only five miles away, how little involved people were in their daily tasks. I was immersed in the charm of my freedom, struck with pity for the condition of the people about me, but I let this feeling go by me, looking into their faces, accepting their ways.

Excitement surged in me. We were on the bus and I noticed people did not touch each other. We were not in prison yet no one talked to each other. For them, the world was normal. For me, it was new as never before. I detected in them a sunken individuality, a no-touch unspoken law. In prison everyone talked. Here in the world was a quietness and the inhuman noise of the city. The people were quiet. They were a kind of steel.

We were met at the bus depot by a parole officer. In his car he escorted us, Nick the Russian and myself, to the airport. Nick was flying to Maryland. I was to stop in New Mexico for a week, visit my people, then move on to North Carolina where I had planned to live and write in the country.

We purchased our tickets and then P.O. Jones left us, with a curt handshake and a warning to be on our planes. Nick and I entered the airport restaurant, ordered some tomato and cheese sandwiches, a couple of beers, then a couple more.

I had promised myself I wouldn't drink anything. I was never much of a drinking man unless I set myself down to lose myself righteously in the fire water.

Nick knew me and cautioned against drinking. He said he was accustomed to drinking and that he had to drink a beer for each member of the club in prison. He was the war lord, an important position in the club. He decided whether his club went to war with another one and he meted out the punishment to individuals in the club, sometimes infractions so severe death was called for.

I couldn't let him drink alone — both of us being friends, having experienced the same horrid conditions together, both of us fighting to the death and breaking on even ground and respecting each other after that. We found it ironic, two respectable enemies, let out together. He opted for the lounge and I agreed.

Two beers. Two more. Two different brand beers. Nick saying, now hold on Jimmy, I'm gonna pick you up off the floor. Two more beers. Me saying, well, I don't drink much, but let's switch to some harder stuff. Two boiler makers were delivered. Two more. We clutched the whiskey glasses, he'd ring out a toast to some poor biker in the joint, and we'd gulp. Then order two more.

It was 1:50 p.m. Nick had a plane to catch at 2:00. I put his arm around my neck and we staggered out with my comments on how he had to hurry. He could stand up and maybe he could walk but he certainly wasn't in shape to run. Unfortunately, to make his plane, we had to run. So, through the metal-detector lady we passed, and proceeded to slip and stagger on the run down this long corridor. Nick, flushed red with heated excitement and unable to mumble his destination, fell forth in a wobbly run at my side.

We got the checkout desk in sight, stumbled up to the clerk, said — with heaves and heavy pauses — where's the plane for Maryland? The clerk pointed to the plane taking off on the runway. It was in the air now.

The clerk offered an alternative. Another plane is leaving in five minutes at the other end of the airport. Take your ticket there, trade it in and you are on your way.

We ran back up the corridor. We arrived in the lobby and Nick could barely lick his lips without falling face first on the floor.

I guided him to a chair. I went outside and saw a black baggage porter rapping with some other ones. I said to him, say bro' can I borrow your dolly? You don't have to carry my luggage just let me borrow your dolly for a minute. He said he couldn't. I said, hey, you know I'm from that place bro'? You mean dat place? he asked. I said, yes, dat place. I have to get my partner on the plane for Maryland and he isn't going to make it if I can't roll him there quickly. The black gentleman helped me roll Nick on the dolly and we started, all three of us, running along the sidewalk with Nick crumpled up in the dolly.

I got Nick up, stuck the ticket in his hand, and said try to sober up. We got to the ticket desk, I took his ticket, exchanged it. We ran again, passed the metal detector lady who said they wouldn't allow Nick on the plane, but she let us past her anyway. I had Nick around the shoulders, hugging him close to me and running.

I saw the last passenger boarding the plane. I gave Nick his ticket and explained to him in very severe and clipped words that he had better do the best he could and get by that stewardess. Once past her and in a seat he'd be all right. I watched him move across the black-top, staggering, attempting to look sober and seeming preposterous. Then he paused with the stewardess, they were engaged in conversation, he pointed to the plane, she motioned her head to one side and opened her arms, he shook his head vigorously. I saw him staggering and clambering up the steel stairs and disappear behind the little hatch door. Goodbye Nick. And I've never seen him again.

I was on the plane. Everything had been quietly enlarged. I could sit back now and contemplate the hectic world-fair of daily life in America.

From Sky Harbour Airport in Phoenix I flew to Dallas. I got lost in the airport but gradually needled my way to the correct gate and waited among servicemen, businessmen, travelers and tourists. We milled at the gate and boarded the plane.

I took the last seat, settled in and we blasted off. In the monotony of the engine roar, with my eyes on the open sky, I watched the fancy land of clouds. Then, shifting my gaze below, doubts and questionings filled my heart.

It was so impossible at times trying to fix one's fate according to game plan. Escaping the great giant man-eater that prison is, I felt compelled to a deed of grandeur; I thought I should at least have something, a solid truth, gained from all the roundabout mazes and torture systems. But nay, not an iota. Instead, I was merely a man, my box of books under my seat. I was riding in the clouds. I was thinking of Neruda's poems, where a horse and rider gallop across the sky. Outside the window, I drew on the air legions of marching soldiers, golden helmets and silver spears, their white stallions stamping over the clouds in a parade for my release.

What would happen now? In prison you are given a number. Here in the world, your name means little more than a number. So my name, Jimmy Santiago Daniel Baca, meant nothing. The powers that grind out our sweat are hidden and removed. So if I were to scream, stop! stop the world! those faceless, logic-thinking, fateless compatriots that are the other people on this plane would only turn around, look at me, and either be disgusted or amused.

It was a fine thing to have one's own house, to up and go when one desired, to eat selected foods, to dress up, to mingle with friends. Still, what I felt in the world about me was that people lacked a certain reverence for themselves. I envisioned opening up on the outskirts of town a house with solitary rooms. Each individual would step inside the room for thirty days and nights. The crude rudiments of a board bed, a small basin, and a small window were all the furnishings provided. In this atmosphere, people could re-know their feelings. In the isolation they could embark upon contemplation. What and who they had been would be stripped away to silence. One would be able to look at it as a new job: going into an office of rock and working the silence in one's heart for priceless wages of spiritual struggle.

We bounced through a cross-current of high winds and it shook from me my thoughts. It seemed strange that no one, absolutely no one in this world, could live by themselves, alone. We all need someone in war and peace. And though no one understands us because we keep changing, the fact remains that we need people. I couldn't make it alone out here. It's what friends and acquaintances one has that tell the story of one's life. Cordoba and Alexander the Great are dust under our boots. There is not a finality to one's life, yet I was expecting one, a sign of my growth, of my change and struggle. And what I found was the dissolution and non-entity of being thrown out into a world where even the most contemporary scholars are baffled by what they see out their windows each day.

I thought I had learned a little of life living in the rock quarry, socially ostracized, hammered with daily neglect and disrespect. Then, when I arrived in Albuquerque, and spent the night with my sister, all changed for me. We sat in the living room all night and she took out old photos of me. I was shocked. In all seriousness, I looked up at Martina and asked if this was really me. It was beyond belief that I could not remember my teens. But the testimony was here in black and white. My God, how was it that I didn't recognize myself? Was my change so drastic? What a world!

It was frightening and provoked such an immense wonder for life in me to look at those photos and not recognize myself. I had pushed myself in prison to awaken in me an understanding in life, a passage through hell, learning by blood-letting and tearless endurance to judge and select, to admire and praise, to scorn quietly. How was it possible after such an all-encompassing struggle to see that I was totally blind now?

My family said I was thin and pale. It was beautiful weather in Albuquerque. They fed me to the bursting point. I had not seen my family in seven years. They all remarked how I had changed for the better. Every time I had to meet a cousin of mine, an uncle, an aunt, I grew flustered and nervous and spoke little. My face muscles were tense. They were all impressed with me. Everything I had planned to do in Albuquerque, visit old friends, old places, write a poem, walk, breathe in the grand air, suddenly felt meaningless.

I wanted none of this world, none of its habits, none of its traditions, its courtesy, its values; I only wanted to be alone and not step into this world. What little sense of certainty I had gained of myself now left me. What purpose I carefully mapped out for my living burned away. I was in a world now that sucked at me, in a world overwhelmed with uncertainty and purposelessness. The norm was indirection, and people everywhere were mere shadows behind their material goods.

The satisfaction of being out was now gone. I realized now that the struggle was to begin twofold from what it had been. In prison the violence is outright, painful and direct. There was reason to struggle, to sacrifice, and the situation could be dealt with no matter how severe: the line was always marked clearly and it was only a question of you stepping across that line. It was never hidden from view and each prisoner knew you directly, knew how dangerous you were, what you could do. This set up an understanding between us, crude and aggressive, from which we could strive forward, for deeper bonds, more loyal friendships. We wasted life inside if life is to be considered material goods and responsible positions. But if life is meant to be a learning every day of ourselves then we had life in abundance.

Nonetheless, I kept my head up and tried not to think too much. As far as novelty went, I enjoyed seeing the outside world again. It had little to offer me except in the way of an amusement park. The resonant echo kept battering me: life is not serious, but vacuous and futile. Life is bound and gagged in pleasures and we are its victims, curled in honey, spiced with social quips, minted with alluring designs of positions and importance. In this candy shop of a world, I wanted to walk out the back door and know and touch a tree and speak to it, be human again, have something in me, find a definition to the clatter and gaudiness of this masked ball, where the dancers dallied in idle conversations, and behind their silken robes and black suits their flesh was stale as old parchment, and their hearts were but knick-knacks to ponder at leisure.

Old Mr. Scrooge I was. I rebuked myself not to ponder the faults of this world but to set about constructing another life for myself from all the garbage around me. So much resource we have at hand and yet funnel it to weaken and decrepitate our humanity.

The law is a hoax, imprisonment as well, and the world a court jester. A joke has been played on us. Legislators and governors are elves and fairies, living behind a political smokescreen, fabled for their riches and magical power. We are mice in the fairy tale. A fairy tale with phones, banks, buildings, and flashy holidaying good-times. In the fairy tale the whole town sells its soul. Disaster after disaster befall the once-rich and content inhabitants. They sell their hearts and minds to the elves and fairies. They are dominated, led, convinced of their powerlessness. Then an ogre descends upon the hamlet. He has come from a place where he learned the true character of the elves and fairies. None want to listen. Instead, he is dressed in clothes of the town, pitied and admired. The feast begins and he drowns out the many words on his tongue with wine. His virtues learned in the desert are rusted. His feelings are distant and unclear.

I was going to North Carolina now. On the last leg of my trip, the tumultuous activity of the past week in Albuquerque left me drained and quiet. I embraced my aunt Jesusita, my sister Martina, my uncle Julian, and I galloped over the blacktop to board my pale white red-striped plane.

I sat between two people, a gentleman to my left and a woman with her sleeping child in her arms to my right. And what dearly grasped the core of my being was the feeling that all magic had left the world while I was doing time. What to me had been love, kindness, struggle all changed now. There was a sort of madness in me now that found something lacking in those things that before comprised my oasis on this Earth.

Things had taken on a stern residue and now that I tasted life again it was bitter and flat. The glory of snow, the macabre dance of black boiler rooms I loved to stare at, with the hissing pipes and orange rusted joints, the stuttering needles on meters, the charm of old radiators, a woman's words, were now fallen feathers when before they filled out to a plump dove or town square pigeon. The linen of an old house all these intimate pleasures seemed now, an old house that I once inhabited, with profound solitude and promise: not again could I sleep and dream as once I dreamt.

The people on the plane — the plane droning strictly through bunches of clouds, over mountains and gorges, over windmills and desert ranches, then green forests and riverways, trolleying on air right along — a batch of people with gorged lives, correctly worded, a history we were on this plane, our lives only a flight, a sudden jump, going blindly but for red alert instincts through clouds. We sped forth. . . .

Who was I then, beginning my second life, after shedding snake-like my past? My small dream bubbles, once lit to milky turgidness, were rocks that lined my path, and now the rocks ended, and every direction was open to me.

I was coming out to North Carolina to work at my writing, to take notice of the world again, to diagnose my turns through the years, to dissect my changes and find the germ of mistake that fashioned my ill-wrought temperament.

I was going to disguise myself as the wind, and whirlwind my passion into remote caverns and canyons and reveal the inscriptions on the rock of my heart. I was going to take the coming months like a whetstone and sharpen my senses to sift the purest images on to paper, sand soft, where the reader's attention would fall, its print upon my beach as I disclosed the island, the lost island of the heart. And I would then speak to you as one native to another, of the secrets in the water and air, of the throttling strings of death and life that hinder and help each of us to sing out our lives in simple words and lies and impulses and emotions.

But there are no sterilizing chambers that would wipe deep recognition and experience from my heart. I am no longer innocent. I pause twice now when thinking of the rose and politics, when seeing the nuclear plants and the sunlight, when seeing a child and an old woman.

I put my hat and coat on and go ramble about the leafless trident branches of Winter trees. I read poetry and prose books. I know woman with the suddenness and ferocious reality of her earthly needs, of her blood and bones and beauty all thrashed together like a forest on fire at night, and sudden shotgun blasts that are our biological needs, leave us bleeding and victimized and utterly more humane, dreamless, with dirty dishes in the sink, and kisses that pale with Autumn to yellow dirty snow in the gutter of our remembrance. I am living in a world getting older and older, one that conceals its secrets and jells its mysteries under my feet, from the shyness of a country boy to a startling pure-faced black-browed woman, with her balance of sensuality and womanly violence preying off deep instincts of my manhood heart. I am captured like a slave of war by common days and their jail of rusty hours, I continually work to free myself from the smallnesss of this world, with which this era has branded me, as though scalding my tongue out to silence. And in the silence the lone breathing of a wounded creature, huddled in himself, afraid, surrounded by snow and cold, living on the fiery fat of faith.

So it is: the disobedience of our young ones who, as lost as the rest of us, step knee-deep in muddy sight; the savage forays of our country into the diplomacy of other countries. There is not a wise man in the land anymore I fear. Lovers assimilate like foreign recipes in the golden bowl of their illusions, the tart tingling of new flesh touching grows stale, and soon the quiet smiles and filled brown eyes are clear and strong, no longer needing sustenance from each other.

What is this land America I have come to? And what is it I must do? How do I work within this world to fully express myself, whether it be bad or good, to choose a center and a robe and claim my words true, to jive talk with the dude on the corner, to turn and be bruised by the early flowers, to speak straight on issues, to be concerned for people, to re-learn the value of never winning, of never gaining a pinnacle to prop my flag, to forever be at the starting point, and speak not of the race but learn the dreams of each racer, that must lose and be overtaken eventually by greed, temptation, by age, by booze, by the weaknesses of the spirit and flesh. The undrained passion that is marginless fills my hands today and wind is but a wind mimicking my yearning, the cold and colder night cools my blood, and in bed I think at night that I am even with all the elements of Earth that forever give and take, that forever come and go, forever renew and age again, in a circular style of dying without crying and birth without prerogative experience. The beautiful blindness of learning to blossom again! Like an old man's fingers smoothing a child's cheek, something presses against us inside, something old and gentle soothes us in our defeat and simplicity, our innocence and hurt. There is a root driven like a spike through my tongue that never lets me forget my origin, that I am human and not a full-grown God, and the dust of life and death blows into my eyes as I try to see outward, far beyond the horizon to what may be.

I am here, scratching for an unmedicated romance, non-idyllic, grossly shortcoming of my upper pursuits, pampered by Winter heat. I've made a few clay cups, scribbled out a few tin-can poems from the alleys in my hearts, a man of many hearts I am, all tested and challenged.

Now the world calls out another heart in me, a stronger one, more faithful, tender and open. A heart that will be able to face the world full-faced with all its mistakes and disconsolate meanderings, a rock well cracked blooming weeds from blue rain of North Carolina.

I made it out here Gray-Fox, Juan-bone, Clifton, Mascara, Wedo, Gambo, and Tommy "Mata," and I've seen the land we used to dream about together, and that you all still strive to get to. No, I've not forgotten you. The world is not so large that it diminishes my friendship for you all. The gray-fox-Corky, his motto of life as junkie: out by noon and in the spoon. Gambo's "ojalá que dios te bendiga carnál.[1]" Clifton the hustling man with his wares, choochoos and bangbangs.[2] Wedo with his friendly young green smile and "Órale es carnál, O sí!"[3] Juan-Bone with his jump shot in basketball. Mascara with his quete[4] or filero[4] or ice-cream on store days (I always passed him one). And Tommy, heart-broken and trying to comfort his woman who is in prison, too. Your three minute showers, the garbage food, the tight security and daily violence. All of you like starved warriors, fifteen years in prison, seven years, five years, all wondering when you will get out. . . .

(February 1979)

[1] *I hope that God blesses you brother.*
[2] *Slang for pastries.*
[3] *What's happening, brother, O yes!*
[4] *Gun and knife.*

James Magill

Morning Shastra

eggs on a plate
light sleet rattles fenders in the parking lot
  no coffee today, stomach burns
"if meaning is not everywhere
it is nowhere"
  waitress tumbles tips
  into a styrofoam cup
  ballpoint "cindy" on the side
from the way she mutters
she loves the work.

cold falls through
  the swinging door;
change tables to dodge the draft
  sleet comes to rain sky like sludge
"cuppacoffee"
what the hell.
"his miracle is
  when he is hungry he eats,
  weary, sleeps"

(March 1977)

We Killed Them

Ron Jones

Friday, June 19, 8:30 A.M.

"We're gonna kill them bums, Mr. Jones. Kill 'em. That's right. You'll see. Right, Mr. Jones? We're gonna kill them!" Michael Rice is sliding into his cushioned airline seat, jabbing words at me through a confident smile: "You'll see. We're gonna murder them guys!" My eyes follow Michael into his seat and watch Eddie Cotter help him with the safety belt. I count to myself. Michael and Eddie in the seats in front of me, Joey next to me, and Audie and Jimmy across the aisle. Good. Everyone's here. I count one more time. All five are on the plane. In the past hour I have mentally lassoed these five a dozen times. In the next two days, I will count to five perhaps a thousand times. Together, we make up the San Francisco Special

That 26 points scared me. On the basis of our warm-up shooting, I calculate it would take us three games to score that many baskets. And that's without a defense.

This story is included in an anthology about teaching and children called No Substitute for Madness *(Island Press, Covelo, California 94528).*

Olympic Basketball Team.

Michael twists in his seat so he can reach back and grab my hand. Just as I think he is going to change the topic of conversation, he smiles and reminds me of our mission. "Coach, we're gonna kill 'em."

Michael is the team's leader, mostly because of his size and generosity. When standing, Michael bends forward like a top-heavy tree, and in motion he shuffles his feet as if on a slippery surface. Like the other players, Michael cannot add a row of numbers or write a sentence. He has not learned about Racism, Republicanism, East or Westism. The social baggage we carry is irrelevant to Michael. Michael welcomes strangers into his thoughts by throwing his arm around them and courting their interest with a barrage of enthusiastic chatter. His thoughts are disarmingly honest and to the point, even if they are repetitious. And though his words are predictable, his enthusiasm and affection are always a wonderful surprise. So I hold hands with this kindly giant who is talking of murder and smiling of life. And I wait to be hugged by him at some unexpected moment. I know I will find myself jumping excitedly into the air with Michael over some soon-to-be accomplishment or commonplace event. I am stuck between two worlds: my world of educated reason that tells me to pay attention, and Michael's world of open enthusiasm and affection that tells me I will perform miracles. His world reminds me that the miracle is waiting in Los Angeles and it will not be orchestrated by reason.

Michael's seatmate, Eddie Cotter, doesn't like the idea of Michael standing. Eddie points all around the cabin, showing Michael that everyone is seated. Then he tells everyone about seat belts. "Put on your seat belt. Like this! Here, Michael Rice, put on your seat belt like this." Eddie is the team's lawyer. He worries constantly about what is "right" and the performance of "rightness." "Isn't that right, Mr. Jones? It's time. Come on, you guys. It's time to put on your seat belts. Joey, you put on your seat belt like this. This is the way you do it." Joey will have none of it. He is listening to Michael's jabber about mayhem on the court. And every time Michael says the word "kill," Joey yelps his approval and shakes both fists in the air. So I reach over and buckle Joey's seat belt.

In between Michael's game plan and Eddie's seat belt plan, I ask Joey if this is his first time on an airplane. Joey nods yes, and punctuates the nod with a great gulp of air. Continuing our conversation,

Joey throws a hand in the air, schoolboy style, and slowly bends his fingers, until one finger points skyward. "Yes," I answer, "We're number one. We can't miss with these killer black uniforms, now can we?" I know my words will make Joey smile. He can't hide his feelings or form words, so he "talks" by flooding you with his emotions. And it works. His smile and raspy sounds are telepathic. At the mention of our uniforms, Joey's eyes light up. He tilts his head back and lets loose with a choking laugh. Then, with his eyes still glistening, he directs a question at me. He points at his uniform bag, then rubs my shirt. "No," I respond, "I don't have a uniform. I'm the coach — remember?" Joey grins in acknowledgement. Eddie continues talking about seat belts. Michael talks on about winning. Joey uses his clenched handkerchief to catch saliva rolling from his open mouth. I count to five.

Other passengers are now boarding the plane. They look stunned at row after row of athletes, wearing bright yellow hats, blue warm-up jerseys, and disabled bodies. The Olympians snap their stares by applauding them. A ripple of clapping greets each passenger as he filters toward the rear of the plane. These travelers are not expecting applause; they smile nervously as row after row of Olympians reach out to touch them or wave hello. Within moments, athletes and passengers are shaking hands, exchanging sign language, and sharing destinations.

"Where are you kids going?"

"To Los Angeles!"

"Who are you, I mean, who do you represent, all dressed up like this?"

"We're going to Los Angeles!"

"What's going to go on down there?"

"We're gonna kill them!"

"Oh. Good luck."

"You too!"

The stewardess is reading the mandatory emergency procedures. Each precaution is met by wild cheers. Methodically, every yellow hat turns upward to find the invisible oxygen mask, and looks to the rear of the cabin for the emergency door, and under the seat for the mysterious flotation cushion. Then the attention of the Olympians turns to the sensation of movement. The plane is beginning to tip-toe. Great applause from the yellow cappers. We are on our way to

Los Angeles. Like some winged horse, the plane glides down the runway, and with a final push sails cloudward. More applause. And yelling. This time, *all* the passengers are clapping.

I count heads. Michael and Eddie. Joey. Audie and Jimmy. Audie grabs my counting finger. His eyes are wide with fear. "I'm going to fall! I'm too high!" "Audie," I say, "It's all right. It's all right. Audie, the plane has wings — see, out there. Those are wings and the air 'lifts' . . . um, the motors push the plane . . . we're riding on waves of air created by — Audie, look at me. Audie, if you fall, I promise to catch you!" My explanation of air travel doesn't exactly calm Audie's fear. It doesn't exactly instill me with confidence either. Fortunately, for both of us, the stewardess arrives with Coca-Cola.

Audie enjoys his Coke. He taps my hand and asks, "Bathroommm. Bathroommm." I point to the line at the front of the plane. Audie stands up and moves to the front of the plane as if something important is about to happen. Actually, something important does happen. Audie is perhaps the strongest and fastest athlete in this contingent. As a basketball player, however, he has trouble with direction. When he rebounds, he returns the ball to the closest basket. About half the time his shots are aimed at what Eddie calls the "right" basket. The rest of the time, he is a fantastic scoring threat for the other team. Any basket sets off a spasm of delight — pure joy that is hard to stifle with the message that, "Audie, you have just scored two points for the other team!"

Audie lives in high gear. Nothing he does is slow or deliberate. I guess that's why I selected Audie for our basketball team. When he shoots down the floor like a grinning rocket, I can point to the ball he leaves behind. I hope basketball will help Audie get a little control. Slow down. Run in the right direction. Well, he's going to the front of the plane and that's an accomplishment.

I do a quick body count. Michael has his arm around Eddie, talking about the right uniform to wear. Joey is gulping his Coke. Audie is in line. Jimmy Powers, his seatmate, is asleep. It's 8:50.

Friday, 7:00 P.M.

We are in a sea of color. Three thousand athletes from all over California are assembled at Drake Field on the UCLA campus for the opening ceremony of the Special Olympics. Jimmy is the shortest player on our team, so I hold his hand as waves of athletic teams move about us. Joey holds my other hand. Michael, Eddie and Audie walk ahead of us, arm in arm, like the Three Musketeers. Pride and friendship are on parade. Just as we hold each other, the sky and earth seem to move closer — brushing softly against the banner, listening to the muffled sounds of excitement and peals of laughter, joining us in this celebration.

Michael is the first to let the air out of Camelot. "Those suckers are big! Mr. Jones, do you SEE those suckers? Oh, brother, those suckers are BIG!" Sure enough, Michael is right. I stop dreaming and start being a coach. I count several towering figures wearing the red warm-ups of Fresno. And there's a giant wearing the orange and white of Tri-Valley. Michael Rice is our tallest player at six feet, four inches. These guys look closer to seven feet. "Mr. Jones, see that tall dude over there? Those suckers are mean."

I begin to question myself. I mean, asking Joey to play on our team was unavoidable. I know that you're not supposed to have favorites in teaching, but Joey and I are best friends. We liked each other immediately. I think he liked the fact I played sports, and I loved Joey for the *way* he played sports. Joey moves like a mechanical soldier. His arms are stuck in a bent position and his gait is an awkward side-to-side gallop — a gallop that races full tilt, unable to change direction or stop. To slow down, Joey often runs into things or throws his body on the ground. I guess it's that will to charge ahead, full speed, knowing you can't stop, that I admire. He has more spirit than an evangelist on a hot Summer night, but he can't even catch a ball, much less dribble or shoot.

And Jimmy. Little Jimmy. He can dribble and shoot if no one stands in front of him. It's going to take more than Joey's spirit to help Jimmy even see the ball. I wish Jimmy were two feet taller. And Audie a lot slower. And Eddie — well, Eddie might be able to get the ball to Michael if he can stop debating with himself about what's the right thing to do.

It's time to start some reality therapy.

"You know, you guys, I've got an idea." Michael, Eddie, Joey, Audie and Jimmy glue themselves to my side. "I was thinking, we need a team motto — you know, something special that we can share, like a secret." The conspiracy thickens as my thoughts are welded by a uniform "ALL RIGHT!" "Good, our secret pledge for these games is *togetherness.*" "YEAH!" I lower my voice, "And instead of shouting all over the place that we're number one, I think it's better that we become number five." I put up five fingers and give each finger a player's name. "In this tournament, let's not worry so much about number one. Our job is for each player to go as hard as he can. Instead of saying we're number one, let's say we're number five."

I stretch all five fingers in the air and hear a roar from my cohorts. "We're number five!" "We're number five!" This attempt at humility is followed by an unprompted, "We're gonna kill them! You watch." Eddie tailors his words. "We'll win, right?" "You'll see, Mr. Jones. We'll win those big guys." Everyone agrees with Eddie. "We're gonna murder them," Michael adds. "We'll clobber them big suckers. We're number one!" The whole team shouts with Michael, "We're number one!" Joey smiles; Eddie shakes his head in the affirmative; Audie jumps up and down; Jimmy holds both small fists in mid-air; Michael holds up one finger — which is greeted by a unanimous "We're Number One!"

I look around and every team in my circle of vision chants a similar claim. The big players from Fresno and Tri-Valley have their arms in the air. I fantasize that they can dunk the ball without jumping. Everyone around us is yelling, "We're number one! We're Number One!" I join the chorus and close Camelot's drawbridge on thoughts of Xs and Os and tall centers.

We're Number One.

We're Number One.

I hope.

Saturday, 5:30 A.M.

I'm right in the technicolor part of a great dream. Good outlet pass. Fill the lanes. Here comes Audie. Pull up. Float a pass rim high. Audie slams it through. Joey and I are playing the tuff defense. We double-team the ball. Joey tips it free. I'm after it. So who's knocking? What has that got to do with defense? A seven-foot center skittles in my way. The door is being pounded like a drum. Bang–Bang–Bang. Thoughts of fire drill, aerial bombardment, and a loose ball race around in my head. Bang–Bang–Bang. I place a hand over my eye sockets to end the mental filmworks. And slowly, very slowly, find the barking door. When I open it, I am assaulted by a blast of cold fluorescent light. And something else. At first I can't quite make out who or what is standing in the hallway. Moving figures look like members of some assassin cult come to get me in the middle of the basketball game. They're talking about death. When my squint becomes an eye opening, I find myself staring at five basketball players in full armor. It is 5:30 in the morning and the entire basketball team is outside my door, dressed and ready to kill.

On close examination I notice that these warriors are not all that ready. Michael has tied Joey's shoes, but Joey has to hold up his pants — actually he is pinching his arms against his hips. Audie's pants are on inside out. Jimmy is holding his supporter in one hand, asking where it goes. Eddie is telling him. "It goes in your bag. Right, Mr. Jones? It goes in your bag." I shake off a dozen questions and ask one of my own. "Are you guys going to breakfast in your uniforms?" It's a silly question. Of course we go to breakfast in our uniforms. White jersey tops, with black numerals, black silk shorts trimmed in white, Converse All-Stars and white high top socks with three black rings. When I ask Michael why everyone got into white tops instead of black, he answers matter of factly, "We're saving the black tops for the championship game."

Game One, Saturday, 10:00 A.M.

Our warm-up consists of everyone getting a free shot. Every careen of the ball prompts applause and excited yells of triumph. Joey and Audie have to race for the bathroom or risk peeing in their new uniforms. Michael rebounds each shot with a thud. Eddie paces. Joey returns to give encouragement. With each shot, he waves his crooked arms in the air like an official signalling a touchdown. When someone makes a basket, or comes close, Joey violently throws his arms down and lets out a gutteral sound of pleasure. Michael pounds the loose ball and announces, "This is it, Mr. Jones. This is the moment we've been waiting for. This is it!" Joey roars agreement. Audie runs around in a circle under the basket, with both hands in the air, yelling, "Now. Now. Now!"

The first game is against Tri-Valley. It's scheduled to last ten minutes, and then the team with the most points will be declared the winner. The purpose of the game is to place teams into divisions of equal ability. The score at the end of ten minutes is 16 to 2. We get the last two points when Michael sinks a twenty-foot running hook, our only two points. Nobody seems to care. Michael roars off the court and picks up Joey. Eddie congratulates Michael and asks what the score is now. Audie is still running down the court, unaware that the game is over. Jimmy takes a Muhammad Ali victory pose and asks if he did O.K. I answer, "Man, you did, everyone did great. Just great! I was proud of you. That shot of Michael's was superb. I think if we work a little more on our defense we'll. . . ." Michael finishes the sentence — "We'll kill them!"

Actually I'm worried. We've been blown away sixteen to two. That places us in the lowest ability division, but even that is poor consolation for someone who hates to lose. I can't help my feelings. For too many years I have played and coached basketball. Something happens when I get inside a gym. I love it. Love to play and love to win. Every intuitive and intellectual antenna clicks into automatic at the sight of another team doing lay-ups. I find myself scouting our opponents, scrutinizing the line-up of teams, pushing my team on the floor to practice at every available free time. It's that extra effort, that extra lap or free throw that will make the difference. That's what I think while I have everyone take defensive positions and attack the movement of the ball. We practice holding our hands up, cutting off the baseline, stopping the dribbler. If we play defense, we just might have a chance. Defense is something you can teach. Offense is an art.

Game Two, Saturday, 2:00 P.M.

We draw Southeast Los Angeles. You can tell the course of a game in the first few seconds. The Los Angeles team executes a tip-off play, streaks the length of the floor and scores the first two points. Then steals the inbound pass for a quick four-point lead. Michael tries to take command of the game. He dribbles the length of the floor and casts off from the top of the key. The ball banks off the backboard and into a fast break. The score is six to nothing. I yell at Michael, "Get underneath, let Eddie handle the ball, get underneath!" Jimmy gets the ball. He tries to advance the ball up the court, but is surrounded by a wall of red uniforms. The ball kicks loose and a Los Angeles player sinks a jump shot. "My God. Did you see that shot — that kid could play for the Lakers!" I call time out.

In the huddle, I explain what I think is our only hope. "Look, Eddie, you dribble the ball up the court and feed the ball in deep to

Michael — you got that? Michael, you take the ball and go right up with it. . . . O.K., Michael? This is the time — go for your sky hook!" The team explodes back onto the floor loaded with confidence and visions of Michael's sky hook. I sit down, then stand back up. Michael is dribbling the length of the floor. "No, Michael, No. Get in the key!" It is a set shot from thirty feet. The ball hits nothing . . . but net. "Two, Two, Yahoo! What a shot! Nice going, Jimmy. Now we're going. . . . Come on, you guys, defense. Get back. Get back. Oh, no." Following our basket, the entire team races to congratulate Jimmy. The other team throws a court length pass for a lay-up.

During this seesaw war, Michael never did get in the pivot. I point. Jump up and down. Even run along the sidelines screaming instructions. "Michael, get under the basket. No, no, no. Don't dribble the ball." They have another steal, and another. It is xerox time. "Michael, let Eddie bring up the ball; get underneath. Michael — down there, get down there where you belong. . . ." The five in white run around officials and past the bench and to the key, and back across the center line to the other end. Drop the ball. Kick it. Roll over it. Only to do it all over again.

We lose 58 to 6. The score doesn't bother me as much as what this humiliation might mean for my killers in white. Michael played like a lion. He sensed the onslaught and tried all by himself to balance the score. No one could have tried harder. Eddie was simply unable to calculate the right place to be or the right pass to make. You could feel his hesitation as he rocked his arms, looking for someone to pass to or some place to run toward. Joey valiantly chased the ball the entire game. No matter where the ball went, Joey was in pursuit. Throughout the game, he didn't touch the ball. Not once. Several times he galloped right past a loose ball, grinning all the way, both arms waving like iron gates. Audie circled during most of the game, with both hands raised above his head, signalling for someone, anyone, anytime, to throw him a pass. Jimmy tried and tried and tried. I am afraid the team's heart will be broken.

The tournament official comes up to me and stuffs a large brown envelope into my hand. "Here," he says in a soft voice. "Here are the participation medals for your team — your guys might need a little pick-up." Together we crank our heads to see how my team is taking their loss. What we see hits us with a jolt. Michael has led everyone over to the roll of mats at the end of the next court. The team is kneeling on the mats, cheering for a game in progress. Whooping it up for baskets made and passes completed. And in the midst of their yells, we both hear a spirited challenge — "We're gonna kill you guys!"

The official hangs on to his envelope. "Maybe you don't need this. I mean, where did your team get its spirit? They might be the worst team in the tournament and here they are challenging everyone in sight to a shoot-out at high noon." My shrug doesn't answer his question, so he continues. "Do they know they just lost?" I offer an idea. "I don't think they know the difference between winning and losing!" We are both shaking our heads in admiration and disbelief. The official takes back his envelope. "Well, coach, you've got one more chance to get a medal. If you can win this afternoon at four against Sonoma, well then you can play tomorrow for a third place medal in your division. Who knows, those characters might yell themselves a medal."

I walk slowly over to my team. They are bubbling with enthusiasm, pointing to good plays and shouting familiar directions. "Get back, get back, you turkeys. Hands up! Hands up!" They seem wired to the play. Every nuance and gesture is picked up. A player's happiness and success is immediately known and shared by the observers. It is almost as if my team were playing another game. By throwing their voices onto the court, they participate in the game. I have always seen the game as a match-up of strategies. If one team throws up a zone, you move the ball and overload one side of the court. If an opponent is superior in ability, you slow down the game tempo. If you get ahead late in the game, you spread your offense and force your opponent to play man-to-man defense. If behind, you double-team the ball and pressure the offense. . . . My team is watching another game and enjoying it as much as any game ever played.

I want to know more about this other game, when Joey jerks in front of me. He points across the floor — and then jabs his hand into his chest. I nod, yes, expecting Joey to romp for the bathroom. Joey runs straight into the game in progress. He simply joins in; chases the ball around trying to vacuum it up with his mechanical arms. I jump after him. In between passes and fast breaks, I chase Joey around the court. When I catch him, we both join our team. They are cheering Joey and me. And the game in progress. And future games. And their own prowess. If an alien force were to ask me about the game of basketball, I don't know who I'd send forward . . . Alvin Attles or Joey Asaro.

Game Four, Sunday, Noon

This is it! The big game. We've made it by accident. The Saturday afternoon game with Sonoma was a forfeit — their bus broke down. So we played against ourselves and won. Actually, several nieces, nephews and parents joined me in playing our Olympic team. It was the most enjoyable basketball game I've ever played. The sidelines were like rubber bands. We chased, pushed, pulled each other. Ran with the ball, passed it, tripped over it, and hugged it. Kept our own score. Forgot the score. Made up a score. Took pleasure in all manner of accomplishment.

Our self-imposed win places us in Sunday's game for third place medals against a San Diego team. As far as our team is concerned, we have won and now we are about to play for the championship of the world.

Saturday night's waiting seems interminable. Five uniformed players hover about me like moths at a lamp. Every moment is filled with poking fingers, pumping hands, and landslides of conjecture. Eddie, weighing every possibility . . . over and over. "We should wear our black uniforms, right? We can wear them now, it's all right now, we can wear our black uniforms. Isn't it all right, Mr. Jones?" Sandwiched around Eddie's thoughts was Michael's insistence. "Too much for those guys. They don't stand a chance. Not against us. We're gonna annihilate those turkey legs from San Diego." Piercing into this constant din is Audie's fix: "What time is it? What time tomorrow? Do we play, what time in our black uniforms?" These three sentiments chase each other around and around. I feel I am being eaten alive by enthusiasm.

"Look, you guys have got to calm down. The game isn't until twelve o'clock tomorrow." Like an endless string of firecrackers, the mention of the game simply kicks off another round of excitement. In desperation, I try hallway exercises. After an hour, I am beat. Audie wants to go to the bathroom and the remainder of the team keeps doing windmills, while jogging in place. Now in greater desperation, I try a late night food raid. I figure if they eat something, anything, the talking cycle will be broken. Dressed in killer black uniforms, we attack the candy machines in the dormitory lobby. Evidently, we are not the only team in training. The machines are overdosed on athletes plunking in odd assortments of coinage and then pushing all the buttons as fast as possible. The telephone in the lobby has been reduced to a sound that cries the end of the world. It isn't a dial tone or a busy signal but a steady whine. In this night before the BIG GAME, even God must be a little confused.

Announcing "lights out," I discover Joey kneeling, bent in prayer, crossing himself over and over. When he finishes, I ask softly, "What are you praying for?" Joey gyrates with his hands. My mind is answering for him — what a wonderful moment, he's saying the Lord's Prayer. The urgency of his gestures serves to question my assumption. His hand is in a fist that stirs the air. Then a finger straightens to point at me and the Converse shoes placed at the end of his bed. I offer, "Joey, you're praying for the basketball team." No, his head thunders. He hits toward me with clenched hands and lower lip curled into a grimace.

"You want to win tomorrow," I suggest. No, goes his head. Michael enters the room and joins my interpretations. He knows immediately what I don't want to see. Joey sweeps into motion. He crosses himself in a spastic fashion and then smiles and hits outward. Michael knows what Joey is praying for. "We're gonna kill them, right, Joey!" Joey grins in the affirmative, then, like the other players, crawls into sleep wearing a starchy black uniform.

So here we are, at last. This is it. The Big Game. The San Diego team is a little shorter than we are, but they have a pair of good shooters. And to get into this game, they've actually won a real game. Scored twenty-six points against Butte County. That twenty-six points scares me. On the basis of our warm-up shooting, I calculate it would take us three games to score that many baskets. And that's without a defense. I contemplate putting Michael and Eddie on the San Diego shooters and letting everyone else run around in a zone. No, it's not a time for match-ups, or strategy. It's a time to play hard and enjoy whatever happens. I decide to let Michael bring the ball down the court and give the team a simple rule: "If the ball comes to you, shoot!"

Both teams line up, not sure of which basket they defend or hope to shoot at. Michael gets the tip. The ball goes straight up and when it comes down, he is waiting for it. He dribbles straight ahead, full speed. Right for the basket. No one is in his way. When he stops to shoot, the trailing players pour by him. He is still alone. His shot rolls around the rim and falls off. Michael stretches his body and catches the ball with his arms extended. From this flat-footed stance, he pushes the ball once again at the target. This time it goes in. "Holy Hot Potato!" Pure exhilaration. The first two points are ours. "Get back. Get back!" Five players clad in black race backward. "That's it! That's it! Hands up!" They form a straight line. One behind each other, like some picket fence. It's a new defense called stand-in-a-row. I am tempted for just a moment to yell instructions, to spread them out. No. "Hands up!" The fence grows a row of points that steal the pass. "Audie, this way." "Audie, dribble the ball." Audie dribbles. He isn't running full tilt without the ball. Or circling. Or surrendering with his waving hands. Audie has his head down and he's dribbling. Dribbling under control past the half court circle. "Keep going, Audie. Keep going."

Audie picks up the ball to run around several defensive players, but then puts it back on the floor in a controlled dribble. Within radar range of the right hoop, he jumps into the air and flings the ball toward the metal ring. The ball kisses the ring and almost skids in. Audie is jumping up and down. Joey is tracking the now loose ball. In the rebound effort, it kicks loose and is bouncing toward our basket. Joey is right behind it. So is a San Diego player. The other player scoops up the ball and veers for a sure lay-up. It's too hard. Joey is now running the other direction full speed.

All the players on the floor are running after the San Diego lay-up attempt. Joey and the ball are flying past them, going the other direction. The two forces almost collide. Joey is now by himself chasing a ball that he has been pursuing for three games: "Go for it!" "Joey, get in front of it!" All the players realize that they have just overrun the ball and they begin to chase. At the three-quarter mark, Joey lunges at the moving ball. His momentum only serves to push the ball further beyond his reach. "Joey, slow down. Let it go out of bounds. Let it go." Joey can't slow down. And doesn't want to try. He continues to run toward the wall at the end of the gym. I've seen that determination before. I start running after him. Then I see what Joey has in his mind. He dives for the ball. If he misses, he slams head first into a doorway. If he hits it, I don't — Joey lands on the ball. Its forward spin and shape punch Joey's body skyward. His arms wrap around the rubber like a child grappling with a favorite doll. He won't let go or be tossed off. The dive is followed by a bounce upward and a violent roll. Over and over, ball and Joey, Joey and the ball. They slam into the wall. Joey has his catch. He's got that ball. He jumps up in that awkward way he has. And holds the ball against his chest. His face is wide with pleasure. The official following the play doesn't know what to do. Everyone stops surrounding Joey and the ball. They are both a good twenty feet outside the end line. Joey's smile indicates that something wonderful has happened. The official gives ceremony to this catch. He whistles loudly three times. Then, with great NBA flare, he yells, "Out of bounds. San Diego ball."

Joey grins and nods his head, and unconsciously hops on one leg. He releases the ball by pulling both arms aside. The ball drops into the official's waiting hand. Joey races to take his place in the picket fence defense. I'm cheering inside. And crying. Yelling, "Defense. Come on." Joey shakes his fist in acknowledgement.

Somewhere in those first few moments of play, the floor tilts in our favor. It is one of those games where everything goes one way. Players get loose and then unstoppable. Michael, Eddie, Joey, Audie and Jimmy become the players in their minds. They are Kareem and Dr. Dunk, Magic Johnson and a thousand television images. They fly down the floor. Tip the ball in. Throw court length bombs. Make baskets only dreamed about.

Before I can turn around, Audie is jumping at me. I catch his hips at eye level and absorb his crashing body. Joey lands on both of us, pounding us with his handkerchief fist. Michael catches the three of us in a great hug. Jimmy and Eddie join our dance.

We've won — 42 to 12.

Everyone on the floor is jumping up and down. Shaking hands. Slapping backs. Even the San Diego players seem delighted by events. I search out the San Diego coach. I want to apologize for not being able to keep the game closer. In the blur of bodies, waving towels, and flying uniform tops, I find the San Diego coach and express my concern.

"I'm sorry, coach, I couldn't keep things a little more in control." The San Diego coach smiles broadly and points at his team. "Look, you kiddin', my kids think they killed you!"

(September 1980)

The Depths of a Clown

An Interview with Wavy Gravy

Howard Jay Rubin

"*Who cares? Whooo cares?*" *a young girl wailed into a portable microphone. It was 1966, one of the first of the Merry Pranksters' "acid tests." The Grateful Dead were playing on stage while hundreds danced wildly and drank Kool-Aid from large garbage cans. Hugh Romney spent most of the evening saying, "The Kool-Aid on the left is for little children and the Kool-Aid on the right is the electric [LSD-laced] Kool-Aid. Got it?"*

Well, at least one girl hadn't and her screams of "who cares" filled the room. Hugh found his way to a microphone and said, "Some little girl is unglued here and I'm going to try to glue her back together. If anyone wants to help out, meet me at her, wherever she is." He and fifteen others found her in a side room, and joined hands in a circle

Think of all the insanity in the world as a big pressure cooker. Laughter is the little valve on the top. If you don't have that, the pressure cooker is going to explode and you're going to end up with beans on the ceiling.

around her until the glue held and she began to smile.

Hugh (more commonly known as Wavy Gravy) felt he had passed his own acid test that night. His weathered face lights up as he talks about it. "It was like when you hit the very bottom of the human soul and you're sinking maybe, but somebody is sinking a whole lot worse than you, and you get off your problem to reach down and pull someone else up."

If the depths of a clown can be measured by the compassion and tears in his joy, Wavy Gravy may be bottomless. Over the years, he's played many roles, from beatnik poet, author and stand-up comic to children's clown, campaign manager for Nobody-for-President, and all-around-pitch-in-and-save-the-world humanitarian. Perhaps he's best known from his days as a Merry Prankster, and founder of the Hog Farm — the communal family that helped run Woodstock.

But whichever side of him you view, Wavy Gravy is a man of almost comic strip proportions.

Wavy Gravy was born as Hugh Romney forty-seven years ago in Princeton, N.J. When he was young, neighbor Albert Einstein used to take him for walks. Wavy remembers Einstein as a very calm man, who smelled funny, wore sneakers and a sweatshirt and had an incredible twinkle in his eye.

When his parents got divorced he moved to Albany, New York, and then later to Connecticut. After finishing high school he joined the Army and studied theatre at Boston University on the GI bill. He soon began writing poetry. Moving to Greenwich Village, he ran poetry readings at the Gaslight Cafe. He married his first wife there in 1966, in a ceremony officiated by blind gospel singer Reverend Gary Davis and attended by friends Bob Dylan, Tom Paxton and Dave Van Ronk. (Dylan wrote the first draft of "Hard Rain's Gonna Fall" on Wavy's typewriter.)

He later moved to Los Angeles that same year and began a career as a stand-up comic, managed by his close friend Lenny Bruce. As the opening act for jazz great Thelonious Monk he developed his now-famed ability to talk fast, especially when Monk didn't show up and the crowd grew restless.

His first marriage ended about the time Wavy started taking acid ("that little tab that will do you," he calls it), gave away all of his possessions and went to live for a time with the Hopi Indians. She thought he was crazy.

Soon, his life took another turn toward the ridiculous when, coming downstairs one morning, he found his kitchen filled with thirty-five people dressed in day-glo clothes. It was Ken Kesey and the rest of the Merry

Pranksters, arrived to do the big Los Angeles acid test. He joined them in their event as well as arranging some of his own — like the Lord Richard Buckley Memorial Sunset (called because of rain).

He moved to a one-room cabin out in the country with his second wife, Jahanara, and thirty other people. When the landlord saw the pile of them, they were evicted. An hour later a man drove up in a truck and offered them a rent-free mountain to live on in exchange for taking care of some forty hogs. Following what Wavy calls "kitchen synchronicity," or "the hard-on of the heart," they moved on to the mountain and the Hog Farm commune was born.

The Hog Farm started doing psychedelic lightshows for large groups, and soon got hired as extras for an Otto Preminger movie called "Skidoo." With the money they made from the movie the Hog Farm fixed up a few buses and began travelling the country, staging what they called their "Days of Lunacy," large, free celebrations focused on showing people that they were the stars — like the acid test without the LSD. They also became very involved in the anti-war movement. Every thirty miles their caravan would be stopped by police, until finally they were busted for having a quarter of a gram of marijuana ashes in an ashtray.

In 1969, eighty-five Hog Farmers and friends were flown out to Woodstock to help with the festival. They didn't realize that they'd been hired to do security until a reporter asked Wavy, "Well, what exactly are you going to use for riot control?" "Cream pies and seltzer bottles," he replied. "Well, how are you going to do the security?" "Do you feel secure?" Wavy asked. "Yeah." "Well . . . see?" They printed up thousands of security armbands and whenever they saw someone who looked fairly responsible they gave him an armband. They also ran the food kitchen and first aid/freakout tent, mostly by setting them up for people to run themselves.

After working a few festivals, the Hog Farm starred in a rock 'n roll movie called "Medicine Ball Caravan" in England. Hip promoters gave them a bus and they drove off toward East Pakistan. This was right after a major flood. They figured that with all the media attention they had gotten from Woodstock they could start feeding people and so embarrass the large governments that they too would pitch in. At this point the India-Pakistani war broke out and they "hung a left into the Himalayas," as Wavy put it.

Finally, tired of the road, the Hog Farm returned to America and set up a commune in New Mexico. Soon it became inundated with others coming to join their much-publicized good life. It was too much, and after another cross-country bus trip they settled in Berkeley.

Wavy has always had a bad back but the frequent batterings it took at anti-war demonstrations made it much worse. It was while he was recovering from one of his many operations that Wavy had the idea of working with hospitalized children. His back had already earned him an appointment as commune babysitter, and now he started volunteering regularly at the Oakland Children's Hospital. A retiring clown gave him some gear and Wavy's most recognizable persona was born. He wore it well and the clown character stuck, especially when he found that it kept him from getting beaten up at protest demonstrations. Wavy also runs Camp Winna Rainbow, a children's performing arts camp in Mendocino, California.

We talked in the Hog Farm's Berkeley house on Wavy's bunk bed in a room decorated by piles of stuffed animals, toys, memorabilia, and transcendental clutter. He lay on his back, eyes closed, as we talked. At times he looked pained, either from his back or perhaps from the effort of keeping the ol' rational mind working that long. His words were jovial and rambling, his wit keen and fresh (if sometimes absurd), yet beneath it all was a dead seriousness that gave his laughter a genuine ring.

His current project is working as fund-raiser for the Seva Foundation, an international organization directed by Dr. Nicole Grasset — former head of the World Health Organization's successful campaign against smallpox in India and southeast Asia — which is working to prevent and cure blindness, beginning with a pilot project in Nepal. (For information on Seva, write to Seva Foundation, 108 Spring Lake Drive, Chelsea, Michigan 48118).

— Howard Jay Rubin

SUN: Often you're seen in your clown face. What does it mean to put on the face of a clown? What changes?

WAVY GRAVY: It started when we first moved to Berkeley. We had done an event called the Berkeley Freak Fair and there was a newspaper article referring to me as a social worker in freak's clothing. Some doctors at the Oakland Children's Hospital who knew about me from Woodstock saw the article and asked me if I would go by the hospital and cheer up the kids. I was still coming out of my third spinal fusion then. I spent a lot of time chewing sheets, waiting for the synapses to reconnect, and it was just the thing to get me out of my funky space to spend an afternoon with the kids. As I began to go, someone handed me a red nose and someone else gave me some giant shoes — he was an old clown who was retiring and wanted his shoes to go on walking — and gradually I began to turn into this clown. Then one afternoon I had to go to a demonstration right after the hospital so I didn't have time to change. I noticed the police didn't want to hit me any more. So I'd finally come across something that was safe. You don't hear a bunch of rednecks get together and say, "Let's go kill a few clowns tonight." I managed to get the entire under-the-counter-culture dressed up like clowns in Kansas City where the Republicans were having their convention, and the police didn't move because the TV was there, and they weren't going to be clubbing clowns on color TV. The best definition I've heard of a clown is a poet who is also an orangutan.

Going to the hospital to put juice into people who were worse off than I was got me very strong. I certainly got a lot more out of it, it seemed to me, than I put in. Laughter is truly one of the best medicines.

SUN: Is there a problem with that? When you're doing serious work, do people see you as just lighthearted?

WAVY GRAVY: The more serious the work the more important it is to keep the light. Think of all the insanity in the world as a big pressure cooker. Laughter is the little valve on the top. If you don't have that the pressure cooker is going to explode and you're going to end up with beans on the ceiling.

SUN: When you're working with children, how do you get them to open up?

WAVY GRAVY: It's always one on one with me. To have any real impact you've got to be available for them. I have lots of stuff in my bag — a deck of giant playing cards, a bottle of bubbles. Bubbles are real good if kids are crying because their mom just left or something like that. If I step around the corner and blow some bubbles that will generally quiet them, they'll want to blow some, and after they've done that they can hardly start crying again. I have a musical instrument, some stories to read, riddles. I use riddles a lot. If a kid can trick me in a riddle I'll give him a balloon.

SUN: So you've got your bag of props, but you say that's not what does it.
WAVY GRAVY: It's like I said, being pretty much at their disposal, and letting them pick the route to take.

SUN: Do you end up feeling like a child?
WAVY GRAVY: My little boy who's eleven told me I'd never be a grown-up, so I don't worry about that.

SUN: Let's talk about Winna Rainbow.
WAVY GRAVY: Camp Winna Rainbow is a circus and theatre arts camp that we've done for six years. It started out as a babysitting service for the spiritual community, because it always seemed terrible to me that parents should be penalized spiritually because they have kids, and can't attend these various hoohas. So we started as a day care thing. After one year we decided to do our own camp, at the same place, and we put together an amazing staff of folks, the top people in the Bay area in dance and music. We taught motor skills like juggling and tightrope and trapeze, along with dance and music. The clowning arts. I refer to the camp as survival in the twenty-first century, or how to duck with a sense of humor, which I think in this day and age is important. I think if those things were taught in the first or second grade — juggling, tightrope, like that — that the kids would be different somehow.

We've just acquired 500 acres of land in northern California. The original vision was to do it in a circle of teepees with a big circus tent in the middle, so right now we're in the process of trying to raise those bucks to get that together because all of the available cash is involved in paying for the spread. It's hard for me to hustle for myself. I hustle for No Nukes, I hustle for the native Americans, for the wildlife, but to ask people to do something for me is hard.

SUN: What makes it hard?
WAVY GRAVY: Because you've only got so many asks for everybody, and it seems that my kids camp, no matter how nifty it is in the realm of right livelihood, doesn't seem to be the maximum impact for that ask. So I'm floundering a little bit here, but I know it's going to be just fine.

SUN: Tell me what Seva is about and what you're doing with it.
WAVY GRAVY: Seva is a Sanskrit word that means service. It's mostly made up of health workers who spearheaded the fight against smallpox, which is the first disease in the history of the world to be eradicated. Now they look for other ways to make a major change in people's lives. Presently it's unnecessary blindness. It seems eighty percent of the people in the world that are blind are unnecessarily blind. And eighty percent of that is reversible. In other words, at the going rate today, for fifteen bucks an eyeball you can restore sight. So my particular area has been FUNd raising, big f, u, n, small d. And putting on concerts, first at Carnegie Hall in New York, that was the first one. I call them Sing Out For Sight. Then with the Grateful Dead here, and Garcia and Weir. And then last year with Jackson Browne, Graham Nash, Holly Near, Robert Hunter, Kate Wolf, Country Joe, like that, down in L.A. We've done pretty well. We've also initiated a tee-shirt, and we're trying to disseminate information as best we can from our California office. The main office is in Chelsea, Michigan. I'm on the board of directors, I guess so they won't get bored. And this is not just limited to the blindness thing, although we have a major commitment in Nepal to get them self-sufficient in eye care by '87. We're looking at a tremendous cataract backlog too. And we were also able last year to teach advanced first aid at Porcupine and Pine Ridge Reservations for women of all red nations. What we're trying to do is help to alleviate human suffering.

SUN: When was the magical or not-so-magical moment when Hugh Romney took on the Wavy Gravyness?
WAVY GRAVY: Oh my goodness golly. The first festival we did after Woodstock was in Texas, at Lake Dallas. I remember about

twenty thousand bare asses, people who had never taken off their clothes before, and the judge told us they were going to call the National Guard, so I had to get everyone to put their clothes back on. I got in a little boat with my Mae West and my cowboy hat on, jumping into the water and yelling, "Ahoy amigo, the judge is going to call the National Guard. If you want to stay high put your pants back on. Swim over and tell that guy, tell him to tell someone else," until about sundown. As the sun was going down I was certain we had pulled it off, and at that moment, here came a naked water skier. We chased him around the lake until we ran out of gas. It was pretty funny.

At some point I wandered on to the stage while these eleven-foot dudes with filed teeth were playing drums and I lay on the floor and started hooting into the microphone, for no apparent reason, "This is Wavy Gravy on the floor, don't dance on the Wavy Gravy." And the guys started dancing around me. And I looked out and saw someone selling a joint for six dollars on the dance floor and I said, "This is Wavy Gravy on the floor, all the dope on the stage," and we started getting this mantra going, "All the dope on the stage, all the dope on the stage." And this big pile of dope started appearing, so I said, "OK, if you can roll good, come up on the stage." And the drums are going, these guys are naked to the waist, rolling one-handed, tossing joints off the stage, and this big cloud of smoke went up over Texas. And B.B. King was there, and this was just before one of my multitude of operations and I was getting up slow, and I felt this arm around my shoulder and it was B.B. King. He said, "You Wavy Gravy?" and I said, "Yes sir." He said, "Well, Wavy Gravy, we can work around you," and he leaned me up against his amplifier. I knew at that point that I was going to be Wavy Gravy for a while. Johnny Winter came out, they played till sunrise. It was everybody's reward for picking up the trash and putting their pants on. A tiny tip of Texas went to heaven there.

SUN: Let's go into a little Hog Farm history. What's the Hog Farm and what brought it together?
WAVY GRAVY: An extended family. I guess we've been doing it fifteen years.

SUN: How big is the family?
WAVY GRAVY: About fifty folks. It was a spinoff of the

Pranksters' old traveling road show. Then Kesey hotfooted it for Mexico with the FBI breathing down his neck, and all these Pranksters were abandoned. My wife and I were living in this one-room cabin in southern California and these Pranksters started drifting in until there were about thirty of them in one room, and the landlord said we all had to leave. About two hours later we heard about a place for free on a mountain nearby. We just had to be caretakers, slop some hogs. And every Sunday we'd have a celebration on the land with a different theme and people would call up from all over southern California and ask, "What's happening this Sunday?" Saturdays we'd put on light shows at the Shrine Auditorium, for the Cream and the Dead and the Airplane, to make money. Sundays were free, and we tried to figure out how to take those Sundays and move them around. I guess the first bus evolved out of that. We got this old schoolbus and painted it up. We took the pig with us, one little pig, that we later ran for President. She was the first female black and white candidate for President and she became pretty famous. And we would travel around and put on the show. I would go into a college and get sponsors — like I would get the Interfraternity Council and the SDS to sponsor us; it was the only thing they ever agreed on all year — and we'd get as much audiovisual stuff as we could, art supplies, musical instruments, and just pile it all up in the football field and fall asleep. And then they'd come up and say, "Hey, when does the show start?" and we'd say, "Golly, we'd better do something. You got a screwdriver?" And we'd put up this sixty-foot dome and thirty-foot dome and set up the picnic, but most of it was getting people to play with each other. It's a very hippie scam.

SUN: Do you have a good story that comes to mind from one of these shows?
WAVY GRAVY: I remember one show we did to raise money for various foundations. It was called "Meet The Pudding." We wheeled out this thousand-pound vat of chocolate pudding, and everybody got spoons. The concept was that everybody would feed each other — some people's idea of heaven. But we got bored with that after a while and pudding was flying everywhere, ladies got pudding on their mink coats. I heard this sound, "Phttt." There was a guy covered with pudding from the top of his head to his navel, and he grabbed the

microphone from me and said, "I've seen the bottom of the pudding." It turned out that New York University wanted two or three thousand dollars for warping the floor of the student center with chocolate pudding. But we wiggled out of that one.

SUN: Let's backtrack a little. Looking back on the whole Prankster scene, have your ideas about it changed? What do you think was happening?
WAVY GRAVY: It was a rude awakening, but it was definitely called for. The consciousness of the planet was rooted in thousands of years of karmic cement, and we needed to blast through it, somehow, so the universe provided this substance that enabled it to occur. And we sort of occurred with it.

SUN: It's gotten a lot of publicity over the years, a myth unto itself. Do you think it's getting overplayed, people going to the myth instead of doing their own trip?
WAVY GRAVY: Once you do your own trip you do your own trip. All the reading about it won't ever do it. It's like one time I threw the I Ching and I got "The Well," and the lines said the water in the well is good water, but it's just water in the well unless you drink it and turn it into light.

SUN: In his introduction to your book, Ken Kesey used the image of a beached whale. How would you introduce Ken Kesey?
WAVY GRAVY: He's like McMurphy in One Flew Over The Cuckoo's Nest. I mean, Kesey doesn't drink just one beer, he'd drink a case. He consumes vast quantities of everything — people, life — but at the same time is real delicate with a delicate strength. He's got a wonderful sense of humor too. He's been an inspiration in my life many, many times over the years. I once used to open as a stand-up comedian for a piano player named Theolonius Monk. He once told me, "Every man is a genius just being himself."

SUN: What about Woodstock? Such a big deal was made of it.
WAVY GRAVY: There have been many deals made about it, including a recent attempt to demystify the pie-in-the-sky out of it, a book called Barefoot in Babylon. Woodstock was created for peace, love, and wallets, not necessarily in that order, and the universe

took over. We were doing security and at one point the producers came up to us and said, "OK, we're going to start charging money now," and there were fifty thousand people on the infield, and five of us. I said, "Do you want a good movie or a bad movie?" because we had figured out by that point that the real bucks were in the movie rights.

There were so many aspects of the scene. It was a wonderful experience for all these Aquarian organizations that were there to drop their weak points and start surviving. Nothing like staying alive to get close to folks. If it was three beautiful days anywhere I think it would just have been rock 'n roll. I said in the movie, "There's a little bit of heaven in every disaster area." But whenever we started to believe that *we* were doing it and pulling it off, we would fall in the mud. If we just let ourselves be moved it's almost like marionettes.

SUN: You also helped run the freakout tent there. What was that like?

WAVY GRAVY: I remember when the first freakout wandered in. There were all these doctors standing around in white coats and shirts and ties, and me, and at that time I had no teeth and was wearing a cowboy hat with a yarmulke inside that Lenny Bruce gave me so I could say, "Howdy goyim." And this guy was coming through the door screaming, "Miami Beach, 1942, Joyce, Joyce." And this 300-pound Australian doctor looked at this guy and said, "Body contact, he needs body contact," and started laying on him and crushing him to death. The guy is still trying to scream, "Miami Beach, 1942, Joyce, Joyce," and this other doctor is saying to him, "Think of your third eye, man, think of your third eye." I decided it was time to make my move and said, "Excuse me, I'd like to make my move," and they backed off. And the guy was still yelling, "Miami Beach, 1942, Joyce, Joyce," and I said, "What's your name?" He said, "Bob." I said, "Your name is Bob," and he liked that. I told him his name and I found out where he was from, and I told him his name again and where he was from, and we went through that one for a while, and then I told him he took a little LSD and it was going to wear off, and he said, "Thank you." They don't want to hear "third eye," they want to know when they're going to come down. And when the guy did come down some more we said, "Hold it.

You see that guy coming through the door with his toys in his nose? That was you four hours ago. Now *you're* the doctor, take over." And he wasn't cut loose until that guy came down and was ready to take over for him and so the whole scene regenerated itself. The same thing with our food trip, where we were feeding ten thousand people a day. People would come into the kitchen and volunteer and somebody would replace them, and by the time *Life* magazine took the pictures of the Hog Farm kitchen there wasn't a single Hog Farmer in the kitchen.

SUN: Are psychedelic drugs still important to you?
WAVY GRAVY: Partly because of my body I don't do it that much. I like to do it at least once a year just to keep honest. But I'll go off somewhere in nature rather than in some rock 'n roll concert, let me tell you. I've noticed that the chemists are coming out with these little bitty hits now which may dissuade some people away from nature's way of telling us to spend money, cocaine. Terrible stuff. If people take psychedelics in limited doses instead of cocaine they'd be a lot better off, it would help them to go a little quicker. And who knows, they might get a little more consciousness to boot.

SUN: How does the Hog Farm make decisions? How do you individually decide what's next?
WAVY GRAVY: I'll be moving through time, space, and circumstance and suddenly I'll start to think well, maybe all the hairs on my arm would like to move to the country. I think that it's like following the hard-on of the heart. We operate our scene by consensus. Folks all get in a circle and something is thrown out there and you can pretty well tell if anyone else wants to do it or not.

SUN: Fifteen, sixteen years is a long time for a family to be together. Any clues as to what keeps it together, what keeps it clean?
WAVY GRAVY: I don't know if it's ever totally clean. You've got to sweep and dust. The initial focus of the bus trip was good. We did seven years of driving around, from sea to shining sea and then that one from London to the Himalayas. But kids were beginning to plug up the aisles of the bus and the third word in every woman's mouth was "house." And so we settled here in Berkeley, and set up a

business that we could all work at. That's important. The real information in any family begins to occur around the kitchen table. A lot of communes have failed because there wasn't a real focus.

We ran a telephone answering service called Babylon. It was different for us and good. We had always been supported by some kind of magic. The buses! God knows how we got them on the road. We certainly didn't. But it seemed that whatever had been taking care of us had better things to do and it was right for us to start taking care of ourselves.

Consensus is good. Folks are starting to learn about consensus through the anti-nuclear stuff. It's real sticky, it takes a while. There are a lot of rough edges.

SUN: Consensus means . . .
WAVY GRAVY: Everyone's going for it. We're creative anarchists, and if we can get something we can all agree on we can get it done.

SUN: What's been the hardest part of communal living?
WAVY GRAVY: Begging off the big movie of the road and taking care of everyday stuff. Kesey has a good line. He says, "The trouble with a superhero is what to do between phone booths." That's what we've been figuring out.

SUN: In the Sixties, "the establishment," "the system" was something to rebel against. Do you feel like you're outside or a part of the system today and how much can you be outside "the system?"
WAVY GRAVY: I don't know. I go to jail much more now than I did in the Sixties. My big line these days is the Eighties are the Sixties twenty years later — old feathers on a brand new bird. Very little of what I believed then has changed. I still think the system sucks and we've got to get another system. Meanwhile we've created this little infrastructure here, and we're starting to create it in the country, because the only way you can make change is to live the change, and if you're having a good time at it someone else will try it. Today there are more communes than there ever were, and people are getting into it strictly from economics. Like, one couple can't afford a house these days. You see a bunch of them get together, you go into the kitchen and look in the refrigerator and every little thing is

labeled — you know, Bob's butter, like that. And eventually either they go nuts and it splits up or all that shading disappears and it's just the stuff and people figure out how to share the expenses and the labor and that kind of thing. It takes time and it's hard, because it's different. The laws of America are set up to help everybody get what they can get for themselves. There are no provisions for people who want to live in a group and share, absolutely none. I think what's going to really change is not our kids but our kids' kids. They're the ones who are going to be different.

SUN: What kind of change is coming?
WAVY GRAVY: I think that all these things that are hard for us are going to be a matter of course to them, if there's a planet to do it in. I used to do a lot of stuff for the whales, and two or three years ago I stopped that. It's just a question of priorities. It think it's important that my kid gets to see a whale, but I'd rather him see *his* kid. Oh yeah, the Save the Humans button, you just picked up on that. At the Brandenberg Air Force Base we did a big protest against the MX, and I did it as a giant bunny. And I had, hanging off a chain, a human foot for luck. Mutant bunnies for peace, save the humans. Little things like that. The Nobody for President campaign really shakes people up. It gets them to think about what this whole popularity contest presidency is.

SUN: What's the Nobody for President campaign?
WAVY GRAVY: Look at the issues. Nobody totally understands the economy, nobody's abolished the draft, nobody's put an end to nuclear war, nuclear power. Even though nobody wants him elected, nobody's done most of the work. People say we've got nobody in there right now, but we say no, if nobody was in there right now it would be a lot different. We've got all the slogans: nobody lowered taxes, nobody bakes apple pie better than mom, let nobody run your life, if nobody runs, nobody loses.

SUN: Is nobody really qualified?
WAVY GRAVY: Nobody knows everything, nobody is over-qualified. As I tell the Native Americans, nobody was here first. And you can just go on and on forever. It's fun. It goes all the way back to Aristotle at least. We have these great rallies where nobody

arrives in the back of an open convertible, a lot of rock 'n rolling, and the crowd parts and we bring nobody up on stage, on a pillow, these little plastic teeth. And everybody gets quiet and nobody starts speaking, the teeth start clicking. That's essentially it. At the Kansas City Convention I was given a press pass by a friend, so I put on some straight clothes and started handing out press releases from nobody to the press. I got spotted by a plainclothes cop, who called the Secret Service and the FBI. He started patting me down and felt this bulge in my pocket. He said, "Is that a gun?" and took it out and these teeth started clicking on his hand. I said, "Quiet, our leader is speaking," and he gave me back the teeth and said, "Get out of here, you're too weird to arrest." I've been using the Get Out Of Jail Free card a lot. I've been Santa Claus for several of the busts. I usually do that in the warmer weather. He's more of an anachronism then.

SUN: What do you get arrested for mostly?
WAVY GRAVY: Weapons, nuclear energy. I put in for insanity last time.

SUN: How did that work?
WAVY GRAVY: I told them it was insane to put a reactor on an earthquake fault. You know, they get a little chuckle out of it and they think. If you laugh at something your defenses go down and you're able to hear it. Otherwise you're filtering it through all these models you have and you can't hear the sense to it. But if you laugh you've got a clear channel that leads to a mental breath. That's all it takes sometimes.

SUN: What has changed for you since the Sixties?
WAVY GRAVY: I've put on a little weight. (Laughs.) Six or seven years ago I was down to seventy-eight pounds and was probably not going to make it. And these polarity people and acupuncture people and wheatgrass people pulled together and saved my life. It was after much surgery from getting bopped down by various police, National Guards, that kind of stuff, back when I was a fool. I was very enamored by the fool in the Tarot who is one foot on the cliff with the dog at his heel. He's always walking off that cliff. I was that fool, and I fell on my ass a lot. I'm a clown now, that's different.

SUN: You've spent a lot of time flat on your back over the years. What has that meant?

WAVY GRAVY: It's a great teacher. There's nothing like good, hard-core suffering. I remember Ram Dass told me how lucky I was to carry all this suffering. I wanted to punch him in the nose. He was right. It's a great teacher. You learn a lot of patience. I'm much more kicked back saying the same things I was then. When you first tune into the planetary SOS and you think you're the first one who's heard it you go around shrieking to everybody and they don't hear you so much. But if you're a little more kicked back and you say it then people pay a little more attention. I'm not quite so manic. But you know, they had me full of opiates, barbiturates, steroids, everything on earth. That's what took me down to seventy-eight pounds. Now I just take aspirin and a lot of hot and cold showers. I'm not supposed to be able to walk around without morphine, and I don't take any of that stuff anymore. If I'm going to do something I have to pace it to the point where I'm not going to blow myself out. But when I started getting chopped by the doctors, nobody even knew what an acupuncturist was. When we first started taking psychedelics, nobody knew what a guru was. Now the kids come up, sure, it's just one of the things. Now survival is what's bringing people together — that's what is producing the peace movement. People are really starting to feel it. In Europe especially, because we're going to shoot those things in their backyard.

SUN: If there was one change you could make, what would it be?

WAVY GRAVY: Well, for years people used to ask me, "Wavy, can I get you anything?" and I used to tell them I wanted a Bentley for my birthday. Then about six or seven years ago I was working on rebuilding this hospital in Southeast Asia. A TV producer wanted me to have a car to get around in, so he gave me a car, had it parked in the driveway of the house I was staying in, and I woke up in the morning and my wife said, "Happy birthday," and I looked out in the driveway and there was this big chocolate brown Bentley. Oh no! So now when people ask me if they can get me anything I usually ask for peace on Earth.

SUN: What are your feelings about spirituality?

WAVY GRAVY: Your politics, your religion, it's all the same mumbo. It's how you live your life. Everywhere I see it's just intellectualized. Mostly it's just the Golden Rule.

I like all the teachings, all the tricks. Many spokes and one hub, I guess. Anything that will get you there. I do something every April Fool's day called the First Church of Fun. And one of the teachings has to do with the funny mantra, which is the basic Bronx cheer/raspberry type noise. You take a paper bag that just fits over your head and do the funny mantra. The bag will vibrate and make you turn into a human kazoo. And I gave it to the kids in the hospital and said, "Put this under your pillow, and when it really gets bad, put the bag over your head and do that, and it will change everything." And they do it, and they're very careful about when they do it. Harpo Marx said, "If all else fails, stand on your head." Well, you can just stick a bag over your head and do the funny mantra.

SUN: What do you do when things get to that point?

WAVY GRAVY: That's what I do. And it works.

(May 1983)

News from Hacker City:

Some Considered Opinions On The Electric Bass

Richard Gess

1. Intro.

It's been three years this June that I've been playing the bass, and after three long years of attempted music-making I am still not a musician. I do not expect to become one, either. A musician, by my definition, lives and breathes music, just as a writer should live and breathe writing, a painter painting, and a preacher God. A certain element of obsession is necessary to do anything truly well. I could very easily become obsessed with the bass, but I cannot allow myself. I'm twenty-four, and the moment for obsession (in the musician's compressed time scale) passed when I was thirteen. Before I got anywhere close to *good* I'd be thirty, and thirty is no age to set out to be a rock-and-roll hero. So I am not a musician; I am, instead, a hacker. Just hacking around. I flirt with the

When I hit a good low bottom-string A and shake the ground and force wind from the speakers, I'm playing the planet through my bass . . . I'm wired into deity.

bass, but I will not be seduced. What follows are some musings about that flirtation.

2. Looks. My romance with the bass is partly physical. The damn things are beautiful. Sometimes I just open up their cases and look at them. I have two basses: a Gibson EB-3 and a Fender six-string. Each represents an opposite school of design. The Gibson is a Musical Instrument; its dark heavy woods are lacquered in such a way that the grain, under the right light, appears incandescent. The body is carved so subtly that some of the edges must be searched for. Each screw and knob is placed deliberately. The controls are laid out with careful regard to ergonomics; the pickup selector, for example, is a four-position switch that's wired so that you never need to flip it more than one stop at a time while playing. The consciousness behind such thoughtful construction is Old World: intelligent crafts-manship and good taste speaking for themselves. The esthetics of the Fender are radically different; it is a Machine, late-Fifties-American-type. In its own way it is very attractive, but it is attractive more as an expression of a style than in and of itself. It is the embodiment of Guitar Rococo. Each corner of the swoopy body juts out in a different direction, and the total effect is of some ornate sci-fi starship straining upward against gravity. The finish is "sunburst" — simulated flame — and encrusted over its reddish glory are three pickups, four toggle switches, a pop-up mute, two lab-variety knobs, a huge imita-tion tortoise-shell pickguard; and no fewer than forty shiny Phillips head screws to hold everything in place. Almost every metal part is chromed. The flesh-tone maple neck is capped by the classic glans-like Fender peghead, and each of the six chrome tuning machines has a big "F" stamped into it. One suspects this device of being hallucinated rather than designed, but I find it curiously lovely. If the Gibson is the Old World, then the Fender is Americana. Owning them both is like having a guitar gallery. When the electricity goes out for good, I will hang them on my wall and admire them by candlelight.

3. Sounds. The Gibson is a bass: four strings, bass viol style. The Fender is a bass guitar: six strings, tuned an octave lower than the standard guitar. The history of the Gibson merges backward into the history of the bowed bass, but the Fender's bastard lineage goes back only as far as the Stratocasters, Jazzmasters, and Jazz Basses that were miscegenated to make it. The sounds of the instruments faithfully reflect their backgrounds. The EB-3s notes are fathomlessly deep and sonorous, with a bowed sounding sustain. The sound is natural; the music seems to originate in the heart of the wood. The Fender's voice, conversely, is pure technology. Its pickups seem to synthesize the notes instead of amplifying them. Mysterious resonances abound; the body is as solid as a coffee table, yet the notes ring with sourceless harmonics. Playing the six is sometimes disorienting, because it can be difficult to connect the sounds with the instrument. One feels one's fretting and picking have nothing to do with what comes out. This synthetic quality makes the Fender ideal for use with add-on gadgetry. It can be plugged into wah pedals, fuzz tones, bass boosters, dynamic compressors, and envelope followers to create a menagerie of sounds limited only by the adventurousness of the player. Such distortions of the Gibson's sound would be unseemly, but with the Fender they're quite all right. The natural direction for technology is toward more technology; that's the electric Tao.

4. An Esthetic. A reed-playing neighbor of mine recently explained the prevailing concept of the bassist to me. "You play the root," he said, "and you play it on one and three." Bass players are often told to just shut up and keep time. Amazingly, most of them acquiesce. Why? A bassist with any melodic ability at all can transform an ordinary rock or jazz group into an electric chamber ensemble — assuming, of course, that his or her colleagues are interested. Most of the time, they won't be. In the playing-for-a-living world, counterpoint takes a back seat to danceability. If you can't rock 'em (or at least sway them gently), you don't work. Working bassists have not yet been liberated from the rhythm section, but their hacker counterparts are free to play as they like. As a hacker, the only standards I must ultimately conform to are my own. My esthetic: the electric bass is the full equal of any other instrument. Properly played, it can simultaneously provide both a solid rhythmic punch *and* a complex countermelody. Look: any note you play through multiple fifteen-inch speakers at eighty-plus decibels minimum is going to have rhythm. The task of the bassist should be to transcend mere metronomics and push his/her playing out in front. Where it belongs. The best bass players — the transcendental bassists (TBs) — are up front every time they plug in. Consider some of my heroes. . . .

5. Heroes. Whoever it was in the Cyrkle (remember the Cyrkle?) who played those nifty little two-bar breaks in "Turn Down Day." And whoever tightened up with Archie Bell and Drells. These were the first bassists I ever noticed. They weren't truly transcendental, but they stood out because they were given a bit of space for themselves. No one else impressed me very much until I heard Douglas Lubahn on the Doors' *Strange Days* album, floating hauntingly through "You're Lost, Little Girl," and defining transcendental bass in the two breaks in the title song. Dust off your copy and listen: in the first break he holds back, coolly playing the equivalent of foot-tapping, waiting. Then in the second break he explodes into double-time, sliding for his life and playing — *mirabile!* — a lead line. Terrific stuff, except that Lubahn wasn't really in the band. In his own group, Clear Light, he was just another bass player. His Doors work is important as definition, but to experience transcendental bass at its best you must experience Jack Casady's work with Jefferson Airplane. Jack Bruce (Cream) was more accessible, and Phil Lesh (Grateful Dead) was more cerebral, but neither they nor the other trailblazing TBs (Chris Hillman of the Byrds and Rand Forbes of the United States of America) can compare with Casady in terms of being so consistently fascinating for so long. None of them ever recorded anything to compare with "Spare Chaynge;" this cut on *After Bathing at Baxter's* is the perfection of the rhythm/lead bass concept. All of the instruments, in fact, are functioning as equals here. Guitar, bass, and drums are balanced, and not locked into a hierarchy. Paul Williams (the critic, not the singer) aptly compares the players' interaction to ballet. This loosened structure allows Casady to let his imagination run, and the range of moods and genres he explores is dazzling. There are Fado progressions in these bass lines, and heavy-metal power chording too; there are slide runs, call-and-response episodes, counterpoint tag games, stretched measures, squished measures — an entire encyclopedia of TB techniques. Casady is the quintessential TB, and the *Baxter's* album is his peak. Six years after I first heard it, I went out and bought my first bass, and Casady was on my mind as I plunked down my money. If I could do half of what he does, I thought — chord half as effortlessly, play half as fluid lead, make half as much booming thunder for rhythm — if I could get half as good as Casady, I thought, I'd be more than good enough for myself. Three years, three bands, and five basses later, I'm no closer to that goal than I was when I took home bass number one. This confirms my faith in Casady; what good, after all, are approachable heroes?

6. Yggdrasil. Hackers, because of their resistance to commitment, seldom cross the line to become musicians. To be a hacker in the hopes of becoming a hero is delusion. Hackers can play the bass, but heroes have to live it. One must choose, so I've chosen to hack, because in hacking there is the hero's freedom. No bars, no boogie, no "Tie a Yellow Ribbon" (ever played in a Holiday Inn?); just the simple high of soundmaking, without any compromises. And there's something more: something spiritual. In the liner notes of *Crown of Creation* Casady is listed as the Yggdrasil bassist. The Yggdrasil, in Norse mythology, is the tree of life; to play the Yggdrasil bass is to play the low notes of existence. And the low notes are the sweetest. When I hit a good low bottom-string A and shake the ground and force wind from the speakers, I'm playing the planet through my bass. No one's cheering or writing me checks, but it doesn't really matter. In these moments I'm wired into deity.

7. Dichotomies. If bass playing, then, is playing the Earth, then writing is just as surely playing yourself. One frets one's neurons as facilely as one can and then strains to hear what's produced. The Earth's note is that bottom string A; the mind's notes are these sentences. The difference is in feedback intervals. A clinker on the bass is obvious in the instant it escapes the amp, but dissonance in prose sometimes isn't heard until a good while after it's written. It now occurs to me, three afternoons into writing this, that I've been dealing in dichotomies here. Hackers vs. heroes, wood vs. chrome, rhythm vs. lead, the natural vs. the synthetic — everything I've pondered has emerged in polarities. And all those polarities eventually boil down into the nagging old dualism of emotion (rhythm) vs. intellect (lead). Which is not what bass playing is about. Remember the TB ideal: rhythm *and* lead. Spirit and mind cooking together. Being a TB is being someone who lives and creates as a whole person. Academics cannot be TBs; neither can the Fabulous Furry Freak Brothers. Or myself; if I'm still thinking in twos instead of ones, then I can't qualify either. I'll be here in Hacker City until the obvious finally dawns on me. Gotta practice more. . . .

8. If You Get an Outfit, You Can Be a Hacker Too. Phil Lesh, in *The Dead Book*, notes that the first time he played something electric, he couldn't put it down; he played for seven hours, and then couldn't sleep. Electric playing is immediately addictive; electric basses make thunder with lightning, and forces that strong are very hard to resist. Maybe *you* should pick up something electric. If you think you'll like it, you probably will. My only advice would be to please be sure. This is because your minimum investment, new or used, will probably be in the neighborhood of $400 for a decent bass and bass amp. If you spend that on new equipment, you won't be getting much; you'll do better for your money with used instruments, but only if you or someone you know knows enough to avoid getting burned. Be wary, because you have no way of knowing where all those fingerprinty old basses have been before they got across the counter from you. Rent or borrow first, if you can, and then go at it for at least a month. Your first week will be depressing; your fingers will want nothing to do with those sharp-edged strings. The second week, after you work up a little callous, will be all overconfidence; the logic of the fingerboard will begin to reveal itself, and you will play along loudly with your punk-rock records and begin to think about gigging. Disregard these moods. When your month is up, you will only have learned two things: the immensity of what it will take to get good, and the depth of your desire to continue. If you're hooked at this point, your next step will be obvious. You will abandon your vices, drain your bank account, and buy yourself an axe. Good luck; don't forget to eat.

9. Fade. Sound is the audible variety of the energy which moves everything from our heart valves to the galaxies. To coax it from wood and chrome and tubes is to celebrate it. Every song is a hymn — even the rough songs of the hacker. In church, as a child, the only thing that interested me was the organ. When our would-be-Biggs choirmaster stomped on his pedals to begin the postlude, he shook the whole block. Now with my basses I can shake my own block, and when I do I think: ah. Worship. And I reach out and crank up the volume. Loud. To hack is sometimes to pray.

(September 1977)

Lord Shantih

Thomas Wiloch

Stones Upon The Path

One day the Lord Shantih was approached by an aged beggar who carried a staff.

"May I walk with you, my Lord?" said the beggar.

"And what path do you wish to follow?" Lord Shantih asked.

"I wish to follow the path that leads from today," said the beggar, "for today I have killed a man."

"No path leads there," Lord Shantih said, dismissing him. "Your staff shall grow branches before you can leave your deeds behind you."

Days later, the Lord Shantih saw the beggar seated beneath a tree by the roadside.

"My Lord," called the beggar, pointing to the tree, "behold my staff."

And Lord Shantih looked and saw that it was the staff grown into a tree.

"Who did you kill?" Lord Shantih asked.

"I killed the man who sold my family into slavery."

Lord Shantih removed his sandals and gave them to the beggar.

"Wear these," he said, "for there are many stones upon the path."

The Forest of Shalaen

There are as many trees in the Forest of Shalaen as the number of hairs in a sage's beard. Much of the forest is yet unexplored, at least by man, and so it is the site of many legendary stories and heroic tales.

The Lord Shantih once lived in the forest and knew some of the places the legendary stories speak about. He had slept beneath the tree in which the warrior Barola was imprisoned for his gruesome crimes. He had drunk from the well the elves drank from when they journeyed to the Islands of the Outer Realm — the well whose water sparkles even at darkest midnight. He had walked the twisted, stony paths the trolls are said to walk upon when the moon is full and the blood-thirst is high. But he never saw the warrior Barola, the travelling elves, or the dangerous trolls men speak about.

"Perhaps these legendary characters are merely hiding from me," Lord Shantih mused, "between the sturdy covers of the books of men."

The Sacred House

The teacher Harmal held that his house was sacred. He pointed out that each facet of his house could be interpreted as a symbol of truth, and in this manner a thoughtful man might gain useful insights into the nature of life.

Harmal believed that the doorway to his house was a symbol of both birth and death, as those who walked into the house through the doorway were born into the world of Harmal's house, while those who walked out were dead to that world.

The windows of the house were carefully placed, Harmal showed, to allow a viewer to see specific, symbolic scenes. He spent many hours seated at one window or another, studying the views to ascertain their obscure but weighty significance, much as other arcane scholars study the visual teachings of the Tarot deck.

In many ways the structure of Harmal's residence held great and sacred meanings for him. The walls, floor, and ceiling represented the faith that protects the seeker from the evils of the world. The morning sunlight on the window sill or the star-patterns seen while lying on his bed were manifestations of the inherent joy and potential of the universe. The shiftings and weavings of the shadows in his house corresponded with the personal thoughts and emotions in the mind of man.

Students of occult philosophy still remember Harmal. Harmal the eccentric hermit and teacher who lived centuries ago and was but little heeded by his fellows. And whose house burned down the very afternoon he ascended bodily into heaven.

There Is No Cave

There is no cave.

But if there were, the cave would contain someone. Someone old and bent and dressed in robes. Someone with a gray beard and gray hair and a wrinkled face. Someone whose voice cracked and crackled whenever he spoke. Someone who saw all things and knew all things and understood all things.

But there is no cave.

But if there were, you would visit the cave to speak with him who lived within it. He would greet you with a nod and a twinkling eye, clasping his hands in front of him. You would speak to him, calling him father or master, and you would plead with him for answers to your questions. With a patient smile he would answer your questions, solve your mysteries, and reveal all the tangled threads of your hopes and dreams.

There is no cave.

But if there were, it would contain the answer you most desire. The answer that makes all things understood and meaningful and yours. And you would guard the answer and guard the cave so no one could ever take it from you.

There is no cave.

(August 1981)

Hot Dogs

Karl Grossman

I was compiling a list of what I would take with me in the coffin when along came a dog wearing a hat.

120 Hershey milk chocolate bars. Two cases of Fox's U-Bet syrup. What would heaven be without some chocolate?

"Hey, buster," this dog with bright blue eyes, a somewhat snooty bearing, and a fedora, yelled.

Four pounds of Colombian. Certainly that would be a necessity for such an extended trip.

"Let me ask you," said the dog, who introduced himself as Morris, "how many dogs are represented among the ranks of veterinarians?" I told him I had never met a vet who was a dog. "This is anthroposexism!" Morris argued.

Spaghetti. But how to cook it? I would take *already cooked spaghetti.*

What would heaven be without some chocolate?

With my mind on spaghetti, I suggested to Morris that we step into Gluttonia's Pasta to talk further.

Over a bowl of spaghetti marinara on which he most noticeably used no fork, Morris spoke with considerable emotion about the domination of "most aspects" of animal life by people. "Humans even concoct this Ken-L-Ration crap," complained Morris. "Not one chef of canine persuasion has been retained. Ask any dog what he'd like — you think it would be Ken-L-Ration?" Morris spoke so loudly that people at other tables were looking.

"And what do you prefer?" I asked.

"Spaghetti marinara, of course," said Morris, as he kept gobbling.

Some books, I thought, and some records, I must have my favorite book, Dr. Bruce Spencer's *The Fallacy of Creative Thinking*.

Morris was waxing on about Ken-L-Ration. I mentioned that during recurring periods of poverty I had lived — for months — on Ken-L-Ration, bolstered sometimes with tropical fish food. "A dab of ketchup was nice," I said.

"Dogs eschew ketchup," said Morris curtly.

"This might be a matter of communication," I said. *The American Beauty Rose* album of The Dead, of course. "Most dogs don't have the kind of command of human language you do," I explained.

"This is true," said the dog. "Mostly dogs bark. Some dogs also prefer ear twitching." *A motorcycle.* A motorcycle to drive all over heaven. "But there's been no sincere attempt to translate dog language," said Morris.

"Morris," I told the dog, "I am convinced you are an honest, well-meaning animal. What can I do to help?"

"Take me to the nearest veterinary school," said Morris.

A flashlight.

We reached Cornell in four hours. Morris bounded from the car. I followed him through a maze of halls. Morris got pissed when we passed the cafeteria, wafting of frankfurter smoke. "Some of those pigs and cows had families," Morris said.

A receptionist in the office of the school's president asked whether we had an appointment. We said no, but she was able, somewhat reluctantly, to schedule us "for just a few minutes" with a Dr. Pinsky.

A telephone. Dry socks.

Pinsky conceded to Morris that there were no dogs among veterinary students, or animal representation among the administration or faculty at the veterinary school other than a Persian cat, an eye-ear-nose-and-throat specialist.

"This is rank anthroposexism!" charged Morris, and the talk immediately plunged downward with Morris ultimately biting Pinsky's leg and Pinsky chasing Morris around the office with a chair trying to bat him over the head.

As we were fleeing, Pinsky was calling the dog catcher.

Matches. And toothpaste and toothbrush.

As we were heading back, Morris was saying how he might have to move through organized politics when a Collie came prancing along. Morris leaped out the window.

A typewriter. A wok. Friends.

I didn't hear from Morris until a few months later, when I got a phone call from him. He said he was running for the town council in Ringworm, N.J. as a reform Democrat. *Swiss Army knife. A heavy jacket*, just in case.

I told Morris I thought this was a wise move, and that I had stopped wearing shoes. Morris stressed that he, in fact, had no possessions. "These are human illusions," said the dog.

(March 1977)

Californicated, Santa Crucified

Rob Brezsny

Sammy Davis, Jr. says: "All men are created bland." And I would add: "But they can, and usually do, get even blander." Case in point (never thought I'd see the day): me. At the end of my second year in California, I watch with fascinated horror as I become *nicer* and *nicer*, more polite, more congenial, more *well-adjusted*.

I do my T'ai chi on the beach, write my haiku about inner tubes and the boardwalk and the crescent moon, glide over to my polarity therapy class, throw the bums a dime in my prime, cop a feel, catch the latest in New Wave fashions down at the thrift shop, pick up my free money from the ever-beneficent state, call my mother and rap about reincarnation, and fall asleep in the arms of my best friend's wife. Hey, this is easy, no

Later, I perfected the involuted style of bragging about not bragging to such a degree that I became able to brag in reverse, exalting what I couldn't do and didn't have.

hassles, no bummers. Hey, I'm in Santa Cruz, what year is it? Have a nice life. *Dear Diary: Almost fell in love yesterday, and again today.* Let's go down to Esalen tonight and get naked and take some drugs.

I can almost remember pre-California: setting my hair on fire to scare and horrify my old girl friend, what was her name again, the one who said she'd get her father to kill me after I threw coffee at her, after she threw my Tarot books out the window, after I raised an eyebrow to some *other* witchy woman. That was a different life, filled with jealousy, suffering, terror, awe. Like the time brother Tom and I ran into that very white Baptist church in South Carolina, in the middle of the Sunday service, and shivered and howled and fell on the floor, screaming *Jesus has come again to judge the quick and the dead, but he's black this time.* Or when my friend Ellen got so demented and distracted over a story I wrote about her (*pornographic*, she said; *erotic*, I said) that she half-sliced off her little finger while cutting vegetables, and blamed me. We never spoke again.

Rock and roll was religion to me then; I *dwelt* in the power and glory of it all. There was Janis Joplin and me and a lesbian roadie crashing on the same filthy mattress in March 1969; the cousin of George Harrison's ex-wife giving me hepatitis in '70; Johnny Winter punching me in the jaw in '71. I mean, I *worshipped* at the shrines. I was pure, I was holy, I was blasphemous and *bad.*

When I see those neat beards and bell bottoms marching in circles in front of PG&E on the Mall, I am calm and Buddha-cool. I do not snort, I do not judge, I do not compare. With supreme detachment, I remember gathering with the Black Panthers in downtown Durham, N.C. to throw Molotov cocktails at the cops; or making love with a *real* Marxist from Czechoslovakia; or — I don't know why, exactly — falling asleep in the outhouse one Winter morning.

In March of 1977, on the day before I left North Carolina, my friend Richard said to me: "You ready to regress, boy? Do you realize that Californians are ten years *behind*, not ahead, of the times? Why do you think they talk so obsessively about spirituality? They know nothing about it, they're innocents, that's why. Look how we tend to the spirit here. No full-page newspaper ads, no remedial gymnastics for the inner eye. It's all blended into the daily routine here. We don't have to call attention to it, we just do it. You just see how fast you lose touch with the moon and the cycle of the seasons out there. They're half-terrified of the earth, the land's too wild and unstable.

They keep their distance — they have to. Why do you think they talk so obsessively about Mother Earth? Because they know nothing about her, they fear her."

Well? Two years later, Jerry Brown wants California to have space bubble communities orbiting the Earth, before the U.S. government figures out how to do it. We'll have gay vegetarian re-birthed jocks in one bubble, and Taoist hermaphroditic scholars hermetically devoted to the study of Baba Ram Dass's sexuality in another bubble. "OFF THE PLANET!" will be the California state slogan by 1985. (Do I smell decadent anti-terrestial sympathies, fear and loathing of the Great Mother, a bizarre exaltation of ignorance and abuse of the Earth?)

And meanwhile, dear old Tim Leary wants not only his soul, but his *body*, his actual, physical, flesh and blood body, to live forever. Is this the next radical development in human evolution, or the supremely effete, deluded ideal of rapidly devolving patriarchal culture?

Psychic Centers

There is a new organic enchilada sauce on the market allegedly more pure than any enchilada sauce ever made. I found it in the Food Bin the other day. According to the label on the side of the plastic container, its ingredients include water, onions, garlic, soy sauce, spices, sea salt, and "unsprayed dry red chilis from the Mesilla Valley, one of the seven psychic windows of the world." Is this a radical new evolutionary development in the history of food?

I wouldn't bet on it. At least not until the makers of the enchilada sauce or some reliable trance medium provide better documentation for this claim. Most everyone I've ever talked to agrees that there are no more and no less than seven "psychic windows" on this planet, just as there are exactly seven chakras in the human body. But according to my own informal survey, fifty-four geographical loca-tions, as of Sept. 1, 1979, have already laid claim to the title, including Santa Cruz. The Mesilla Valley is number fifty-five.

As I understand it, a psychic window is a supercharged place in the body of the planet where the veil between this dimension and the next is parted. Strange and miraculous things happen there. Planes and ships disappear into thin air. The skies are cluttered with fantastic colors and images. Animals talk. Clairvoyance and tele-kinesis are commonplace. People are obsessed with the occult. UFOs come and go freely.

The most celebrated of these places — which also go by the titles "energy vortex," "planetary chakra," "spiritual center," and "circle of light" — is of course the Bermuda Triangle. In more esoteric circles the popular sentiment remains with the hidden magical city of Shambhala (where the Buddha will supposedly be celebrating his birthday on the Full Moon), which some observers have located in the Himalayas, others in the Gobi Desert.

I don't think I've ever lived in a place that hasn't been identified as a psychic window, and that includes sixteen different cities and towns. Which means either that my very presence bestows some sort of divine grace, or else that some of these places are faking.

During my stay in North Carolina, I lived in two cities, only eight miles apart, that *each* claimed to be the center of a psychic win-dow whose boundaries most definitely did not extend as far as the rival city. It always seems unlikely to me that the Earth would squeeze two separate chakras into an area only fifty square miles wide. But when I lived in Durham I believed in the divinity of Durham, and when in Chapel Hill, the divinity of Chapel Hill. It gave me a kind of civic pride not much different from the chauvinistic glow other people drew from the success of the local universities' football and basketball teams.

Of those fifty-five places I know to have been called psychic win-dows (and there are probably more) I have visited forty-one, so I feel eminently qualified to offer a list of seven locations in the United States most likely to be psychic windows. These are just the possibilities; I doubt that we actually have more than two, since the seven must be distributed pretty evenly over the face of the earth:

1) The Bermuda Triangle. The odds-on favorite of the people; the darling of the *National Enquirer* and pop-occult crowds. (This should not, however, be held against it.)

2) The Cleveland-to-Columbus Corridor. This section of Ohio is visited more frequently by UFOs than any other place in the world. It is also the origin of several of the most notorious punk rock bands.

3) Fairfield, Iowa. The Transcendental Meditation organization has made this its "levitation headquarters." Advanced meditators

are brought here to be taught the power of flight.

4) Forestburg, S.D. It's often mentioned, by subjects progressed through hypnosis to their future lives, as a great center of North American civilization from the twenty-second to twenty-sixth centuries.

5) Durham-Chapel Hill, N.C. My own sentimental favorite.

6) Los Angeles. Who can possibly deny that the entire world is being created in the image of L.A.?

7) Santa Cruz. The evidence is impressive. The Dalai Lama himself has said that the new spiritual center of the world will be between San Francisco and Monterey. According to the U.S. Geodetic Survey, this area has a strangely low amount of electromagnetic activity — thunderstorms are abnormally rare. Several psychics on the east coast who have no special stake in glorifying Santa Cruz have made references to this area as an "energy vortex."

In June, 1968, several years before I had ever even heard of Santa Cruz, I dreamed of a tall, yellow-eyed, winged man who told me, "Go to the holy place, Santa Cruz." Recently, while researching this article, I discovered that the native Ohlone Indians, who regarded this land as holy, had legends of a giant bird man who appeared periodically and foretold the future.

I have only one reason to question the evidence. And that is that there seems to be almost *too much* spiritual activity in Santa Cruz. Sometimes the proliferation of spiritual schools, movements, and organizations is so excessive that I'm sure someone must be playing a joke on all of us. But then a cosmic comic sense might be the one and only essential symptom of life in a psychic window.

I Like Reich

A blonde-haired black woman in a *Close Encounters of the Third Kind* tee-shirt approached me on the Mall last Friday afternoon and motioned for me to follow her. Her eyes had the snuffed-out blaze of certitude common to fanatics, and I always enjoy the company of fanatics, so I went with her.

Usually I can guess the nature of the obsession from the posture, hair style (or lack of it), facial twitches, and uniform of the obsessed, but this one had me stumped. She wore pants I was sure had some sacramental significance; sacramental, because although they were highly stylized, they were not very stylish. They were ordinary navy blue corduroy Levis except for the conspicuous bulge of a codpiece, such as I have seen on the line of men's pants marketed by Eldridge ("Born Again") Cleaver in Oakland.

She wore three home-made buttons on her shirt at the neckline, which plunged sharply. Button number one said simply, "I LIKE REICH" (the first evidence I have found to support my theory that Wilhelm Reich and Dwight D. "Ike" Eisenhower were one and the same person). The second button bore the likeness of a whorey-looking Madame Blavatsky, her lascivious lips half-parted in an eternal seductive invitation to the most suave of the spooks and spectres who slither in and out of the material plane. The man whose face graced the button that straddled the cleavage looked like a short-haired, clean-shaven Christ, getting ready to sell me some insurance. (After a minute I realized he was actually Werner Erhardt.)

I thought at first that this woman might belong to one of those very esoteric sects of Jesus Freakdom, the Children of the Saucer, a group that combines the best of Christian prophecy with Erich von Däniken, *Close Encounters*, and the punk band Parliament. They believe Christ is an extraterrestrial being, who on Judgment Day will land in the heart of the Washington, D.C. nightclub district in a condominium-sized flying saucer, where he shall judge the quick and the dead. And when he's through with that, according to the Children of the Saucer, he will circulate among the bars and discos of that city with his entourage, the twelve extraterrestrial apostles (presumably Judgment Day falls on a Saturday night), until he finds the earthly woman suitable to be the mother of the 144,000 "children of the saucer." He will take her away to his divine kingdom, on a planet much like the Earth, located somewhere in the constellation of Virgo.

I was sure this woman's first words to me would be something like "Do you know the Lord?" Or maybe (who knows in these increasingly matriarchal days?) "Do you know the Lord's Mother (or lover or wife or sister)?" And I was ready to unveil the dazzling, convoluted, righteous rap I have used to deprogram fifteen different fanatics in four different countries of the world. (Note to parents and friends of fanatics: I will deliver this rap to your fanatically-programmed loved one free of charge. Contact me here. Offer good for a limited time only.)

She took my hand but did not speak as we covered the distance between Bookshop Santa Cruz and the County Bank. As we crossed the street toward the Cooper House, she stopped, turned to face me, placed her hands firmly on my shoulders, and said softly, "Have you heard of the Circle of Gold?"

My nose began to run and my eyes began to itch. My legs broke into a St. Vitus Dance, but my arms and trunk insisted on the Latin Hustle. I remembered with a twinge of passion a valentine I had made for the Virgin Mary back in the third grade, but had given to little Gail Musa instead. The words and music for an original song exploded full-blown across my limp synapses. The title: "Punks in Redwood Tubs." All in all, I felt I was on the verge of a religious experience that would cure me forever of hunger, poverty, and humiliating need.

And then for an instant I was in perfect sync with all the money everywhere on Earth. I knew all money. I had all money. I *was* all money. Money was what flowed through my brain. Money was what pumped from my heart. Money was what vibrated with a lush and crystalline radiance in my chakras.

"It all comes from the same inexhaustible source, Krishna," she was cooing to me, her hands sending hot flashes from my shoulders down to the ends of all my limbs. (For some reason she addressed me as "Krishna," even though my real name is Rob.)

"It's all the same eternal energy, Krishna. Food, sex, knowledge, spirit, money: they are all One. And I can help you to know and remember this always, if you will let me."

She licked her lips like the Blavatsky on her button, and I shuddered.

"I can help you make $100,000 without any risk, Krishna," she continued. "Thousands of people like you have done it. Let me help you, let me share my prosperity with you. Do you have $100 that you are willing to invest in yourself for one day?"

With a perverse burst of willpower I broke free from her squeeze and bolted at full speed toward the Catalyst. I arrived in time for happy hour, during which I managed to slowly come down from my money trance. It wasn't easy. I had to get rid of more than $100, buying drinks for friends, before I felt like myself again.

In Tune With the Tao

I ended my week-long vigil at the food stamp office last Friday with a meditation on bragging. I'd devoted forty hours in five days to the task of observing the behavior of food stamp recipients, for clues to the current state of the Santa Cruz collective unconscious.

At about 3:30 p.m., I was half-asleep on the patio listening to an Elton John look-alike as he bragged to nobody in particular, and the female sex in general, that he was the lead singer in a punk band that was secretly funded by the CIA. The arrival in the main waiting room of a woman wearing a baseball jersey jolted me from this exotic reverie. A beautiful astrological union: she walked like a Scorpio and talked like a Pisces. She reminded me of a girl I'd had a crush on in the fourth grade, and my memory circled back to those simple days, when I bragged and boasted without guile or inhibition.

When I was ten years old and wanted to impress a female, I might have given her the unadorned account of my prowess on the baseball diamond, or my grade on the latest history test (today I would say *herstory* test). But by the time I was twenty, after three years in the New Age incubator with Alan Watts and Lao-Tse, I was incapable of a blatant, straightforward, out-and-out brag. Instead of praising my own virtues and calling attention to my accomplishments, I had learned to drop broad hints that I was too highly-evolved to brag.

The climax of the conversion came three years after I had utterly renounced baseball, the game that had brought me so much glory in earlier years. In June of 1972, obeying an impulse, I renounced my renunciation and joined a semi-pro team in Vermont. In my first game I had five hits, including two home runs. I quit immediately. There was nothing more I hoped to accomplish. I could have dropped dead right then and there, completely happy with my life. Not because I had proved what a virile jock I was, you understand, but because for those two and a half hours I had achieved perfect harmony with the *Tao*.

When I spoke of the game later, and I often did, I bragged that I could never even consider bragging about my phenomenal success, because I cared nothing for it. *I* hadn't gotten five hits. The *universal life force* had gotten five hits. It just happened to be circulating through me with consummate power and freedom exactly when I needed it. Of course, it couldn't have happened to a nicer, more deserving, more *highly-evolved* guy.

Later I perfected the involuted style of bragging about not bragging to such a degree that I became able to brag in reverse, exalting what I couldn't do and didn't have. My proudest moments in recent years have come while bragging about my chronic poverty. But at the food stamp office I saw the art I considered my specialty raised to its most ingenious, if somewhat decadent, form of expression, and I realized it was being practiced skillfully all around me.

The woman in the baseball jersey sat down next to a bare-chested, rednecked hippie. For the next fifteen minutes he held her spellbound with stories of his exploits as a beggar. She was most visibly impressed when he told her that this was the third state in which he'd received foodstamps this month. As soon as he left this place, he said, he was headed for Nevada to score another $54 worth. Did she want to go with him?

Thirty minutes later they left together with a combined fortune of $108 in stamps, joking about what food they would buy for the road: oysters, pickled baby octopus, marinated artichoke hearts, and ten pounds of ginseng.

(September 1979)

US/Readers Write About . . .

Drugs

Seventh or eighth acid trip, I can't remember which, my trip-pal, Blue, was spewing a lot of crap about love being imminent and ever-present and I was starting to tune him out; the acid was starting to tune him out (I and the acid being two distinct people, maybe more), but before he dissolved I heard him say *acid is a tool*. Now that made sense. I used the tool that trip. Anyone who's done the drug knows the way you can look *into* things, enter things. The trip went on and that was the theme. *Acid is a tool.*

It was in a dorm room that the tool did its best job. A crowd of people were drinking, smoking, babbling, eating fruits and meat (not me . . . that meat was alive!). I stood back and watched them all turn into apes in the mirror across the room. Yea, I had a snout and pointed ears too. I wasn't eating or drinking. But I was sure as hell abusing the tool, using it for kicks. But what else is it for? The thought, the image got lost in the evening (somebody's car, some beer, some reefer, the night spread out, I came down on a sunny Saturday in Spring which I was too burned out to appreciate).

But I realized there was more to the drug than just the high and the kick. It took a few years to incorporate that realization into my living. Although I could see that it was wrong to waste so much time and so much of my soul and body in the narrow pursuit of *highness*, the *desire* couldn't be told to leave. But acid I eventually swore off. Too far, too long, too much. But the *desire* needed fulfilling somehow. So back to the standards: booze, pills, the drugs of our fathers and mothers. Not too many insights, but a lot of action. The trouble was that I began to lose control of the action. The pills frayed my nerves. A little pot and I'd freak: body shake, head spin. Teeth ajar, eyes all bloody, stomach torn up, legs weak, I'd reach a point where I'd say no more pills. That would work for awhile. I'd smooth out. But I'd come back. *A tool*, I'd say. I could write pretty well on speed at one time. But the *tool* quit working. Lucky for me I can throw some things away. I reach a point where I've had it and I shovel whatever it is that isn't doing its job into the shitcan. So eventually, out went the pills. Two out of three. One more to go. (Don't count marijuana in this. It's just too benign, or to me it has been; or is that another joke on myself?) *Alcohol.*

I've seen alcohol do a number on so many people. We all have. It was hard to realize that it was doing one on me. The thing about alcohol is the thing I've heard about drugs like heroin, cocaine and morphine: you come down off the high, but the drug still controls you; that is, if you're susceptible like I am. Alcohol is a liar as far as I'm concerned. It says I ain't going to hurt you, all you got to do is behave. You learned your lesson last time. You're not going to embarrass yourself any more, you're not going to alienate any more people, you're not going to wake up with that cold paranoia squatting on your chest tomorrow. THIS TIME IT'S GOING TO BE DIFFERENT.

Like I say, he's a liar. After thirteen years, I said no more. It was like kicking someone out of the house. The last time I got drunk (I don't drink if I don't get drunk) I saw the devil . . . a very nasty, very ugly person. The same guy I saw in the mirror on acid. Myself of course. It was a cold Winter night and I had finished my last beer, finished a half gallon of wine, eaten some kind of slop that drunks are famous for throwing together (one time a mixture of tomatoes, celery soup, bacon, mushroom soup, ketchup, mayonnaise, oregano, lemon juice, salad dressing, potato chips, American cheese, black-eyed peas, eggs, croutons, wine, spam, all on rice . . . it made me puke . . . the dogs wouldn't get near it); I went to the bathroom and I saw the devil.

The next thing I knew I was waking up. I remembered cussing someone over the telephone. I remembered an angry woman's voice. I remembered my best friend (at least he was until the night before) leaving as I threatened him. I jumped up and the room started spinning. I took a shower and started thinking. I said, buddy, you've reached a point of crisis. Something has got to be done. Something was done. I told the guy in me who drinks to get his shit together and get the fuck out. He got out. Every now and then he comes to the edge of the yard. I get out my blackjack and he splits. I've decided I don't like him, don't care about his feelings. . . . It wasn't easy to get him to leave, but he's gone. I feel a hell of a lot better for it.

So now, if I need to get high I smoke some pot. Blessed the gentle hemp. It's never caused me any problems.

The whole thing about drugs is this: you've got to realize what *you* can handle. Young people do it because it's a fad. Older people do it because they need it. You can't escape drugs. You don't have to. Time is the teacher. If you survive, you can learn. If you don't learn, you don't survive. I've never been one for useless pain; the problem is being able to tell when the pain is what used to be pleasure.

What's the main thing I've learned from drugs? The same thing I've learned everywhere else: stand up, be strong. Don't let anyone push you too far. Don't let anyone else control you. Once anyone or anything gets their grips on your person, do like the Dolomite: bust out their teeth, kick 'em in the ass, get 'em a night job pumping gas.

Name Withheld

□ □ □

Today would have been Einstein's 100th birthday, and the media are taking us aside to Explain What He Meant, lest our continuing bafflement (why do they assume we must be baffled?) dampen the celebration. One pathway to understanding Einstein's cosmology that the newspaper hasn't discussed is chemical alteration of consciousness. Marijuana, psilocybin, and LSD, by changing our relative viewpoint, can bring us an emotional understanding of Einsteinian truth that just isn't available in, say, high school physics. My own chemical enlightenment about special relativity took place a few years ago in Mt. Auburn Cemetery in Cambridge. Late in a Sunday of tripping (marked by reverent visits to the graves of Henry James and Margaret Fuller and a less-than-reverent wander around the tomb of Mary Baker Eddy), I leaned back against a tombstone and slipped into reverie. The acid was revealing the immense deliberations of nature — how the cirrus clouds above and the branches of the trees and the swell of the hill I sat on were not random but ordered, symmetrical in themselves and seamlessly interlocking. Clouds and trees and hills were all one entity. And I'm in it too, I thought, and so thinking I (as myself) ceased to be. I stopped being illusorily independent of the universe. Now I was the hill, the tombstone, the sky. No borderlines of body or mind. I felt the true I, heard the one note that we and all we sense are merely harmonics of. I did not disappear; I became manifest. Since that moment I've never understood how Einstein could baffle anybody. $E = mc^2$ simply means that there is one energy that is everything. "All graceful," as the Grateful Dead once sang.

Name Withheld

(July 1979)

David Spangler says there are some advantages to being known as a spiritual teacher. "It doesn't get me cheaper fares on airlines or an honorary ticket to the Superbowl . . . but it does give masters of ceremony at conferences something to say about me."

Since the age of twenty-one, Spangler, who is now thirty-six, has been lecturing on spiritual growth and the birth of a new age. From 1970 to 1973 he was co-director of the Findhorn community in Northern Scotland, famous for its forty-pound cabbages. Spangler had a lot to do with leading Findhorn beyond the garden and into the community it is today. During the time he was there, it expanded from twenty-four to 170 members — in his words, "a working organism seeking to accomplish what no human group has yet accomplished in the history of mankind."

Author of Revelation: Birth Of A New Age, The Laws of Manifestation, Towards A Planetary Vision, *and* Reflections On The Christ, *Spangler, since childhood, has been able to enter an altered state of consciousness ("going upstairs," he calls it) and draw information from non-physical beings. The power of Spangler's writing and thinking derives, in part, from these experiences. "Having been born with this ability," he says, "I can claim no particular merit for it; it is simply part of my life, like seeing and hearing . . . though having it has meant needing to learn how to live with it and use it properly."*

Born in Ohio, Spangler spent most of his childhood in Morocco. He returned to the U.S. at the age of twelve, lived in Massachusetts and studied genetics at Arizona State University. Right now, he's working with the University of Wisconsin in Milwaukee, teaching and designing courses about spiritual transformation. The Lorian Association, which he founded, is also active in creating a network of educational programs focusing on spiritual growth.

These remarks are excerpted from a talk Spangler gave at a spiritual healing conference in Leicester, North Carolina.

— Ed.

Something Does Push The River

David Spangler

It's interesting that, in our culture, the Christian pattern is the dominant one, and yet when we reach out to build a new culture, it's often the last place that we look. I can readily understand why that's so, given the experiences that many of us may have gone through with institutionalized religion. Also, when we're reaching out to discover our own thresholds and our own new dimensions of growth, it's good to break away from the familiar. Having done that, it's useful to come back and take a second or third look at the Christian tradition, and today I will be looking at a particular aspect of it.

Christianity is based on the idea that God took flesh, that divinity incarnated as a human being. This has caused endless controversy and problems for the Christian Church —

Letting it all hang out in a personal way is not necessarily the same as providing a nourishing diet, and is sort of the inner McDonald's.

the argument over the two natures of Jesus. Was he a man? Was he a God? Was he both? If he was a God and just simply took on the form of flesh, and went through the psychodrama amongst us, then in some way he doesn't really participate in our humanness. Where is the connection, then, that is needed for redemption to take place? On the other hand, if he was a man, how could he participate in the divine estate? What Christianity ended up with was this doctrine of the two natures, man and God, sort of a cosmic amphibian. He is somehow both, thereby providing a bridge between two otherwise separate estates: the human condition of being a creature, created, and the divine condition of being the creator, the one source. The reason that many of my Christian friends don't consider me a Christian is that while I say God did incarnate in Jesus and Jesus was divine, I say that's true for all the rest of us as well, that's true for all life — which is a very pagan point of view, pagan in the best sense of the word, in terms of the ancient, mystery religions that saw a divine spirit resident in all things.

Here I am, in a body. The fact that I have been born does not necessarily mean I have incarnated in any meaningful sense. I could go through my life as a blank, perfectly embodied — which is what incarnation means, to take flesh, to take body — but not interacting with the world in a definitive fashion. The movie "Being There" is a story of a wonderful fellow named Chauncey Gardner, who in some ways is not incarnated. He has grown up watching television, he has lived inside a house all his life, and he's in his fifties when he gets kicked out. He is the archetype of the totally passive individual. Anyone can see anything they want in him. As he goes out into the world he becomes acclaimed as a wise person, because people see reflected in him what they want to see. He is such a total blank that other people take their incarnation through him. Chauncey Gardner is like a living mirror. He has no will of his own, he is not active in his world, and for that matter, he is not reactive, but totally neutral.

For me, to incarnate means that I take on a body, not just of flesh, but a body of purpose, of relationship, of thought, of will and awareness, a body of interaction and community with the life around me. Another way of saying that is that I can't really incarnate myself only as myself. Incarnation doesn't happen in a vacuum. I only begin truly to incarnate when I become part of our whole incarnation. I begin to work to incarnate others and I'm open to their incarnating me. That is the process of relationship. By relating with you I am assisting you to become what you are. By your relating to me, you are assisting me to become what I am, part of a web of life, a network. That is what is incarnating: the entirety, the wholeness. My ability to incarnate runs through my capacity to work in consciousness with that whole, that community, however restrictive that may be for me.

Back in the Sixties, it became a catch phrase to say, "Let's go with the flow, let's surrender to the process." And the image that was often used was that of the river. The river just sort of does its thing, goes from the mountains down to the ocean. Nobody has to get out there and push the river. But, like all analogies, it's somewhat limited. It suggests to us an image of passivity, when in point of fact, that's not the way it is. The river is a very dynamic system. It's part of a whole cycle of water upon the earth, rain, evaporation. Something does push the river. The river gets pushed and pulled and tugged by various forces. The river meanders, and there are many alternate routes that it could take. Sometimes it takes all of them — we call that a swamp, or a delta. In the dynamics of our life, we are involved with both being part of a process — an unfolding process, if we wish to see it that way, a flow — and we are involved with choice and the act of will, which is also part of that flow. We are presented with the need to make choices; we cannot encompass everything. Even saying, "I will not make a choice, I will just go where it takes me," is a choice. It is much better to make that choice deliberately and to say, "Right, I am deliberately going to go where it takes me and I do this with consciousness, with conscious acceptance of where it takes me." In order to have the privilege of coming here I had to make a choice. There are things that you are not doing in order to be here, there are sacrifices you've made. You may not see them as such, you may make them willingly, but they are sacrifices nonetheless.

There is always consequence. There is always the result of our action, and those results become our body. The consequences of our choices are our body. We explore the body that we are creating in order that we can become more incarnate within it, more at home within. Incarnation is a dynamic process of will and spirit and responsibility and choice-making, and of response to others, of participation in the community of life. The extent to which I am incarnated is the measure of the extent to which that spirit and that involvement is actually present in my life. In the image of the Christ, we say that God incarnated in human form, and in the sense that I'm speaking of it, that does not mean only that God took on a human body. We could say God always takes on a human body and all other bodies as well. We say that through the incarnation a divine will, a divine consciousness, accepted the consequences of creation and became part of that, and participated deliberately and with involvement in the human community.

For me or you to incarnate divinity is a similar process. In what way can I make my involvement in life, my relationships, my participation, my community, a reflection of, a connection with, an embodiment of what I consider to be divinity? What is this divinity? The question really cannot be answered, if by "answer" we mean some final kind of definition. But I would suggest that one element of this divinity is our capacity to embody infinity. What does that mean? Consider for a moment, as I am rambling on up here, an angel appears in back of me and I begin to wonder why you all suddenly start staring at me with rapture. Is it the brilliance of my presentation? Is it my good looks? And I turn around and see the angel. Crestfallen, I ask this being, "Why have you interrupted my talk? I thought angels had a sense of timing." And it says, "Well, the time is up, and it wasn't that good a talk anyway. I'm Gabriel and here's my flugelhorn. Now is the moment when infinity breaks upon the Earth." I never thought it would happen at a conference in North Carolina. "Now, what we're going to do, ladies and gentlemen, is file up before me and offer me one day of your life, and on the basis of that day, you will be given your heavenly assignment. This is where you will find your niche for eternity, based on what you did and expressed on that day." Gosh, Gabe, couldn't we have at least two days?

The problem immediately becomes evident. What day would I pick out of my life that expresses me? I don't know. I don't really have a day that does that. Each day I discover something new about myself. Some days it makes me very happy, other days I wish I hadn't gotten up. Each day offers an opportunity to express something new. We need many days just to begin to approach the fullness of what we are as human beings, as personalities, much less as divinity. The problem becomes insurmountable if I attempt to tackle it only in a finite way. Hence, the desire for immortality. There are just not enough days for me to express all that I can be, so let me have all the days there are and then some more, let the days never stop. But I can look at it another way and say, suppose we pool all our days. Suppose we each take the best day we can think of and we put them all together and we come up with a universal day that is the conglomeration of all of us. Even that might not be wholly suitable, but it would come closer to saying something about who and what we are. I would like to learn to paint, but I have yet to learn how to draw a straight line. But undoubtedly someone of you is a fine painter. So I have one of your days, when you have painted like you never painted before, and in your day I become the painter that I would like to be. Perhaps one of you is a fine singer, or a scientist, or a mother or father. Perhaps two of you have discovered a profound beauty in human lovingness. We have so much that we can share in our great days and moments that by myself I'd need more than a lifetime to experience. I don't need immortality, what I need is community and the ability to share deeply and the ability to discover an identity capable of participating in that sharing. So here we are, blending our days, and we've outfoxed good old Gabe and he's going to have to give us all of heaven to express in. And if we reach out to all humanity, we're going to come out with an awful lot of different days, some of which are not very pleasant but are still part of the human experience of the moment.

So, incarnation is a shared process, and for me to incarnate divinity, I want to incarnate that sharing, so that we aren't a bunch of little separate lives struggling for infinity, but we are a shared life in which infinity becomes visible because we're sharing our finiteness and through that sharing creating a space through which great potential can emerge. And, as I said before, that doesn't have to stop with humanity. What is a day in the life of a great tree like? Or a day in the life of a dolphin, or a day in the life of an ant? Then we get into wholly different perspectives.

If we imagine all the days that ever were and all the perspectives that ever could be, and days yet to come, and lump them together into one view, we would begin to have a shadow of what divinity is like. Yet, that great consciousness is that participation of all these others. It is incarnating itself. We are part of that process. So, on the most simple level, to incarnate divinity becomes an exercise in relationship, an exercise in how to expand relationship along many dimensions, not just three, not just human or social. Love, openness, defenselessness, sharing, these are the tools we use and the qualities that help us to expand those relationships.

Which brings me to the communion. The image of the Last Supper, when Jesus says here is my body and here is my blood, here is the bread and the wine, in this symbolic act of the communion — to me Jesus is saying, here is the essence of incarnation, here is how divinity becomes flesh, by sharing itself. He was saying, here is my vital substance, here is what makes me what I am, as symbolized by body, form, the flesh, and the blood or the spirit, the life-giving essence that flows through us. The mystical body of Christ is the body of divinity, it's the body of life itself. In my particular approach to this, Jesus is saying not just partake of my being, but he is saying, here is the formula for incarnation, for partaking of divinity by realizing divinity in our earthly life. And that is, put colloquially, to nibble on each other, to be able to share our substance and essence. Now, our substance can take many forms. It can be tangible substance, possessions, clothing, finances or what have you. It can be emotional and mental substance. But the point is that we are all nourishing each other and we are nourishing our world, or at least we should be. That is a key.

As we develop in the whole sphere of our being, we provide nourishment, substance, energy, vitality that enriches the world about us, or at least so we hope. Communion represents the act of deep and profound sharing, a sharing of identity. You may be what I am, I open my identity to you, and I would like to partake of your identity. This can be a very scary process, because we all have, or think we have, parts of ourselves that we really wouldn't wish anyone to partake of, and we might not be all that willing to partake of some of the juicier aspects of someone else. Back when the human potential movement and encounter groups began to develop, it was a kind of humanistic communion, a sharing of feeling, of being defenseless and vulnerable to each other. One of the people at that time defined communication as the art of sharing vulnerabilities. I've always liked that definition. On the other hand, letting it all hang out in a purely personal way is not necessarily the same thing as providing a nourishing diet, and is sort of the inner McDonald's. In fact, I had friends who got very involved in the human potential movement, for whom sharing became a fast-food process and they had their ready-made encounter group personas which they could warm up in their inner microwaves and dish out on a moment's notice. They became consummate actors. But the kind of sharing that I have in mind is a bit deeper.

Identity is two things. We think of it in terms of content. Here are all the things that make me up. Here's my list of experiences and memories, the things I own, the things I do, the content of my mind, which I trundle forth upon inquiry in order to define myself. Some of us have short lists, some have very long lists. Behind that is the context that helps to organize it. Sometimes that context is very subtle and hard to get our hands on. What are the organizing principles of our life and our identity? Why is certain content selected and other discarded as being unimportant to our make-up, our definition of who we are? And even perhaps deeper than that is what I call the will. The will to me is not just force — I will do it — and action, but it's something more related to being. When I get right down to it, I will do most effortlessly that which I am, and the most powerful will in the world is the will of what is.

What is the energy that makes me what I am? That energy is what links me in participation with the co-creative processes of my world. What I am is a point of creation, the creation process, continually fashioning itself. Now, that's the substance and nourishment I want to share. To say, "Here's what I did when I was ten and eleven, and here's my job, and here are pictures of my children" — all that may be very wonderful, and it's the grease in human interaction, the wonderful small talk that lubricates things until we can get our gears to mesh in deeper sharing. But that sharing of identity is not the same as communion. It's just the hors d'oeuvres.

At some level of our being, we are convinced we are divine. We know that whatever Jesus did, we could do it as well, probably better. That's what he said, we could do it better. That was a very beautiful thing to say, evoking the promise of eternal evolution. But how often do we allow that to surface? Sometimes when it does surface we don't know what to do with it and it becomes pathological, because we don't know how to integrate it into our daily life. What in heaven's name would a God be doing working in this factory or doing these dishes? What is a God doing in the midst of all this trivia?

In God's perspective, nothing is insignificant. Consider the time frame of a blade of grass and its growth. It is filled with all the drama and power that our lives are filled with, just expressed differently. In *The Once and Future King*, Merlin is training Arthur to become king, and he does so by transforming Arthur into various forms — fish, bird — so he can experience what life is like as an animal, as another form of being. All of us have had that experience too. We may not remember, but it's there. We share it with the life around us, if we can pause for a moment and be sensitive enough to entertain a perspective different from the human. We glorify nature, we romanticize it, but we don't actually participate in it. We go out into it and say, "Gee, it's wonderful, it's lovely, it makes me feel good." But to actually get into nature, touching some things that aren't groovy at all by our standards, that are very strange, not human, alien in some respects, and to try to think like a tree, a rock, a river, is not an anthropomorphic exercise.

A very close friend of mine went through a period when she became convinced she was the bride of God, and was to give birth to the Second Coming, which would not be a physical birth, but a birth in her. Then she would become the Second Coming. Under normal circumstances, she would be trotted right off to the local place where Second Comings are assisted in their mission without overly disrupting society. But she wasn't that way all the time, and she had a long involvement with metaphysical studies and had some clue as to what was happening to her. And more importantly, her family, her children, and her sisters also realized that she wasn't going round the bend, but rather touching a very deep wellspring which her personality was having great difficulty integrating. So they performed something like a vision quest, a dance, in which they didn't exactly confirm her in a delusion, but they sought to take her starting point — "I am the bride of God" — and to help her draw it out and work with it so she could incarnate it as a personality. One of the things they did was to go through a ritualistic pattern that lasted all night; they celebrated a marriage, a birth. At times the children would take roles that they thought were important and at other times she would give them roles. "You will now be the Holy Spirit, or you will be this angel," and so on. In this particular case, they weren't trying to humor her, they were literally trying to take on and to objectify the principles and powers that she was experiencing in order to get them out of her head and into her environment, so they could dance with them together and anchor that power a bit. Well, that helped a great deal, and over a period of time, the whole process became a very transforming one. But she could not have done it without the help of her family or someone who could help her balance that out and not be pulled into it.

The emergence of our divinity is something that requires all of us. We all need to participate in it. It's not something I can do only on my own. I can touch my divinity and you can touch yours, but to actually incarnate it is a community process.

In the Zen tradition there is a beautiful set of paintings, the Ox-Herder. The story is of an ox-herder who seeks enlightenment, has various adventures, becomes enlightened, and returns to being an ox-herder. The first picture and the last picture are identical. At the end of the quest he is back where he started. From an outer viewpoint there is no difference. From an inner viewpoint, they are worlds apart.

We may find that the incarnation of divinity in a world of everyday trivia is not all that much different in appearance — though in some cases it might be — from what we now experience. We still have to relate to each other, we have to relate to people who are different than we are, who don't always share our perspectives, and shouldn't share our perspectives. We have to relate to form, process, pain, hope and struggle. It's just that we relate to them differently, and we help each other relate to them differently. The process of incarnating divinity as a community project transforms the world in a very deep way by transforming our ability to nourish each other. At the very least, it helps us dispense with a number of things we now use to indirectly nourish each other or to grab nourishment from each other when we think we're not going to get it, and that would ease things a lot, just getting rid of some of those games. But the everyday drama of living on this physical earth will remain one of always seeking to honor the finite as a gateway to the infinite, and to work with limits, those limits that are necessary at any given moment to provide the next step for the infinite.

Redemption follows from that. Jesus the Christ is considered in Christianity as the saviour of humanity. This is the third element necessary to being a true Christian: to accept the Christ as a saviour, to see in the crucifixion-resurrection process some kind of redemptive act. Creation is an ongoing process. And evil — that's what we're being redeemed from, by the way, evil, and its effect upon us — is simply the unfinished business of creation.

There is an unintegrated stuff in our world, and that stuff is the source of power if we want to tap it and utilize it. I can work out of positions of unintegration as easily as out of positions of integration, maybe more easily, because the power may be more accessible in some ways in a state of chaos than it is in a state of order. This is not always the case, though. There is unintegrated material, and it needs to be taken on. In a personal way, I have it in my own life, things that I have not yet quite dealt with in order to be a whole being — my jagged edges. And occasionally they catch on things in my life, and I get hooked or bruised or turned around, or somebody gets cut from one of my jagged edges, or I get cut from one of theirs. Some of these edges, some of this jaggedness, I'm not going to be able to integrate all by myself. Others need to help me and vice versa. There are some places that itch that are very difficult to scratch, so I look for someone else to scratch them. There are some places where I hurt that I can't quite get a hold of. Someone else may be able to, in an act of love, forgiveness or understanding, or just a neutral act of saying, "Yeah, I see that you hurt there and this is how I see it. I have no judgment about it one way or another, but acknowledge it and affirm your ability to deal with and heal it." I may find that inaccessible place has suddenly become accessible. In a sense, the Christ represents the big scratch, the fingers that can reach just about anywhere. He said, I forgive the world. Wherever it hurts in there that you can't get to, I can get to it and I've already forgiven it. I have already acknowledged it. I am a healing process at work, so work with me.

There is this little cartoon — you can get it on tee-shirts — that says, "Have patience with me, God is not finished with me yet." That being the case, we are in a process of struggle to learn how to come together in new ways, in appropriate ways that do honor to us as individuals, to us as a group, as a species, and to our world life as a whole. And the energy that we bring into that struggle, that process, that communion, is a redemptive energy. We are redeeming ourselves from stopping in the process, from becoming caught in our own non-integration. We don't have to think of it in terms of sin or not sin, unless we choose to. We can think of it in terms of realizing that we are an unfinished project and that evil in one way comes out of our unfinishedness, and evil might be perceived as the attempt to pass off that which is unfinished as a finished thing. Perhaps the great tragedy of evil is its cheapness. It cheapens everything, by passing off what is incomplete in the name of what is perfect.

Part of our challenge is that we have an abundance of images about the Christ — historical, religious, philosophical. Sometimes you just have to let all these images go for a time, because in confronting the Christ within myself — each of us does this — we are confronting our divinity, and it is the most intimate and sacred confrontation. It is unique. It has not happened to anyone else the way it happens to us, nor will it happen to anyone else again the way it happens to us, nor is it a one-time happening. All teachings, everything I learn and study, the benefits I receive from great teachers will only bring me to a point and at that point I have to step off into my own abyss, into my own faith. There is a point beyond which no teacher, no teaching, no guidelines, can really tell us what it's going to be like or what's there. We need to discover that for ourselves.

In Ursula Leguin's *Earthsea Trilogy*, the magician is saying, "An act is not as young men think, like a rock that one picks up, and it hits or misses and that's the end of it. When that rock is lifted, the earth is lighter, the hand that bears it, heavier, and when it is thrown, the circuits of the stars respond, and where it strikes or falls, the universe is changed." All forms of magic, or spiritual endeavor, or living endeavor have that quality. We are part of an unbreakable and unbroken system. So when I come to that edge, the universe comes there with me, and when I step over, everything steps over with me, and I step over into everything.

That edge is in our minds. It could be called the edge of growth, because when I grow, change, take on a process of transformation, however modest it may be, I'm really undertaking a very courageous act. In its pure nakedness, I am saying, I will now be different, and because of that difference I accept the possibility that the universe will be different, particularly the universe that interrelates with me. To shield myself from that nakedness and what it represents, I may surround growth with a lot of support structures and jargon, but it does come down to the fact that I am changing reality. In that process I will be changed and I may find myself in a world that is unfamiliar to me when I look at it through the eyes of yesterday.

I work for the University of Wisconsin in Milwaukee, where we are trying to develop a series of courses that reflect New Age themes — spiritual, transformational themes. One of the courses we just completed was called "A University for the Future," which was a critique of the existing university system, in an attempt to revise it. What would a New Age university be like? And how to go about creating it? Time and again, it was brought up how modern education tends to stifle, to confine people. One person brought up the idea of the hidden curriculum: you go to school, but what you really learn is obedience, punctuality and respect for authority. There is another way of looking at that, which is that we all gather together in a sort of unspoken conspiracy to make growth non-threatening. Education is a doorway to growth, or it can be. All these data, new relationships, new insights come to us, and conceivably can shatter what we have previously believed or accepted. Education can be very frightening. But we conspire to make it less scary, by saying, "Let's learn things, but let's not change too much, let's establish some limits." Perhaps the first stage toward a New Age education would be to confront that feeling directly, and ask, "Am I willing to go whole hog with the potentials of education, to accept the consequences of radical transformation if that's where it leads to? Am I willing to bear the pain of discontinuity with the familiar for however long I may need to bear that?"

The Christ, on a personal level, is that force which brings us to the edge and then steps over with us, in order that a profound continuity may be maintained, in order that the bonds of love and communion are not shattered by the appearances of growth, and also to have the courage to take those steps, to risk that. The edge is in our minds, and is really the confrontation with our fear of growth, our fear of change. Everyone does it with me and I do it with everyone else. I realize that I am growing, not only for my own sake, but I am the Earth, the spirit of the whole moving forward. When I feel that I grow for myself — this is *my* growth, in much the same way that this is *my* college education or *my* car — it is a more scary proposition.

That edge is much more personal. I am growing in order more largely to share a process that is the growth of all things. I need to grow in the same way that plants need to grow, that leaves come out in the Spring, that rivers flow to the ocean, that winds circulate about the Earth. To explore the seasons of my humanness, to see where my roots and sprouts will go, is part of a great ecology of growth, of unfoldment, of life. It expands our awareness, gives us a new context in which we can see the processes.

Sometimes we embark on a venture, like starting a community or a spiritual project, and it fails. The form does not coalesce properly, and disperses, so we say it fails. But out of that process can come very deep knowledge and experience that will reweave itself into future forms that will not fail. It's a matter of perspective.

My physical body in my mother's womb goes through a process of recapitulating many earlier forms. They appear and reform and appear and reform until my human shape develops, and I don't think anything of it there in my mother's womb. In the womb of society, of a larger life, similar things are happening. We recapitulate earlier stages of consciousness. I've seen this in most groups and can't think offhand of an exception. The evolution of individuals is often more advanced than that of the groups that they form, so they come together to form a community and immediately they're at a quite different level of group expression. They begin recapitulating human history in one way or another, sometimes very fast, sometimes more slowly. Different phases of human government, different phases of human relationship. Groups have their embryology as well. We realize that a particular stage or form may come into existence briefly only because it's a step toward what is actually trying to emerge, and when it dissolves, it is not that anything has failed, it is that the process is working. I feel very fortunate the fish stage of my embryological development failed. Of course, I did get trapped at the human stage, but that's the way it goes.

This process of forming and reforming, dissolving, dying and rebirth, of going back and forth over these edges, is very much a collective one, and we struggle to form together the kind of collective that would represent our values and vision for a new world. Because it's collective I can't assume that the success or failure of my growth and my efforts are wholly and totally my own responsibility. That's not quite the world I want, but — all roads don't lead to David.

Sometimes things that I would like to bring into being, parts of myself that I would like to touch, may be in timing for me as a person but are not in timing for me as a collective person. So, that's partly what I mean by not being able to cross this edge just by myself. In crossing it I may take a step that has very little to do with my own growth, but has to do with the growth of someone around me. I call it the spirit of the Christ that coordinates all that, enables it to happen. It is that spirit that says to me, "I am this personal divinity within you, but I am also a universal spirit. I act that you may grow, for your well-being, but also for the well-being of all that is." This doesn't mean that I necessarily have to do an inventory of everyone around me whenever I choose to make a growth step, but it does mean that I have a perspective that my growth is in a context. I might say, I'd be so much farther along if it weren't for so-and-so whom I have to deal with, and I'm just being held up because of him or her. But sometimes being held up is the best thing that could happen to us, in order maybe to look more deeply into our process and be more fully in touch with it.

All of us have our rough times, our moments when we think, "I don't want to get up this morning." Sometimes those moments are not when something horrendous is happening, but it's the weight of trivia, of the familiar, that is just too much. It is at that moment that we draw on that resource, when we say, "I'll just take one step in front of me." That's being heroic. And we are heroic. It's that power that lets us do that, when we don't want to get out of bed but we do. It's what underlies that power that we share with each other when we talk about, "Here is my body, here is my blood."

It is said that one of the persistent images in many of the great religions is that of sacrifice: the Buddha renouncing all of the treasures of the world in order to achieve enlightenment, Jesus sacrificing his life, Osiris being ripped to shreds in order to be reformed, Orpheus descending into the depths in order to be reformed. This is a powerful image in which a greater life gives itself in order to provide energy, vitality, nourishment to lesser lives who are struggling with inertia, finiteness, form. So in communion, we participate in that. We say, like Osiris, Orpheus, Buddha, Jesus, "I renounce, I surrender. Rip me apart, eat of me, get energy and let's do it. Be nourished that we can go on, and let me be nourished by you." In redemption, that is also a collective experience in which we take on the unintegrated matter of our lives and we work, integrate it, form it, heal it. All of this requires our mutual power and our ability to generate that mutual power, to be mutual. The personal Christ is our ability to touch those qualities in us, as noble or as mundane as they may be, that at any given moment we can rise to the occasion and do what's necessary to preserve or express our human community.

Which leads on to the image of planetary healing and the avatar event. I have a little challenge talking about the Christ simply because I don't like to give an impression of exclusivity. The Christ to me is an avatar, or a divine incarnation, a divine expression. There are many other avatars. What we are dealing with is a great planetary event, in which we are trying to touch and become aware of and expressive of our wholeness, our inheritance, our remembrance that we are princes and princesses of the kingdom.

There was a wonderful book written years ago called *Flatland*, about the adventures of the beings in a two-dimensional world. The hero of *Flatland* is a square, who has a dream in which he is visited by a three-dimensional being, and has great difficulty trying to grasp the third dimension of depth. But eventually he does, and goes out to proclaim to the world the existence of the third dimension and ends up being committed to a mental institution. Consider for a moment what the interaction of a three-dimensional being with a two-dimensional world — say, a table — would be like. Imagine I have a basketball and I pass the ball through the plane. At any given moment the inhabitants of that plane are going to experience that ball as a plane. They are not going to see its depth, just its surface, and what they're going to see is not a ball but a series of different events. You slice the tip of the ball and it's just little, and then you slice in the middle and get the whole diameter, and then it starts getting smaller again. So you get this bell-shaped curve of an event. They would experience a basketball in terms of duration, as a process, but we would experience it as just a ball. Trying to communicate that to somebody living in this two-dimensional place would be difficult. They would tend to see the ball as history.

Well, that's what I feel about the Christ. The Christ is the manifestation of a basketball passing through the table of our universe. It's a multi-dimensional event which we are trying to grasp four-dimensionally. We would see it as history, as a succession of events. Which means that the event is still happening. It is not *in* history, it is history, it is still happening. We are in the midst of it at this moment. I don't know just where we are along the basketball.

I think of all the great prophets, spiritual leaders and avatars. Quite a bit of conflict tends to develop around them all and around different spiritual teachings. Different groups happen to be active in experiencing the event when their bit of the table interacted with it. Naturally that's going to seem the most real and powerful aspect of that event. To a person in Mecca in the fifth or sixth century A.D., talking to Mohammed is going to seem a lot more real than listening to somebody tell about someone named Jesus who lived five hundred years before. And it is a logical assumption to say, this is the reality and what comes after will be the reflection, and what came before was preparation. As this polydimensional basketball dribbles its way through our universe, we keep encountering the real thing over and over again, to which everything else is preparation and everything following is consequence. We may miss the point of view that is is really all one thing, it is one event. Part of that event could be described as the incarnation of spirit within our world, our world going through a process of birth or of incarnation, a consciousness coming to birth within our planet, our world-soul becoming more integrated, and a process of spirit interacting with the world just like our own soul interacts with us, to draw all our scattered parts together in a process of remembrance, to where we become whole.

Perhaps the point which we are reaching is where we approach the diameter of this basketball — obviously my metaphor may begin to break down here — but let us say we approach the point at which the avatar event becomes a collective event as it has never been before. We are talking about planetary healing, the incarnation of wholeness within our world, where humanity is not separate from itself, nor from nature. All our dreams and visions of the future that somewhere in our hearts we know will happen are going to happen. It is happening now, because it is the basketball. The new age, or the golden age, or utopian age, is the same as the avatar event. In the past, culture has not been able to embody it. People have been able to embody it; collectives have not been able to embody it, except in small degrees. We do not have civilizations that express the Buddha nature. We have civilizations that believe in Christ, in Buddha, that practice Christianity or Buddhism, but not civilizations that are the Christ, that are the Buddha. But it is such a civilization that has always been trying to emerge — it is the human civilization. At some point it must become a collective process.

How do we heal our planet, give birth to this planetary culture? I believe the first step is a recognition of this avatar event and that it embraces us, that we are now that event. We have great teachers that come to us, who have the luxury, the ability, because they are only dealing with themselves, to bring it to a clear focus, to catalyze it, to keep reminding us. But how can I look into myself and say I am divine? That may be a particularly Western problem, the struggle with the identity of divinity. How can we say, "I am one with the Earth, I am one with the stars"? How can we look at each other and say, "I want you to know I am the Christ, the Buddha, the Earth, and I take responsibility for that, so I will seek to act out of that reality?" And you say, "I accept that, and I am the Christ, I am the Buddha, the Earth, and I take responsibility for that. Let's live out our fantasies." To share on that deep level is something we need to learn. But the sharing is not in words. Nature provides the perfect example of it. A tree does not say, "I'm divine, so here's some color, some shade, some food." Just, "I am a tree." A tree may do this, from our point of view, unself-consciously. Our challenge is to learn to do it self-consciously. I love myself, and I offer myself to you as nourishing food.

I am an optimistic and upbeat person. It is not that I do not see that in pursuing the avatar event we are confronting a whole history of fears which can generate stress, but that is not the operative reality. What we've been engaging in this weekend is the reality. It is customary at many of these conferences to come to get one's batteries recharged. We also come to do a piece of work and to be co-workers. It is nice to have our fellowship and be affirmed, but we are workers and we come because here we get a taste of the collective we are trying to create, and hopefully to evolve enough momentum to let us go out and see it and evoke it out of our world. It is useful to remember that the great representatives of the avatar event have always worked in the world. And they are infinitely accessible and very human.

So, if we are taking on the avatar event, our tendency is to say, as a person, I really would like to come together with others who share this event with me, and live somewhere where we can pursue it. But as a collective consciousness, we work in the world. The world is our marketplace, not just the Western world, but the whole world.

Sometimes people in the most unlikely places, for a shining moment in their lives, become outposts of the avatar event without even knowing it. It can become a game to look for that, to look in the shadowed corners and say, is there an avatar lurking in there? At the next desk, in that church down the street? How we work out our relationship to this is something that each of us needs to do, but my contribution is simply to say that there is a planetary process of healing going on and it places an extraordinary demand on us to learn to see ourselves as part of a collective event, a polydimensional event which in order to make itself known on our level has to become collective. If we truly want to celebrate the avatar event, we end up celebrating the spirit in all of us.

(August 1980)

US/Readers Write About . . .

Growing Older

"Getting older" — an evocative notion as full of resonances as some great bell struck just once. As it fades, it changes, becomes subtler, less deafening, and its components of sound emerge a little at a time until, just as I am about to congratulate myself that I "understand" each molecule of this melody there is . . . silence.

Among my molecules:

— At forty-two, as the teeth lengthen, the bottom sags, and the white hairs multiply, I recognize a little what I did not know when I was younger, namely, that what makes aging a pleasant process is that it is richer. Not that events are very different or the intellectual shenanigans less varied or the emotions less interesting, but there is a richer context in which to fit it all. Success is not quite so successful nor devastation quite so devastating when it has been lived a few times. Not-understanding seems to take on a good deal of the lustre once exclusively reserved for understanding. The need for beliefs-judgments-opinions-etc. slips slowly-slowly away (they're possible, yes, but not really necessary) and life becomes more . . . "interesting" is the best word I can think of. "Love" and "freedom" are real things that cannot, thank God, be named.

— A couple of weeks back, an Indian who was selling his astro-logical appreciations said I would live to be "eighty-three or eighty-five." That's nice. Whether it's true or not, I don't know. That's nice too.

— The Japanese have a character to designate "death" which

can be translated as "speaking the truth from another place." Always liked that.

— Am I afraid of death? Only to the extent that I am afraid of life, which is plenty sometimes.

— As this body decays, there seems to be a growing (concomitant?) sense of some entirely lively entity within, an entity unchanged from milk-and-crackers in the first grade through lumberjacking, Popsicle packing, book publishing, news reporting, sexual encounters, spiritual exercises, loving and angry relations, laughter until the tears came and vice versa, and on and on until right this minute. When I was younger, I thought references to this entity were the mere mutterings of those who were afraid of death, afraid to see things clearly. I still think belief systems are counterproductive in the long run but they are a good place to begin. For me, this "entity" is not just wishful thinking, but it is impossible to name. My experience is that it is incapable of piety or misdeed, intellectual or emotional acrobatics, yet it informs all things. Or as one fellow put it, "When you can't say it, it's there; when you don't say it, it's not there." It is, perhaps, just a sense of my life's life. That sense is the same one which can cause the aging to resent youth's exuberance and grumble with (was it?) Churchill, "Youth is wasted on the young." To which it is not difficult to reply, "If that is so, age must be wasted on the aging."

— Who was there in my youth to help me identify with this nameless life? No one. Everyone. So now I will take responsibility for this time and place myself, do my best to experience the integration with what-is and what-is-not, set aside heroes and villains, and find the joker in the deck, the one who is everywhere at home, yet claims no home itself . . . express my own life's life and see it as it is . . . graying hair, added weight, sunshine on my bare feet, death as possible and exciting as birth. These are fine and easy things to write and think, but they are not so easy for me to do. Can I do them? Don't be ridiculous!

Adam Fisher
New York, New York

(*January 1983*)

Roger Sauls

The Weather This Morning

The weather this morning makes me think
I've wakened in one of those countries
where the women are seen
walking out of a cloud of blackbirds
carrying apronsful of geese:
the women are heartless,
the necks of the geese sway like tulips.

The point is:
it's fine weather for slaughter
not so much because it's cold
but because all I can see
is snow, snow that's fattened
the valley's hungriest fields.

The clouds are showing up now,
one by one, like the curious
at a public spectacle.
I think of my uncle, lame,
who dragged one leg behind him
in perpetual hesitation,
facing off the stares of bystanders
as he hurdled grotesquely
through knee-deep snow.

The ability to remain unmoved
by the most commonplace cruelty —
that's what weather teaches.
You know how on some mornings
snow will spread beyond
its own comprehension,
how it remains blameless, hushed,
its depth
simply an aspect of repose.

Advent

Month of slate gray skies
& the religious promise
of snow. Every morning
we wake to a world
drained of color, both of us
a little older,
a little less comfortable
with the view of hills
assembled beyond the window
like an old man's knuckles.

Our breath clears a space
in the frost. Together,
we watch as Autumn
wears to a thin edge.
For weeks we've cleared
the wide fields, cut back
frail limbs on the fruit trees.
Bramley apples, Portugal quinces
all gathered & darkening now
in the cellar, piled in wicker
baskets, each one a province
spared from the season's hardness.
A little light elbows
its way through

the peeling limbs
of the sycamore, blackbirds
fret the powerlines.
It's cold. The days are short,
close to the bone.
It's become a question
of our hold on things.
We could rise up like plainsong
through the hayfields
in the last frayed hours of daylight.
We know that weather itself
is a form of worship.

(February 1980)

If the high priests of American society are its white-robed doctors, with their seeming power of life and death over the rest of us, Dr. Irving Oyle is a renegade urging us to reclaim our power, to take responsibility for our own health.

"Don't put me in the spook section," Dr. Oyle says. "I'm just a family doctor turned medical researcher trying to find out what it is that gets people well — and approaching the job with an open mind."

Dr. Oyle's books include: The Healing Mind; Time, Space and Mind; *and, most recently,* The New American Medicine Show. *He earned his doctor of osteopathy degree in 1953 at the age of twenty-eight, and for the next fifteen years had a private practice in New York City.*

In 1966, he went to Mexico, to run a clinic for the Tarahumara Indians. Then, returning to New York, he set up a clinic on the city's Lower East Side for Puerto Rican and black children. He now lives in Mendocino, California, and is a teaching associate at the University of California, Santa Cruz Extension.

For the last ten years, he has investigated different models of reality and consciousness, exploring their application to health. Disease doesn't "happen" to us, he suggests, nor does health. Our power to heal ourselves is greater than we've been led to believe.

What follows are excerpts from a talk Dr. Oyle gave in Asheville, North Carolina at a conference on education and health.

— Ed.

A Medical Doctor Diagnoses Reality

Dr. Irving Oyle

There's an old Buddhist story about the teacher who holds up the staff and says, "Look, if you understand this, you understand everything." If I were to take a holographic picture and cut it into a million little pieces, and shine a light through each, each one of those pieces would show you the whole thing. Now that totally changes our concept of reality. What about you, the guy who's looking at that? What they're saying now is that all that is in *you.*

Your brain, which we're just now beginning to understand, is between five and fifteen million years old, according to the latest theories. And if you want to take a computer analogy, the fastest computer that we have on the outside, which will tell me what seat my Uncle Louis is sitting in when he flies from London to Zurich on

TWA, has about fifteen million bits. A bit is a point of light that is either on or off, and by the arrangement of the ons and offs it carries all this information. Does anybody have any idea how many bits or cells your brain has that are on or off? Twenty *billion*. You have in your head at this minute a twenty billion-bit, fifteen million-year-old computer. Know what it does? It creates reality.

That's what we talk about when we say reality goes from inside out. Now to deal with these kinds of questions we did a program at the University of California, called Transition 21. What I'd like to do is frame my remarks within the information that came out of that conference. What we wanted to know was: what ideas are kicking around now which represent the twenty-first century? In case anybody hasn't noticed, we're living at the turn of the century. The twenty-first century is already here. You hear all the talking about apocalypse, the end of the world, the disaster. Who's going to experience that? Those who insist on living in the twenty-first century with twentieth-century notions, let alone seventeenth-century notions.

There's a paradigm shift happening in our society. What does that mean? The last time the scientists pulled this they told us the world is not flat but round. So there were meetings like this one and somebody like me got up and said, "Hey everybody, the world is not flat." You know what they're saying now? It isn't *there*. There's nothing out there, it's all happening on the back of your eyeballs. So if you want the basic message from me to you, as a family physician, if it's all happening on the back of your eyeballs you might as well write a light romantic comedy instead of a heavy tragedy. And that I think is the basic message.

One of the speakers at our conference was Brian O'Leary, a physicist-astronaut who was on the moon. Dr. O'Leary said that we are living through a change, equivalent to the time when life first crawled out of the water onto dry land. What's the nature of the change? The nature of the change is the paradigm shift. What no longer works is the idea that this universe is composed of separate entities and that you can know anything about it by analyzing it, by breaking it down to its smallest bits. We used to believe that atoms were the smallest bits, and then we found out atoms are made up of protons and neutrons and electrons spinning around, and then Heisenberg comes along and says, well, they're not always there, and it's mostly space. Now we know that the smallest little bit is a quark.

Do you know where the word comes from? The word doesn't mean anything. It comes from James Joyce — three quarks from us to Mark. He had to have a word to rhyme with Mark so he made up the word quark. Dr. Fritjof Capra says that quarks, which make up the basic building blocks of our reality, don't exist. As a physician I was interested in what this physical body that you bring to me to fix is made of. You say, listen, this pile of quarks isn't working, fix it. Well, what am I supposed to say when Dr. Capra comes along and says quarks can't possibly exist? So this physical body is made up of a bunch of things which have no real existence.

Another of the speakers was Dr. David Finkelstein, the physicist from Georgia who came up with the idea of black holes in space. Dr. Finkelstein looks like Ram Dass. We had Ram Dass, too. They look alike, and they're essentially saying the same thing. Dr. Finkelstein's thesis is that physics was given the task of examining the physical world. And its job is complete. It's examined the physical world and found that there's nothing there.

One of the other speakers we were supposed to get was Dr. Eugene Wigner, who won a Nobel prize for working on the atom. And he couldn't come for some reason, and I called him up and I said, "Well, Dr. Wigner, what would you like to tell the people?" Dr. Wigner's message is that consciousness is all there is. Just consciousness.

And that's what Dr. Karl Pribram is talking about. Dr. Pribram says that your brain takes in information from your five senses about the physical world out there, puts it together in the form of a three-dimensional picture, a hologram, and projects it as if it were out there. That's what I mean when I say it's all happening behind your eyeballs. And he's running around the world telling everybody that and they haven't put him away yet. They argue with him but his arguments are very powerful.

It's the end of about 300 years of illusion, of an era. Heinz von Forster, a cyberneticist, says the basic shift in our society today is the elimination of the difference between the observer and the observed. The idea that I can study something objectively is asinine. An objective scientist is somebody who watches something very carefully and takes copious notes to find out what it does when nobody's looking at it. Think about that one.

The same is true about the body. We used to think, my body,

which is this pile of quarks, does whatever it does regardless of what I think about it. Carl Jung said back in 1919 that the predominant feeling in medicine is that the brain secretes consciousness the way the kidneys secrete urine. Dr. Jung summed up the Skinnerian attitude beautifully. It's just as likely that consciousness creates the brain. We don't really know for sure. Nobody really knows what's going on. Everybody's got ideas, theories, hypotheses. It's round, flat, it's real, nobody really knows. So what do you do in a situation like that? What I do is retreat into the philosophic position of William James, who talks about truth as what *works*. People talk about truth as though they have seen directly into the mind of God, and find some unalterable verity there. That is simply not possible. The best we can hope for is what works, which is great for a general practitioner. If you have asthma, and you go out and whistle Dixie and your asthma goes away, I don't really care *why* you get better, just so you get better.

We are presented now with two different ways of looking at the world. One is, it's out there and it's doing it to me. I mean, this germ attacks me, I was walking along and suddenly this cold virus comes along and now I've got a cold. I'm not attacking the germ theory, although I find it a little hard to swallow at this point. You know the story of the Legionnaire's disease. There were two guys in the same hotel room, they drank at the same bars, they went to the same places, they ate together, and one got Legionnaire's disease and died, and the other didn't even get sick. It's not enough to find out what "caused" one to get sick; this is the basic transition that American medicine is going through.

What we're beginning to look at now is the guy who didn't get sick. Now this is a complete turnabout. We're not looking out *there* anymore. We're beginning to look at the consciousness. We're beginning to examine the position of Dr. Wigner that consciousness is all there is, that there is no mind-body separation but that the body is a function of the consciousness. You want a simple proof? You ever notice that husbands and wives look alike after they've lived together for a long time — not all of them, some of them. Some people's dogs look like them. How you think creates how your body is.

I want to give you some evidence for this. I want to build a model which can help you in terms of taking care of your own health. Krishnamurti said that we're very careful around rattlesnakes because we know what they're capable of. He said if you knew what your thoughts were capable of, you would be even more careful around them than you are around rattlesnakes.

The suggestion coming down from the best minds in the scientific community today is that the world is crystallized thought. What you think creates your world. There's an old Buddhist image of two mirrors facing each other — each one reflecting and creating the other. That's the way it is with your consciousness and your physical reality.

One of the basic things that's happening, as the twenty-first century comes, is the downfall of the cult of atheistic scientific materialism. There are still some high priests of that cult around, telling us the world is flat, or it's real, or it's objective. But the crescendo of work which is coming out of the best institutions all over the world is beginning to overwhelm that point of view. And you hear that pretty much in backwaters, scientific and medical backwaters where people are still stuck on Descartes and scientific materialism and objectivity.

The cult of atheistic scientific materialism is based on the idea that matter is God, and that the only thing that really matters is matter. The old Greek concept is that matter was put here by God and only the mind of God can change matter, so that *my* mind, a mere mortal's, cannot have any effect on matter. Now that was a mistake. It really isn't like that.

That's why you get religious healings. People would pray to God to interfere with the malfunctioning of matter in their bodies, to change it. Now we're beginning to understand that possibily, in terms of being able to manipulate matter directly with mind, each one of us is God. Now you can move matter with your mind, you know, by scratching your head. You decide you're going to scratch your head and your finger goes up, and scratches your head, in exactly the place you want it. Remember the involuntary nervous system. Remember that old myth? I think they still teach it in some medical schools. I find it hard to believe that there's such a thing as an involuntary nervous system. According to the new science, the new physics, and twenty-first-century medicine, there is no part of your body that you cannot theoretically affect directly with your consciousness.

I can remember when Dr. Hans Selye first came out with his

idea of psychosomatic disease, the idea that the way you think can initiate a disease process. The medical profession in my time, and I got out of medical school in 1953, was led, kicking and screaming, to the idea that a patient's lifestyle and thought processes can actually initiate a heart attack, or an ulcer, or allergies. Now we're beginning to look at psychogenic factors in almost all disease. I personally think that almost all human disease is probably psychogenic — psychologically caused. If you want to look back, Buddha said that the root of all human suffering is attachment, the unwillingness to let go of something. Dr. Selye showed how it worked. He isolated the hormones, and he got objective evidence. What we're saying now, of course, is if you can think yourself sick, you can think yourself well.

We know, according to the work of Bogan and Sperry, that there are two sides to your brain. The left side thinks, does time and space; it's linear. The right side makes pictures. If we presume that they're right, what kind of a mode can we create which will help us stay healthy?

Dr. Selye, who limited himself to the left side of the brain, says that there are two kinds of thoughts that you can have — one kind kind is catatoxic and one kind is syntoxic. Now what is catatoxic thought? Catatoxic comes from the same root as "catastrophe." An optimist is sure that this is the best of all possible worlds. The pessimist agrees and says, "I worry about that." Now what happens when you say, "I worry about that.?" You look at the world, which is just doing what it's doing, there's no good or bad in it, and you look at this and you decide that it's bad. Catatoxic thoughts, through what he calls neurohumoral transducers, translate the electrical impulses you experience as thoughts into hormones, which then create a bodily state which instantaneously reflects your thoughts. You cannot have a single thought in your head which is not instantaneously translated into a bodily sensation. If you have a pessimistic or a catatoxic thought, you make adrenaline. Instantaneously. You have a worried or a frightened thought, you get a squirt of adrenaline. That's the connection between mind and matter. The other thoughts you can have are syntoxic thoughts, from the same root as "symphony," and when you have syntoxic thoughts, you create cortisone-like hormones. He calls them the doves among the hormones. So if you happen to be an optimist and you think everything is fine, you're constantly bathing yourself in these syntoxic, happy hormones.

Let's include Dr. Meyer Friedman's model, too. A cardiologist from Mt. Zion in San Francisco, Dr. Friedman wrote *Type A Behavior and Your Heart*, in which he worked out his Type A and Type B personality concept. The Type A personality is a person who is constantly struggling against time and other people for survival. Type B personalities don't do that. They know how to relax. And he's been doing a study for seventeen years, and he has a standing offer that if any Type B personality dies of a heart attack, he will pay for the funeral. He says he has not had to pay for a funeral yet.

You've got two kinds of people in the world and you see them every place. You've got the hard-nosed realist who knows how it is; I mean he or she is *objective* — "I know how it is and how it is is terrible." On the other hand, and I see a lot of them in California, there is the pollyanna whitelighter. "Oh, I can cross the street and I can put white light on myself and the bus won't hit me. Everything will be just fine." The hard-nosed realist says, "Well, listen, you're going to get killed, you're just not going to survive." Well, the facts are interesting. It seems that the hard-nosed realists die twice as fast of heart attacks as the pollyanna whitelighters. So if you think about the survival of the fittest, you know, it's almost as if Nature herself through heart attacks is eliminating the hard-nosed realists. Practical application, see, because the pollyanna whitelighters really know that the white light is going to protect them and bathe themselves in cortisone and does not put the body under what is called chronic stress, which is a killer.

Now, there's one other basic piece of research, and this will nail it down: it happened last year at the University of California Medical School in San Francisco, by Field and Associates. And set next to the Nobel work of Guillemin and Schally, who proved that the human brain secretes hormones, which affect the pituitary, it's a revolution in medicine. Western medicine will never be the same. It's a work on placebos. A placebo is an empty capsule or an injection with nothing in it, no active chemical. Mind you, we're proceeding on the assumption it's the matter, it's the atoms, it's those little quarks in that syringe or in that pill that are really going to fix you. And what you think about it doesn't really matter. So that if somebody has a pain and I give them an empty capsule which has no quarks in it, just nothing, maybe milk sugar, and the pain goes away, the general feeling is that the pain is in your head, right? That you didn't really have the pain. Dr. Field took fifty-one people with pain in their head. They had pain because they had just had teeth pulled. So that there's no doubt that they had *real pain*. What he did was to give them placebos. Eighteen out of those fifty-one reported complete relief. Now, what happened? I give you an empty capsule and I look you straight in the eye and I say, "I'm the doctor, and I'm going to stop your pain." You know what happens? Your brain makes morphine. They're called endogenous morphines. Now, I don't know what the limit to that is. Which means that as a physician it totally changes my approach to a patient. I no longer care about the objective disease that the patient has. Right now, I do care, because I could get sued. You still have to touch the base of objective reality because we are in a transition time.

Dr. Carl Simonton, who was one of the people in one of the early conferences that we did about five years ago, says what is killing his cancer patients is the notion that they have an incurable disease. The idea that they're supposed to die. Implications in geriatrics are enormous. Dr. Rosenfeld talked about evidence that this body is built to go at least 150 years. I remember being told that after twenty-five it's all downhill. Well, that's what creates it. Just like Field giving you a placebo and saying your pain is all gone, if all the doctors say that after twenty-five it's downhill and you have to expect to get old and feeble and senile, that is a direct command to your body to do that.

Mary Leakey found human footprints exactly like ours in Africa in a stratum of rock that was three million years old. Three million years ago, people at least with feet like ours were running around on the planet. Now why should just the *feet* be like ours? The idea occurs: well, how did we survive, let's say three million years without drug stores? How did we do that? I mean, running around with the dinosaurs, what got us through it?

For that I have to adopt a model of Julian Jaynes of Rutgers University. He brings in the function of the right side of the brain. The right side of the brain makes pictures, it's the image-making side of the brain. What are these pictures that your brain makes? You have a dream, or you close your eyes and you see a picture, what is it? Well, Dr. Jaynes believes that the images — Carl Jung calls them the archetypes; Jaynes calls them the gods — are actually hallucinations spontaneously produced by the right side of the brain to guide us and direct us. He says, for instance, if Org was walking along and came to a split in the road, or was walking along and had to eat, he wouldn't say, "I'm hungry now, I think I'll go kill a dinosaur." Rather, the right side of the brain would create an image and Org would see this god standing in front of him who would say, "Org, take spear, kill dinosaur, and eat." You begin to think of these ancient images of hunting scenes in the caves at Altamira. Dr. Jaynes suggests that the Trojan Wars were directed by hallucinations. Most of our major religions are based on hallucinations. It's quite conceivable when Moses saw the burning bush, or Bernadette saw Our Lady of Lourdes, it was a hallucination produced by their right hemispheres to guide them.

There's an old Indian legend that when the first primal parents were born, when they were first walking on the planet, they didn't know what to do. So they asked the Great Spirit. And the Great Spirit said that they were to watch the animals in their dreams. And the animals in their dreams would direct them. The animals taught them how to hunt, fish, build shelters and plant corn. The information for how to survive on the planet came from spontaneous visual images which arise in the right-hand cerebral hemisphere. Jung codified this into the method of active imagination, and I've been playing around with it for ten years, and let me tell you, it's dynamite; I think it'll cure anything.

At another program we did, Elisabeth Kubler-Ross talked about how the consciousness does not die. At the end of life, she says, the body is cast aside like an old overcoat and the consciousness continues. What the consciousness is, we really don't know. What some people are beginning to feel is that what we call consciousness and light are the same phenomenon. You begin to think about Einstein's "$E = mc^2$." Energy is the same as matter. Einstein told us several times that there is no difference between the thing that's moving and the motion. That the thing is crystallized form of the motion. Things are crystallized energy, just as ice is crystallized water. What they're saying now is that the continuum is not just energy and matter, but it's mind, energy, matter. Consciousness, energy, matter are a single continuum.

I'm a general practitioner and I'm operating on the implicit agreement between patient and physician that goes on today. I make a house call, and the problem is that my patient has a pain in the right buttock. I do a careful examination of the patient, and being a very astute physician, I discover that my patient's rear-end seems to be impaled upon a tack which is sitting on this chair. Okay, so now I'm going to do twentieth-century medicine. The job is to get rid of the symptom, using the finest technology available. Going to give you a shot of morphine. Not only is your pain going to go away but you're going to be one happy fellow for about three or four hours. Great, you're a great doctor, fantastic. But I know that after about three hours the pain is going to come back, and I don't want to make another house call. So I'm going to leave some codeine tablets. I'm going to say, "Take two codeines and call me in the morning." I leave the codeines, and when the pain comes back you take two codeine tablets and every four hours you take two tablets and your symptom will be destroyed using the finest technology available. Of course I get a call, maybe the next day, maybe two or three days later. "Well, I don't know, the pain used to go away, now it's back every *two* hours, and I've got to take six tablets, and it only goes away partially, and I'm sick to my stomach and I vomit all the time, and I don't know, I don't think your medicine is working." So I say, "It's not my medicine, it's Eli Lilly's medicine. Don't blame me for the medicine." However, if it's not working, I have to presume that our pharmaceutical technology has not solved this problem. We have here a medical failure. What do you do when you have a medical failure? " I've got a friend, Sam the Surgeon, he's really good — it costs a little more than me, but Sam is a specialist, he's very good a cutting sciatic nerves. He'll cut the nerve. Your foot might drag a little bit, but it won't hurt." "No, I don't like that one." "Well, I have a friend, Norman the Neurosurgeon — he can do what's called a dorsal root rhizotomy. He'll just cut the sensory nerve. Of course if Norman hiccups or sneezes while he's in there you might have a lot of trouble, if you survive the anesthesia. And it is expensive." Well, he doesn't like that. "Well, we can go on the thalamus, tha pain center. We can stick a needle in it, we can fry it or freeze it. And most of the time it works. If you don't like that we can do the *pièce de résistance*, which is a pre-frontal lobotomy. In that case your rear end would still hurt but you wouldn't notice it. It wouldn't matter. Or I can send you to a psychiatrist who can teach you to live with your pain." Of course, I *could* say, "Why don't you get up off the tack?" I could say that, right? But you know what the answer is? The answer is, "But Doc, I make my living sitting on tacks." Now, that sounds dumb. Not let's extrapolate this to an executive with an ulcer, or with anginal pains, a truck driver with a bad back, a housekeeper with arthritis, okay? That's the approach we have been using to destroy the symptom using the finest technology available. Using this approach, we spent approximately 192 billion dollars last year without significantly affecting our mortality rates at all.

Now, imagine the way this twenty billion-bit computer works. The bottom part, which is the part we share with lizards, is the computer. And it doesn't think, and it's pretty good. And that's as old as life, because lizards have this computer which can detect a fly, shoot the tongue out, and swallow it. Fully automatic. It doesn't need anything — no consciousness as we know it is required of a lizard to perform its function. So you've got the computer, which is running your whole body. Now the question is, if the body is malfunctioning, whether there's some bad program in there. There are two ways you can change the program. You can give your computer direct instructions from either side of the brain. Either side will program with thoughts, which is the old power of positive thinking. "I will get well." There's a lot of evidence that you can actually command your body to get well. The other side of it, which is worrying about what it might do, is also a command, because computers are stupid.

I can remember when I was in general practice, I used to get from the drug companies beautiful little three-dimensional models that would show you all the horrible things that can possibly happen to you. And those are just suggestions. The doctor says this is going to happen, and sure enough, it happens. It happens because you have put a program into the computer. What we're saying now is if we can make morphine, why can't we command a diabetic pancreas to secrete insulin? How far does this go? The other way is to make a very clear picture of how you want your body to be. And this is for pain relief, and I've had a lot of good experience with it, and a lot of people all over the country have been doing it. Let's say you have pain in your back. The right brain works through pictures. So you can't tell your right brain, I have rheumatoid arthritis, fix it, because it doesn't know what you're talking about. If you have a back pain, and it feels like there's a knife stuck in your back, a very clear image of the knife coming out of your back, in *my* experience on a general practice level, will work ninety-eight percent of the time. It really works for pain relief. Beyond that, what we need is to understand why you got the symptom. What is it trying to tell you?

We did a program on that: Birth and Rebirth. Two of the speakers we had were Arthur Janov and Frederick Leboyer. And the reason for having those two was to describe that there are two ways you can be born. You can be born kicking and screaming, or happily floating around in warm water with the lights out. Now that's on the physical level. If everything is a hologram, where everything is in everything else, we say, if this is the physical model, it must be reflected on the psychological level. Now, how is it reflected on the psychological level? Let's look at an infant at term, at nine months. This happened to all of us. For nine months we were floating around, upside down, if we were lucky, in our mother's womb and protected by these huge muscular walls, and this nice thing of water surrounding us, attached by a stalk to a root which sunk into the maternal soil and sucked up nourishment. You hear your mother's voice, and you slosh around in the water and everything is fine, you know? Great, it couldn't be better, it's perfect. And one day somebody pulls the plug. The water runs out, and the same walls which protected you try to kill you. Then, the next thing you know your stalk is cut and your roots are pulled up and some idiot has got you upside-down and is whacking you on the backside. This is the old medicine, it's not the new medicine anymore. If you try to resist that, you die. Any creature which does not go through the birth process dies, and in terms of the forces to which you were subjected — if your head today were subjected to the forces that it was subjected to at birth, it would be crushed like an eggshell. So, that's birth. You're out, and you look around, and okay, somebody takes care of me, somebody feeds me, well, this isn't so bad. I see these two big people, Mommy and Daddy, and they take care of me, it's fine, I think I really like this, and as soon as you decide you like this, off to school you go. There you are in school, and finally you get used to that, and you get to play with the boys and the girls, and then one day you notice there's a difference between the boys and the girls. And you have to deal with that one, right? Sex. Okay, you go through the problems and trials of adolescence, and going from childhood to sexually active adolescence. You go to see the psychiatrist or whatever you do, and you make it, you even decide you like it. As soon as you decide you like it, you've got the hang of it, poof, it's gone. Finished. *That* one's over. Well, what's happening? I'm getting older. I'm older but people ask me questions, they listen to me now, they think I know something. As soon as you've got that one down, you die. That's the human condition. We have to go through these phases. We are constantly turning into somebody else. As soon as you think you know who you are you've got to give it up. And if you don't give it up, you suffer. So you begin to realize that disease, suffering, pain is an ally, it's a friend, it's goading you to evolve. Of course, the one thing that consciousness does is evolve and change. It simply does not stop. Each one of us is the means by which the human race evolves. There's nobody here but us. It's possible there's nobody here but you. You're making all this up so I can tell you this, right? If you don't evolve, if you try to stop, you simply get recycled, you know, back to the drawing boards and start all over again.

There are two ways you can program the computer — you program it with thoughts and you program it with visual images. The left side thinks and the right side makes pictures. Both sides serve a dual function. A) it will carry messages from you to your body and will tell your body what to do. B) it will carry messages from your body to you, which will tell you what your body wants to do, why it made the symptom. For example, your body gives you pain in your rear-end because it wants you to get up off the tack, or a heart attack because it doesn't want you to keep that job anymore. It has direct effects in your day-to-day life.

John Lilly talks about programming and meta-programming, that the universe knows what it's doing and it means us no harm. When Albert Einstein was asked, "What is the most important question facing the human race today?" he said, "Is the universe friendly?"

If you decide the universe is not friendly, then that's harmful to your health; if you have to fight the whole universe, the odds are really against you. If you decide that it's friendly, whatever happens to you, you decide that it's happened for a good reason, for your own edification, your own evolution.

There can be no inappropriate pictures in a perfect universe.

The left side of the brain that looks at the universe and says, "that's inappropriate," is about three thousand years old. Language started three to eight thousand years ago; until we had that we could not have any opinions at all about the image. The part that makes the image is about five million years old.

How can there be an inappropriate picture in a perfect universe? It has been my experience that there are no inappropriate pictures.

(March 1980)

The Eleventh Man

Leonard Rogoff

"Our life resembles the process by which the world came into being."

— *Rabbi Abraham Isaac Kook*

Rarely do I awaken before my dog. When I do, obligation demands it. For the past two years I have risen at six on Thursday mornings to attend a *minyan*, the prayer quorum of ten Jews. The *minyan* was originally convened at the behest of a Peruvian Jew whose father died in South America, so that he might properly recite the mourner's kaddish for the twelve months in which the soul may linger in the lower spheres before its ascent to higher domains: "Exalted and honored be the name of the Holy One, blessed be He, whose glory transcends, yea, is beyond all praises, hymns and blessings that man can

"When I die and face the heavenly tribunal," Rabbi Zusya used to say, "they will not ask me why I was not Moses; rather, they will want to know why I was not Zusya."

render unto Him. . . ."

We meet in the family room of a professor's home. The men don skull caps, bind themselves — chest, head and arm — with phylacteries, small leather cases containing scripture passages, and wrap themselves in prayer shawls, all with the appropriate blessings. Then we open our prayer books and pray. The Hebrew word for prayer — *daven* — means not "to beg" as in English, but "to attach."

The prayers are in Hebrew, which I half understand. Plodding slowly, I lose my place frequently. Often, my mind wanders to last evening's basketball game, to that waitress at breakfast, to my dog sleeping, rest assured, on my empty bed.

A Hasidic tale tells of a disciple who travelled many miles to visit the court of his master, Sholem of Belz, so that he might see the Rebbe, palm and citron in his hand, recite the Hallel prayers on the Feast of Tabernacles, celebrating the harvest. The disciple looked up to the Holy Ark of the synagogue so that he might gaze upon the Rebbe's wondrous face. Such was the fervor of the Rebbe's prayers, however, that the Rebbe had disappeared, having incarnated himself in the citron. Other tales tell of Hasidim who pray so furiously that their bodies erupt into searing flame, and one gazes upon their blinding light only at great peril.

I had not seen Alex since our high school days in New Jersey. He had been an end on the football team, an artist, and because he rode a motorscooter, was regarded back then as a "beatnik." My contact with him in the intervening years was intermittent and indirect: a cousin knew him when Alex was a mailman in Berkeley. I had seen his picture on a record album of Shlomo Carlebach, the Hasidic troubadour. The parental grapevine passed word that he and his wife had emigrated to Israel where he devoted himself entirely to his painting and religious studies.

Searching a map, I located the moshav (agricultural co-op) of Migdal on a bus route north of Tiberias. Once there I am told to ask for Elyah Succot or "Redbeard," the American artist.

As I trudge up the road from the bus stop, I pause to catch my breath as well as the view. Before me loom towering white cliffs; beneath are the lush fields and orchards of the moshav, and beyond them is the Sea of Galilee or the Kinneret, as it is called in Hebrew, "the violin." The curving road is lined with small stone houses; I had been told that Elyah's was the last hut, the highest on the slope.

I climb the steps and peer into an open door. Elyah and his wife sit at a homemade table while more children than I can quickly count scurry about. My journey of thousands of miles climaxes in a moment of complete and mutual non-recognition. Though I know who he is, physically even, he seems changed, much thinner, with scrawny beard and earlocks. So I introduce myself. Still, the atmosphere seems a bit awkward until his wife motions toward my head. Then I realize: muttering a lame excuse about the severity of the climb, I reach into my pack and push a skullcap on my head, and the atmosphere relaxes. Blessings are recited; hospitality is offered; cold drinks are served; old friends and family are recalled. Elyah introduces me to his wife and children as a classmate from his Hebrew school days, a fact which, indifferent student that I was, I have entirely forgotten. A small part of our past suddenly grows very important. Elyah has rewritten much of his own life.

The walls of the hut are covered with Elyah's paintings, fantastic paintings with frames in the shape of wings. Elyah studies *Zohar*, the cabalistic texts, and draws his themes from them. Lines of scripture weave in and out; an eyeball encompasses a world. The colors — vivid reds, bright blues, living greens — swirl and dance.

We stand in his garden and talk. In a glance I simply cannot absorb the totality of the view, not just because of its magnificence but because of its scope and variety. The Psalmist, I should have realized, had glorified this land sometime before my arrival. Elyah points to the cliffs above us. They contain caves, he tells me, where nearly two thousand years ago the saintly Rabbi Akiva hid before his capture and martyrdom, teaching Jewish law to children during the ill-fated rebellion against Rome. One expects that of Israel, that nature would breathe history, but I was unprepared for the pure physical beauty of the land: the palm trees and citrus orchards, the blue water, the quality of pale light. The Edenic setting seemed so perfectly attuned to the peace Elyah emanated from within himself. "Come live in Israel," he urges me. "In America you'll live in a wooden house; here you can have a house of stone."

The following is from the *Midrash Pinchas* by Pinchas of Koritz;

it appears in *Nine Gates to the Chassidic Mysteries* by Jiri Langer:

Everybody has a special light burning for him in the higher world, totally different from the light of every other person. When two friends meet in this world, their lights up above unite for a moment, and out of the union of the two lights an angel is born. However, the angel is only given sufficient strength to live one year. If the two friends meet again within the year they give the angel a further lease of life. But if they do not see each other for a whole year the angel wastes away and dies for lack of light. The Talmud bids us, when we see a friend whom we have not seen for a whole year, to bless God for "raising the dead." This is a strange commandment indeed, since neither of us have died. Whom then has God raised from the dead? Surely none other than the languishing angel whose lease of life is renewed each time we meet.

According to Talmudic legend, four rabbis were permitted to enter the Garden of Divine Knowledge. When they departed, one died immediately; one went mad; one turned to heresy; and the fourth — Rabbi Akiva — left in peace. Saturday mornings we gather, four or five men, one or two women, to discuss Talmud, Jewish civil and religious law, with Dr. Schlessinger, who is a rabbi as well as a philosopher.

For thirteen years now Rabbi Schlessinger has proceeded through the seemingly endless volumes chapter by chapter, line by line, word by word, translating from the Hebrew or Aramaic. Our class size fluctuates, often declining in number, never quite dying by Zeno's paradox that a fraction of a fraction can never reach zero. Such is the state of Talmudic study in Chapel Hill.

Since by and large we are a less than observant group, why is it that we expend our energies arguing the smallest point of law: what objects may be carried outside the household on the Sabbath? How can the exact second of dusk be determined so that the festival candles may be lit at the proper time? What regulations govern the harvesting of the first crop of tomatoes? The Talmudic arguments are copious and tireless, centuries upon centuries of commentators, not dogmatic pronouncement but interpretations, often conflicting, which are argued with a finesse that borders sometimes on the fanatic, sometimes on the inspired. The scrupulousness of the Talmud's subject — on praying and planting, on astrology and personal hygiene — at times repels by its self-conscious regimentation, its seeming denial of spontaneity. Despite an occasional enlightened opinion, its attitude toward women is frequently narrow, if not repressive. Yet, the cosmic breadth of its concern reveals an insatiable spirituality, the conviction that every event, however seemingly insignificant, reveals a divine purpose and must be consecrated, blessed, and elevated to the holy. Nine hundred years ago, Maimonides, the Rambam, wrote, "If thou find in the Torah or the Prophets or the Sages a hard saying which thou canst not understand . . . place it in a corner of your heart for future consideration, but despise not thy Religion because thou are unable to understand one difficult matter."

Here I am lost in Safed, the holy city, for centuries the center of Jewish mysticism. I have climbed the hill from the bus station, clutching in my hand a slip of paper, a note from Elyah to his friend Yakov, as if it were a map, a guide through the maze of Safed's labyrinthine streets. The alleys of Safed twist and turn, climb and drop, broaden and narrow, sometimes dead end. Safed is stone, stone, stone: despite its antiquity and the solidity of its buildings, the old city sits precariously on the edge of a hill, a fortress against war and earthquake. At its foot is a medieval Jewish cemetery, containing the graves of the revered cabalists (as well as those of several dozen children massacred when Arab terrorists ambushed their school bus). Beyond Safed are the valleys and hills of the Galilee.

Dusk gathers quickly, and I know neither my destination nor the means to find it. Turning in an alley, I start down an endless stairway and spot two Hasidim, in black frocks, hands clasped behind their backs, enjoying their evening stroll. Perhaps in my rudimentary Hebrew, they could point me to the address on the note.

"Rehov Zipporah?"

"So vere are you goink?" they answer in perfect Brooklynese. "Come, vee show you."

In this, the 5740th year since creation, the Lubavitcher Rebbe, may his name be blessed, sends two of his Hasidim to bring the light of Torah, the body of Jewish religious teaching, to the Jews of the American South. Yossi and Shlomo are two Hasidim like other Hasidim. Despite their beards, they are uniformly businesslike in their dark conservative suits. Their trick: beneath their fedoras they wear skull caps. They are aggressively, but not impolitely, pious.

Their "discussion" groups are, in fact, lectures, and with each successive visit, a pattern emerges. They seize upon someone's question or a remark — the meaning of an approaching holiday, life in Brooklyn — and begin their talk, ascending the ladder from the mundane to the holy, and just as adroitly, returning down the ladder to the here and now. Then they pass around schnapps and sing. Sometimes the ambience is genuinely spontaneous, even joyous; other times, the mood is argumentative, divisive, forced.

This particular evening we sit in the elegant living room of a Hungarian Jewish woman, a touch of Vienna on Westwood Drive. Someone asks, how bad are things in Brooklyn? We read in the newspapers about fights between blacks and Jews, Hasidim storming a police station. Not with local blacks, Yossi demurs. His own sister plays jump rope with black children and has taught them Yiddish rhymes. His very own mother, however, was attacked by a knife-wielding assailant in the laundry room of their apartment house. This event provokes a discussion of evil and of the divine purpose of evil. We must see how evil fits into the divine scheme. Then Yossi moves on to the Godhead; how we must approach *ha-Shem* ("The Name") — God's name itself is too holy to pronounce — through reason and emotion. The head must inform the heart. The heart must enlighten the head. (Lubavitch Hasidim is founded on the three pillars of ChaBaD, an acronym for *chochma, binah, dat* — wisdom, knowledge, understanding.) We must purify our acts to conform to the divine spark within ourselves, to raise the physical world into the realm of the spiritual. So we recognize that even evil contains a Godly element, a kernel of holiness, if we can break through the shell of the material world. When his mother was assaulted, she grabbed the attacker's knife and broke the blade with her hands, turning this instrument of evil into a token of divine power. The policeman who took her to the hospital was amazed at her miraculous strength. That's how things are in Brooklyn.

I walk through a small courtyard, a neat flower garden, and knock on Yakov's door. It opens. Before me stands a Hasid in round hat, thin, tall, and dark, with black stringy earlocks and beard, frock and knickers. This is no counter-culture, guitar-strumming Hasid but the genuine article. "Yes?" he inquires. I hand him Elyah's note. "Ah, yes." He pauses thoughtfully.

"I am sorry but I cannot offer you the hospitality of my home this evening." He is embarrassingly apologetic. "My wife is soon to give birth, and I have house guests for the holiday. Come, I will take you to a place." We walk briskly down a narrow street. The conversation is awkward as he continues to apologize. "You must understand, because of my wife's condition, I must first respect the sanctity of my household . . . and these house guests for L'ag B'omer. . . ." In turn, I apologize that in truth I had come only to deliver the note from Elyah, that I had no intention of asking for a place, and so on. Secretly, I regret that I had not waited until morning to deliver the note. Yakov takes seriously, I soon realize, the biblical injunction to give comfort to the stranger in his land, and he obviously feels discomfited about his inability to perform this deed, this *mitzvah*. He invites me to return at nine the next morning, but for now he takes me to a nearby pension which, it turns out, is owned by direct descendants of the Baal Shem Tov, the Master of the Good Name, who in eighteenth-century Poland founded the mystic Hasidic movement.

The pension is entirely charming, set in a luxuriant green garden. The great-great . . . granddaughter of the Baal Shem Tov, a middle-aged woman with a cigarette dangling from her lips, gives me a key to the room while in the small lobby her son and her mother argue over who controls the television dial.

Elie Wiesel is one of those writers with whom the reader makes a personal compact, and, as I enter Page Auditorium, I am somewhat jealous of the large audience which is intruding on what I really regard as a personal encounter, the two of us. But I know, too, that Wiesel will somehow insist on his unapproachability; as a survivor of Auschwitz — harrowingly evoked in *Night* — Wiesel will build a fence around himself. The darkness of his knowledge, of his experience, shuts out our daylight world, hides some awful power that was inaccessible to all others. "And yet, and yet," he frequently writes, he sees himself less as a spokesman for the dead than for the enduring, though he saw his mother and sister led to the crematorium and watched his father die painfully days before liberation. *Souls on Fire, Messengers of God, A Jew Today*, all Wiesel's books, are less testaments to a vanished world — the thousands of spiritual centers and millions of Hasidim ("pious ones") that vanished in the

Holocaust — than to the vital continuity of that tradition. Wiesel quotes the Hasidic master Rabbi Nachman of Bratzlaw who issued edicts which specifically forbade Jews to despair in the midst of a savage pogrom. In *Souls on Fire* Wiesel recounts stories of Hasidim dancing for joy in the cattle cars as they were driven to their deaths. More than one critic has described Wiesel's writing as beyond literature; others accuse him of self-dramatizing.

I am late. I stopped to pick up a hitchhiker, a Duke cheerleader in uniform who also is going to the lecture. Walking down the balcony steps in the darkened auditorium, Wiesel spotlighted on stage, I feel the illusion that we are face to face. He sits alone behind a long table, an open book before him. He looks long and lean, contorted, severely angular. An unruly lock of hair falls repeatedly from his forehead as he gesticulates expressively with his hands and arms. I recognize the pose: the Rabbi expounding Talmud to his students.

He has written, "God created man because he loves stories," and so he begins this afternoon, as Jews traditionally do, with a story. When Pharaoh decreed the death of Israel's firstborn, the angel Michael swept down to Egypt and grabbed an Israelite child. The angel took this child before the divine presence and confronted God with the potential victim of his severity. When God gazed upon the sweet face of the child, in mercy He relented in his judgment.

He had first heard this story, Wiesel tells us, when he himself was a child, a young Hasid, and he was proud. He was proud of the Jewish child who entered into the court of the Lord. He was proud of the angel who demanded justice of God. Most of all, he was proud of God for his compassion.

Now, what kind of God — Wiesel leans forward, unclenching his fist — permitted the murder of two million Jewish children in the death camps of Europe?

We sit despondently in the hospital lounge, my family and I, on plastic chairs bolted to the wall. Before us is my grandfather, strapped to his wheelchair. With one arm he pushes a wheel, inscribing semicircles on the floor, while the other arm dangles uselessly. His head hangs loosely, bobbing and weaving, and he makes gurgling noises. Death will be only weeks away, yet even now it seems his higher soul has departed from him, leaving before us a creature of the lower depths.

The elevator doors open and Rabbi Kellner steps briskly out. His black suit and brimmed hat accent his white beard and ruddy complexion, his crystalline blue eyes. I cannot tell whether Rabbi Kellner is an old young man or a young old man. He places his brief-case on the floor, opens it, removes a skullcap which he places on my grandfather's head, and takes out a cellophane bag of cheap vanilla cookies. Kneeling before my grandfather, he slaps him gently on the cheek. Bending over, staring him in the face, he recites the blessings in Hebrew over the bread: "*Baruch atah adonai . . .* Blessed art thou, O Lord our God, King of the Universe, who bringest forth bread from the Earth." He sticks the cookie in my grandfather's mouth, and it is eaten. Placing his hands on my grandfather's shoulders, he sings to him in Hebrew and Yiddish, pious songs, folk songs. Slowly, my grandfather's lips move and then mumble; noises grow into syllables; syllables form words, until my grandfather sings. He pulls himself up in the wheelchair; now the two of them sing lustily, joyfully, not singers but only song.

Rabbi Kellner kisses my grandfather on the forehead, packs his briefcase, picks it up from the floor, and without waiting for thanks, walks briskly down the corridor. There are other rooms to visit. He is a very busy man.

Hillel used to say, "If I am not for myself, who will be for me? And if I am only for myself, what am I? And if not now, when?"
— *The Talmud, Pirke Aboth I, 14.*

I am looking for the entrance to Yad Vashem, the museum and memorial of the Holocaust, on Mt. Herzl in Jerusalem. I enter the wrong gate and lose my way in a military cemetery. The cemetery has the feel of a park, meticulously maintained with neat shrubs and gardens. Each grave is a raised rectangle of brownstone with a cover of greens or flowers. The headstone itself, the shape of a pillow, reposes at an incline, as if the grave were an empty bed for an antici-pated guest. These are not the ancient stones of Jerusalem; death here is new — 1948, 1956, 1967, 1973 — and those buried here, almost alone in Israel, are safe from the archaeologist's spade. The effect of the cemetery as a whole is almost indecently suburban, spic and span, a housing development of expensive graves, as if some overly-zealous do-it-yourselfer had embarked on a frenzy of patio-making.

I take the obligatory photographs.

Walking the rambling paths, seeking a way out, I find myself deliberately lost. The enormity of it all tolls. Here, in one area, shipmates are buried side-by-side. On some graves comrades have placed polished artillery shells, engraved with a message. Occasionally, memorial candles flicker in lanterns. Other tombstones are topped by pebbles, placed there by mourners according to custom. More haunting are the small, framed photos of the victims, mostly it seems of Sephardim, Jews from Arab lands. The faces tend to be young, dark and smiling, incongruously casual for funereal portraits, candids from a party perhaps.

Climbing through a fence, I tear my pants slightly on barbed wire. Enough. I would leave if I could find a way. A gray man, dressed casually in the Israeli fashion, approaches up a road.

"Excuse me, sir, could you tell me how to get to Yad Vashem?"

"Please," he says, waving away my question with his hand. "I come to visit the grave of my friend." Under his arm he carries prayer shawl and phylacteries, the mourner's gardening tools.

The Holocaust and Halakhah by Irving J. Rosenbaum contains rabbinic responses to such questions as: may a Jew desecrate the Holy Torah to save his life? May he accept a forged baptismal certificate, effectively denying his Judaism, to escape capture by the Nazis? Is it permissible for a father to bribe a concentration camp guard to save his son from extermination, knowing that another will be selected in the son's place? What is the proper blessing to sanctify God's name before one's own execution? This excerpt comes from the Warsaw ghetto diary of Hillel Seidman, dated October 2, 1942, the seventh day of the Succot festival, describing a scene in a slave factory:

Now here I am in Schultz's "shop." The people are driving in nails and saying Hoshanot *(prayers). . . . Here you see sitting at the wooden block and mending shoes . . . the* Kozieglower *rebbe, Yehuda Arieh Fromer. . . . This Jew is sitting here, but his spirit is soaring to other worlds. He does not stop studying from memory and his lips keep moving all the time. From time to time he addresses a word to the* Pleaseczna rebbe, *the author of* Hovat Hatalmidim, *who is sitting just opposite him. . . . Gemarot and biblical texts are quoted, and soon there appear on the shoe block, or rather in the minds and mouths of the* geonim, the Rambam, the Rabad, the Tur . . . *and who cares now about the SS men, the* Volksdeutsch *supervisor, or about hunger, misery, persecutions, and fear of death! Now they are soaring in higher regions, they are not in the "shop" at 46 Nowolipie Street where they are sitting, but in lofty halls . . . !*

The basement of the Duke Baptist Student Union is an unlikely place to celebrate Simhat Torah, the holiday commemorating the "rejoicing in the law." On this holiday and Purim the rabbis command us to drink until we can no longer distinguish between good and evil.

Yossi lets us know rather overtly that he is with us only at the command of the Lubavitcher Rebbe himself. For tonight in Brooklyn he is missing an occasion of singular importance. One year ago the Hasidim gathered by the thousands, as is their custom on Simhat Torah, before the Rebbe's home on Eastern Parkway, closing the street, where they sing and dance all night. Before their perfect master, the Hasidim aspire to a state of *bittul*, self-obliteration. Last year, however, as the festivities began, the Rebbe collapsed, struck by a severe heart attack. The Hasidim fell silent as the Rebbe was taken to his bedroom to be attended by physicians. They stood in the street, stunned, awaiting word. From his sickbed the Rebbe passed a message: he could not hear the singing of his Hasidim. And so they resumed the revelry with renewed fervor until the return of dawn. (In such matters Jewish law is unequivocal: if a funeral and a wedding procession cross in a street, the mourners must yield to the celebrants.) A year later, to his regret, he is not with his Rebbe to celebrate his miraculous recovery. But here at a Methodist college in the basement of a Baptist student union, he will bring to us some of the spirit of Eastern Parkway.

The evening begins with a prayer service; in deference to the audience we are segregated by sex not back to back (as in a conventional orthodox synagogue) but side to side. After we *daven*, we move to a table in the back where lie two covered Torah scrolls and enough bottles of scotch, gin, and bourbon to stock a small-town ABC store. Yossi begins the procession, carrying a scroll and chanting a lovely Hebrew melody: "We beseech Thee, O Lord, save us. . . ." Then we drink and toast *l'chaim*, "to life." The Torah scrolls are passed around. In the center two men lock arms and swing around in a tight circle; around them the other men join arms and dance in a larger circle, and another circle of women forms around them. The Torah is passed from arm to arm, as each takes a turn in the middle.

Periodically, we break to resume our drinking. Yossi and Shlomo resume the procession, chant another prayer, and once again, the singing and dancing rekindle.

Into the night the drinking and dancing take their toll, and the decorum of the service rapidly yields to frenzy as we circle and spin to the point of dizziness. Old Dr. Brodie, silver-haired and patriarchal, dances alone in the middle of the swirling circles, clapping his hands and singing songs of his youth in Galicia. His wife sits and chuckles.

With each renewed bout of drinking, one by one the weak drop out in exhaustion. Not so our Hasidim who, despite their dark suits, seem not to show a drop of fatigue. When well past midnight the festivities die a natural death, Yossi and Shlomo can scarcely conceal their disappointment. "You should only see what's going on tonight on Eastern Parkway," Shlomo mumbles.

Shortly after Elyah's arrival in Israel in 1973, war broke out. A musician as well as a painter, he was dispatched with a friend to entertain the troops. They arrived at a kibbutz, which, unbeknown to them, had been overrun by the Syrians, who had been driven out only moments earlier. Even as they pulled up, the kibbutz defenders were emerging from their bunkers. Corpses and pieces of corpses littered the ground. Though still heavily armed, the soldiers demanded that Elyah and his friend play their guitars. Shaken and shattered, they refused; it was impossible. The soldiers ordered them to play, and so they played. Throwing down their weapons, the kibbutz defenders, men and women, joined arms, singing and dancing.

Menahem Mendel of Przemyslany used to say, "Three things are fitting for us: motionless dancing, upright kneeling, and silent screaming."

When asked in a recent interview (*Quest*/80, July-August) if he is a Jewish guru, Adin Steinsaltz is not amused. "Basically, it's revolting," he answers, for people to stare at him with cow eyes. Surely they have never met him. Pure attachment, he says, is death, as much as is pure detachment. Self-mastery, not unquestioning deference, is the Jewish way, and that is a process, an "oscillation" up and down, a movement "heavenward and earthward, like breath; this is life." To be Jewish implies struggle, and he quotes Tolstoy who said that a Jewish non-believer cannot exist whether inside or outside the tradition. "Israel," Steinsaltz reminds us, was the name given to Jacob, the ancestor of the Jews: in Hebrew it literally means "one who wrestles with God."

Adin Steinsaltz is a phenomenon as much as he is a person. He was raised in a militantly socialist family on an Israeli kibbutz and received a secular education, acquiring degrees in physics and mathematics. Obsessed with religious questions, he embarked on a task of awesome monumentality: to translate by himself the entire thirty-three volumes of the Babylonian Talmud and to add his own commentary, the first wholly new edition of the Talmud in 700 years. As well, he has written *The Essential Talmud*, a primer; *Beggars and Prayers*, a retelling with commentary of the mystical tales of Rabbi Nachman of Bratzlav; and *The Thirteen Petalled Rose*, a personal — and highly accessible — exposition of cabalistic theology. Additionally, he has written on archaeology, science fiction, cats, and politics. He founded the Shefa (Abundance) Institute to bring traditional Judaism to secular Jews, and publishes its journal. Last year Jean-Paul Sartre and Simone de Beauvoir invited him to Paris for a dialogue with Palestinian Arabs. He is forty-two and has a wife and two children. He suffers from a genetic disease which has severely taxed his health.

Recently I met him. Though I had heard vaguely of his scholarly reputation, I knew little of him personally, whether he was a dry academic or personally devout. He is, in fact, a pious man, physically slight, a mystic, who exudes that curiously compelling blend of gentility and liveliness, modesty and authority, that one sees in the truly religious, in those who sojourn in other worlds. Despite his Promethean labors — another Jew forcing the Messiah's hand — he maintains perspective.

Question: Rabbi Steinsaltz, what brings you to America?
Answer: To meet Woody Allen.

"When I die and face the heavenly tribunal," Rabbi Zusya used to say, "they will not ask me why I was not Moses; rather, they will want to know why I was not Zusya."

9 a.m. I open the iron gate of Yakov's courtyard; his wife, a fair

woman and very pregnant, waters the flowers. (Later I learn that she will give birth that very day.) She calls to Yakov. I am apprehensive, never having chewed the cud with a Hasid before. He again apologizes for his inability to extend hospitality the previous evening and invites me upstairs to his studio. Climbing the steps we are bedeviled by his young son who mischievously steals stares at the stranger. The father firmly but gently tells the child to apply himself to his prayer and studies. He explains that his child is home today from the yeshiva in Meron because of the festival of L'ag B'omer. On this holiday thousands of pilgrims visit the tomb of Simeon bar Yohai, the legendary author of the *Book of Splendor*, the *Zohar*, but he refuses to expose his son to the idolators among them: hawkers selling cheap wares, beggars, pimps, and as he puts it, "women immodestly dressed." He ushers me into his studio.

The walls are lined with his paintings, geometrical abstractions in the current international style. Some are shaped canvases, repeating a Star of David motif. Other designs, he explains, he borrows from ornamentation on ancient synagogues. The forms are based on cabalistic numerology. On one canvas ten rays, corresponding to the *sefirot* (the channels of divine emanation), pass through four blocks (the four levels of being), and disappear into white light (the *ayin sof*, non-being, the Infinite Itself, the Godhead). Yakov removes a battered catalogue from beneath an easel. His colors he has borrowed from Ben Cunningham, a British expressionist of the 1930s.

We retire to his balcony — a long view across the valley — and recline on two plastic chaise lounges. How is it possible, I want to ask him, to be a geometrical abstractionist in this ancient holy city? In his person, in his art, time past and time present seem to conjoin happily. He drops names of artists and dismisses the reputations of ungodly self-promoters. He himself will sell his work only to and through people who are "Torah-centered." He has found a rabbi in Haifa who owns a gallery. He discusses the prophet Micah and tells bad jokes about Jimmy Carter. He is curious about American Jewry. "How is it possible," he asks me, "to be a Jew in North Carolina?"

When the Baal Shem Tov was troubled he would go to the forest to meditate. There he would light a fire, pray, and — miraculously — what he asked was done.

When his disciple, the Maggid of Mezeritch, sought heavenly help, he would go to the same forest and say: "I cannot light the fire, but I do know the prayer." And what he asked, it, too, was done.

In a later generation Moshe-Leib of Sassov would return to the same forest as his predecessors and pray: "I have no fire. I do not know the prayer, but this is the place in the forest, and it must suffice." And so, too, what he asked was done.

Finally, Israel of Rizhin sat at his home and beseeched the Holy One: "I cannot light the fire nor do I know the prayer. I am unable to find the place in the forest. All I can do is tell the story, and it must suffice."

And that, too, was enough.

(September 1980)

Autobiography No. 34

Carl Mitcham

An ox had been lost somewhere. He
heard about it, and wanted

to join with others in the search. He imagined
himself as a hunter

who had caught sight of the tracks
or instinctively knew the secret

watering places, and was able to wait
patiently nearby, concealed in a blind.

He could also imagine himself as a cat
single-mindedly stalking its prey,

or as a lizard or walking-stick camouflaged
on the branches of a tree,

as a flamingo standing on one leg for hours
in the marsh. He imagined himself

sitting so still
that he could hear

his own blood coursing through his veins,
that listening he would fall

in with the very rhythms of creation,
and through these rhythms

into the mind
of one who knew everything,

even the whereabouts of the ox.
If only he could be like a snake

warming itself on a rock
or like a bear hibernating in Winter,

like a tree which stands for 200 years
and only sways in response to the wind,

like the grass growing low in the fields,
being grazed by cattle, eaten by insects, withered

by the sun — all of which,
of course, know the whereabouts of the ox.

Or if he could just be like some plant in the garden,
a seed buried in the ground,

a stone at the edge of the road, like
one of the stars hanging in place for a million years,

like a fossil
entombed in the earth.

O the glory of thus finding the ox!

But dreaming all these things
he never caught sight of the ox.

(June 1979)

Three Photographs

Priscilla Rich

Of God, And My Father: A Memoir

David M. Guy

When I was ten years old I passed through a period when I could not sleep. Probably the first sleepless night was an accident, or perhaps the first two, but I began to worry about them, and soon I couldn't sleep at all. Long before bed-time I would start feeling anxious, and however tired I might have been all evening, by the time I was ready for bed I was awake and alert. In my anxiety I would go to my parents, try-ing to laugh, make light of it all, and they would laugh with me, aware of my worries and wanting not to add to them. We would laugh at my comic arrival in their bedroom, at ten o'clock, eleven, eleven-thirty, at twelve; when it got that late they would say, "Oh David, are you *still* awake?" and I could see the concern behind their smiles, and perhaps a

It may be that I was just afraid of dying . . . but somehow I was equally afraid of eternal life.

trace of annoyance, as they let me come with them into their bed, and promised that if I were too tired the next day, I would not have to go to school.

My memories of my father are vivid from those years. I particularly remember the long, hot Summer evenings, when we would have opened every window and door, trying to catch a breeze (my father announcing its arrival with a shout like a command: "Feel the breeze"); by the late evening it did get cool, and quite comfortable, as we sat reading in the living room. He would still be wearing a white shirt, rumpled by then, from work, and an old pair of khaki pants that he relaxed in. He did not smoke at the office — I think he felt a doctor shouldn't smoke in front of his patients — but in the evening would take some cigarettes from my mother's pack and smoke them between the hours of his nap (he always took a nap after dinner) and his late bedtime. He had a can of beer beside his chair, which through the evening must have been two or three cans; he was not a heavy drinker, but would have a drink before dinner and those several beers afterward. My father sitting with several buttons of his shirt open, so the thick graying hair of his chest showed; his light occasional sips from the beer; the three or four long, quiet exhalations of smoke from his lungs (when I later took up smoking, I would try to duplicate exactly those sounds); the rustling sound as he turned a page — I sat on the couch less to read than to be enveloped in that atmosphere. I was too old, by then, to sit with him in his chair, feel the warmth of his breath on my head, smell the faint odor of his sweat, but being just a few feet away was almost as comforting.

Those nights when I could not sleep I began to ask the unanswerable questions. I don't remember whether my sleeplessness was a result of the anxiety they caused me, or whether, already awake, I stumbled upon those questions that were to cause me so much anguish. At first they did not exist in my mind as questions, simply an attempt at comprehension: I was trying to understand eternity, and I could not. I would picture endless blackness, like the utter darkness I had experienced once in the depth of a cavern; I would imagine myself moving through it with no end to my movement. I would try to imagine existing with no expectation for tomorrow, next week, next year, or the end of time, because there would be none, only an endless present. I would try to understand how

God could exist with no beginning to his existence, how there could be an existence with no beginning, and then, by analogy, would try to conceive of my own life with no end, but I couldn't do it; I would imagine myself, in that eternal blackness, thinking, "But it all must have started sometime, so it must sometime be going to end," and if it all did end sometime — the universe, God, everything — what would be there in its place? What had been there before it began?

It may be that I was just afraid of dying, that I had suddenly discovered death — certainly the thought of eternal non-being terrified me — but somehow I was equally afraid of eternal life. What I could conceive of it — an existing with no particular purpose, goal; a thousandfold anxiety at its indeterminate future — seemed impossible, incredible, grotesque, an existence no one could want to lead.

Great thinkers have said that of all the eternal possibilities, endless life on this mortal Earth would be the worst. Yet, I also think that in those days what I most wanted was an assurance that my life as it existed then would infinitely continue, that there would be one after another of those quiet Summer evenings with my father.

I finally took my fears to him, late on one of those nights when I couldn't sleep. I have calculated: he died when I was sixteen, and I was told then that he had known of his illness for more than six years. I was experiencing those fears at the same time he had discovered the disease in his body that was to kill him. I can remember my mother telling me of his long silences in those days just after he had been to the doctor; she had to wait several days for him to tell her what was wrong. I have often wondered if, by coincidence, I was asking him those questions at the worst possible time.

I remember his first reaction, a laughing, quizzical concern, as if he were amazed I had brought those things up. I don't remember exactly how he answered me. I don't remember, either, that what he said particularly set my mind at rest; there was a long period when I could only get to sleep in bed with my father and mother. But I do remember something he told me, and perhaps it was the most important thing, just because it is what I have remembered through all the years.

He must have sensed my solitude. For as I tried to imagine eternity, I did not envision a physical location, and therefore did not picture anyone around me. I knew that eternal life was to be spent in communion with God, but I didn't know what that involved, what activity could last through eternity. I pictured only myself, in endless space and time, and the answer my father offered me — not as a little story you tell your son to allow him to sleep, but as a belief so much a part of him that it came naturally to his mind (if he had believed there was no eternal life I think he would have said that) — was that I was not alone, that I lived in the presence of God. It's odd as I think of it: he didn't say that I would some day live in the presence of God; in a way he wasn't answering my questions at all. But he said that when we are young we are unaware of God's existence, of any existence, in fact, but our own; as far as we are concerned, the universe revolves around our being. It is only as we grow — perhaps he said if we grow — that we discover we are not the center of things, that the core of existence lies elsewhere, and, inasmuch as we continue to grow, we move out from concern with ourselves, try to center our existence in that core. The whole process of growth, in fact, involves that moving out from ourselves. Inasmuch as we grow at all we are involved in a search for God.

Those few words — it took him only moments to say them — did not make the universe any smaller or simpler for me. I have no memory of immediately putting what he said into practice. I doubt that I really understood it; I had never thought of God in anything even remotely like those terms. But it must have impressed me. It is what I have remembered through all the years, even more than my fears.

Those fears have not disappeared. It seems the nature of human existence that, no matter how well we once explain them away, they do return, because they are not rational concerns. I still sometimes envision the darkness, feel the leaden weight of eternal time. But I think of my father, facing death straight on, devoting even his last days to his family, patients; I think of my wife, son, friends, the many lives that I touch just by being alive; I think of God, in an infinite universe, calling others into being that He might love them — just as, by loving, even we can call others into being. And my fears are not dispersed (I must learn to live with the fears within me always), but I do see a shadow, a hint, of the nature of eternal life.

(May 1977)

Seeing The Gift

An Interview with Hugh Prather

Sy Safransky

I interviewed Hugh Prather in Virginia Beach, where he was giving a talk at the Association for Research and Enlightenment, set up to carry on the work of Edgar Cayce, the sleeping prophet who predicted that Virginia Beach would be a haven during the coming global cataclysms.

Resort hotels and restaurants encroaching on the dunes, a tidal wave of ugliness, suggest another kind of cataclysm in Virginia Beach — the rape of the eye and the ear, Resort Town U.S.A., built on nobody's fault line, the bottom line. Amidst it all, the corporate splendor of the A.R.E., looking like an insurance company, or a church, its bookstore crammed with every variety of spiritual literature, a cacophony of truth, a hotel of the mind for every journeyer, no reservations please.

I spent several hours with Hugh

Often, students of truth feel they have to test their faith and I went through a period like this. . . . I shouldn't wear seat belts in the car because it was a negative thought and it would draw accidents to me. But who would get in a car with no brakes and expect God to brake the car at every stop sign?

Prather in his motel room across the street from the A.R.E. It might have been a thousand miles away; the materialistic and spiritually materialistic worlds he travels in — and he travels a lot, giving thirty or forty talks a year — seem to have little hold on him. He's learned to love himself. And to love others, without advertising it. Wise words you expect during an interview. Genuine words of concern, before and after an interview — that's not on the menu, but that's what makes the difference.

Best known for his earlier book, Notes to Myself, *a diary of observations about his "struggle to become a person," Prather has more recently written* There Is A Place Where You Are Not Alone, A Book Of Games, *and* The Quiet Answer. *They're about love, and the power of forgiveness. In* The Quiet Answer, *he writes:*

Fear is a distraction. It is mental turmoil. It does not focus. It does not even know exactly what it fears. Fear is pure avoidance without direction. Calmness dispels fear by restoring the willingness to look. Through either direct or gradual means, the thoughts and exercises in this book urge you to look, to be honest, to be calm, so that the grounds for happiness can be clearly seen. And these grounds will never be comparative. True gratitude is not based on the perception that others have less or suffer more. It is the recognition that spirit instead of flesh holds all that is of value and that there is no end to spirit. Because love does exist, you are free.

A counselor and teacher, who has worked in the fields of alcoholism, divorce, suicide, rape, battered women, and child abuse, Prather lives with his wife, Gayle, and three-year-old-son, John, in Santa Fe, New Mexico.

— Ed.

SUN: Does writing about God take you closer or farther away from God?

PRATHER: Writing used to be a struggle. I would have schedules and I would quarrel with the thesaurus and do multiple drafts and I was never able to adhere to the schedule but always felt I was supposed to.

About a year ago, I realized that there were several gifts in my life. Of course everything is a gift. But there were certain ones I could recognize. My wife and my little boy were unquestionably gifts from God. Another was my particular talent to write and to speak. The gift is given to you to make you happy. And at that particular time I decided above all else I wanted to establish the peace of God as my single goal in all that I did. That's just my way of phrasing it. And that I was not going to do that unless I began simplifying my way of life and enjoying the little windows to heaven that I could recognize. There are a few places where the rays of peace and love shine into our lives and we must begin there.

I realized that I wanted to put the happiness of my wife first. She was unquestionably my spiritual partner. In so doing I would learn that to give is to receive. You have to begin some place. It's nice to say to give is to receive but unless you're practicing it, you don't really believe it. It's just a concept. So as I did that, and began to realize that John was the expression of our love, the extension of our love for each other, then the theory that they were gifts became more and more fact. And I saw that speaking and writing could become the same thing if I let them.

We took a little room in the house and made it as comfortable as we could, without any regard to whether the contents were spiritual, because wall-to-wall carpeting is not spiritual. We just made a peaceful little nest. Very simple. And in there we do only two things. We write or we meditate. Gayle and I go into that little room usually three times a day. It's not a ritual but usually works out that way. Almost always in the morning and usually also in the evening and in the afternoon. So I just go into this room and I sit down there in peace. And I write in peace.

Now, at the time this change took place — and it was a subtle, gradual, gentle change — I was ghost-writing a book, which is something I've done several times. And I was about a third into this project when it became clear to me that either the book would not be published, or, if it were published, very few people were going to read it. Here was a case where my ego had all it needed to have a little fit. I was not going to get any credit. I was not going to get any money. And the thing probably wasn't even going to be read. Now did I want to continue writing? This was a very important turning point for me. The answer — after meditating and thinking about it, calmly and peacefully — was yes. I wanted to continue writing because I enjoyed writing. And that was a sufficient reason. It didn't matter what happened to the material.

I had to begin doing things out of peace. I had to begin following my peaceful preference regardless of what my ego said the consequences would be. I didn't know what the consequences would be. The fact that it was a peaceful thing for me to do was sufficient reason to continue doing it. I love writing. The moment there is any distress in the writing I just get up and leave it. I go about my day until I feel I can sit down happily and begin writing again. And once again, if there's any distress, I get up. In other words, I refuse for it now to be anything else but a thoroughly enjoyable experience.

SUN: You talk about how everything is a gift. With something in your life that is really a struggle — some scare, some craziness — what process do you go through to see the gift in that? If you could be specific that would be helpful.

PRATHER: I don't think anything in our life has to be messed with unless it is disturbing our ability to turn to God. This includes illness, even terminal illness.

If I had a terminal illness, I don't believe I would do anything in particular about it unless it was disturbing my ability to turn to God. I look at everything that comes up in my life — or try to, at least — in a similar way.

When I turned forty, I was running sixteen to eighteen miles every day, in sand. I was doing more than 100 sit-ups, I had one of these rowing machines, I was lifting weights, and I was watching my calories, and I had been doing that for as long as I could remember. I'd always enjoyed running but now the whole thing had become absurd, because I was having to spend almost an hour every day doing exercises to lengthen the muscles in the back part of my body which the running was shortening. I was now spending almost half my life fighting this battle to hold my weight down. So I was out running one day and I asked myself, "Why am I doing this?" And I couldn't think of a reason. I just stopped right there in the road.

Now what often happens in these situations where we think we've found an external solution is we simply go from one extreme to the other. And that is what happened. I stopped all exercise. And I allowed myself to eat everything, all the time. I'm forty-four now. Over a period of about four years, this gradually became a problem. My health was not as good as it was. And I started becoming self-conscious in public, especially when I would meet friends who knew me before. I would find that I was thinking too much about that. So that's an example. I now recognize that while this has definitely been a step forward — it was consuming much less of my mental and emotional life than it had been — it still was a big chunk of something that I hadn't let go of. So the way I went about solving that problem, or anything that's interfering with my ability to turn to God, was to pause in peace and then act with assurance. I believe that the peace of God is the best guide back to peace. In peace, something will come to us to do. And it's very important that we do something. If we don't do something, we don't want to go past the problem. So here was the problem. What was I willing to do?

I had not gone to a doctor for twelve years and a certain amount of pride had developed, that somehow I wasn't supposed to go to a doctor. That I was beyond this. That I should be able to work out all my problems internally. I wasn't working out this problem. And in my prayer, there was a particular doctor who kept coming to mind. He had been Gandhi's physician, Krishnamurti's physician, and he had moved to this country. He had his own ashram. Aside from all that he was an extremely loving and gentle man. I'd met him on one occasion and I'd heard a number of people speak of him. And it was my conviction through my prayer that he was a healer. And the minute I decided to go to him I felt instantly better. I can remember making the decision and suddenly feeling better because I had let go of this pride. And in going to him, it turned out that the simplicity with which he was living was very inspiring to me, and to Gayle. So as a result of going to him I began eating much more simply, we began living much more simply. Not that he told us to do this. He didn't. It's just that we looked at his life, how simple it was, how happy he was all the time, how he seemed to love everybody's personality. I had not seen that point. I was thinking of the ego as the personality and thinking that the ego is something that we relinquish and not realizing that you can love people's personalities just as you can love the personalities of different dogs or different bird songs.

So what happened was I went to my peace. From the peace came the thought of something to try and I tried it. Now it happens that this began to work right away but what I've found is that it doesn't always work and that doesn't matter. It does matter, though, that I then go back to my peace, see what else I want to do and try that. And then if that doesn't work, go back to my peace and try something else. And I continue this until I move past the problem. So the decision is: I will move past this problem because it is interfering with my ability to turn to God. And I will do something.

SUN: Talk about your marriage: what happily married means; what happiness means, for that matter.

PRATHER: Gayle and I have been married for almost seventeen

years. I'd say about fifteen of those years we had a sort of typical marriage, which means it could have fallen apart at any instant, even if we didn't think so. All of us look around and see people who have been together for a number of months or years — ten, fifteen, twenty years — and suddenly they're breaking up, not speaking to each other. It seems like they were each other's best friends, sharing everything. A month later, nothing. As if there's no love in their hearts.

It's very much like trading in a car on a new model. You had this car and you loved it so much when you got it and you took it out and had it washed, kept it up, got it fixed. And suddenly there's a new model, something that is more special, and the new car replaces the old car in your heart and you have very little, if any, remorse in letting the old car go. Most relationships are on that basis. You form a new relationship that replaces in your heart the old relationship and there is surprisingly little remorse that the old relationship has gone by the wayside and everyone is left with their mouth open. You don't understand how this can happen, but the fact is that it happens over and over. And it is, in fact, the given. It's only because you thought there was real friendship and trust and loyalty there that you're surprised. Because it shouldn't surprise us, it happens all the time.

There is another foundation on which a relationship can rest. I touched on this before in saying that I decided that I would put Gayle's happiness first. A year ago we made the decision to form a holy relationship. The *Course in Miracles* goes into great detail on this. But it still, once again, is one of those concepts. I'm not recommending this. There are people who are obviously not ready for this and for them it would simply create a war. But if two people wish to form a holy relationship, and they're together on this, it's quite simple to do.

The praying together is very important. We begin the day together, with the recognition that we are walking home together, hand in hand. We will always be together. That's oftentimes not easy for people to see — that they're going to walk home with this individual. And I can't tell you how you see it, it's just sort of a quiet inner recognition that grows within you and you understand finally that you are with this individual. You're of course with everyone else but you realize that you're not going to get home unless you treat this individual with all the love and kindness that you have within you, that you respect this relationship and the fact that the universe has brought you together.

So we begin praying together, setting our purpose for the day together, realizing that we want to make each other happy and exert a different kind of pressure on each other. Instead of a pressure that would make each other guilty — that kind of manipulative pressure in which you try to get that other person to do something, hold up their end of the bargain, change this particular thing about their body or their personality — there's another kind of pressure in which you see sometimes how your partner has gotten onto an unhappy road. Maybe they're all caught up with something a clerk said to them in a store and this is ruining their day. It could be any number of things. It's as if there are these two roads: one is a very happy road and the other one is the usual, unhappy road. So you exert this very gentle pressure for them to be peaceful and happy. That is not chastising or correcting. It's a pleading for their happiness. After we've been with someone for a certain period of time we know what to do to make them happy and lead them back to peace.

So we may make an effort to do this. And their ego may be so caught up in whatever is going on that they reject our first effort. And that is just fine. We step back in peace and we love them. And then we make another effort. We're literally there to usher them into heaven. We can do that. We know how to do that. That person, of course, does the same thing for us. Such acceleration of progress can take place when two people are actively working for the same goal and trying to assist each other.

This is a game I sometimes play: I can't get to heaven but I can get Gayle to heaven. Now by "heaven" I mean a state of mind. Heaven, I think, is here and now. It's awakening in God. It's a state of natural happiness and peace that is ours and somehow we've mentally looked away from it. I'm not speaking of heaven as a physical location to which we must journey on some bloody, self-sacrificing path. It's like in *Alice in Wonderland*, when she turns to the doorknob at the end of her journey and says to the doorknob, "How can I get out?" and the doorknob says, "You can't get out, you're already out." That's what I mean by heaven. It's a recognition that we're already there. But it feels like a journey and seems to take a certain kind of effort. So the praying together is important. It sets the purpose. And it flows from this gentle pressure.

The second thing that is important is what I mentioned before — you put the other person's happiness first. Here's how that works. Before I do anything during the day, I first ask myself, "Is Gayle happy?" If she's not happy, I don't do it. I first make her happy, then I do it. I literally put her happiness first. This can sound like some form of self-sacrifice but it actually teaches me that to give is to receive, because when I make her happy the happiness I receive is ten times greater. What often happens in the usual relationships that we've all had is that each person carries on in quite a selfish way. By selfish I mean that only the ego is served. People who may have formed a pretty good alliance ask themselves mainly, "What do I want to do? How can I manipulate my mate so that I can do it? How can I do it so my mate won't have too big a fit about it, or get in the way?" You will see, for example, one person who may be a writer and one person who is a potter, so the person who is a potter is always looking for a time to go throw pots. The other person is looking for time to do the writing. And they have put throwing pots and writing before their relationship. Now to them this is a very innocent thing to do and it is innocent. There's certainly no guilt in it. But you can't form a holy relationship or a great love relationship as long as you do that. The only thing that is difficult about this is seeing the importance of it because it's not readily apparent that it is so important. It's easy to say, "I need my space and I need my time, I need this, I need that. And it would be a great sacrifice to make my mate happy, although I can see that my mate is in a lot of trouble right now. I can't mess with that. I need my own energy."

The third thing that we recognize is the typical ego ploys to distract us from a holy relationship. Because a holy relationship will produce the kind of peace in which the ego will melt away. This imaginary identity will defend itself because that's the way we've set it up. One of its ploys is, "There are so many worthy things to do." The ego adopts a new position.

The higher ego adapts to the spiritual path and cites truth in order to cause conflict. Here's some worthy project you've been offered. I was approached about doing groups at the penitentiary for inmates before they left and then again to have groups for them outside. And at the same time I was being offered an opportunity to start a group for juvenile delinquents. At the same time I was being offered the opportunity to start a public access television station, which would appeal more to the heart than to the ego. And on and on. There's no limit to it. In addition to the television station, I'd just started a little church, the Dispensible Church. So one of the ploys is worthy activity. This is "very important," the ego meaning: this is more important than your great love relationship.

What can also come up in the guise of spiritual truth — because the ego will use words like openness and unconditional love — is the idea you should go out and have a relationship with every person of the opposite sex you could think of. Or, in Santa Fe, a person of the same sex. It doesn't matter. And the ego will say, it's not important if you go ahead and have this relationship because love should be universal and so forth. That all sounds very good, but it simply isn't the way it works. It certainly isn't sinful, but it does stop the forming of this holy relationship. I've seen people try to work this out in a thousand different ways. Open marriage is one of those wonderful concepts because it has the word open in it. It sounds like it must be very spiritual. Some couples have been amazing in their ability to sort of accommodate each other. But you don't see this deep peace growing in the relationship as long as that's going on. Now, of course, there are simply people who can't help it, they're just at the stage where they've got to do that. And that's fine. So I'm only talking about those people who sincerely want to form a holy relationship. The ploy of the ego that they might want to notice is that they will be offered some substitute relationships and that if they see this or if their mate sees this as a form of disloyalty, then they're not putting their partner's happiness first.

Let me say this also — not everyone needs to form a holy relationship. There are people who will awaken without someone by their side. Mother Theresa is an obvious example. But Mother Theresa has this constant dialogue with God. She's formed a holy relationship with God. She talks to God all the time. It seems apparent that there are people who will not awaken without their holy relationship. And there are people who will awaken with another kind of holy relationship. They've formed a holy relationship with God, or they may call God something else. They may call God "Jesus" or they may call God their "spiritual guide." There's this sense of going beyond the confines of their body. They're now uniting with something else, which is, of course, simply a recognition that they are more than just their body. This isn't literally bringing two things that were previously separate together but it feels like it's a bringing together. Because we start out thinking we're nothing but a body and we're actually inside a body looking out of these little holes in our head, hearing out of these little holes in the sides of our heads, we really think that's what we are.

I find it's very helpful to have a plan of operation. So in our moments of sanity, Gayle and I have said to ourselves a thousand times that above all we want the peace of God. Above all, we want to give a gift to our awakening and to the awakening of all our brothers and sisters. So whenever one of us gets caught up in something, some jealousy, some anger, some bitterness, some grievance, some depression, some sickness, whatever it may be, it's understood it's all right for the other one to come and help or suggest we go off and meditate. Now if we are both caught up in it, what I've found is that one person is a little more sane than the other. They're not more advanced or better or anything. And this changes all the time. But usually in these situations there's one person who suddenly sees the insanity of it and can suggest that there's got to be a better way and wouldn't you like to sit with me for a moment and let's see if we can't find a better way to do this.

SUN: A friend of mine, a therapist, wanted me to ask you how you deal with dependency on your wife. But the terms you're using to describe that relationship, the assumptions about who the two of you are, suggest to me something quite different from emotional dependency.

PRATHER: There is a sort of sick dependency and it's characterized by a great deal of anxiety. What will I do if I lose this person? We sort of tiptoe around the other individual and the relationship is like walking through a mine field. We don't know if any moment we might say something that will set the other person off. Or maybe there is a dependency on some aspect of the relationship, such as getting your mate to cooperate sexually with you. You think, above all, you've got to have sex three times a week, so you can't do anything to anger your mate, who might say, "No sex."

But that's always characterized by a ground of anxiety. There's no deep trust in it. Another thing I didn't mention that is part of a holy relationship, a very fundamental part of it: complete honesty and openness. But this isn't the kind of honesty practiced in the late Sixties and Seventies in which you list — honestly list — the other person's faults. You tell the person, very honestly, that they're a son of a bitch. That's not honesty. What's happened is that these angers have built up and now, instead of being honest, you're simply using the opportunity to attack and you're attacking in the name of honesty. It has nothing to do with this instant. True honesty has to do with this instant. So we may, for example — and we do this quite frequently — sit down and examine, not analyze, but look at our ego positions on a particular subject. Most people who have come together have opposite ego positions on a number of subjects. Now, that is a disguise for spiritual strengths that complement each other, but on the ego level it shows up as one person who always wants to spend his money, and one person who always wants to save her money. One person wants to be gregarious and have lots of people and go out and the other person likes to be quiet and spend a quiet evening at home. One person wants to be very firm with the child and the other wants to let the child be free and learn for itself. Always the individual's ego is arguing the rightness of its separate position and to us our position always seems right. And if we're on a spiritual path we can justify spiritually what we're doing, because we've temporarily forgotten that truth has nothing to do with behavior. It doesn't imply anything about behavior. It implies something about our heart. But it implies nothing about our actions. Because the same action can be loving or unloving. So I cannot form a holy relationship while hiding things from Gayle. I cannot in the name of kindness be a little deceitful.

SUN: Are your dreams important to you?
PRATHER: The greatest of all hymns — "Row, row, row your boat, gently down the stream. Merrily, merrily, merrily, merrily," — that's very important, you see, there are four merrilys to every three rows; even though you're rowing gently it is still more important to be merry — "Life is but a dream." Every major philosophy and religion says the same thing. Even our own Bible says Adam fell asleep and never woke up. There's no account of his waking up. So it becomes obvious as we journey back toward God, what we are actually doing

is awakening in God. We are asleep in the arms of God, dreaming that we are bodies just as we do at night. And at night we can dream that we are a body that is quite different from the body in bed. It's no less convincing to us while we are asleep. And we still think we're confined in this body and we have all these problems and we try to solve them, even though we ourselves have set the problems up. It's very important in the dream. We wake up and see it wasn't important at all.

I have a friend who had a dream that he was in the house and his wife asked him to go out and check on the spoons. So he did and sure enough, the spoons are jumping over the wall. And this was a problem. What were they going to do about this? They didn't know whether they should build the patio wall higher or hire a spoon trainer. They decided they would build the patio wall higher. But what was going to happen? Would the spoons get hurt? You know, if they jumped over the wall. You know how it goes. It goes on and on. There's no end to it.

A *Course in Miracles* says that when you awake in the morning you merely pass from one dream to another. One of the most important recognitions is that this dream is never going to end in and of itself. It will just go on and on, like the soap operas on TV. It will always be something else. And it will always seem important. Sooner or later we have to make a decision to begin very gently to turn away from the dream. Not from our brothers and sisters but from the dream. A dream at night is a mimicry of what's going on. The daydream or the waking dream is once removed, but the night dream is twice removed. And when it's seen that way it can be extremely useful. For example, who holds a grievance against someone who did something in a dream, once you have awakened, and realize it was just a dream person? You can't stay angry when you realize it didn't happen. We realize what they did in the dream was just dreamed and so anger is dropped immediately. A *Course in Miracles* says that what you think your brother did to you did not happen. That's the basis of forgiveness. It's not dishonestly saying, "Well, somehow it was all right," or, "It will benefit me," or, "They didn't really mean it." Of course they meant it. They really were trying to hurt you. If you step away from the whole thing rather than trying dishonestly to manipulate the interpretation of it, then it is possible to let it go because you realize this grievance has nothing to do with your walk home.

I find dreams extremely helpful as an analogy to what's going on during the day. And they also suggest the solution, because we've all had the experience that we're dreaming at night and then suddenly realize that we are dreaming. We suddenly know in the dream that it's just a dream. And the whole thing becomes very happy, even if we're being chased by monsters. We now know it's a dream. It isn't the change in the circumstances of the dream that makes us happy, but the recognition that it is a dream, and that we are safe, and can't be hurt by any of this. What that analogy points to is that all we need to heal, all we need to change, is our heart. The way we are looking at things is the only change that is needed. If we can look at all things in love and peace, then we can enjoy all things until we awake. Another thing this analogy can teach you is that once we realize we are dreaming at night we also realize that our awakening is inevitable, and is not very far off. So no one panics once he realizes he is dreaming at night. It doesn't even occur to the dreamer to think, "Oh, will I ever wake up from this?" because now he realizes it's a dream. In that recognition comes the certainty that you will wake up and that you will wake up very soon. So you don't start running around in the dream forming committees to get everyone in the dream to wake up.

So, what do I say to my friend, whose spoons are jumping over the wall? Just sit quietly in peace. If you want to do something in the dream, that's fine, but this is just a dream and see what it is you want to do, because it will all be over very quickly. And so he sits quietly and maybe he does something about the spoons and maybe he doesn't. Why would he decide to do something? Maybe on the basis of whether or not it was disturbing his peace, which is his awakening process. To do nothing has consequences as well as doing something, in the dream. You can't do anything in this world, you can't do anything in a dream, that doesn't have ramifications. So, it's not possible to retire from the dream in the dream. This is a mistake that many people make. They go off and try to isolate themselves from the world, while still being in the world. And often people come back quite discouraged because they took the world with them in their mind. I'm not saying people shouldn't become nuns or monks. What I'm saying is that you do not awaken from the world by trying to isolate yourself from the world. You awaken from the world by accepting the peace of God within your heart.

SUN: How does someone keep in touch with the truths you're talking about, and be effective politically. How do *you* do that?

PRATHER: I help the people I can help. I take regular duty on the crisis line. I have two groups in Santa Fe. One is a grief group, people who have had a child or husband or wife die. I have a general open group in which we have mugging victims, battered women, alcoholics, people who are suicidal, people who are going through the breakup of a marriage. Then I have a Dispensible Church, which is a completely volunteer organization. I receive no money for it. I do a lot of counseling with individuals. I don't charge for that. So those are the things I can do. That's the beginning — helping the world in the way I can help it now rather than running off after some broad project that somehow never gets done and causes as many problems as it solves. When Mother Theresa was in India at a big conference they passed around a petition for the speakers to sign — a very mild statement, as those go, opposing nuclear proliferation. Mother Theresa and Baba Muktananda, without having gotten together on this, declined to sign it because they said they did not want to take part in a controversy and they did not want to side against the people who were for war, for nuclear proliferation. Now this to me is a truly helpful position. Love doesn't take sides against those who don't believe in love. One mistake people make — and they're well-intentioned — is that they think to solve some problem they're going to have to walk over a few people. Some reputations are going to have to be destroyed and certainly a lot of feelings are going to be hurt but it's all in the name of this cause. We can see in our own government these very well-intentioned things literally accomplish nothing. We've had all these projects in Washington that were very well-meant but didn't do anything, they just sort of shifted the whole thing around. There was a good deal of love and compassion and sincerity behind it, and that was very helpful — seeing that children were starving, that there were mothers that needed medical care, that there were streets that needed cleaning and all that. And they did what they thought they could do to help the situation. But often that sort of manipulative approach doesn't net anything. Whereas one individual working from his heart and doing what his intuition guides him to do can obviously relieve misery. And he may be doing it on a large scale or a small scale and that doesn't matter. Because the love is in helping us to awaken from this dream and not the overt form that it takes.

SUN: You refer to *A Course In Miracles* a lot. Tell me how it's been important for you.

PRATHER: *A Course In Miracles* itself states that it is *a* course in miracles and there are thousands of courses. So it is simply one statement of truth. It is a tool, a teaching aid that I personally find very helpful. But the course itself says it is not for everyone. It says if you're already praying you don't need this course. It makes statements like, forget this course and turn to God. So it's very important for your readers to understand that I am not recommending *A Course In Miracles*, for to do that would be against the very teaching itself, which is that a universal theology is not a possibility, but that a universal experience is a necessity.

It's very important that we stop shopping around. People really cause themselves a lot of unhappiness by trying this and that. There's just no end to it. The ego has gotten in there. They're looking for the perfect spiritual tool. And on that level there is no perfect spiritual tool. When I first started reading *A Course In Miracles* I was so impressed with the content. Then I ran across a few mistakes in punctuation and I was horrified. Well, this is the ego. Does that mean I throw out the books because of whoever was proofreading it? It was important that I stop shopping around. That's what I did when I came across *A Course In Miracles*. I said this is the best thing for me that I've run across. I'm going to settle on this and start. Maybe it will be useful for several months, maybe several years, maybe the rest of my life. That's irrelevant. It's useful to me now so I will use it.

It's a set of three books. The second book contains 365 lessons that offer specific suggestions on how to remember God as you go through the day, along with some very simple meditation techniques and even suggestions on how to word certain prayers or certain affirmations. So *A Course In Miracles* presents a teaching — a very theoretical, abstract thing — and then shows you how to incorporate the teaching into your mental process. And that was the thing that made it so helpful to me. It gave me a specific way of using it. The third book gives the answer to a number of questions that would commonly arise with anyone that studied the course. And it gives a general tone of an answer, so that from reading the third volume — a manual for teachers — I can get a sense of how to be very gentle with someone who is asking for help. Or someone who is obviously making a mistake. So often, we want to rush in and try to convince a person that they're not doing it right or point out their error. And it becomes clear that it's never necessary to confront the ego directly. A person may be embarking on what we know will be a very unhappy course, but it also may be apparent that there's nothing that can be done about it. They're just not ready to see that. But we can help them in this other area of their life. We don't even have to get involved in that thing. But here's this other area where they are ready to see something and so very gently and happily we can present them with something truly useful to them. I don't study the books in the way I used to because I now realize that truth is simple and whether we understand how *A Course In Miracles* is using this term or that term is not important. There's simply the dream and there's reality. And the question of which do I wish. Do I want to be happy, or do I want to be right?

SUN: If you see your child is about to fall down a flight of stairs, you've got to act on that. You might feel anxiety. That seems natural to me, although in your terms it's also within the dream. On a more global level. . . .
PRATHER: It's bringing love into the dream to save your child, and love is the awakening. And it's more loving to catch your child than to let him fall. By expressing that love and protecting his peace you are then part of the answer rather than part of the problem.

SUN: How about those who view the presence of nuclear weapons, for example, as humanity tottering on the stairs?
PRATHER: Anyone who feels strongly about nuclear proliferation or nuclear power plants or anything else should obviously follow the deep feelings within his heart. If someone sees how he personally can be of help in that situation, it's fine for him to do that. We're always doing something in this dream, even if we're just sitting in a chair. And sitting in a chair has consequences, as I said before. This is something that's so often misunderstood. For example, *A Course In Miracles* says, "You need do nothing." But it doesn't say, "Do not act in this world." There's nothing that you *need* to do. Your way home

does not consist of certain prescribed, overt behaviors. But obviously it's not calling for no physical action, just to vegetate in a bathtub.

SUN: Are you afraid to die?
PRATHER: I'm less afraid than I was. As long as my ego is capable of acting up and controlling me, I'm still going to be afraid, to some degree. But I am decidedly less afraid. Often, students of truth feel that they have to test their faith and I went through a period like this. I had to leave the front door open because everybody should be trusted. I shouldn't wear safety belts in the car because it was a negative thought and it would draw accidents to me. But who would get in a car with no brakes and expect God to stop the car at every stop sign? One of the main ways the higher ego makes the spiritual path so hard is by telling us that truth implies certain behavior and that the behavior is the way home. Therefore, if you're spiritual, you shouldn't lock your door, you should never take medicine, you should never have an insurance policy, and so on. Which has nothing to do with truth whatsoever. For some people taking aspirin would be the way for them not to be thinking of their body. For other people, who are against any kind of medication, taking aspirin would cause them so much mental guilt or anguish it would be best for them not to take it.

SUN: To what extent do we create our own reality?
PRATHER: This is a concept that's presented in almost all teachings of truth — that we are responsible for our experiences. Once again, the higher ego steps in and uses this to cause all kinds of distress. I heard someone say recently, about a mother who had a blind baby, "She created her blind baby." Now this is not helpful to the mother, and it is absurd. Did Jesus create the crowds that stoned him? Did he create the stones? Did he create the Pharisees who railed against him? Did he create the corrupt system in Rome? Did he create the crucifixion? Did he create Judas? Did he draw Judas into his life? And make Judas betray him? When we take spiritual truth and try to apply it to the world we just make people very unhappy and this, of course, is the ego's purpose. It makes people become disenchanted with spiritual truth and they drop away for a while because they've been spending all their time manifesting parking spaces near the front door.

We do create our own reality in the same sense that when we fall asleep at night we choose to dream. But within the dream itself all of the circumstances are already set up so we choose the dream as a whole. But to go into the dream itself and look at the dream as if part of it is healed and part of it is unhealed and to say, "I am choosing that part which is unhealed, and this other part is OK" is absurd. There's no way to wake up by approaching it that way.

A time comes when we recognize that we don't need to get into this absurd application of truth to the details of this world. For example, let's take sugar. Sugar is a very fearful thing right now. There are so many articles and books. Everybody's scared of sugar. So someone says, "I create my diabetes. Diabetes is a decision." Meaning, sugar shouldn't hurt me, therefore I will eat the sugar. Well, that's crazy. Disease *is* a decision. It is true that if we understood this, no food would hurt us. We could walk in the sun and not be burned by the sun. We could leave our front door open and never be robbed. That's all true. The fact is there are certain things we have not gone beyond and if there is any anxiety about leaving the front door open, it shouldn't be left open. If there's any anxiety about the seat belts, then put the seat belts on, because the peace of God is more important than the issue the ego has raised. It doesn't matter that certain foods *shouldn't* hurt us. It does matter whether or not at our particular stage they *are* hurting us.

SUN: I know people who go through a cycle of smoking a lot of pot, for example, then deciding it's not good for them, and stopping it, and then, predictably, a few days or months later, they're doing it again. The same with coffee, tobacco, or diet. There's much conflict.
PRATHER: Once again, the body is not important. Do whatever allows you not to think of it. Finances are not important. Do whatever allows you not to think of it. I see people, for example, refusing to get jobs because God's supposed to take care of them. Well, it's true that it's possible to reach a state of mind where you can get money out of a fish's mouth. But if the person hasn't gotten to that point then it's ridiculous for him to sit home while the collectors beat on his door.

It's all coming from the higher ego. This has nothing to do with truth. So with smoking, drinking coffee, smoking dope, and various mild addictions, first of all this is not a big thing, not truly important. Alcoholism can be causing quite a bit of a problem, but smoking isn't causing that much difficulty with most people. Drinking coffee isn't. Beating your spouse or your children is probably causing a great deal of difficulty and should be taken care of quickly and easily and it can be. If the person will just try something, they can move beyond it. They can try neuro-linguistic programming or AA. There are so many organizations, so many approaches to solving those problems. The individual just has to decide that he wants to move beyond this, go out and get the help. If that help doesn't work, he goes to someone else until the problem is behind him. Because he realizes he's not going to make any more progress until he does that.

But it's possible to make tremendous progress while you're continuing to smoke cigarettes or drink coffee or take medicine or masturbate. I once had a woman call me up who was beating up her daughter. It took her half an hour to tell me that. It took her almost a year to tell me she'd had an affair with her minister. It took her two years to tell me that she masturbated. That was the worst of all her confessions, that she masturbated. Obviously the ego has made an issue out of something that is not important.

Now, if the individual finds that he is thinking a great deal about the smoking thing or being overweight, he can go ahead and do what he needs to do to move beyond that. But I would not advise anyone to do that unless they are sure that this is keeping them from turning to God. If it's not interfering with their meditation and their praying, and they have a sense of progress in their lives, it will take care of itself in its own time. One day, you'll wake up and you'll realize, "Oh, I'm not masturbating anymore, I'm not eating meat anymore, I'm not gossiping anymore, I don't have a craving for sweets anymore." Those things just fall away. There's no effort, you just happen to notice them in retrospect. So the best policy is to let it take care of itself — unless it is consuming a large amount of attention and then, try something.

There's a friend of mine who's very religious in a conventional sense and he's very religious in a real sense, too. He doesn't think he's supposed to look at women's bodies. So when he walks down the street, he will turn away from an attractive woman who is passing. Passing a store window in which there's a girlie magazine, he'll turn his head away. It seems to me he's creating an unnecessary war here. He's trying only one solution and it's obviously not working.

There are other things he can try if he wants to move beyond that. For example, this is a little meditation that I used. Let's say I had suddenly seen a woman whose body had startled me. I'd look at the body, and then I'd look away from the body, and say, "Is this the only place I'll find God?" Then I'd look back at the body. Often it's not the body, it's some particular part of the body that seems to contain all the power, which means the peace, all the peace of God we long for. And we think that we're going to be able to find it in another body, or a particular part of the body. So I would shuttle back and forth. I would look at the body. There's no war there. I'm just looking calmly. There's nothing to be afraid of. And what almost always happened was I would see the faults in the other person's body, meaning that it was just a body among all other bodies. Instead of being some sort of fantasy — which it would have been had I just glanced at it and then tried not to look at it — I am now looking directly at the woman's body and I say, "She's got fat thighs or she's got a pimple on her nose." And this makes it, of course, just a body.

Then I tried something else, because I didn't like the fact that I still could not walk down the street without being preoccupied by women. I wanted to be able to walk freely without worrying about this, or worrying about whether Gayle would see me do this and it would hurt her feelings, or that people would feel uncomfortable because I was looking at them. I just wanted to go beyond that. So Gayle and I took our pickup truck to Baskin-Robbins — Gayle knows about this; it's helpful to talk about these things to your spiritual partner — and we sat in front of the door. Everybody in the world goes in and out of Baskin-Robbins. I had this experiment I wanted to try, which was every time anybody at all — a little child, an elderly person, a buxom teenager — walked by, I would say to myself, "Is that a good body or a bad body? No, it's just a body." What I thought would happen is that this would make me have a neutral feeling about bodies. But what actually happened after a few minutes was that I fell in love with all the variety of bodies. I had never seen the world that way. All the different bodies we have. These wonderful tall people with bald heads, different colored people, eyes going in different directions. I had never seen that and I just loved it. I was still in this state of love and we started driving home, down this road in Santa Fe where all the fast food places are. I loved the motels with the half-broken signs. I thought it was the most charming thing I had ever seen. So when we look directly at the ego, it melts and there is love. Love is already there.

Another thing I found very helpful is this little statement from A Course In Miracles: "Your brother's body is of no more use to you than it is to him." What I would say to myself is, "Her breasts are of no more use to me than they are to her." For some reason I found this helpful. I knew if this society had covered elbows we would have dirty little shops where they would sell magazines with closeups of elbows. What we've singled out as the parts of the body that contain all this power over us is so arbitrary.

The breakthrough for me happened to come when I realized there is so much more in life to look at. I just didn't want to be preoccupied with that. I wanted to look around and see the different things on the street. So that was the breakthrough for me, though it's hard to know just how free you are of it. I'm quite free of that, compared to the way I used to be.

SUN: What role, if any, can drugs play in someone's spiritual growth? What role have they played in yours?
PRATHER: Gayle and I were in Berkeley during the days of the Free Speech Movement, the People's Park and all that. We partook of everything — psilocybin, mescaline, acid, marijuana, and hashish. In those days, these drugs were a religion in and of themselves. The idea was that if you could get a straight person to smoke a little dope they would become enlightened, loosen up, and enjoy their life so much more. And because it was looked at that way, it did seem to have that effect. And people did seem to have genuine mystical and spiritual experiences at that time.

The reason it didn't last was because it was all hinged on an external agent. Any time we think it is something out there that's bringing us the peace of God, we become controlled by the thing. If we think we can only be peaceful in a church, then we cannot be peaceful if we're not in a church, and we have to go across town to church, and maybe it's only a particular church. Or maybe it's only one church when there's a particular person giving a sermon. The ego will keep reducing this. We have to sit in the third row. It keeps narrowing the agent. It can only be when we're in nature. When we're walking in the woods and smelling the pine leaves or when we're walking on the beach. That's the only time we can be peaceful. We think it's the ocean that's causing the peace. It's the backpack and the pine leaves. Then we're tied to it. Although those can help someone start on the spiritual path, a time comes in which he has to move beyond that or else his progress is extremely limited. Many people turn to truth today to become healthy, wealthy, and wise. If they study metaphysical truth, then this will increase their income. And they'll have some sort of super health and of course they'll be wise because they know more than other people. There's nothing wrong with that, because it draws people to the truth to begin with, but a time comes when they have to see we don't apply the truth, we enter the truth.

SUN: Define love.
PRATHER: People often mistakenly think they have to love other people. You find yourself at a party and someone is holding a drink, telling you of the great illnesses in their life. And you think, "I'm supposed to love this person," because of the teachings or whatever guru says since you're supposed to love everyone. That's a useless battle, because when we are in the presence of an ego we don't like, it's very difficult to see beyond the ego to the child of God. And it isn't necessary. If we simply make peace our goal, being comfortable in that individual's presence, often we will feel some love come into our heart.

SUN: What about loving yourself? How do you distinguish between your own ego and the child of God in you?
PRATHER: Once again, the higher ego uses spiritual truth to cause as much trouble as it can. It is true we must love ourselves, but this is Self with a capital "S." The way the ego translates that is "I must love my body." People spend time going to the spa, doing things they don't want to do. If they enjoy doing those things, that's fine, but so many people put themselves through torture because they think that to love themselves their body has to reach a certain ideal. I was once bitten by a spider and a little growth started to form on the bridge of my nose. So I went to a plastic surgeon to take off the growth. Before I got there I noticed this other growth that had always been there and I said, "Could you take that off too?" He took that off. I went home and started looking at my body and noticed a

number of things that could be corrected. I went back to him. It was about two months before I woke up. I was standing in front of the mirror one day filing my teeth.

That's what happens when we think that the self we're supposed to love is a body or a personality. You think you've got to be witty. Or suddenly somebody's decided they're not funny enough or that they're too boring. Now they're studying everything so they can pepper their conversation with interesting facts. Or they're too short.

The Self is a joy to love. There is this deep river of peace that flows through the heart of every one of us, still waters that connect us all. There is no distinction between loving ourselves and loving another. There's nothing to choose between because the Self that we are is the Self that unites us to all living things. And it doesn't even occur to us that there could be a choice between what is in our interest and what is in someone else's interest. But if we think it's this body we're supposed to love, then we think we constantly have to make choices between our interest and someone else's interest.

SUN: What particular spiritual teachers are important to you?
PRATHER: The spiritual teacher that is important to me is this man I was telling you about who was Gandhi's physician. I'm not naming him. People then think that there is more of God in one body than another so you would have people running to Santa Fe to see this man and they would be disappointed. This just happens to be the person who came into my life at this time. The way he lives and the way he loves people's personalities is very inspiring to me. He was once with a group of people and there was one woman whom everyone seemed to find very obnoxious. She dominated the conversation and she asked endless questions. Everybody tried to point this out to her and that hadn't changed a thing. He immediately saw her personality and started calling on her. He would make a statement, and he'd say, "Tell us what you think about that." And so she would talk and he started kidding her, not in a way that hurts but in a way that makes people relax and realize they're welcome. Everybody was laughing and the woman felt happy and loved. After a while she quieted down and became part of the group.

So at the moment I guess he's my teacher and I would say he's almost in the same category as my son John. John is such a wonderful teacher to us. Children see that everything is for fun — the knives and forks and the salt shaker on the table. They're not interested in the past. They don't want to tell you what they did today. That's why they can forgive so quickly. Here they can have an awful argument with their friend and two minutes later you see the kids playing. The present is more important to them than the past. Whereas the past is the only thing that the ego believes is real. That's why it holds on to it. When we're caught up in our ego, we look at another person and instead of seeing that other person we see what they did to us. Their body is a symbol of all the unfair things and we're not even looking at them. This is why we have such a hard time in letting people change. Old friends have a hard time realizing that we're not what we used to be. And we can see their egos trying to make us be the way we used to be, even though we've moved beyond that.

(September 1982)

US/Readers Write About . . .

How I See God

God looks much the same to me as He did in 1955. Then, when I was six, God looked a lot like a combination of an elderly Abraham Lincoln and Uncle Sam. He wore a white stove-pipe top hat, and a freshly-pressed white tuxedo. I was impressed how a man as busy as He surely was could always look so neat. He had shoulder-length white hair and a long Rip Van Winklish beard. He was impressive, but not in the least unapproachable. I'd see Him when I was supposed to be taking my nap, but instead I'd find myself staring up at the ceiling, and, sometimes, I'd see this elegant grandfatherly figure before me. He never looked particularly at me, but I always felt welcomed and loved nonetheless.

I didn't see Him again — indeed, I hardly thought of Him — until January 1979. At first, I didn't recognize Him. His hair and beard had been neatly trimmed, and he'd grown a fine, full mustache. His suit, still freshly ironed, was a handsomely tailored three-piece outfit, soft and cream-colored.

He entered the hall of the lodge with an old and dear friend of mine whom I'd not seen since college. I thought He was Hal Holbrook. For a short, silent time, we three gazed out over the mountains, my friend in the middle. Then, as if on cue, I turned to look at Him, and He at me. I knew instantly I was in love with Him, and that He loved me. My friend was forgotten as we came together, embracing with intense passion and fervor. I was startled to realize I was falling, and that I *longed* to fall, to surrender myself to this stranger. Nothing else mattered to me but my desire to merge completely with this man. I fell backward, floated downward, revelling in the waves of orgasm, although I felt no physical penetration. When it began to rain, an umbrella was immediately lifted over us.

Later, I carried my sleeping bag to the dormitory where I would spend the night. All the bunks were taken. Then, from a bed in a corner, cast in shadows, a man said to me, "Here, you can sleep with me." It was Him. I went to His bed, without pause, without fear.

Next morning, we drove down the mountain together in my sports car. He was telling me all the things He had to do. I was oddly relaxed and at peace, even though I sensed I would not again see this man I had loved so mightily. I let Him out on a street corner and we said goodbye as though we were old friends.

I was in good spirits when I arrived at my therapist's house, pleased that for once I had a "good dream" to work on instead of the usual nightmare. As soon as I brought back the scene at the mountain lodge, I was immediately engulfed by the same intense passion and love of the previous night, yet I had no more understanding of its significance than when I dreamed it. As I emerged from the happy, semi-hypnotic state in which I had relived the dream, Linne said, "Who do you think that was?" I hesitated a moment, still puzzling over His identity. Then, a distant memory came to me and I began, "He reminds me a little of what I thought God looked like when I was six. . . ." As the words left my mouth, I knew with absolute certainty that I had met, embraced and loved God.

Suddenly, a year and a half of therapy was over. I knew I would no longer need the sanctuary of Linne's house, the warmth, understanding and wisdom of her counsel, to make my own way. In those few short moments of recognition I had received an inner knowledge that I now had to go out in the world on my own, to stand on my own two feet, and that I'd have the strength to do so.

To my surprise, I burst into tears as I said goodbye to Linne. I wept for knowing I wouldn't see her again as my protector, my teacher, and the nurturer of my pained soul. I wept for a happiness and peace I'd never felt before, for the sense that I'd discovered an unshakable Truth in which to put my faith and trust. Most of all, my tears were for an overwhelming gratitude for the gift Linne had given me — a gift more precious than life.

Virginia Mudd
Alamo, California

I see God through the hole in my throat. He's very big and very old and very loud. He's the loudest sound. He lives everywhere but He's on the finest, most refined level of perception. When I can see out the hole in my throat I see Him hovering all over His Creation. He's the biggest Santa Claus I ever saw and it's true that He'll give you anything you want — anything. He's the Creator of everything there is, so He owns it all. He's the landlord, and He's most certainly jealous, tender and very careful.

He doesn't waste any time, so He doesn't come knocking until we're ready to shake His hand. When He finally does come, He comes because we appreciate everything on the same level He does.

Meeting Him for the first time — that's something to get up for. First He casts His shadow. I thought: "Wow, this is my Creator coming in my room, I'd better ask for something, quick, before He goes away." But right away I realized He's the Creator, so when He comes, there's nothing to ask for. It's all there, every inch of it. God. He can't stand it if you don't recognize that everything belongs to Him. He literally doesn't tolerate such behavior. That's called pain, suffering, longing and despair. It means not giving everything over to Him.

He made each of us to fulfill His plan — to witness the Absolute, where we all come from. He came from there, too, and He made us to experience the Absolute. That's what we're here for and He expects us to do it.

If we want to meet Him we have to start by taking off the dark glasses and letting in the light. He's certainly real and no poet's fancy or philosopher's argument. He's the owner of it all, striding over it like a huge, crashing waterfall, the President of Life. The sound that encompasses it all. Being with a capital B.

Kathleen Snipes
Carrboro, North Carolina

(February 1981)

Teachers

Francesca Hampton

One hundred thousand Tibetans, including many high lamas, fled to India after an abortive 1959 uprising in Lhasa against the imposition of Red Chinese rule. This short story is based on a stay at the monastery of Ganden, now re-established in a refugee settlement in south India.

In the small kitchen behind the meditation room, the fire was going even in the afternoon, heating milk and water for Tibetan tea in large dented aluminum pots set in the grill. The ventilator shaft above the flames was curved, and the smoke curled up to it lazily, discouraged by every small draft back into a tour of the low-ceilinged room. Walls and ceiling had long ago taken on a thick fur of soot, and the fading light that crept into the kitchen made little impression on the midnight walls. Even with his face turned partly toward the door, the young monk did

He offered up himself: his body which was useless if it were not used to help others; his speech which had no point if he could not teach others the Way. . . .

not notice when the foreigner came into the room.

In the farthest corner, away from the fire, the foreigner settled down on his haunches, his long, thin knees in the air, his back against the wall. He stared, as he always did, mercilessly, without any politeness, at the person who had claimed his interest.

It was the intensity of the stare that made Sherab aware of the man. With a start he looked up from the orange basin of half-washed cups and saucers on the floor. The man's pale, long-jawed face under its raft of red hair, the furious question in the blue eyes, sent a shock through him.

"This one is a little crazy," the guestmaster had confided the day before. "And he has no passport."

As well as he was able under the Westerner's gaze, Sherab kept his face still. But he stood up, and in a motion unconsciously defensive, flipped the trailing end of his red linen shawl expertly over one shoulder.

"Chu tsapo?" he inquired. "Hot water?" The water for the kitchen came from a good artesian well, but the Western visitors seemed to regard it with suspicion. Another pot, full of hot water, simmered over the fire all day to keep their minds at rest.

The man shook his head.

Sherab stood perplexed.

"Cha? Would you like tea? I am make Tibeti tea now." The troublesome man made no answer; he had covered his face with his hands. Sherab studied him indecisively, then searched along the line of battered aluminum utensils hung on the walls, past a neat row of flower-painted thermoses on the table. Some simple diversion might satisfy the foreigner and encourage him to leave.

The man's sudden movement shifted his attention back. With horror the young monk realized that the foreigner had begun to weep. There was no sound. The man's hands remained over his face. But his body was shuddering with the effort of suppression. Sherab watched him, feeling foolish.

At last he went to the man and squatted beside him, tucking his monk's shirt back between his ankles. He put out his hand and lightly touched the unsteady shoulder.

"You are sick?" he asked softly. He knew the man was not sick. He struggled to remember other English words that would express sympathy better. The man had not answered.

Sherab looked uneasily at the open entrance to the kitchen. The last crash of cymbals and trumpets had died away. The prayers were over. The monks in the meditation room would be expecting the tea. And Rinpoche was with them. He could not fail to bring tea to the household's master, the most famous lama in all the monastery.

He began to rise but the madman clutched his hand.

"Please don't go yet," the man pleaded. Sherab was unsure of the meaning of the word "goyet" but "please" and the look in the eyes were clear. He stood, nonplused, between his new responsibility and his old one.

Within the door frame of the kitchen a small head had appeared. The knowing, impish face of the boy-monk, Ngawang, was bright with questions. Before Sherab could explain his plight, however, the normally reliable little boy had flicked out of sight like a startled sparrow, back to the meditation hall.

Sherab knew he had to do something quickly.

"Please come," he said. Pulling gently but persistently on the man's arms he got him to rise and took him to the long bench under the window.

"You here," he told him. "I make tea." The man looked at him, his eyes vague with unhappiness, but Sherab turned away. Working as rapidly as he could without an outward display of tension, he cut a thick slice off the black brick of Assam tea that Ngawang's father had brought for the Rinpoche and dropped it into the boiling water. He churned the hot milk in the butter churner until it frothed with air and then, more quickly than he would have liked, added it with butter to the boiling tea. He was struggling with the salt, trying to loosen it with the butt end of a knife, when he sensed that someone was at the door. He froze with his hand still buried in the long container. The senior monks of the household were going past. They had not waited for the tea.

Through the open door he could see the old Rinpoche being helped up the stairs to his room. The other monks were dispersing. No one had looked through the wide doorway to the kitchen, not even the three who were to help him with dinner. He didn't move. What did this mean? The foreigner was watching him again closely.

Sudden as a grasshopper, Ngawang reappeared in the room. With childishly deft motions, he slapped two cups and saucers onto a small tray. He poured a large dipperful of butter tea into a flowered thermos, waited poised for instant motion while Sherab pinched salt into the steaming opening, and was gone.

As the little monk disappeared, the foreigner stood up decisively. On his feet he stood a head taller than Sherab and weighed a fourth again as much. Against his will, the sixteen-year-old monk felt a tremor of fear.

The man was talking now.

"He pretends he doesn't know who I am but you know, don't you?"

Sherab looked at him noncommittally, struggling to make sense of the rapid words.

Restlessly, the man was circling the small room. He muttered as he went, slapping his open palm for emphasis against the sides of the pots. His words sounded like nonsense to Sherab.

"The Indian holy man knew me. And the dreams cannot lie. I am his teacher and he knows it. Why does he say he doesn't know it?" The foreigner sounded vexed. He pounded the last pot with violence and turned to face Sherab.

"Is it because the policeman touched my head?" The man's voice was suddenly plaintive. With hesitant fingers he reached up to explore his head, as if it were some precious relic.

"I am the one who was lost," he said hopefully.

Sherab had understood at last but said nothing.

The man's confident posture was slowly fading. He did not seem to notice that Sherab had not answered. Another thought claimed him and his expression curled into a scowl.

"The bitches won't even talk to me. Those American bitches." He circled the room once again.

"And the Rinpoche said, 'Go out.' He dared to say to me, 'Go out!'" His voice was rising in frustration. "He's the one who should go out!"

Silently Sherab watched him circle the room a third time. He could sense the rapid fluctuations of pride and sorrow and anger. And he flinched as the man began to curse the high lama. It was terrible karma this Westerner was sowing. It would bring him much pain.

Searching his memory, the monk strained for a simple teaching he would be able to say in English that might calm the man. Often enough he had observed the effects of pride in the monks around him. He himself had felt, briefly, symptoms of the illusion that gripped the Westerner. It was sweet to dream in secret that you were an unrecognized "tulku," a highly evolved one who had taken birth only to teach others. You knew you were wrong, yet you yearned for the lama to acknowledge this quality in you. As a monk in the monastery you were quite safe. Sooner or later the lama would destroy your fantasy, as mercilessly as other people swat flies. He would scorn you, or he would mock you in public, or he might refuse to speak to you at all. It was a great humiliation. It hurt like fire. It cured you at once.

With sudden pity, the young monk realized that among Westerners who studied the Teaching very few had such a close spiritual friend.

Coming close to the man Sherab took him by the arm.

"You here please," he said gently. He pushed him back to the bench and the rambling monologue ceased. Fresh tears filled the Westerner's eyes. His moods changed as quickly as the Spring wind in the mountains.

"I make tea," Sherab reassured him.

Together they sipped the hot, rich, salt-laced tea from metal mugs. Sherab watched the madman discreetly. In the light of the kitchen lantern, the tension that pulled at his face seemed to have lessened. He looked tired.

"All beings have Buddha-nature," Sherab offered at last. He placed the teaching lightly into the air between them, not looking at the Westerner, with a humility he hoped would not arouse the man to pride again.

"All beings hate me," the man whispered. He looked crestfallen, worn out from struggling with the confusion he himself had spun and cherished.

Sherab stayed silent, sipping his tea. He knew that something very extraordinary was happening. Not one monk had come to help him with dinner. Not even the Rinpoche's attendant had come to complain. In the dark outside, each in his separate room, he could sense the presence of others.

He remembered a verse from the teachings:

> *"When you meet a being of bad nature,*
> *pressed by violent sins and sufferings,*

do not turn away,
but treat him as a precious treasure,
rare to find."

After he had given the man a small meal, he took him again by the arm.

"Now is sleep," he said firmly.

The man looked at him wonderingly, already distracted by a new onrush of thoughts. But he did as he was told. Together, they marched out into the dark, past the well and the low shed where five water buffalo snorted softly at their passing. The stars across the south Indian sky were as distinct as flung embers. A sharp-edged new moon hung low above the horizon.

In his room the man undressed obediently and got into a worn sleeping bag. Sherab went out onto the long veranda and dragged in one of the straw-packed mattresses piled there. On this he sat cross-legged, several feet away from the bed. The Westerner was watching him with a child-like acceptance of all his actions.

"Sleep," Sherab ordered. "I will stay."

The man looked at the ceiling for a while, limp, as if, for the moment, all the energy of his self-preoccupation had spent itself. After a while Sherab saw that his eyes were closed.

Sitting straight on the prickly mattress, he closed his own eyes. He needed to think. He had never before tried to help a person through meditation on his own.

He had memorized many texts in recent years. He had said mantras for dying animals. He had sat with the younger boys through their fevers. But in the ceremonial meditations with the high lama, or in the crucible of the debating courts, he felt that he had failed to become more than the most indifferent student. At least the great lama had never praised him. Not once could he remember praise since coming here at the age of twelve.

With brief shame he pushed the unworthy thought from his mind.

Now he was alone with this stranger in great distress and he must try to help. In the weak light coming from the bulb on the porch, he could make out the man's face. Even at rest it was flickering with emotion, as the mind within followed its dialogues down the tunnel of sleep.

Deliberately Sherab relaxed. His tense legs eased down onto the mat. He straightened his back. Breathing slowly, he let his heart open in sympathy and tried to imagine the experience of the obsession. Subtly at first, and then with increasing power, he began to feel it. A sense of great injustice came, far away from all others, loneliness. But like bright shocks of lightning came the moments of exaltation, rearing arrogance. It had become so sweet, so important for this Westerner to believe he was extraordinary. To give in now to the disbelief of others would be like death. Between despair and excitement the man's mind arced back and forth, self-obsessed, trapped. The stress was breaking down the harmony of mind and body and odd physical sensations and mental images had come to add to his confusion, and his fascination. He had lost even the will to find his way back to the conventional truth and simple curiosity with which he began.

Sadness for the man's predicament and a sympathetic anxiety overwhelmed the young monk. Surely if he meant to practice the teachings, he must at least try to help.

He gathered his concentration, breathing slowly, letting his mind calm and deepen as it rode on the waves of breath — in, out, in, out. Then, with feeling, he prayed to the high lama to help him with his effort.

As he had been taught, he tried to visualize the lama in the form of Chenrezig, Buddha of Compassion. With startling suddenness, the image leapt into his mind, without effort, more clearly than it had ever come to him before. The wide calm eyes of the deity seemed actually to regard him from the center of the room. Its graceful limbs were shaped of white light. They radiated light throughout the room, bright rainbow colors that shimmered in a soft halo. Easily, Sherab could visualize the four hands of Chenrezig, holding on the left side a pure lotus, a crystal rosary on the other, and in the center, the great sparkling jewel that fulfills the wishes of all beings.

The clarity of the figure, the powerful sense that it was really there, sent a shiver of excitement through the young monk. But he caught himself. Without breaking concentration, he let cool awareness wash excitement away. He must not let his motivation become debased.

As his mind grew quiet, his concentration on the image deepened. In visualization, he made prostrations to it, and then made symbolic offerings of all beautiful things for which he himself had ever yearned. He offered flowers, fresh water, sweet smells. He offered light, food, sound, caress. He offered up himself: his body which was useless if it were not used to help others; his speech which had no point if he could not teach others the Way; his mind which was the root and heart of suffering if he could not see clearly the true empty nature of all things. And then he prayed to Chenrezig to grant him the real ability to help another by meditation.

In his visualization, that now seemed so real, a bright piercing light began to glow in the heart of the awakened being, shining right through the transparent body. He felt a stretching in his own heart, a sense of energy pouring through his chest. And then in a shower of light, the image of the Buddha dissolved and poured into him, through him, around him. In the intensity of the experience he forgot himself completely. "Sherab" fell away like a dream.

All that was left was simple awareness that filled a vast expanse of infinite clarity.

With the clarity there was a low hum without source or direction, an all-pervasive gentleness. Its sound was OM MANI PADME HUM. . . .

Very gradually he let himself conceive his own mind as that sound. Sound became light. In piercing focus, light became the letters of the mantra and the secret syllable of Chenrezig.

And out of that the mind of Sherab itself became Chenrezig.

For a long time he let consciousness rest there, feeling, without holding, the bliss of it, the marvel. He looked down at the translucent clarity of his body, the luminous, light-sculpted perfection of fingers, feet, flowing blue-green robes and white lotus. He sat in space as open as the dawn sky.

Then he focused inward. Chenrezig focused inward. He felt himself opening to care that extended throughout time and space, without limit. He let himself love, cherish every being in existence as tremulously as a mother loves her new child. Their faults did not matter. He loved them fiercely, as a general loves the city he goes out to defend. He loved each one particularly, watchfully, shrewdly, as a teacher loves a favorite pupil. And he saw them with delight, his precious peers, as the awakened beings they did not yet know they would become.

Remembering his purpose, Sherab visualized the Western man

in front of him. He put him there as he looked, unkempt, his hair long and unruly, his face tight. About the man he caused his obsession to become visible as a foul, dense smoke. Repeating the mantra to himself, Sherab began a slow inhalation. With the breath he took in the smoke, pulling it deep into his own lungs as Chenrezig. When repulsion rose he was ready for it. He took the blackness even further in, and opened his defenses back out into a total concern with the Westerner. The black smoke at his heart was transformed. With the outbreath he exhaled light, an elixir of wisdom that gradually penetrated the figure in front of him. With each completed breath, the darkness around the Westerner cleared and his inner light grew. With all the strength of his concentration Sherab/Chenrezig pulled from him arrogance and self-pity and fear. Vividly, he imagined the man changing as the massive confusion settled and evaporated to nothing. He imagined his features relaxing into tenderness and bright interest. He imagined his body clearing to translucence. With effort that brought sweat to his body, Sherab poured into him, in a wave of spoken mantra and visualized light, all the joyful wisdom that he himself did not yet possess, Chenrezig's wisdom.

When he was done, there were tears wet on his cheeks. His mind felt worn down and wavering with the effort. He knew he had not been skillful. But before he said the prayer of dedication, before he let go of a visualization grown unsteady, he rested in it one last time.

Two fully detailed figures of Chenrezig floated there, bright, facing each other, himself and the Westerner. He let the joy of it, the completion of it, fill him. Then he let go.

Rapidly, he said the traditional prayer of ending. More rapidly still, and with little concentration left, he recited by rote the daily prayers the lama has given him as an obligation.

The foreigner slept, his face at last still.

Sherab closed his eyes and leaned back against the wall. He didn't know how long he slept. When Ngawang's low call woke him in the dark, it felt as if a long time had passed.

"Sherab, please come. Rinpoche has sent for you," the little boy whispered.

Wakefulness came in a shock. Sherab scrambled to his feet and followed the boy unsteadily through the yard. His left foot had gone to sleep.

His heart pounding, he paused before the curtain covering the

Rinpoche's door. Then with a decisive motion, he flicked it aside and entered. He felt as self-conscious as the day he had arrived, four years ago. He only dared a single quick glance at the lama as he made the three ritual prostrations. The lama was not looking at him. He was looking at a rosary that moved steadily between thumb and forefinger in his lap.

"Sit down," he said.

Sherab obeyed, too shaken to think of speaking first. He waited.

In a little while Ngawang came in backwards, his small bottom pushing out the curtain and keeping it behind him as he turned and entered with a tray of food. With an enormous yawn he set it down in front of Sherab. Sherab recoiled.

"Rinpoche!" he rebuked the boy, gesturing vehemently to the high lama who sat without anything in front of him. Ngawang was too sleepy even to remember protocol.

The Rinpoche swept his politeness back at him with a wave of the hand and went on saying the silent mantras.

Awkwardly, Sherab forced himself to eat some of the meal and drink a cup of tea. The old lama was too unpredictable and the night had been too grueling for him to feel any hunger.

"You have been with the Westerner," the lama said matter-of-factly as soon as he had finished.

Sherab looked up, a faint eagerness creeping into his mind. He began carefully, "I tried to help him."

"You have not helped him," the lama said bluntly. "He will be the same tomorrow."

The words came like a blow across his face and Sherab dropped his eyes sharply. With effort, he successfully checked the urge to cry, but he could not stop the inward rush of despair. What was the purpose? If such effort accomplished nothing at all. . . . It was a long time before he could bring himself to look at the lama again. When he did, he started nervously. The lama was studying him with total attention, his old eyes bright with humor.

"He has not benefited, but you, I think, have gained something."

He went on passing the little bone beads between thumb and forefinger.

Sherab stared at him.

"You cannot help him. In the end only he can help himself. All you can do is show the way."

There was another long silence. A buffalo bawled in the distance and a dog started barking. With surprise, Sherab realized that it was almost dawn.

The lama's voice commanded his attention forward again.

"To show him the way you must know the way." The aged voice was precise. "And you must know your disciple perfectly. You may go."

Sherab stumbled to his feet and turned toward the door.

"Come here," said the lama.

Bewildered, the young monk went to him. He bent over as the lama placed a white scarf of respectful greeting around his neck.

"There," the lama said. He touched Sherab lightly on both sides of his head.

Feeling braver, Sherab glanced up into his eyes.

The look of love there stunned him. Warmed to the bottom of his heart, he backed away, hands held to his forehead in greatest respect. And fled.

It was late morning when the foreigner at last came out of his room. He had packed his bag and tied it together with a rope. He whistled as he rolled his sleeping bag on the covered porch. As he passed Sherab's room he peeked through the open door and the whistle wavered. When he saw the young monk wasn't there the whistle rose again. He went on.

In the garden he saw the old Rinpoche walking with a monk at his elbow. A deep furrow formed between his brows and he waited to pass until they had gone, muttering under his breath. Out in the monastery's dusty central lane, he glared at the maroon-robed monks who passed him. But they were all going the other way. At the entrance gate he found himself alone. He stood silent, looking back, until the crying of a buffalo calf caught his attention. A genuine smile lit his face as he went to pet the young animal. He forgot himself. When it was quiet he half-lifted, half-shoved the young animal across a drainage ditch that blocked its way and pushed it toward the monastery. He was whistling again as he began the long walk to the bus station in the Indian village.

Behind him the Tibetan long horns groaned into life to mark the beginning of a morning ceremony at the refugee settlement. Hundreds of prayer flags, hung on ropes from the monastery's golden peak, fluttered in a breeze that came from the distant sea.

(March 1984)

An Interview with Ram Dass

Sy Safransky

To some, Ram Dass's story is as familiar as their own. He is a superb storyteller, with a flair for the dramatic and a keen sense of timing. His humorous tales about his inner struggles have kept us laughing for years.

To others, Ram Dass is unknown — there were no reporters at his talk here last month — or perhaps he's vaguely identified with a carny-world of gurus, teachers, and spiritual leaders, with strange-sounding names and stranger ideas.

There's nothing stranger than his own life, nothing more quintessentially American. At forty-nine, he's one of the best-known, most widely-respected spiritual leaders in the West. His book, Be Here Now, was a phenomenal bestseller; his ability to translate ancient Eastern ideas into language that penetrates Western minds and hearts is

God doesn't go away from you; you go away from God, you go away from the spirit with your own mind.

unique. So is his cultural savvy; first he's talking about pizza and Jimmy Carter and LSD, then he's describing the trance-like state of samadhi or reading from the Ramayana.

He was born into a well-to-do New England family as Richard Alpert. (His father was a lawyer and later president of the New Haven Railroad.) He studied psychology, got his doctorate from Stanford, and became a professor at Harvard. By outward appearances he was happy and successful — he had a Mercedes, an MG, a motorcycle, a sailboat, and a Cessna 172 airplane; he played the cello and hosted dinner parties; he was much in demand as a teacher and as a therapist. But something was missing. The academic world "didn't really have a grasp on the human condition . . . the whole thing was too empty."

One day, down the hall, a new colleague moved in. The new psychology instructor was Timothy Leary. They became friends; Leary began experimenting with psychedelic mushrooms — which triggered, for him, "the deepest religious experience of my life" — and Alpert was invited to share. On that first trip, he went through a profound ego death, watching all his "personalities" — professor, lover, man-about-town — slip away. Then his body started disintegrating. The terror mounted, panic set in. But then he felt engulfed by calm. He had touched the inner "I," the universal essence "independent of social and physical identity . . . beyond life and death."

For the next six years, he kept ingesting psychedelic substances. He and Leary were tossed out of Harvard and Alpert criss-crossed the country, lecturing on psychedelics and the inner realms of consciousness that were opening for him. Eventually, he came to a dead-end: no matter how high you went on acid, you eventually came down. When a friend invited Alpert to accompany him to India, he accepted.

In India, he met his guru — a remarkable saint called Neem Karoli Baba, or Maharaji (in India, the title Maharaji — great king or wise one — is available for the taking by tea vendors or perfect masters). Their first encounter is related in Be Here Now. Alpert kept his distance while the other devotees threw themselves at the old man's feet. At first, Maharaji teased him about the car he was driving, asking if he'd give it to him. Then he called him closer and whispered that the night before Alpert had been thinking of his mother, who had died a year earlier. This was true, though Alpert had mentioned it to no one. He felt a wrenching inside him, and broke down. This was someone who "knew." The journey was over; he was home.

He stayed on to study yoga and meditation for six months. When he returned to the U.S. in holy robes, his father whisked him away from the airport before anyone would see him. But it wasn't long before thousands began to seek him out.

In the decade since, the changes have been less dramatic, but no less important. In 1970 he returned to India, "freaked out by how much I was lost in the world," to have his guru assure him that he would eventually become "pure enough." His guru died in 1973, which deeply shook him, but in the years that followed Ram Dass says he has often met with Mararaji on other planes of consciousness.

In his books and lectures he keeps refining his message: his appeal is no longer merely to hippies and rebels, but to a broader constituency; he wears ordinary clothes again and his beard and hair are trimmed short; his own attachments, lusts and fears are discussed with a candor striking for any public figure, let alone a "spiritual" teacher. A few years ago, he became involved, spiritually and romantically, with a teacher named Joya in New York City. It was a disillusioning experience, exposing to Ram Dass his own spiritual greed. After fifteen months, he disavowed her teachings — he wrote an article about it called "Egg on My Beard" — and many of his admirers were let down. Among the many inconsistencies of his life during that time: he insisted his own students be celibate, while he was making love with Joya, who was married. "Finally," he wrote, "I had to admit that I had conned myself."

In Ram Dass's latest book, Miracle of Love, *he explores more intimately than in his other works* (The Only Dance There Is, Journey of Awakening, Grist For The Mill) *his relationship to his guru, and the nature of this remarkable man. Reading it, it's hard to resist the suggestion that Maharaji was an avatar on the order of Christ or the Buddha; at the very least, he was a saint of extraordinary awareness, with a profound love for all of humanity.*

Ram Dass is the first to acknowledge he himself is no saint. His passion is the quest for God, and everyone I spoke to who came in contact with him was moved by the depth of his caring and the clarity of his consciousness. The poet Jimmy Santiago Baca, seeing Ram Dass for the first time, wrote to me:

"I loved him. More than anything else, I found him to be a poet of living, taking the erring and righteous reflections of life and drinking them, to be the mirror we all see our faces in. He lives himself and it is what he does: on the edge, like the glow of sunset emanating off the blue rims of sky

at dusk. And then he becomes the dark, the distance, the space we inhabit. But he flows from the center of what we experience as life; from the mix and muck and magic of the immense city comes the flow of his being to entangle itself in the starlight and bloodball of sunlight. Take it all into yourself, go from the One to the Two."

—Ed.

SUN: Many people who commented on your talk said they appreciated your not being so self-consciously holy anymore. That resonated because so many of us have been going through the same process. It's always nice to get it mirrored back. . . . For this interview, I asked some friends for ideas for questions. One wanted me to ask, "Who are we, from where have we come, why have we come, and where will we go?"

RAM DASS: Heidegger says, I stick my finger into the soil to find the quality of the soil and when I stick my finger in the soil of existence it smells of nothing. Then he gets paranoid, and asks who's responsible. Generally, the answer is that it's none of your business. The rational mind is not a sufficiently expansive mechanism to be able to comprehend the nature of existence, because even that question has implications of time and space, and actually existence doesn't exist within time and space. It just comes into time, but it doesn't start at the beginning and end at the end. So the rational mind really can't know the answers to those questions. It's like why is the one the many? At one level, it isn't. It's all an illusion. At another level, you could say — like Meher Baba says — God takes form in order to know itself. Part of the totality is the separateness, including the oneness. These are all games of the mind. Actually you stop asking the question. Tell your friend you can become the answer but you can't know it.

SUN: My friend's other question was, "Can words convey spiritual truth?"

RAM DASS: Words are like the finger pointing at the moon. They point to what is unspeakable. They can take you into their method to get you beyond words. They only work if you don't get lost in the content. They start moving you in a certain direction, but then you've got to let go. They're not the ocean, they're the diving board.

But you walk out on the diving board to get into the ocean. So we can convey relative truth, not absolute truth.

SUN: What would be a good antidote for someone who's in love with words?
RAM DASS: To do meditations in which you focus on the silence between words. On the silence out of which the words come. Words are like birds; they come and they go. You can become fascinated with the content, but if you just start to see them as words, not as content — not focusing on the meaning of the words, but on the sound of the words — eventually you become rooted in silence. Then the birds are singing, and the words are appearing. And that's really a meditative act.

SUN: Do you still meditate regularly?
RAM DASS: Yes, I do a prayer to Hanuman [in Hinduism, God's loyal servant, often depicted as a monkey] a number of times each day. It keeps me in that role of servant, listening to hear how it comes through, rather than focusing on my own trip. And then I need long periods too, every few months. I would like to evolve — and I can feel it happening — to the point where the stuff of life doesn't catch me anymore. So I'm at play with it, and I'm always in a meditative space. The thing is that it all has a certain kind of clinginess. It's like static stuff in the laundry. You take it out of the dryer and it clings to things. It's that kind of clinging, not heavy, thick, grabbing stuff. I mean I don't get neurotically depressed, but it just slowly clings. I'm still fascinated, for example, by this or that. And there can be no fascination. You've got to break that fascination, finally.

SUN: When you say that the fascination needs to go, does that mean that the excitement or sheer creative pleasure goes too?
RAM DASS: No. The difference is that there is delight and playfulness and enjoyment and ecstasy, but there is no need for them. You enjoy them when they're there, but when they're not, they're not. The clinginess of the need makes the problem. The fascination is in grabbing for it, looking for stimulation all the time. If you don't need stimulation, you can have it. Maharaji would say, "You need this cup of tea? You want it? Don't drink it." And you learn how to work

with enjoying the cup of tea because you don't need it. Enjoying the play of life, because you don't need it.

SUN: What are you afraid of?

RAM DASS: Well, there are levels of that. When I'm very much in my psychological personality, I'm afraid of being unloved, being rejected, being judged, being laughed at, persecuted, hurt. The minute I quiet down, I'm really not afraid of anything. But I go in and out of those places. Every time I experience fear, I know I've gotten caught in a space, and it's almost just a device for getting me to quiet down. I just know I lost my center. I'm interested that when I get into crisis situations, there's no fear, because I get pulled out of myself. As long as I'm busy being me, I'm afraid almost all the time. Just like a lot of people. It's poignant, and that's about it.

SUN: What difference do you see between your public persona and your private self?

RAM DASS: Hardly any. I have made it a policy to make private public to the point where I don't have to change. Who I am here is who I am on the stage. There are a few things I haven't yet integrated into sharing publicly, because I don't know quite how to do that, because of other human beings that I don't want hurt. I am presently in a relationship with a man, a sexual relationship. I've been living with him for ten months. This is a young fellow, an artist out in California. And I haven't yet figured out a way, because in his world and his life it wouldn't be comfortable for him to be publicly defined as someone who lives with a man. It's okay with me — I don't want to hurt him, so I don't want to focus on him. Because the minute people know there is somebody in my life that way, everybody with that kind of greed for gossip would want to know who he is and what it is, and they'd have his pictures and all that stuff. I don't think that's fair to him. So, it's only out of that reason. But it's not a difference in the quality of my being. He's as much my work on myself as anything. As far as I'm concerned, my game is going to God. That's all I know. I know that more and more clearly all the time. And I've said to him, I'd give you up in a second if I didn't think this was useful to get me to God. I love you and you're wonderful and I yearn to be with you and I'm happy when I'm with you and I love the intimacy and I yearned for it for years, and I'm finally letting myself have it and it's wonderful. And it's not worth shit if it doesn't get me to God. And that's really the way I feel about my life now. I think that if these lectures weren't a payoff for me, in terms of me having to deal with power and fame and money and all this stuff, and trying to deal with it compassionately and consciously and without attachment, and working with my attachments to it, if it was not feeding that process, I wouldn't do it. It's not out of altruism. Because I realize now that those things are so interwoven that the work you do on yourself is what makes you free to liberate — you become a force that liberates other people. And you're not a force that liberates other people if you're too attached. So, I really can only work on myself as my offering to other human beings. I'm not doing it for them, nor am I doing it for me. I'm doing it because it's what I do. But it has that effect. At one lecture recently, I got up and said to everybody, "I don't want to be here tonight, to tell you the truth. The only reason I'm doing it is for the money." And it was interesting, because there were a couple of thousand people who came to hear me. I felt that they should deal with that truth. If I don't start from truth, forget it. Because every time I phony it, in the first few sentences of a lecture, I have to live the whole lecture with the phoniness I created. It was like last night, I really didn't know how to begin. I didn't know where I wanted to go, or what I was doing. So I said, well now you could start this way or that way, and I was just sort of figuring, let the audience deal with this issue, too. Why should I sit inside, making these decisions as if the audience is them. They're not — they're us. With us, you don't have two personas, you only have one. I don't have to straighten up and smile and look holy and get it together. I went into a gay club in some city I was in. It was a private club and you had to join, and to do it they took a picture of you to put on a little card. So they were taking my picture and the guy say, "Hey, aren't you Ram Dass?" It was such a beautiful moment. It was like, Maharaji, you couldn't have done it better.

SUN: That reminds me of your Deep Throat story.
RAM DASS: Standing in line to see the movie when the guy came down the street and recognized me. Those are all the same story. And they're just about getting rid of that private stuff. Listen, if I've got lust to deal with, I've got to deal with it. We've all got it. So, why should I assume that everybody in the theater has got it and I don't?

SUN: What's been your greatest disappointment in the past couple of years?

RAM DASS: Well, disappointment is a funny thing. Disappointments are exquisite clues to where you're holding. And if you want to awaken, a disappointment becomes a great thing, so you get to love them as much as you hate them. They're hurting you, and at the same moment they are awakening you to how you're clinging. I really wanted Hanuman in America and I went to India and I had a 1500-pound statue of Hanuman prepared. A beautiful thing. I had it shipped to America and thought that the American satsang [communion, or spiritual community] would create a land and a temple, and so on. And then I realized that they couldn't quite get it together. At the moment, it's in a beautiful room in a home where we all come and visit it in Taos, New Mexico, and that's the way it's supposed to be. I can feel that now. But there was a period where I still had the model that everybody should get together and create a space, and they couldn't do that because there was just too much dissension within the group. And there was disappointment in that. Then I saw that was just my model of how everybody should be a certain way, and I really enjoyed the fact that they were what they were, rather than what I thought they ought to be. I think I've been disappointed when I've wanted to share intimate space with someone who didn't want to share with me. Not having fulfillment as a lover. I've had disappointment like that.

SUN: Do you get jealous?

RAM DASS: Yes, I get jealous, but I never get totally jealous. I don't lose the space. The jealousy is part of my human conditon, of my separateness from wanting that intimacy. I'm just beginning to experience what the quality of intimacy is with another human being and how it keeps me from God. And that's one that I'm just beginning to play with now in my relationship. Because I see that intimacy is something that preserves your separateness. I don't know how to describe that. It's not union, it's intimacy. When somebody I would like to have oriented around me orients in another way, and I lose that, my separateness screams. My spaciousness notices it. That part of me that wants God is in a way delighted. There's all these different levels going on in me at once. Can you hear what I'm talking about?

SUN: Yes. When I experience that, the sense of how far I am from God in that moment hurts so much.

RAM DASS: Yes. But you get over that one. You stop picking on yourself so hard. Because otherwise, you're using everything in order to become unlovable by God. And actually, God loves you all the time anyway. So, it's only your mind, your guilt, your own stuff that's taking you away from God. I realized that God doesn't go away from you; you go away from God, you go away from the spirit with your own mind. So to feed anything that keeps you away from God is silly, which includes not only the jealousy, but the guilt about the jealousy or the self-pity because you're so far from God — all those thought forms. It's not the content of the thought, it's just the thoughts themselves that keep me from God.

SUN: What do you do when the teachings go dry, when your inspirations don't nourish anymore?

RAM DASS: There are three alternatives. You can sit with the dryness because it is all spiritual materialism and the dryness is as much a teaching as the wetness. So you sit with that because that is God, too. And to assume that the dryness means you have fallen from grace is just another part of the journey. People come and say, "I have fallen from grace, I've lost it," and I say, "That's interesting, what does that feel like?" And that's part of it too. So one strategy is you just sit with it. Another is, you reinvest your method. Like sometimes Maharaji becomes a mechanical name I recite, in a mechanical set of rituals, and then I really stop. Like when I bless food, sometimes I am sitting around a dinner table or at a restaurant with my father or other people, and the food comes and everybody starts, and I want to bless the food but I don't want to interfere with everybody so I do a quick blessing and I realize I did it mechanically and nothing happened. Then I stop myself and close my eyes and sit there and start the whole thing all over again. I demand it come alive. I demand Maharaji come. In order to do that, I have to let go of time and space and the whole scene. I have just got to go into that. And I demand it of myself before I will eat. I will only take food that has genuinely been offered. So that every time I eat, which is numerous times a day, is a good opportunity for me to see how close I am to the living truth and I have got myself trained now so that I won't eat until it turns living. So in that sense I reinvest it.

Another strategy is to realize that there are other methods and sometimes you move into another method for awhile. Like if it is not working as a heart method, I may turn to study and read some Vedic books for awhile. Or if I am bored reading books, I might hang out with satsang or go sit with Hanuman. Or take a meditation course or something that will come in from another oblique angle and cut through. Those are all different types of things and I use them all.

SUN: What do you read?

RAM DASS: Well, mainly I read books that people want me to write comments on, or write prefaces for. I'm becoming the world's leading preface writer. Which throws me into interesting material. It's as good a way as any to read material. That's the new material. Then I have my old tried and true things that I read. I reread the stories about Maharaji, I reread Ramakrishna, I reread *The Third Chinese Patriarch*, *The Diamond Sutra*, Chuang Tzu. I mean, I've got dozens of those kinds of books around that I read and reread and pick up. *Bhagavad Gita*. The *Ramayana*. And in a way those books about God are always feeding me. And that's what I'd rather read than almost anything else. I also read murder mysteries. I can read two murder mysteries a day very easily. I read those as a way of extricating myself from the dramas of the rest of my life. There's always the point between wanting to go more into God, reading about God and being by myself, and trying to stay in the world and do my thing. There are always those kinds of pulls in me. Maharaji says, "There will come a time, Ram Dass, when you will be with God and you won't want to lecture anymore." Well, that time obviously hasn't come yet, because here I still am. And when I don't want to lecture, it's usually because of ego reasons, it's not because of God. I'm still at the stage where the higher I get, the more I want to share it.

SUN: Telling others what I've discovered has always been important to me, which is why I do what I do. But I ask myself, sometimes, why do I need to share this, rather than just experience it?

RAM DASS: In René Daumal's book, *Mount Analogue*, they climb the mountain of consciousness and at each plane there are cabins and farms. Each day the party goes on, leaving behind one of its members to keep the fires going and milk the goats. You go up a way, and you share. Then you go up, and you share. That's a cycle of processing. On the other hand, when I was silent for six months or when I'm alone for a long period of time, I go into much farther out spaces than I ever do when I'm sharing. Because I'm a people junkie in the sense that I still need people, and part of my sharing is my needfulness. I can hear the statement, "Your life is your message." I can imagine people saying, "Whatever happened to Ram Dass? Well, I hear he's off in a cave somewhere. It's been five years since we've heard from him. Well, what happened?" And that's the statement. I'm not sure that isn't a statement that would have as much power as all the other little games I'm playing. So, I think it's a much more far-out dance than I'm yet playing it to be. I'm just getting up the courage to let go of some of the cultural, habitual ways of expressing consciousness or love or being or something, to explore more far-out ones.

SUN: What do you think are habitual ways, in terms of your lectures and writing?
RAM DASS: That when you have something that is useful to society you share it. That's a good one. That's a cultural thing. Good guys share it. But what happens is, by doing that, you settle at a certain level of sharing. While if you'd hold back a little more, you'd just be sharing from another level. But the question is, what's your tolerance for holding back? I can imagine getting to the point where I just sit in one place and people can come or not, but I don't care. I don't even notice whether they come or not. But now if I'm in one place and they come, I'm suddenly in the hotel business. Where are you going to sleep? What are you eating? So I keep moving all the time so I don't have to be in the hotel business.

SUN: How much do you feel sense your guru's presence?
RAM DASS: More and more and more all the time.

SUN: Do you see him?
RAM DASS: There are different levels of seeing. Every now and then, I have a vision in which he actually comes. At other times, I create an image of him — a visualization. At other times, most of the

time, I merely experience his presence, more or less thickly. And that gets to be a good deal of the time each day. Like last night, when I was lecturing, there were moments when the lecture started to get very spacious. While I'm talking I'm also talking to him about the whole thing. He's really right there. I mean, he comes. The thing has taken over. It's no longer me doing it. It's just another quality. And I ask him to do it. I say, this is your trip, not mine; I don't know what the hell I'm doing here. If you want to share dharma with these people, do it. I'll try to stand out of the way, but it's your business, not mine.

SUN: What does being Jewish mean to you?
RAM DASS: It's certainly still a very active issue for me. I still feel there is a lot of reactivity in me about it. I am always open to a new possibility of finding a heart doorway through, into the living spirit of Judaism. But every time I try and open it, I end up meeting a lot of belief systems and a lot of proselytizing and rigid stuff that turns me off again. My way would be through a Hasidic rabbi, for example. There's someone in Palo Alto who brought over a rabbi from Israel who has an ashram or monastery there where people gather just to study the Rabbi Nachman stories — wonderful stories. I helped pay for his trip. We had brought him out to California with a translator to this gathering of liberal growth movement-type people who were sort of Jewish, but not quite. He ended up giving his lecture about the Jews as the chosen people, in which everything in life was designed — everything, I mean — to help the Jews become the chosen people. I couldn't believe it. He couldn't have picked a topic that would have been more inappropriate to the situation. The rabbi that brought him was absolutely appalled because he could see how he was losing the whole scene. So I ended up just giving money to the center because I love the Rabbi Nachman stories. But I realized that wasn't my route through, so I'm waiting. I've never even gotten to Jerusalem yet, because I just haven't felt in my heart the rightness of it. I know that there are things about Judaism, in terms of a quality of emotion, a quality of love of intellect, a quality of compassion, a quality of long-sufferingness, that are deep within me, and I know that I am incarnated as a Jew just this time. I mean, I'm not always a Jew, and I am not a Jew. I am in a Jewish form this time, and that's what the Jews find offensive — that my identity

isn't first as a Jew and then as a man, human being, and everything else. Because that's the thing about Judaism — it's a . . . first you're a Jew — and I don't feel that at all. I feel it's merely part of the dance this time. And it's interesting to be part of a persecuted minority group, and so on. I think that's a certain kind of work one does on oneself through that.

SUN: Someone wanted me to ask, in line with what you said last night about goodness, what you feel about Mother Theresa.
RAM DASS: I don't think she is a saint. I think she is a good woman. A very good woman, but I don't think she is a saint. When she was told she got the Nobel Prize her first statement was, "I don't deserve it." And then she corrected herself and said, "In Christ's name," or whatever. She is a good woman out of the deepest sense of good. She is really far out. She is a very lovely, very high being and I am glad she is around. But I don't sense a freedom in her. See, my standard is always Maharaji, that sort of cosmic playfulness where life and death are all to be laughed at. The ultimate goodness comes from non-attachment to goodness. It is very hard within the Christian metaphor to get beyond good and evil. Hardly anybody does, because the mystic Christ is so hidden within Christianity. I think that is one of the hardest metaphors to get through, that ultimate polarity of good and evil. See, Krishna is much easier than Christ. The *Ramayana* is hard also, because that is a good and evil book too. But Hanuman is more like Shiva. He breaks the fruit trees, and he is like a kind of rascal or the trickster in the American Indian tradition. Those are different from the Christian. You never get the feeling of the trickster or the playfulness. Christ isn't playful. He is never laughing. You never think of him as having a good time, or cuddling up either to Mary or to John. That is really terrible stuff to say. Sacrilegious. I think the good and evil issue is just so subtle. It is very hard for any of us to get outside of it. I think that a lot of people think they get outside of it by spurning righteousness or spurning goodness, and that isn't it. I can feel people continually pulling on me with a sense of, "If you were good you would do thus and so." Like they will call up needfully: "If you were good you would fill my need." And I sit with it, watching it act on me, seeing that at the level of my personality I really want to be good, I want to be known as good. The less I am in my personality the more I notice that I am

willing to pick up this discrimination and act in a way that is dharmically useful, even though it isn't seen as good. And it gets exciting. It gets interesting at that point. And that is why in the last analysis I have a hard time judging people like Trungpa Rinpoche, or Muktananda, or others. Because they are not good. Muktananda is a little goody, sort of, but he is also a tough customer. And that toughness can come out of clarity. Someone said of Trungpa, when you go to the top of the mountain with a bird and the bird flies, don't think you can. I realize that there is a certain kind of tantra that I am afraid of, because it is not rooted in good, in good and evil. good and evil.

SUN: Are you still a good Jewish boy?

RAM DASS: Yes, that's the one. And I go in and out of it all the time. You've got to deepen your meditation a lot to get through that. You have really got to invest in your meditative stance.

SUN: Did Maharaji ever say anything about the future in terms of world catastrophe, nuclear war?

RAM DASS: He didn't ever give me the sense that the demise of humanity was imminent. Maybe it was so trivial to him that he never bothered to mention it. But he never gave me the sense of it being imminent. He would say things like, "India is like a golden bird and it can survive and it will go on," and you got a feeling that like your car, it just sort of will go on, sort of clunking along. That kind of quality about life and the world. And that periods come and go, dark ages and light ages. You just got a feeling from him that there was a much more profound root and wisdom in it all than we could see. Somehow from him I got the sense that I would live to an old age. I don't remember why, but whatever happened that gave me that feeling, the result is that I never, like on airplanes, think I am going to die, because it just seems irrelevant to me. He never talked much about world conditions. When somebody said to him — it was a great line — somebody said, "Maharaji, what can we, from another culture (this was during the Pakistan-Indian war), learn from this war?" Maharaji said, "Learn how to be peaceful."

SUN: So, you don't get hooked by all the scary stories?

RAM DASS: I am in a funny situation. One of the ways I pick up information is that I have a lot of friends who are very deeply involved in this and that. I can sit down with Dwayne Elgin, who is just finishing a book on voluntary simplicity and was a presidential advisor on issues of lifestyle and worked for the Stanford Research Institute. In Santa Fe, David Padwa is one of my closest friends. David is probably the most brilliant human being I have ever met. He can look at a page and then close the book and tell you the whole page. He never forgets anything he ever knew. David went to the University of Chicago at fourteen. Had to wait until he was twenty-one before they would give him his international law degree. He was working for the United Nations after that as an advisor in economics and maritime law. Started his own business called Basic Systems. Built it up to a business, sold it to Xerox, took his five-million-dollar profit. He took off, went and studied Buddhism in India in the mountains, and so on. Then he started another business a few years ago called Grassland Seed Corporation. He is now perhaps the largest independent seed owner in the world. And he is interested in things that can change the entire food chain supply system in the world. He is a very conscious being. He is tuned to oil, politics, structures. He knows Russian history. So I will go and take a hot tub with him and we will sit for a few hours and I will have just saved up a series of questions like, "What is Russia's predicament at this moment?" He'll discuss the political, the economic, the Chinese rice fields on the border of Russia, how much grain the Russians can take in through their ports. How many metric tons and what kind of drought they would need before they would have to invade China to survive or their government would crumble because of food riots, and how thin the chains of food are around the world. We will just have discussions for hours and I will use him as a resource — like reading the encyclopedia, except it is up-to-date. Now I have him on one end and he is in the business world, the money markets, has a tremendous grasp of history and political, economic, stock market manipulation, stuff like that. On the other hand, I have all of these friends who are very active in anti-nuclear things, in social action. And as I run my questions through all these different people I find all these different opinions, held with great dedication and honesty and integrity. I am very tempered by the nature of the resources I have to work with, because I keep finding that everybody has an ax to grind. The anti-nuke people, of which I am more or less one, deny certain information which makes the issue not exactly the way they present it. There is an emotional reactivity that gets in there that makes you distort what you are hearing. As a scientist I know that stuff is not clear enough — those data aren't clear enough yet. I mean Allen Ginsberg, who is one of my resource people, will come and say, "Well, I was at a meeting and the waste toxicity is over the critical point. We have done ourselves in now. It is all over." So I'll say to David, "Hey, David, Allen says . . . ." David says, "Oh, that is a crock. We have this and this and there is this safeguard and this is happening and this is happening." And I say, "Are you sure you are not just hiding from it?" "No, no, we have got this waste possibility, and you know. . . ." And I say, "But what if there is an earthquake?" I end up without a clear view, so I can't say that is bad, that is good. And I realize that this isn't good guys and bad guys either. Not at all. I was one of the people in 1948 who was thrilled about peaceful use of atomic energy because that was going to change the starvation levels and the freedom of people. Suddenly free energy for everybody with atoms forever. And we did that out of goodness and then we saw we had made an error. We hadn't anticipated the fallout from it. The people that are committed to technology, obviously, have a certain blind spot — David is one of these people — where they feel technology can solve every problem. The people that are anti-technology are committed to the idea that technology will slowly do us in. The relation between our intellect and our wisdom is what is at stake here. A lot of technology can be reabsorbed and redirected through wisdom. And I feel that it behooves people like me to work on wisdom and not get caught in reactivity to these issues. By reducing the size of technology we are putting humans back into perspective in a certain kind of way . That is changing the game again. When I first worked computers, the 650 I used was two huge rooms. Now that same thing you carry in your pocket, which is bizarre. The intellect itself can be a master or servant, and technology is merely the stepchild of intellect. It, too, is a master or servant. We are almost hypnotically entranced by technology. Just like by psychiatry, just like by drugs. There is an addiction to technology that we are just coming out of now. Wisdom undercuts addiction.

SUN: Even positive addiction?

RAM DASS: Even positive addiction. All addiction. I mean the last addiction is the addiction to God and even that must be undercut.

SUN: Would you be President if the job were offered to you?
RAM DASS: I just did a lecture with William Irwin Thompson, who gave a long discourse about separating authority and power. When I was twenty-four, my father became president of the New Haven railroad. I became assistant to the president. I was the route through to my father and he was handling the financial end, and I ended up running the railroad at twenty-four years of age. Seventeen thousand employees. And I didn't know what the hell I was doing, and the power of it was so corrupting to me, I finally couldn't stand myself and I had to get out. But there was a point where everybody was nice to me because they wanted something of a worldly nature. When you have power suddenly people are coming toward you and orienting you for something worldly. When you are not in the power domain, they don't. You are irrelevant to power players. You are only relevant to people who want something else. Maharaji kept calling me Guru Ram Dass. That was the guy that lived in the mud hut next to the palace. And when the king offered him his kingdom Guru Ram Dass said, "I accept it. Now you run it for me." And I think I would much rather be a friend of the President than the President. I would rather have no power at all. You know, I would rather simplify my life and simplify and simplify. I really feel I am in training to be a wise man, not to be a powerful man. I mean Mahatma Gandhi is much closer to my model. He never held public office. He was a friend of it. He was the spiritual guide. And that is a much more appealing role to me.

(June 1980)

Random Notes On Spiritual Life

Adam Fisher

This essay is dedicated with deep respect to the Rev. Dokai Fukui of Shogen-ji Temple in Japan.

The disagreements between so-called mystics (those who seek experience of their god) and orthodoxy (those who perform rituals calculated to serve their god) is old, endless, and sometimes delightful. Either path, followed exclusively, carries both dangers and rewards.

And yet I wonder how much spiritual life has to do with either danger or reward. Perhaps that is one of the central dangers.

For all that, it seems to me that a human being, to the extent he is interested in spiritual life, must eventually pull up his own socks, leave the precincts of the wise and the precincts of the learned, and find his own way. It may be wonderful and sometimes

The first sign that a man is getting religious is that he is getting happy.

useful to hear of saints and other unusual people who seemed to accomplish marvelous things, appeared to lead clarified, rarified lives. It may also be wonderful and sometimes useful to know texts and liturgy, the warp and woof of ritual. But, given the swiftness of life, the impermanent nature of all things, the change that greets us in every moment, the losing of that which we long to keep and the keeping of that which we long to lose . . . eventually, if a human being wants to live his life at ease, the sweetness of others must be set aside. That to which authority has been granted must be seen and perhaps loved, but, finally, for the serious student, it must be set aside.

My own experience is not long — twelve years of spiritual activity, three studying a branch of Hinduism and nine practicing Zen. Still, over that time, I seem to have created a series of notes for myself, some based on observation, some based on experience, that may be of tentative use to others.

HAPPY. The first sign that a man is getting religious is that he is getting happy. A good line from a Hindu. Often happiness is interpreted as meaning the imitative, glue-y smile, the active suppression of "negative" aspects like anger, envy, or greed under the misapprehension that this is a better way to act. But "negative," like "positive," follows even into the highest and holiest of mountains. There is no hiding place. Luckily, there is also no reason to hide. Feigning anything — from serenity to gloom — is not necessary to spiritual training. Walls that shut out will eventually and invariably hem in, and looking to achieve something *else*, anything *else*, will inevitably boomerang. Happiness is not so difficult: take good care of things, watch closely, and the joy will assert itself.

INSTITUTIONS. Obviously, it is a good idea to pick an institution that more or less suits you. Shopping around is fine, but not forever. As one Hindu put it, if you want water, you don't dig 100 little holes, you dig one deep one. There may be many who lay claim to the ecumenical spirit, but very few have the vaguest idea of what they are talking about. It may be nice to say with the Upanishads, "Truth is one, wise men call it by many names," but it is quite another thing to know what this means. Talk is cheap even when it feels good.

To find a more or less palatable institution (perhaps only three or four things are a real turn-off) is important. Institutions check pride even as they offer laziness. But perfection of the institution is not the point. Pick one, find out everything you can, practice hard, and see for yourself. Beware of personal bias, but do not be too self-critical: after all, who is this for? An institution that perpetuates its connection with the student forever is probably no good. If an institution, implicitly or explicitly, suggests, "You have to stick with us if you want to get to heaven," be very, very careful. Probably better is the group that in some way asserts, "This institution, with any luck at all, will self-destruct in five seconds."

LAUGHTER. Care should be taken of places in which laughter is missing. Gut-wrenching, falling-down laughter is what I mean. There may be many who specialize in a kind of controlled heh-heh-heh and others who give a great imitation of the knowing smile. Leave these people to their own devices.

The whole thing reminds me a bit of a woman I once knew who admitted that at one time she had been enthusiastic about men who were "tall, strong, and silent."

"It was all very sexy," she said, "until I found out that too often tall, strong, and silent types were tall, strong, and stupid."

It is easy to ascribe virtue to another, but that doesn't mean the virtue is there. Laughter is all but impossible to fake, and, although spiritual life may be a serious matter in an individual's life, still, it's not *that* serious. If it is *that* serious, there is a serious problem. The seriousness with which some students approach their practice — prayer, meditation, or whatever — is more often a sign that they take themselves seriously than that they take spiritual life seriously.

TEACHERS. Teachers are named by other people. The best teacher is still a student — very probably the last student. Be careful of teachers who think too much of themselves or their teaching: they are not thinking hard enough. It may be difficult not to think of one's own practice — into which so much effort is poured — as the "best." Many groups in history and even in the present single themselves out for a higher station: they are the "chosen," a term elected by a surprising number of tribes through the ages. Or perhaps they are the only recognized "human beings" or are on a "higher" road. All such nomenclature will impede the honest student who is far better off being his own brand of so-called slob or so-called failure than to associate himself with such preening.

How is it possible to know the true teacher? It isn't. The true teacher is the one who began before I did. He or she is also the one about whom it is impossible to know if the title "teacher" is deserved. The only way to find out is to practice. It takes a thief to catch a thief. Becoming a good thief is important.

My own first teacher was a proud liar and a nasty womanizer. When I discovered these things, I felt many things: anger, betrayal, guilt, suspicion, sorrow, etc. But for all that, still his teaching put me along the way. He was good for a beginner. He had no laughter and he loved power, but he emphasized practice and the practice proved to be no liar, so eventually I was able to say "no" to his weed-choked garden. For this I am grateful. From this I infer that it is more likely that a teacher will be a human being than a saint and that the student looking for a saint will have about as much luck as a dog chasing its own tail: what the hell would he do with it if he caught it?

DEATH. This death business needs attention. Luckily, since in our environment death is so often hidden and lied about, it gets a great deal of sub-surface attention, frequently in the form of fear. Being afraid of death is being afraid of life — one aspect (so-called) of life. The serious student is not the one who chooses one thing and rejects another — choosing life over death as if they were opposites. Discrimination of this sort is very painful. So somehow, with courage, doubt, and persistence, the student will need to face his own life, his own death. With practice, it is not so difficult. After all, who dies?

SEX. I always like mentioning sex because it gets people's attention. Paying attention is *sine qua non* of spiritual practice.

SPIRITUAL LIFE. Great teachers the world over have proclaimed the benefit of spiritual discipline. Such discipline benefits not only the student, but the whole world, the whole universe. The fact that these things are true does not need to concern the student. "Better your own truth, however weak, than the truth of another, however noble." The blessing of spiritual life is not that people say it is true, but that it is true. Even a bird can be taught to recite wonderful words.

TEXTS. It can be a lot of fun to read books about spiritual life or to hear others read and explain them. Heaven knows there are a lot of them. In my own case, I read between 300,000 and 500,000 pages and went to any number of lectures and sermons before I made up my mind to do something about spiritual practice. I decided in two forms: 1) If they (those teachers, saints, gurus, etc.) can do it, so can I, and 2) I want to know, really know — for me, not for anyone else — if spiritual life is bullshit or not.

Doing is a lot slower than thinking. The intellect is so agile, so in love with itself, so praised in our society, that to ask it to shut up for a while may seem slightly more difficult than to ask the sun not to rise. How to begin? Where to begin? Where are the handholds, the grips with which to start the climb? My experience is that it doesn't matter where the beginning is. What matters is that there is a beginning. Perhaps here. A beginning of doing something. Doing what? Who knows? Many people tease themselves along with some goal: "getting good," "clarifying the mind," "seeking God," "longing for enlightenment," etc. And if that's what it takes to keep going, to keep doing, then seek your heart out. But in the midst of it all, it is best not to get sucked into thinking or believing that this effort is for something *else*. "Else" and "other" are false.

Keep doing. Doing what? If the discipline is prayer, pray! If meditation, meditate! Be constant. Doing — over the seconds and minutes and hours and days and months and years — has one singular and amazing advantage over thinking: for once there is the possibility that the student will *know* what he is talking about. Like riding a bicycle or playing the piano, there is no particular harm in reading books about the subject, but only a fool would confuse intellectual accumulations with the ability to ride or play.

So keep doing. Practice wholeheartedly. At first there may be terrific feelings of foolishness or unworthiness or, more difficult still, of great understanding. These things need gentle attention, but not too much attention. The important part is to keep doing. Pray. Meditate. There will be plenty of time later to fit angels on the head of a pin or to speak marvelously. Comparisons and contrasts will assert themselves. Fine. Keep doing. Never mind *other* states of being, worlds beyond worlds, consciousness divine, serene looks on other faces, words spoken in a mellifluous foreign tongue, the wisdom of paradoxes, healing lepers, walking on water, levitating . . . all those *other* things. Do *this* thing.

A calligraphy in my apartment says: "Drinking green tea, I stop the war." Such a saying may not be pleasing to the socially or ethically attuned intellect, but then, ethically attuned intellects have never shown themselves to be especially effective in stopping wars. Perhaps a little unethical investigation would be useful.

So, texts are fine up to a point. But for the serious student, I think doing is more effective — careful, wholehearted doing. The wonderful thing about spiritual life is that, contrary to a suspicious inner voice I think everyone needs to harbor, it is not a crock of shit. Even though I say it's wonderful, still it really is wonderful and no one has to say so. It works all by itself, like flowers opening in Spring — not by explanations, quotations, analysis, love, or anything else.

Here comes Spring. Here come the flowers. BOING!

PAIN. According to our society, pain is one of the most unpopular of sensations. Whole industries are dedicated to fleeing from it. But, since there is no place in life that pain cannot reach, fleeing pain amounts to fleeing one aspect of life. ("One aspect." Ha! How many lives does a person lead? How many "aspects" can there be?)

Flight from pain is screwy — common enough, perhaps, but screwy still. At some point it will be necessary for the honest student to investigate pain closely, to turn around and look, not with some fearful, cursory sniff like a dog near an uninteresting fire hydrant, but very, very closely.

The invitation to investigate pain closely is sometimes criticized as "masochism." But masochism is the active seeking and enjoyment of pain whereas the serious student only investigates what *is*. Aversion and attraction may be possible, but what *is* has nothing to do with possibilities. Perhaps the true masochist is the one who flees from what *is*: running from things gives them more power than they actually have, and those who run make themselves slaves to what they claim to dislike. This is first-class masochism.

One popular pastime is to distinguish physical pain from mental pain. With practice, this distinction shows itself as false, but it probably doesn't do much harm as long as the student maintains the courage, persistence and doubt necessary to a thorough investigation: where does this come from? Whose pain is it? Mine? Who is this "mine?" Etc.

The same close scrutiny will eventually be necessary for pleasure, but, since pain has a way of getting a lot of initial attention, it is best to start there. The desire to avoid pleasure is not exactly common.

BENEVOLENT SUICIDE. It is really quite amazing how many people seem to think spiritual life is out to take something away from them. Out with all the fun! On with the glum or superficially serene face! Lousy food, no sex, a set of pursed lips . . . but it's good for you. This is one attitude.

For the student beginning practice, this attitude may seem to come from the advisors of his ritual, the teachers or advanced students. What teachers or advanced students advise may become holy writ in the student's head — an article of faith never to be changed or transgressed.

OK. But it is also important for the student to know that, except for those teachers and advisors who have their own difficulties, no one really wants to take anything away. While it is true that spiritual life doesn't mean doing anything you want, it also doesn't mean not-doing anything you want. Possibilities like anger, greed, sorrow, pride, and vanity that the student may seek, or think he ought to seek, to eradicate have a way of simply disappearing when a constant, strong practice is exercised. Instead of tossing things out the window, it is more likely, with time and practice, to see them simply jump.

PSYCHOLOGY AND PHILOSOPHY. Both psychology and philosophy offer profound insights. (It is sometimes true that people who immerse themselves in spiritual life are more in need of a good psychologist. A certain health is required.) But for all the profound insights, the excellent observations, even the truth as ascertained in one form of discipline or another . . . still, there is nothing that can reach or attain or match the tacit, silent, go-about-your-business understanding in which "understanding" plays no part.

VOID. Together with the lurking fear that spiritual practice may not be true, there is often a deeper lurking fear that it is true. Both fears are based on ego, the sense of the self as real. It is not a good idea to bad-mouth the ego: where would spiritual practice be without it?

Still, getting a clear understanding of the ego is important. Understanding has nothing to do with seeing, hearing, tasting, touching, feeling, thinking, or consciousness. It is with these elements that fear arises. From the point of view of spiritual life as nonsense, these elements resent being told they are not primary. From the point of view of spiritual life as sensible, these elements, again, resent being set aside, threatened with imagined annihilation. They fear their own death at the hands of something (something?) that precedes and postdates them, that informs them yet refuses to participate in their self assertions. It is not entirely soothing to these elements to be told, "If the eye were not empty, how could the eye see? If the ear were not empty, how could the ear hear?" etc. Emptiness sounds very threatening, like death, a vacuum where nothing grows. But this is not emptiness. This is imagination.

Someone once said, "Just because the window is dirty doesn't mean there isn't something behind it." Probably a Hindu. Certainly true. Practice is necessary. Cleaning the window is necessary. But the attitude will be important. Best would be just to clean the window, just do the practice. Goals are great hindrances in the end. If, with the goal in mind, I were to actually reach the goal, I would be thrown back as surely as a fisherman throws back the little ones. Ideas, hopes, and goals cannot enter. It takes courage to enter here. Courage, constancy, doubt. But it certainly isn't somewhere else.

Another approach: there is often fear of the unknown. But how is it truly possible to fear the unknown? What we fear is always known. So what is it, exactly, that is known? Likewise there are goals. Students speak easily of "enlightenment," "God," "void," "mind," "no-mind," etc. Questioned closely, students will admit they don't know what they're talking about. But how is it possible to have a goal that is unknown? Of course, it is possible to pass such questions by with intellectual posturings or emotional outpourings, but really there needs to be some sure understanding, a quiet admission of what has never been unknown.

POWERS. There are so-called powers attending spiritual

endeavors. Wanting them will bar the way just as wanting to keep them will bar the way. They are available, like the popcorn ad before the movie — connected but not central.

A Hindu story tells of a man who one day set up his dyeing vat in the center of the village. The townspeople came to him one by one with their bolts of undyed cloth. The first said he would like his cloth to be "blue." Into the pot it went, and out it came, "blue." The next villager was interested in "red." Into the same pot that had produced "blue" went his cloth. It too came out as desired, "red." And so it went through the colors of the spectrum. Each time the cloth went into the same pot. Each time it came out a different color.

At the end of the line of villagers came a man with a bolt of cloth that he handed to the dyer, saying, "I'd like my cloth the color of what is in the pot."

Those seriously inclined toward spiritual life would be better off finding out what's in the pot.

COMMANDMENTS, PRECEPTS, ETC. It is true that a sincere student will have to change his attitude and activities slightly as practice enters his life. By "slightly," I mean just that. Students who attempt to wrench themselves violently into some mold perceived as "better" or "more holy" will probably burn themselves out. Laziness (doing anything you want) and pride (doing anything you want) need some clarification.

Precepts like "don't kill," "don't steal" and "don't lie" are important in spiritual practice. But paying too much attention to them will only manage to vitiate their true meaning. By making rock-hard principles, we only invite shattering. Such carved-in-stone monstrosities are frequently praised in the social setting because there is an assumption that if we don't have these cages, the raging beast in all of us would get loose. Social improvement may be a by-product of serious spiritual practice, and certainly a student will strive to avoid doing evil, but to make social distinctions and judgments will always stand in the way of an honest student.

It is best, as regards precepts, to practice. Pray, if prayer is the practice; meditate, if meditation is the practice. With time and effort, precepts once only spoken with the mouth, once only repeated at the behest of others, will begin to keep themselves. They keep themselves because they work, not because they are "good."

Not so complicated after all: things do themselves. No need to convince, cajole, impress or convert. Things do themselves. Isn't that enough? Isn't that really enough?

(May 1983)

Illustrations and Photographs

Contributors

JIMMY SANTIAGO BACA went into a maximum security prison at the age of twenty-two to serve five years for selling drugs. He'd had only two years of formal schooling; he taught himself to read and write in his cell. The author of a book of poems, *Immigrants In Our Own Land*, he lives in the Southwest with his wife and two children.

LIGHTNING BROWN is a poet, computer programmer and political activist who lives in Chapel Hill, North Carolina.

ROB BREZSNY is the author of *Images Are Dangerous*, a collection of "born-again pagan Marxist poetry and lascivious feminist prose." He wrote for **THE SUN** under various names — Medea, Lamellicorn The Clone, and his own. He lives in Santa Cruz, California, where his band — Tao Chemical — has put out an album on its independent label.

CHRISTOPHER BURSK is a poet who lives in Langhorne Manor, Pennsylvania. He's the author of a book of poems, *Place of Residence*.

ELIZABETH ROSE CAMPBELL worked for **THE SUN** from 1976 to 1982 as a magazine distributor, typesetter, subscriptions clerk, assistant editor, contributing editor, and flower bed manager. She lives in upstate New York, where she publishes her own writing in *The Rose Reader* (P.O. Box 149, Tivoli, NY 12513).

DAVID C. CHILDERS is a new wave lawyer practicing in Mt. Holly, North Carolina.

DAVID CITINO teaches at Ohio State University in Marion, Ohio and edits the *Cornfield Review*. He's the author of *The Appassionata Poems*.

C.B. CLARK is the pseudonym for a writer from Chatham County, North Carolina.

JOHN COTTERMAN is a graphic designer and typesetter who runs Lunar Graphics in Chapel Hill, North Carolina.

CINDY CROSSEN is a songwriter and singer who lives in the country near Chapel Hill, North Carolina with her husband and son.

RAMESHWAR DAS lives in Amagansett, New York.

HAL J. DANIEL III is a professor of speech, language and auditory pathology and an adjunct professor in anthropology at East Carolina University in Greenville, North Carolina. His books of poetry are *As Long As You're Not Cold* and *Leave of Absence*.

ADAM FISHER paints houses in New York City.

ROXY GORDON is a writer and artist who lives in Dallas, Texas. His work has appeared in *Rolling Stone*, *The Village Voice*, and other publications.

KARL GROSSMAN is a journalist and the author of *Nicaragua: America's New Vietnam*, *The Poison Conspiracy*, and *Cover Up: What You Are Not Supposed To Know About Nuclear Power*. He lives in Sag Harbor, New York.

DAVID M. GUY is a novelist and essayist who lives in Durham, North Carolina. He's the author of *Football Dreams*, *The Man Who Loved Dirty Books*, and *Second Brother*.

FRANCESCA HAMPTON lives in Santa Cruz, California, where she's working on a historical novel about Tibet.

RIC HAYNES is a freelance illustrator who lives in Ardmore, Pennsylvania.

LESLIE WOOLF HEDLEY lives and writes in San Francisco, California.

ART HILL lives in Birmingham, Michigan. He's the author of *Booze, Books, and the Big Deuce*.

FRANK HOLYFIELD is an artist who lives in Chapel Hill, North Carolina.

RON JONES is a writer and teacher who lives in San Francisco, California, where he's physical education director at San Francisco's Recreation Center for the Handicapped.

HARRY KNICKERBOCKER lives in Seattle, Washington. When last heard from, he had just bought a twenty-seven foot sloop named Maya and was dreaming of sailing to the South Pacific.

DAVID KOTEEN is a writer who, after thirteen years of land-oriented communal living, now makes his home in Eugene, Oregon.

STEPHEN MARCH is a writer and photographer who lives by the sea.

LORENZO W. MILAM is the author of *The Cripple Liberation Front Marching Band Blues*. Instrumental in setting up many listener-supported radio stations, he's been called "the Johnny Appleseed of listener-sponsored radio" by *Broadcasting* magazine. He lives in San Diego, California.

STEPHANIE MILLS is a writer who lives in Maple City, Michigan.

CARL MITCHAM lives in New York City and is at work on a book called *Studies In Marginal American Piety*.

LESLEA NEWMAN is a poet who lives in Jericho, New York. She's the author of *Just Looking For My Shoes*.

PETER RAY believes "the unaltered life is not worth questioning."

PRISCILLA RICH is a photographer and mother of four who lives in the country near Boone, North Carolina.

J.W. RIVERS lives in Rock Hill, South Carolina.

LEONARD ROGOFF is a writer who lives in North Carolina.

JOHN ROSENTHAL is a writer and photographer who lives in Chapel Hill, North Carolina. He does a weekly radio commentary on WUNC-FM, the public radio station in Chapel Hill.

HOWARD JAY RUBIN is a professional magician who lives in Chapel Hill, North Carolina.

VIRGINIA L. RUDDER lives in Hurdle Mills, North Carolina. Her books of poetry are *After The Ifaluk* and *The Gallows Lord*.

ROGER SAULS is a poet who lives in Chapel Hill, North Carolina. He's the author of *Light*, a book of poems.

MICHAEL SHORB lives in San Francisco, California, where he writes poetry, short stories, and novels.

KATHLEEN SNIPES lives in Chapel Hill, North Carolina.

PAT ELLIS TAYLOR lives and writes in Austin, Texas.

BARBARA TYROLER is a photographer who lives in Silver Spring, Maryland.

MARK WEINKLE lives in Durham, North Carolina.

IRVING WEISS teaches at the State University of New York in New Paltz. He's the translator of Malcolm de Chazal's *Sens-Plastique*.

THOMAS WILOCH lives in Westland, Michigan. He's the author of *Stigmata Junction*, a book of prose poems.

Inevitably but regrettably we've lost touch with some of our contributors. Where are you Steven Ford Brown, Richard Gess, Ken Girard, Gerald Hutchinson, James Magill, David Royale, Barbara Street, Enrique Vega?

THE TEXT OF THIS BOOK IS SET IN A TYPEFACE KNOWN AS GOUDY.
THE DISPLAY-FACE IS GOUDY HANDTOOLED.
GOUDY WAS DESIGNED BY FREDERICK W. GOUDY.
ALTHOUGH NOT A FARMER,
HE WAS OUTSTANDING IN HIS FIELD.

THE TYPESETTING WAS DONE BY JOHN COTTERMAN'S
LUNAR GRAPHICS OF CHAPEL HILL, NORTH CAROLINA.

THE SUN LOGO WHICH APPEARS ON THE COVER IS BY TOM CLEVELAND.

PRODUCTION BY SEAN BROWNE AND KEITH YARWOOD.
THIS BOOK WAS DESIGNED BY DOUGLAS CRUICKSHANK.

ALSO AVAILABLE